LYING IN PLAIN SIGHT

THE FINAL BOOK IN THE MOMS WHO LIE PSYCHOLOGICAL THRILLER SERIES

BRETT MONK, MCKENNA LANGFORD

BIG WHY MEDIA

Contents

Foreword by Brett Monk

Welcome to *"Lying in Plain Sight"!* The **fifth and final book** in the *"MOMS WHO LIE"* series. As in all the other books, McKenna and I are just having a blast working together to bring you this story.

In addition to the five full-length novels in the series, there's also a special FREE bonus novella called *"The Lying Begins"* that's not available on Amazon or anywhere else other than the link below. It tells the story of just what happened twenty years ago, the night of the prom when Maddy and Amelia were in high school together. Once you're thoroughly hooked on this story, you're definitely going to want to read it, too.

When you join my reader's community, you will not only get free books and other content by me and some of my friends, but you will get the inside scoop on discounted products and upcoming releases. Plus, I share some personal thoughts and "behind the scenes" photos and notes about my life, media adventures, and favorite grilling recipes. :-)

Community members also get to vote in polls and make suggestions for upcoming books and projects.

You might even want to consider being a "beta reader" or an "advance review reader", both of whom get to read the books before they're available to the public.

https://www.brettmonk.com

But for now, enjoy *"Lying in Plain Sight"*.
- Brett

CHAPTER 1

WARNER

I am a liar.

"Just—tell me straight, Warner. Do you have feelings for my sister?"

Lyla stands in front of me, her head tilted and her arms crossed, the two of us out in the cold under an orange tree. She's tense. She's hurt. She wants the truth from me.

But I also think I now know exactly what she's hoping that "truth" is.

"No," I say, my stomach dipping because it's angry at me for what I'm doing, "I—I don't."

In a town like Toxey, where lies seem to just be swarming through the atmosphere, creating those cumulonimbus clouds in the sky that hardly ever seem to leave, I find myself wondering if maybe lying is a learned trait. If it's something you're destined to start doing once you live here because you learn the most from the people you surround yourself with.

As I stare at Lyla, who looks like she's far, far away from believing my bull, her ice-blue eyes as stormy as the sky above us, I think about her family. They're all liars themselves. It only adds to my "learned trait" theory.

Still.

Maybe lying is a gene I inherited from my mother. An incessant one. A gene passed down to help keep me protected from all the bad in the world that might reveal itself to me were I to tell the truth.

"Warner." Lyla's tone is full of warning.

But don't let me get ahead of myself.

Nine days earlier...

When my phone vibrates in my pocket, I almost don't want to see what bad news I am going to receive next. Still, it gives me something to temporarily distract myself from what is currently happening in front of me, so I take the chance and pull it out.

It's a text message on my old iPhone 8—the one that needs my thumbprint to unlock it—from Audrey:

Audrey: *Um... Warner. Stop dodging my calls. Can we please talk? Like... ASAP? What the heck was that?*

My stomach revolting inside of me, I put my phone back and don't answer her. Yes, my lack of response is mainly because I just don't want to—how can I possibly explain to Audrey why I kissed her like a huge idiot after I already told her I don't have feelings for her?—but it's also because I already have a mountain of other problems I am currently dealing with.

"Warner?" The voice is deep and strict and dripping with concern. It's the voice only a father would have—the voice of Dean Reeves. He's standing in my living room.

"Huh? Yeah," I reply, even though I have no idea what he just said to me. I rushed back home immediately after kissing Audrey, and he showed up minutes later with dinner for us and no explanation as to why he left in the first place.

"Did you even hear me?" he asks me.

Crap. I've been caught.

"Sorry," I admit.

He motions to the phone I've just returned to my pocket. "Who texted you now?" he asks. "That your mom again?"

The police found my mom's borrowed car from her current fling, Steven Hall, turned over in a ditch on the side of the road. There were signs of injury, but unfortunately, no sign of my mother. She's still missing.

However, a text I received from an unknown number said otherwise.

UNKNOWN: *It's your mom. I just wanted to tell you that I'm fine. And that I don't want you to worry about me. OK?*

After Dean returned to my house from "running an errand" with Chinese food—bold of him to assume I'd have an appetite right now—I showed him Mom's text.

"No, it's nothing," I lie about Audrey's text, shaking my head quickly. I seriously wish I was telling him the truth—that the text from Audrey was nothing because I never kissed her.

I'm such an idiot!

Dean squints at me but eventually lets it slide. "We need to tell the police you got that text from Maddy. See if they can look up the number or something."

I've already tried calling the unknown number that my mom—if it even really was her—texted me from. There was no answer and no voicemail box set up yet.

But why wouldn't it be Mom?

Or better yet, why is she even missing? Or hiding. Or on the run? Carson Price, the reason for all of this, is dead now.

I shake my head repeatedly to Dean, to really get the point across. "No way."

"No?"

"Not a chance."

"Do...you want to tell me why you don't want to?"

"Don't trust 'em."

And I don't know if I should trust you.

Over in his chair, where he's stabbing at some kung pao chicken in a carton with a plastic fork, his shoulders sag. "You don't trust them?"

"No."

"Warner, Craig saved your life."

I stand from the old, faded, sagging sofa. "You don't get it. It's... complicated."

He doesn't even acknowledge that I am not touching the food he brought. He sighs and sets the carton down on the coffee table, which is covered in laundry Mom once folded but rifled through so many times instead of putting away like she was supposed to that it's now a disorganized mess all over again.

"I know it must be... hard to accept... that after everything he put you through, Carson is dead now," Dean says, "but—"

"Hard to accept?" I glare at his ignorance. "No. More like impossible to accept." I get up and begin pacing. "I...I don't know. I want to, like, see a body...or something."

"I don't think Craig Fritz and Harris Wilde are lying to you about that." His eyes follow my pacing. "I know Craig isn't the most reliable guy—"

"He's not. You can't tell them."

"I just—"

"Look—Dean! Coach. Mr. Reeves—whatever I'm supposed to call you: Mom texted me and only me for a reason. And I told you about it because... because I trust you. Don't make me regret it."

I stop pacing and stare at him. His dark, full head of hair. His five o'clock shadow. His ears that stick out the same exact way mine do...

"Just... call me Dean," he says. "And fine. For now, we won't tell them."

"Thank you."

He nods. I've annoyed him enough that now he looks like he doesn't want the Chinese food either. "But I've made the decision that you're staying at my place—don't look at me like that. I don't feel safe having you here."

"It's fine here." I don't want to go anywhere with him.

"Hurry up and go pack a bag. You'll follow me in your Jeep to my place. At least until we figure out where Maddy is and what's going on."

I give him another hateful glance and then turn to go to my bedroom.

"What's that look for?" Dean asks, catching my expression. "Did I do something?"

"No. Nothing."

I am a liar.

I told Dean he didn't do anything wrong, when I know exactly what he did. He claims he wants to be a family—me, him,

Mom—but how can we possibly be one when he is still in love with Amelia Bailey-Flynn?

CHAPTER 2

Lyla

I am a liar.

But I don't want to be. I want to tell everyone the truth. Scream it at the top of my lungs. Detective Fritz—Freaky Fritz—is dating Nora—my aunt Nora.

I stand outside of Toxey's only detective's house. My mouth is gaping. I'm not staring at Freaky Fritz, who is standing in the doorway in front of me. I'm too busy looking behind him at my aunt, who has her hair up in a towel and a T-shirt on that looks suspiciously like it doesn't belong to her.

I don't know what to do. Or say. Or think.

"Why don't you come in?" Craig asks me. He opens the door wider. Aunt Nora stares back at me, but I can't read her expression. Does she want me to come in? Did she not want me to discover her here like this? What have I just walked into?

"No," I decide, taking a step back. I think I'd rather get in another car accident driving back to my house than deal with...whatever this is. "I'm good."

Aunt Nora practically pushes Fritz out of the way. "Lyla, come on," she snaps. "Just come in." She takes my wrist, drags me inside, and shuts the door quickly, like she doesn't want the paparazzi to spot her.

I hate this so much. I don't want to be here. I feel trapped. Cornered. By a man I hate and a woman—a member of my own family—who clearly has been lying to me.

"What are you even doing here?" Aunt Nora asks. She looks stressed. The always-there bags under her eyes are darker than usual. Her usually smooth forehead has creases. Her grass-green eyes are burning garishly into mine.

Why does she seem mad at me?

I look at Fritz instead of her, surprised that he actually seems like the easier one to address in this situation. "I-I wanted to hear you talk about Carson myself."

"What about Carson?" Craig asks, his tone facile. "He's dead."

I switch back to looking at Aunt Nora. "So, what? Are you guys, like, together?"

Aunt Nora reaches out and clasps Fritz's forearm in a way that looks so...natural. Like she's done it a hundred times. "We... we are. Yes," she answers.

I scoff to show my disbelief. To show my disappointment. "I'm leaving."

I turn to the door, but Aunt Nora grabs me again. "Just wait, okay?"

I glare at her. "Why?"

"Let the kid go, Nor," Fritz says, rolling his eyes. He looks exhausted. No, beyond that. He's like a walking zombie. What exactly happened before he found Carson Price dead in the woods?

"Thank you," I say to him, full of 'tude.

"But!" Craig barks, stopping me from turning once again. "You can't tell anyone about us, okay?"

Next to him, Aunt Nora nods.

"Why not?" I demand.

"We're not ready to let people know," Fritz says.

"Why?"

"It's complicated, Ly," Aunt Nora steps in, her tone finally softening.

But I'm still mad. "Don't treat me like a kid," I snap at her, which feels weird because I don't think I ever have before. "I've been through a lot more than most kids my age. What's complicated about the two of you being a couple? It's not like Carson is around to get mad about it."

"You're right," she tells me. "There's just a lot—we're sort of busy right now. Carson—"

"Nora," Fritz says.

Aunt Nora sighs. "I promise. I will explain more later. Okay? Can you just do us this solid for now?"

"Whatever." Anything so I can get out of here stat.

When I go to leave a third time, they finally don't stop me.

My head is spinning as I race down Fritz's front lawn, just now realizing Nora's crappy car is parked in his driveway.

Ugh, I wish I had noticed it earlier.

I'm nearly to my car when I hear Fritz's front door open and close again behind me.

"Ly," Aunt Nora's voice calls. "Lyla!"

I begrudgingly turn back around. Thankfully, it's just her this time. She's standing on Fritz's unmanicured lawn, in the freezing cold, with her bare feet and wet hair.

"I have one more favor to ask."

"Aunt Nora," I plead.

"Can you not tell anybody what we talked about in my car?"

"Oh—uh, okay," I tell her. "I won't. Not my secret to tell."

I am a liar.

Because I already did tell somebody.

She throws her arms around me and hugs me so tightly that I can't breathe. "Thank you, Ly."

I already told Audrey.

CHAPTER 3

AMELIA

I am a liar.

I don't even know if I've ever told a single truth. Maybe I deserve to be locked up in a psych ward—sorry, "wellness spa." Because maybe I am a compulsive liar, unable to help it. Unable to control myself.

I've lied to Nora.

I've lied to Dean.

I've lied to my husband.

I've lied to my kids.

So much has happened, I don't know where the lying ends and the truth begins. I can't keep it all straight. I don't know who knows what.

It needs to change. It's going to change.

I just have to get out of this place first.

Thankfully, my stay at Maple Meadows Psychiatric Hospital has been cut short. Very short. When it was discovered my anxiety medication had been switched with something that made me act very, very unlike myself, it became clear I didn't actually belong here in a place like this.

Because I'm not actually crazy.

It might take some time for the effects to get out of my system. I might still feel off for a couple of days. But after that, I can start taking the steps to get back on track. I have to.

Carson is dead now. It's all over. I have to make things right with my kids, Gentry, and Maddy, and then we can all move on and get things back to normal.

Whatever that looks like now.

A nurse unlocks the door to the lobby of Maple Meadows with her keycard. I step out in the clothes I arrived in. Waiting for me with a kind smile on his face—even though I definitely don't deserve one—is Gentry.

"You all set?" he asks. We keep our distance. It feels very formal between us. Like he's been paid to pick me up. Like he's my Lyft driver. Not my husband.

"Yes," I reply, nodding curtly.

He holds the door open for me, and I step out into the cloudy atmosphere, holding the plastic bag filled with my belongings tightly to my chest. It contains my dead phone, the jacket I should probably be wearing, and a silver charm bracelet Lyla and Audrey got me for a birthday one year.

Gentry already knows what happened. Once we get into his car and he begins the drive back to the house, which only one of us is currently living in, he opts to keep the chatter light.

"Get any visitors in there?" he asks, keeping his eyes steadily on the road.

"No."

I am a liar.

Dean Reeves came to see me.

And I think he and I are sort of in a secret relationship.

CHAPTER 4

AUDREY

I am a liar.

I'm in Sophia's bedroom. She's just walked in to see me—her former best friend—sitting on her bed, trying to look easygoing.

"Hey!" I cry out, a little too high-pitched.

She looks confused and suspicious. "Did you see who dropped me off just now?" she asks.

"Uh, no, what do you mean?" I ask, sweating profusely. It must be the pain meds. It's not long ago I was in the hospital after having nearly drowned to death. After Carson Price tried to kill me. "Who?"

She relaxes a bit and steps further into the room. "Um...Olive."

"Oh," I reply.

Sophia's a liar, too.

I know it was Jackson who dropped her off. Jackson Mullens. Her homecoming date. And Lyla's ex-boyfriend.

The Jackson Mullens who drives an old gray Mustang that no one knows about.

No one but Sophia, apparently.

"What are you doing here, exactly?" she asks me, taking off her earrings at her vanity. "I thought you were still in the hospital."

"I'm out," I say, getting to my feet. "I, uh..." I came here originally to apologize to her for how she was attacked at the Halloween carnival at our school. I know it was Carson who did it. I thought it was all my fault. I thought that since I got away from him when he tried to attack me, he went after my friend instead. Carson Price was always looking to punish me.

But when I got here not long ago, before Blackfell High School's blonde queen bee arrived, I discovered the camera equipment and green screen in her bedroom, and it made something abundantly clear to me.

Sophia Key—and probably Jackson Mullens as well—are the ones behind the Toxeydramaenthusiast TikTok account, which has gone viral worldwide for exploiting all of the drama occurring in the Bailey and Carpenter households.

It makes total sense as to why. Sophia loves attention. Jackson is mad at Lyla for dumping him and ruining his friendship with Warner. And he's also a bit egocentric himself. Together, they make quite the life-ruining team.

Feeling trapped and slightly worried about what might happen if I tell Sophia my suspicions while alone in her bedroom with her, I decide to keep it to myself.

Just do what you came here to do, and then get the heck out.

I take a deep breath and smooth my short blonde hair. "I wanted to apologize about what happened at the Halloween carnival," I tell her. "I know first-hand what it's like to be... attacked like that. You didn't deserve it. The person who chased you... they were just out to get me."

She rolls her eyes, which I see in the reflection of her mirror. "It's whatever." Maybe she no longer cares that it even happened.

"I'm really sorry anyway."

"Just forget about it. You went through way worse."

You would know.

I don't really know what else to say. Instead, I find myself looking at the green screen again. "I miss making stupid TikTok dance videos with you guys."

She must be uncomfortable. Sophia has never been good at show-ing her true emotions. She's stone-cold. Unaffected. But I dumped her, and I know it has to bother her.

"Why?" she asks. "They were stupid. Like you said."

I'm not getting anywhere with her. And I don't need to. I came here and said what I wanted.

But I can't stop myself as the words tumble out. "Hey, so, are you and Jackson a couple?"

Sophia smirks and says, "We're talking, why?" She looks smitten. I wonder if she really is, or if they're just business partners.

"I'd be careful if I were you," I say.

"Is that a threat or something?"

"Not at all!" I backpedal. "I just...I don't think he's over Lyla."

Sophia is back to rolling her eyes and looking carefree. "Don't worry; he is."

I purse my lips for a moment. Then I ask, "Are you?"

"What?"

"Are you over Lyla? You were both dumped by her."

She's actually smiling at me, like this whole thing is funny. "Whatever. Jeez Audrey, it feels like forever ago that we stopped talking anyway. Jackson and I are done with her."

"Okay..."

Suddenly, the air in the room has changed and Sophia is eyeing me up and down. "So, that Carson guy they found in the woods... he was the one who attacked you? Attacked us? And he kidnapped Lyla and made Warner's mom's car blow up?"

Why should I give her more information for her stupid, cruel social media account?

"It's hard to know, but it looks like it." I sit back down on the edge of her bed.

What are you doing, Audrey? Leave!

"That's so crazy! Didn't he like, go to school with your mom forever ago?"

"Yeah. None of it makes any sense. And with him dead, it's going to be even harder to get any real answers."

She pouts. It looks fake. "Yeah. You'll never get to hear him tell you why he did it."

"Yeah."

We're silent for a long while. Maybe I can finally go. "I guess I'll... see you later."

She just stares me down instead of replying. I step toward her bedroom door. Her voice stops me when I reach it.

"Hey. Just because we're sort of...fighting... right now, or whatever, it doesn't mean I don't care about you."

That's what the stare-down had been for; being sweet is really hard for her. She must have forced herself to get the words out.

"Oh," I say.

"So, are you...okay?"

"Yeah, totally."

But I am a liar. Because I am not okay.

CHAPTER 5

MADDY

I am a liar.

I lied to my parents about what I did with my trust fund. I lied to Amelia about keeping in contact with her sister. I lied to Nora about how Mia and I became friends again.

I lied to Warner about who his father is. Wait—I lied to everyone about that.

I've lied time and time again. And where has it gotten me? And more importantly, why haven't I learned my lesson?

After everything my lies have cost me, here I am, currently lying to the man I want to have a future with.

***

36 Hours Earlier...

I'm panicked. It's pouring rain. The roads are slick. I am not fully used to driving this Audi.

But mainly, I'm just so. Freaking. Panicked.

After hearing Warner's discreet phone call, I couldn't get inside this car I'm borrowing from Steven fast enough. I just got done calling the police, and even though I've been told to stay put and let them handle it, there's no chance at all of me listening to them. This is my son we're talking about. And he's in the presence of a psycho!

I speed toward the school. I don't have a clue what I will do when I get there, or how I will stop Carson from further hurting Warner and Audrey. But that doesn't matter right now. All that matters is that I get there.

Fat drops of water pound on the windshield and the wipers are on full blast, but it's not helping much. I'm speeding twenty miles an hour over the speed limit, and there are hardly any other cars around to slow me down.

What does cause me to slam on my brakes, however, is the figure who darts across the road in front of me. My headlights shine on them, and for the briefest moment, I catch a glimpse of who it is.

A person in a mask. The mask.

But then I'm immediately hydroplaning. The car is spinning out of control. I cry out and try to right myself, but it only makes things worse. The Audi goes off-road. It slams into something, and the airbags deploy, knocking into me with painful force, but still, the car is moving. Falling. Tipping.

Rolling.

I don't know how much time passes before I stop feeling anything at all.

When I come to, I'm inside Steven Hall's incredible mansion. But I don't understand how I got here or why I am in so much pain.

What on earth happened?

All I can get out is a groan.

Then Steven appears, hovering over me as I lay on his sofa. He brushes my hair from my forehead. "You're going to be okay."

I groan some more.

He seems to know what I'm trying to ask.

"I figured it out," he tells me. "It's Dean. Your psycho ex is Dean. He kissed you, and you felt trapped with no way to escape him. It all makes sense now, and I am so sorry you felt you couldn't tell me about him sooner."

I'm so confused. I'm in so much pain.

He continues. "I found the car...and you. Were you trying to escape him?"

"Steven," I manage.

"Don't worry. I loaded you up, brought you back here, and had a doctor friend of mine come and patch you up. He says you're going to be all right."

I remember now.

"But... Warner." Where is he? Is he okay? I couldn't save him. And Steven has no idea that I had even been trying to.

"I wasn't sure if Dean was harassing Warner, too. If he is, tell me, and I'll leave right now and bring him here, too. You guys will be safe hiding out here. At least until we figure out how to deal with him."

He has it so wrong. So, so wrong. I should have just told him the truth from the beginning.

"Maddy," he continues, looking completely besotted with me as he moves some dark blond hair from his forehead. I can't bear to look him in the eyes, so I focus instead on the cute dimple on his strong, jutting chin. "I don't care about the car. I don't care about the lies. All I care about is you. I'm so glad I found you when I did, or it could have been much, much worse."

I need to tell him the truth.

"And hey, maybe it's a good thing you had my car. Imagine if you had been in that accident when you still had your old car. I don't even want to picture it. I'm glad you were driving the Audi."

I dug myself too deep. I'm scared. I'm hurt. I'm tired. So, so tired.

So, for now, I go along with it.

Later, when I make my way back from the bathroom down a very long hall, Steven is waiting for me on the couch. He's waiting for me to rejoin him so we can keep cuddling. So he can keep taking care of me. So he can keep hiding me from my fake psycho ex-boyfriend with not a single clue about what is really going on in my life.

"Hey," he calls out before I've rounded the corner to him. "Some guy who apparently went missing from Toxey twenty years ago was just found in some woods nearby! How crazy is that?" He must have the news on, or maybe he's reading an article on his phone. Or watching a video on the Toxeydramaenthusiast account on TikTok.

So, Carson Price *was* caught. Thank God.

"Who?" I ask, my voice weak.

I am a liar.

"Some guy named Carson Price," Steven replies.

Because I am too cowardly to ever tell anyone the truth.

"Oh, man—that's a bummer," Steven continues, giving me a play-by-play. "They didn't find him alive. They just found his body."

Chapter 6

AMELIA

The first thing I do when I wake up the next morning is check my phone, which is on the charger on my nightstand. Gentry must have plugged it in for me last night. I had been so tired. I hardly remember going to bed. Yesterday had been a blur of talking to Officer Wilde, contacting my doctor to get me back on the right meds, and hugging my girls. A lot.

I'm crestfallen when I find I don't have any missed calls or texts from Dean. I know I was still a little out of it yesterday, and I still feel a little out of it right now, but I couldn't have imagined Dean's visit with me at the psych ward, could I?

So where is he now?

As if by magic, there's a knock on my closed bedroom door, and for some reason, I'm thinking maybe it's him.

"Come in," I say.

The door opens, and the smell of cooked bacon wafts into the room as Gentry smiles at me softly.

"You're still here," I say. I'm not upset, but I'm definitely surprised.

"I stayed in the guest room," he says. "I figured that would be best for...everyone."

"And Joey?" I still feel horrible for what I put him through. The drugs I had been unknowingly taking had coerced me into *kidnapping* him. To ensure Gentry couldn't take him from me. And I only realized the error of my ways when he nearly got hit by a car in a busy street because of me. After that, I decided it's best he keeps his distance from me. I still don't trust myself to be alone with him again. Not yet. Gentry deserves to have custody over him. Not me.

"He's here, too," Gentry says. "Don't worry. He said he's handled worse. You didn't mess him up too bad." He throws in a wink, but his playfulness doesn't make me feel any better about what I did to my foster son. It's a miracle I'm not in prison.

I put my head in my hands. "Ugh, he must hate me."

"He doesn't."

"He should."

"Don't be so hard on yourself, Mia. You weren't... you. I explained it to Joey. Sure, he's still a little...upset. But he understands. He'll come around." When I look up again, Gentry is standing at the foot of the bed. "I made breakfast."

I sit up. It's weird now for Gentry to see me like this, all unkempt and tired-eyed. But the fact that it's weird now is also weird. "You didn't have to do that."

"I did. For my family."

I give him a look. One that needs no words. And all Gentry does is give me that kind smile of his again, then he shoves his hands in the pockets of his sweatpants and leaves the room.

The breakfast goes well. The girls are overly sweet to me, hugging on me and clearing my plate and refilling my juice. Joey doesn't say anything to me, but I catch him looking at me over the top of his iPad screen multiple times.

Once breakfast is over, the kids help Gentry clean up, and even though I was hoping to have a moment alone with Audrey so I can tell her how sorry I am that I hadn't been there to protect her back in her school's pool room, Gentry sends the kids upstairs.

"I get it now," I say to Gentry, who is drying his hands on a kitchen towel by the sink.

"What?"

"You made breakfast to butter me up so that I'm in a cheery mood right before you bring down the hammer on me."

Gentry sighs, and my half-smile falters. I had been kidding. But apparently, I was right. "We should talk," he says, "if you're up for it."

I'm not up for it. But when will I ever be?

"About...?" I know he can fill in the blank without either of us having to say it.

"Yes. About *that*."

I nod. I can't delay this forever.

"Do you want to sit?" he asks.

"Not really."

He leans against the counter. "Okay then."

Quickly, I decide that I want to speak first. "Gentry. I owe you a huge apology. Like... huge." He doesn't say anything. He wants to keep listening. So, I keep talking. "I brought the girls, you—everyone—into this huge mess, and it was wrong. I wasn't honest with you about my past. With Dean. With Maddy. With Carson and what we did to him. It is the biggest regret of my life, what happened that night back in high school. We should have come clean about what we did. There's still so much I don't understand about why Carson did what he did. About why Nora said he was dead when he had clearly been alive all this time. None of it makes sense right now. But I am sure that, somehow, even though Carson is...dead, we will get those answers."

It takes a beat as he clears his throat and scratches his stubble. "So, uh, you and Dean."

It's supposed to be a secret. But Gentry isn't an idiot.

"We're not going to lie to anyone," I say carefully, "but we're not exactly ready to tell anyone, either."

He nods.

I can see it on his face. He knows. He's always known. If Dean is in the picture, there is no one else I can truly give my heart to. I think deep down, Gentry even knew this when we got married. He knew I settled for him after I learned what happened between Dean and Maddy. And I know that it hurts him. A lot.

"Right," he replies.

"But... you're happy, right?" I ask. "With Heather?"

He steps away from the counter and doesn't make eye contact. "Yeah, yeah. I am."

"Good."

"Yeah."

More silence.

There's another thing I want to tell him. No matter how much it hurts me to do it. "Gentry."

"Yeah?"

"About Joey..."

He waves a dismissive hand. "We can figure that out later. Let's not rush to get everything hashed out in one conversation."

"No, listen. I'm not trying to argue with you about him anymore. I'm trying to tell you that... you should have him, G."

He freezes. "What?"

"I love Joey to death—clearly. But you're the one who has always wanted to foster. You're the reason Joey came into our lives in the first place. And, my life is a mess right now. I am mentally well enough now to know that in my life is no suitable place for Joey to be. He needs stability."

"Mia, I... I don't know what to say."

"You don't have to say anything." A tear trails down my cheek. Gentry crosses the kitchen and holds me.

CHAPTER 7

AUDREY

I know I should be resting and recovering from my near-death experience and blah blah blah, but I'm fine.

What I would rather do is finally get ahold of stupid "I don't like you, Audrey" Warner. I've been trying to get him to talk to me since Friday when the kiss happened. Because you can't tell a girl you don't have feelings for her and then kiss her!

And I get that Warner is going through his own issues. I know his mom is missing. I also wish he'd talk to me so I can be there for him. No matter what happened between us, he's still my friend, and I'm worried about him.

He didn't reply to me at all yesterday, and I'd really prefer to talk to him before we're forced to have an awkward run-in at school tomorrow—if he even shows up.

"Ugh!" I yell at my phone inside my bedroom.

"You good?" a voice that sounds very similar to mine calls from the door, making me jump.

"Lyla!" I cry to my twin. "I didn't know you were standing there."

Her shoulder-length blonde hair is pulled back into a super small pony, some chunks of it framing her exhausted face. "You didn't?"

"No."

"You okay?" She doesn't come in.

I stand and click my phone screen off. "I'm... good. Yeah. You?"

She shrugs. "I don't know what I am."

Then she leaves me alone.

I'm relieved. The last thing I want to talk about is stupid Carson Price.

I get changed into leggings and a matching workout top, thinking maybe what I need is to go for a run, even though I've never really been the type of girl who does that, to clear my mind. Usually, I prefer coffee, retail therapy, and senseless teen-drama TV for that.

When I check my phone again, I fully expect to still see nothing from Warner. So, I literally gasp out loud when I see that he's finally replied to me:

Warner: *Our spot today?*
Me: *When?*
Warner: *Doesn't matter. Unless you're free now?*
Me: *On my way.*

Seeing his red Jeep from the 90s makes my stomach lurch. I know I sort of have a "thing" with the cutest senior at my school, Ryan Copeland, but Warner was always my first choice. I only went for Ryan when I couldn't have Warner. But now I'm wondering if maybe there was a chance to be with the one I wanted in the first place all along.

Warner turns off his car and gets out carefully, still injured from when Carson stomped on his ribcage. My mind flashes back to that moment, and for a second, all I can see is the water my head was held under in the pool, Carson's gloved hand tight around my throat while I struggled....

"Hey," Warner says dully as he walks toward me.

I snap out of it and put my hands on my hips. "Don't 'hey' me."

"What?" He stops short of the bench I've just stood from at the abandoned, overgrown, outdoor train station we call "our spot." As far as I know, other than the one time Warner spotted Aunt Nora and Freaky Fritz talking in secret here, no one else knows about this place. Not even Lyla.

"What?" I mock angrily. I'm not really that mad—more just... confused. But it is irritating that he's ignored me for a day and a half but is acting like he hasn't.

"Audrey, I really don't even know what to say."

"Why not?" I ask.

"Come on. I have a lot going on right now. I'm staying at *Dean's* house because my mom is missing."

I drop my hands by my sides, my face falling. I step closer to him. "No sign of her still?"

"I got a text from an unknown number claiming to be her that says she's fine. But who knows what to believe anymore?"

"I think that's a good sign."

Finally, he looks at me. Like really looks at me.

"What?" I whisper.

"I'm sorry I kissed you." He looks like he really means it, which worries me.

I stare at my feet. "Why'd you do it?"

"I don't know," he grumbles, walking past me, kicking some rocks with his old Nikes. "I know it was stupid. I wasn't thinking. I just..."

I watch him walking away from me, but then he stops. His back is to me.

"Warner..." I trail off.

When he turns back around, it's quick. "You almost died trying to protect my mom. For me. I know you want to just forget about it, but I can't forget about what it looked like to see you... like that... after I pulled you out of the water."

"Please," I beg, squeezing my eyes shut. I really don't want to talk about this. "I can't."

"I'm just saying, it killed me, Ree. I think it just made something in me snap. And suddenly... I was super mad seeing you with Ryan. I don't know. It's all so messed up and weird and confusing."

I step closer to him. "It killed *me* seeing you with Jessica Vaccari."

"Yeah... well, I don't think you have to worry about that anymore."

I smirk at him. "We're all confused, Warner. It's okay."

"Yeah, but still. I shouldn't have. I'm—"

The quickest way for me to shut him up is to just lean in and kiss him. But this time, it's much better than the first. This time, he doesn't immediately pull away and run for it. This time, it's real.

CHAPTER 8

LYLA

When I wake up and start getting ready for school the next day, I half-expect Mom or Dad to come into my room and tell me about how I don't need to go. How I should probably take the time to process everything that's happened and stay home even longer than I already have. I've already missed so much. And if I don't graduate on time, it'll set my life back in a big way. The quickest way for me to get past everything that happened is to get the heck out of Toxey.

I'm surprised when I don't hear from them. I go downstairs to find Mom cooking breakfast and Dad sitting at the table with Joey.

"So, you're going today?" Mom asks with a pleasant smile on her face.

"Shouldn't you be resting?" I reply.

"I've done lots of resting. Breakfast isn't some great big task, hon."

"I am going, yes."

"You sure, kiddo?" Dad asks.

"Yep."

"Good for you," Mom says, Dad nodding with her. "I think it will be good for you. Now that this is all over, and nothing's happened all weekend, we can safely say that we know who the person behind all of this madness was. And they are gone now. So, we can get back to how things were."

"Well..." I'm about to tell her how they can't go back to how they were, seeing as she and Dad are separated. But then I remember my list. The things I promised I would do if I got out of that shed. So, I change my mind. I give her a smile instead. "You're right. You're so right." Then I walk over and give her a huge hug, for good measure.

She squeezes me back tightly before letting me pull away. Then she hands me a plate of bacon, eggs, and toast.

Joey's already at the table with Dad, scarfing his food down. He's being very quiet. He has his eyes fixed on his iPad. He has no interest in talking to any of us. And that's okay. He can talk when he's ready.

I sit down next to him and give him a playful nudge, just so he knows that I'm here for him and that I care. But I don't push him to talk. Instead, I eat my meal in silence.

"Is Audrey coming down soon?" Dad asks me.

"Doesn't matter. I'm not waiting for her," I say.

"What do you mean?" He and Mom both pause to stare at me.

"I'm taking my 4Runner to school," I say with a shrug, like it's no big deal and I do it all the time.

Seeing Mom and Dad's eyes practically bulge out of their heads is priceless.

I did it. Again. I drove my car again. It was terrifying. I was extra careful. I went ten miles under the speed limit. But I got behind the wheel. And I didn't get into an accident, I didn't even look at my phone, and I didn't kill anyone—I think the last one is the most important part.

People are looking at me curiously before I even get out of my car, and I know it's because they don't recognize it. Blackfell High School is small. Everybody knows everyone, and what everyone drives is included in that. After my first car was totaled, no one ever got to see my replacement.

When I get out of the 4Runner and everyone sees it's me who drives it, the stares don't stop as I walk through the parking lot. And I can hear the whispers.

"Look, it's The Cursed One.*"*

Some people smile. Some people even give me a wave. But nobody approaches. Nobody knows what to say to me. To say to our family.

The only person who is waiting for me is Wrigley, standing by my locker when I get inside the school.

"Hi," I say, relieved to see him.

He leans against the locker next to mine and rubs my arm in an adoring way. Wrigley and I aren't official or anything, but he makes it clear to everyone that we are an item. It's strange, because Wrigley Hall has never done that with anyone before.

I suppose I should consider myself lucky.

"You're really brave for coming," he says encouragingly. "I'm proud of you, you know that? But also, you don't have to be here if you don't want to. You say the word, and I'll take you home in an instant."

I reach out and play with his brown curls. It's my favorite thing about him. That, and the way he looks at me. "Don't be silly," I tell him with a smile. "I'm not going home. I can't miss any more school."

We start walking, but I almost freeze in my step when, down the hall, I spot Jackson Mullens, the dreaded ex-boyfriend. He is standing with Sophia Key, my ex-best friend, and they both look like they rule the school as they hold hands and stare around, dirty looks on their faces. Jackson is usually pleasant, but his dirty look is because he's staring at Wrigley and me. And I know he doesn't like what he sees. But we've been over this before—I've moved on. And he has moved on, too. With Sophia, apparently.

Classes are horrid. I talk to every single teacher after the bell, and every single one of them tells me I am failing their class, or close to it. That I still have a ton of makeup work to still do. Some give me options for some extra-credit work. Others look at me like they're saying, "Tough luck, kid. I'll see you back here next year." But those teachers don't know what they're talking about. Because I'm not going to repeat my junior year. I'm going to make it out of here on time. I'm going to catch up. I'm going to get at least C's. I'd prefer to get grades that will get me into college, but one thing at a time. One thing on my list at a time. I can be a model student. I can be the perfect daughter. I can be good to Wrigley. I can be the old, happy Lyla.

Danielle offers me a nice smile in Yoga, the class my therapist wanted me to take after Trinity's death. I think it will be fairly easy to get our friendship back on track. I always liked Danielle the best out of her, Sophia, and Olive. Olive, on the other hand, just does and says whatever Sophia wants her to. Danielle has a mind of her own, and she's incredibly sweet.

I smile back at her. She's wearing a sweater that I love. She borrowed it from Audrey once, and I guess she never returned it. I wouldn't either if I were her. It's soft and cozy. I've stolen it out of Audrey's closet myself a few times.

I think back to the old times, the day that Danielle first showed up to school in the sweater after borrowing it during one of our weekend sleepovers.

Audrey, Sophia, Danielle, Olive, Trinity, and I all walked through the hallways of Blackfell High School knowing we were the closest-knit group of friends in our year. We knew people envied what we had. We knew people talked about us more than they talked about other kids. We always got invited to all of the events and parties. Boys were always coming up to us to hang out or sit at our lunch table to get their flirt on.

Sophia was the one who helped us all learn how to do our make-up, along with some tips from my fashionable mother. Olive was the one who cracked stupid jokes that made us all giggle and look as if we were having the time of our lives as we strolled through the school's hallways. And Trinity... she and I would often linger behind the other four, in our own little world as we laughed about something stupid she had done the last time we hung out. She was my favorite. And everyone knew it. It was like we were a part of Sophia's group, but at the same time, Trinity and I had our own little one as well.

It's on my list to get my old friends back. Old Lyla was always with them. But it'll be weird to reunite with everyone.

Because one of them will never be able to return.

CHAPTER 9

WARNER

I hate being at Dean's. It's not that he has a lame house—he has a *nice* house. Nicer than the one that Mom and I are in. It just reminds me of the fact that he spent so much of his life not contributing to mine. Not to mention, he asked if we wanted to ride to school *together* today, which weirded me out beyond comprehension. I immediately told him no, of course.

School is going to be weird, too. I still don't know what the heck is going on with Audrey and me. I don't know why she kissed me at our spot, but I do know that... I liked it.

But I'm still so confused about everything because I know that I really like Lyla. Her twin.

As soon as I walk in through the entrance of school, my eyes fly to Jessica Vaccari. Another girl I have unfinished business with. She's standing by a bulletin board with some of her friends, talking to them with her arms crossed. She seems closed-off. Upset about something. She has every right to be upset. At least when it comes to me.

At the Halloween carnival, Jessica, acting completely freaked, told me to stay away from her. And I have no idea why. But I listened to her, even though it stung. Up until then, she had told me repeatedly that she wasn't buying into any of the rumors she had heard about me. Yet, out of nowhere, she decided she's done with me. Not only that—when she told me this, she had sounded *terrified*.

It's time I start cleaning up my messes. And since I can't figure out how to resolve the one I created between Audrey and Lyla, I can start with Jessica first.

"Hey, can I talk to you?" I ask her. Her friends stare at me with big eyes, which makes me feel like Jessica had just been talking to them about me. Or maybe they were just talking about what happened in the pool room recently, when Audrey and I were almost killed by Carson.

"I don't know, Warner," Jessica says, looking over her shoulders both ways as if she's worried that somebody she doesn't want to see us together is going to spot us.

"Please," I try. "It won't take long."

"Guys, wait for me, okay?" she says to her friends. Then we step outside together. It's frigid out here, making her cross her arms tighter. I try to look as relaxed as possible because I don't want her to think I'm closed-off or angry.

"Hey, I'm sorry that I haven't exactly reached out to you lately," I start.

"Why would you have?" she asks, shrugging. Her curly hair is pulled back and she looks pretty, but I can't help thinking about how she's just not Audrey. Or Lyla. "I told you not to."

What is wrong with me?

"I know," I say. I'm not good at this kind of stuff. "I just... I guess I want to know what happened to make you change your mind about me. Who said something to you? Who convinced you that all of the rumors about me are true? They're not, but I get it. Being with me was stupid."

I'm not looking to reconcile things with Jessica so that we can get back to dating each other. She should stay far away from me and all my problems.

"Wait." Her thick, dark eyebrows furrow together deeply. "Are you kidding me?"

"What?" I'm lost.

"Warner. After what you did to me..."

"Wait, what did I do to you?"

"You..." Her voice turns quiet. "You *used* me."

"Used you?"

"I talked to Jackson. He made it very clear to me."

"Jackson? Jessica—I'm lost."

"You're still into Lyla. You only asked me out to make her jealous."

I don't even know what to say back to that. And she can sense it.

"Tell me I'm wrong," she says.

I can't. But only because I am trying to decide if I should tell her it might actually be Audrey I'm into. I don't freaking know. I tried things out with Jessica because I knew she liked me. She's beautiful. She's sweet. I thought maybe being with her would help me...move on.

I guess maybe I did use her.

"That's what I thought," she says. Her voice is gravelly. "I know my worth. I don't need to put up with guys like you."

Ouch.

"Jessica, I'm—"

She interrupts me. She doesn't want to hear my apology. "Besides. That whole thing with Sophia that happened that night...With that—that person who's been messing with you guys now apparently starting to go after your friends, I think it's best if we just keep our distance, don't you?"

"I... I don't know. You're probably right. I guess."

She starts to turn back to the school.

"For what it's worth, I'm really sorry, Jessica."

"Yeah. Sure, Warner. See ya around."

One of the nice things about being a senior is that I don't have any classes with the Bailey twins. It makes it easier to spend the day avoiding them so I can get my head on straight. I don't want to avoid them forever because I do need to talk to them about everything. I want to know what they think about Carson Price being found in the woods. And I want to let them know that my mom is okay—or at least she *says* she is.

Walking to the locker room after school so I can get ready for practice, I text the new number that belongs to my mom to check in again. And the reply is:

Unknown: *Still fine. Laying low. Will explain soon.*

I have no choice but to trust that it's really her and that she is all right. Because my head can't take anything else. I want to believe that Carson Price was the one behind this. And that he is dead, and that my mom is safe. I want to move on from all of this.

Before I even get past Dean's office and into the locker room, Dean pulls me inside and shuts the door.

"Yeah?" I ask him a little impatiently. I'm still mad about how I caught him driving to go see Amelia at the psych ward. I don't like that he basically forced me to stay over at his place when I would have been fine at home alone.

"Warner, there's no easy way to say this so I'm just going to do it quick. Rip the Band-Aid off."

"What are you talking about?"

"I'm sorry, but you're no longer captain of this team. There have just been too many absences. There is too much going on with you. You don't have the headspace anymore for it. You have to agree with me."

"Are you kidding me?"

"Well... No. I—Warner, you've been skipping practices. You haven't come up with any new plays. None of your teammates are really happy with you right now. It's just not—you've lost your passion for football. Everyone sees it."

My blood is boiling. But what is the point of arguing? "Fine."

Besides, if I start yelling at him right now about it, I'm probably going to let it slip that I know about him and Amelia, too. I'll probably keep going and accuse him of lying when he said he wanted us to be a family.

"I'm sorry, Warner," he says, "But this might be good for you anyway. It'll be one less thing on your plate."

"Whatever. Can I go now?"

"Uh... yeah. Fine." He puts his hands on his hips, standing in front of his chair. He shakes his head like he is frustrated with my reaction. But what does he want? Tears?

"Great." I storm out of his office, throwing the door open and hoping to break it off the hinges as I go. It doesn't happen, but it does catch the look of a lot of my teammates.

I ignore all of them and get changed for practice.

It's not until I get back out onto the field and join everybody that I learn who the new football captain is.

Ryan Copeland.

CHAPTER 10

MADDY

"**S**o."

Steven is sitting on the coffee table, staring at me as I lay on his couch. I just woke up from a very long nap a few minutes ago. Warner texted me again on the prepaid phone Steven went out and bought me. He says I should keep my other phone off in case Dean is somehow able to track it.

I feel horrible about not being home with Warner. I need to get myself out of this mess with Steven so I can come out of hiding. But if Steven learns Dean isn't crazy, is he going to go back to hating me because of that kiss he saw Dean give me? I don't want him to hate me. I just want him to trust me. I want him to believe me about how the kiss meant nothing. Not to me, anyway. I still don't know why Dean did that. It had been completely out of the blue.

"So," I say back to Steven in a groggy voice. My body is still sore. The pain medication I've been taking around the clock makes me drowsy. I have been asleep most of the time I've been here.

"When are we going to go to the police about Dean?" Steven asks. He's apparently had enough of this "waiting around." He wants something done about my "psycho ex-boyfriend."

"I... I don't wanna go to the police, Steven," I say, trying to sit myself up. I manage to do it, but it's not without great difficulty.

"You don't have to get up, Maddy," Steven says, sounding worried as he watches me struggle. "But you've got to tell me what your issue is with the police."

"I don't have an issue with the police."

"No? What about when we ran into that one guy at The Mix? Detective Craig Something?"

My stomach dips. "What about him?"

"When I met him, it was pretty apparent that you two have a problem with each other. I didn't press it then, but I think it's time I know now. Is it because of Dean? Are they friends or something?"

"Definitely not."

"Then what? Come on. We gotta do something about this. It's not like you can just stay hidden with me forever. You have Warner to get back to."

I'm tired. I'm hurting. I'm stressed. My job is probably going to fire me for all the no-call no-shows. But what is scarier than that is how Steven is going to react to what I need to tell him. To what I should have told him from the very beginning.

I really want to be with Steven. I can see myself marrying and settling down with him even. He's the perfect guy for me. And not just because he has a lot of money. I don't care about that. I genuinely like him as a person. And he likes me, too. But that might change once I tell him.

And I need to do it now.

The sigh out of my mouth is a heavy one. "Steven. I... I need to tell you something."

"What is it?"

I hate that he looks concerned instead of skeptical. That he hasn't already figured out I've been lying to him this whole time. He probably thinks I'm going to admit some horrible thing Dean has done to me in the past.

I close my eyes when I say it because I can't bear to see his reaction. "I don't have a psychotic ex-boyfriend."

I don't open them again until I hear him say, "What?" And when I peek, he looks confused. Go figure.

"Dean... He is Warner's father, yeah. But he's not—he's not crazy. I never had a psychotic ex. I just made it up."

Sometimes I really hate myself.

"You made it up." His voice is flat. And his eyes have hardened.

"It was just easier than explaining the truth to you. Because in the truth, I... I did something terrible. And I've been afraid to tell you about it. I just like you so much, and..."

"What's going on, Maddy?" He gets to his feet, which isn't a good sign. I try to get to mine, too, but he shakes his head. "Just stay there," he says, holding his hand out to stop me.

I obey him. I want to cry. But I need to hold it together and get this out.

"You know that person they found in the woods on the news? Carson Price? I know him. When we were in high school, Carson was dating my friend Amelia's little sister, Nora. And he was abusive to her. So, at our junior prom, Mia and I followed him to a cabin, and Mia pushed him off the balcony. And... I thought she killed him. We pulled him out of the pool she pushed him into, and when he didn't wake up, I told Mia to just—to leave him there. It turns out he wasn't really dead. And everything that has happened, the reason *you* were messed with, is because he had been trying to get his revenge on us."

Steven stands there with his mouth hanging open and his wiry brows clashing. I focus on his dimpled chin because at least it is one feature of his that can't look angry.

Scratch that. Yes, it can.

"Steven, I'm so, *so* sorry I lied to you," I say. "I just—I feel terrible about what I did to him and what it led to, and I couldn't bear you thinking of me any differently." I wish I could take a thumbtack and pop the huge lump in my throat.

"Oh, I think of you differently all right," he replies.

It's exactly what I hoped he wouldn't say. But I also knew he would.

"I wish I could take it back."

"I don't think of you differently because of your past, Maddy. I think of you differently because of right now. Because of all of the lies. I can't believe this. I feel so stupid. My car...What happened with my car then, if you weren't trying to escape from Dean?"

"I was driving to Warner because he was in danger. And then... Carson dove in front of me. He must have been running from the police. I don't know."

Can I fix this? Can I get him to not be mad? To understand why I lied?

"You couldn't have just told me the truth in the beginning? I—I would have just brought you to the hospital when I found you if I knew all of that! Instead, I had you bleeding out on my back seat, and I felt like I had to bring you somewhere I could stay by your side and keep you safe in case you were still in danger. I—you scared the heck out of me, Maddy! When I brought you back here, I was worried I was going to have to kill this guy if he showed up at my house again!"

"I know, I messed up."

"Messed up? You didn't just mess up. You're... you're not who I thought you were."

"Steven..."

He shakes his head, and his eyes are sad. A tear falls from mine. I didn't want to hurt him. I don't know why I had any semblance of hope that it would go differently. That he would understand. That he wouldn't be mad. That our relationship would continue.

He sighs. I already know what he's about to say next.

"I think it's time for you to leave."

CHAPTER 11

AUDREY

When I arrive at school and walk through the parking lot, I hate that I have to go through it all alone. The stares. The Whispers. There was a time when Blackfell High only called Lyla "The Cursed One." But I hear it loud and clear when a sophomore, who thinks he's the funniest thing on the planet, jokes with his friends about how my whole family is cursed and they all laugh with him.

When I get inside, even Ryan's friends are gossiping and joking about me. Ryan is at least enough of a gentleman to tell them to shut up. Instead of joining in with them, he continuously asks me if I am okay. He is sweet. Ryan is *always* sweet—but here I am, pining over Warner and kissing him in secret.

After Warner and I kissed again at our spot, we agreed that it was probably better if we just kept it quiet that it happened. And then we hung out for an hour, and we didn't kiss again or say anything about it. In a way, it still feels like I didn't get any answers from him.

At lunch, Kylie Fisher and her friends want me to sit with them. I agree, knowing that if I wasn't involved with Ryan, they wouldn't even be talking to me. I don't say much, no matter how many questions they ask me about what I just went through. Instead, I play the observer. I notice how the more I get to know Kiley, the more I realize she is the Sophia Key of the seniors. She likes attention. She likes gossip.

And she likes Ryan. I can just tell by the way she talks about him. It's pretty obvious.

When school ends, I can't participate in cheer because of my injuries. I would've skipped it altogether, which would have been a lot nicer than trying to dodge Sophia and Olive as they, yet again, try to be friendly to me. I wonder if Olive knows what Sophia is up to with the TikTok account.

Instead of skipping, I sit with my back against the brick wall in the gymnasium, my knees under my chin and my arms wrapped around my shins. I watch Sophia and Kylie act like the same exact person in two different cliques.

I had to stay after school anyway. Because Jackson won't be leaving until he's done with football practice, and I'm planning on following him.

I hide around a corner in the empty hallway after practice. All of the other girls left already, but the football players just got back from the field. I feel disgustingly like how Carson Price must have felt that day he chased me in the school hallway the first time I ever had an encounter with him.

I watch as Jackson leaves the locker room with his buddies. I discreetly follow them outside. In the parking lot, I duck down behind other cars, hoping other classmates don't see me, as Jackson fist-bumps his friends goodbye and then begins walking.

And he's walking off-campus.

I sneak after him, and for an entire block, he's completely clueless about me. He's too busy staring at his phone.

Then, there it is. His stupid gray Mustang. It's parked on the street in front of a dirt lot.

This is it? This *is where he's keeping his secret car?*

This whole thing is so stupid. Who hides the fact that they got a car and their driver's license? What does he get out of it?

I had been too afraid to confront Sophia about the TikTok account before. But now, I want some dang answers.

"Hey!" I yell, jumping out of my hiding spot behind a bus stop advertisement before Jackson can get in his car and speed away.

Jackson, his hand on the door handle, turns to the sound of my voice. I walk toward him, watching his expression transform from surprised to angry. "Audrey?"

"What is this?" I demand, thrusting my hand to his stupid car.

"What are you talking about?"

"Why are you hiding the fact that you have a car from everybody? I knew it was you. I knew it from the very first time you drove past our house when Lyla went missing."

He steps away from the car. "That's stupid. I'm not hiding it from anyone."

"No? Then why are you parking it so far away from school?"

"None of your business, Audrey. Did you seriously follow me all the way over here?"

"Don't try to turn this around. You're being sketchy."

"Look in the mirror!"

"Are you and Sophia Toxeydramaenthusiast?"

He looks like he wants to lunge at me. "Why would you ask me that? Are you kidding me?"

"Are you?" I have to stand my ground. "You know what? You don't even have to answer. I know you are."

"You're delusional."

"Why are you doing it?"

"Audrey, leave me alone! I'm not some stupid gossip reporter for some stupid TikTok account! And don't even think about babbling about this to Lyla, because it's completely false."

"I don't believe you." My head is held high. "And I think I am going to tell Lyla."

"You'll just look like an idiot when the real owner of the account comes forward."

"I guess we'll just have to see then."

We have this intense stare-down that lasts I-don't-know-how-long, and then he scoffs at me, shakes his head, and gets in his car.

Great. I had been so certain that I was right before I followed him here. It made sense. Sophia has the camera equipment. The two of them have been sneaking around together. Driving around in an unfamiliar car, they don't have to worry about being recognized by anyone.

But maybe the real owner of the Toxeydramaenthusiast account is still out there somewhere.

As I glare at Jackson's car while he starts it up, another familiar one slowly drives past us. I look through the window and recognize the person driving it immediately.

Eric.

Carson's supposed father.

That's strange.

What is Eric still doing in Toxey now that he knows what happened to his son? I don't like it. I don't trust it.

What if Eric is still here because he knows something we don't?

CHAPTER 12

AMELIA

After I end the call I just stupidly accepted, I want to throw my phone across Lyla and Audrey's bathroom—I've been on my hands and knees giving their shower-tub a deep clean. Instead, I set it carefully down on the tub ledge beside me. My hands shake furiously. My heart is pounding, echoing in the quiet of this tiled bathroom.

I take a couple of seconds and try to calm myself as quickly as I can, then I pick up my phone again and call Gentry. Thankfully, he answers. Maybe Gentle Hands hasn't called him yet, or he ignored them when they did.

"Everything okay?" he says as a way of answering.

"I-I—Gentry... Gentle Hands just called me and... I didn't know what to do. I can't deal with that right now. I'm—I'm so stupid." I'm rambling. I can't stop myself. I don't even know exactly why I called Gentry. I'm just panicking, and I'm hoping he can help me. Gentle Hands knows what happened with Joey. They have it out for me. They know I am unfit to foster anyone.

"Mia. It's okay. I'm sorry that they called you. I already left a message at their office saying for them to give me a call if they need to talk. Apparently, they chose to ignore it."

"Yeah. Apparently." I put my head in my hand.

"Don't worry. I will handle it. All right?"

"Thank you."

Already, I feel a million times better, just with Gentry's reassuring tone.

"Are you okay?" he asks.

"Hardly," I admit. "Sometimes I feel like everything is getting better. Then other times I feel like I'm still hanging on by a thread."

"I won't be gone much longer," he says. He's been back to staying in our guest room, and Joey is still here, too, even though he's still not speaking to me. Gentry thinks it's important to be here by his daughters' and my side, for now. "I'll pick up dinner so you don't have to cook again."

I close my eyes and nod.

"Mia?"

"That sounds good."

"Everything's going to be fine, yeah?"

"Right."

We get off the phone, and still not feeling totally better, I wander into my bathroom downstairs. I open the medicine cabinet. I pull out the pill bottle.

I should take one. I haven't yet today. But what if after I went to sleep last night, something happened? What if my medication got switched again?

An anxiety pill would help me out so much right now. And my doctor was pretty adamant when he said I needed to take it. But as I stare at the bottle, I'm terrified. It wrecked me before.

Maybe I'm better off just not taking anything at all.

I open the lid of the toilet, dump all of the pills into the bowl, and flush.

CHAPTER 13

WARNER

The pants are nearly scared off of me when the doorknob of our front door starts jiggling. I came home in the first place because I only packed one thing of clothes for Dean's, wrongly anticipating that I wouldn't have to stay with him another night.

Thankful that I had remembered to lock the door behind me, I start looking around for something I can use as a weapon to defend myself against the potential intruder. When the door opens, I yell, thinking that I'm about to be attacked again. When I see that it's Mom, and that she has come home, *finally*, I run my hands through my hair and take a couple of deep breaths.

"You could have told me you were coming home!" I snap at her. My heart is hammering in my chest. I look Mom over. She's hurt. Bruised everywhere. Walking with a limp. She looks like she's in pain. "Mom... are you all right?"

She shuts and locks the door. "Hey, Warner," she greets in a soft, tired voice. She hobbles over to the couch. Worried about her, I rush over to help her sit down. "I'm fine," she says, but I hardly believe it.

"What happened? Where were you? How'd you wreck Steven's car?"

"I'll explain everything," she says. "But please, I need aspirin. Or ibuprofen. *Something* for this pain."

I run to the medicine cabinet and get her some, along with a glass of water. I hurriedly hand it to her, and she takes the pills and then takes her time drinking the water, draining the entire cup while I stand there patiently wanting to know what the heck is going on.

"So?" I ask when she sets the cup down.

"I was at Steven's."

"Okay...why?"

She jumps into her explanation. She tells me how stupid she's been. How she made a fool of herself in front of Steven. How upset she made him and how they're broken up. She sheds some tears over it. I can see clearly that she really likes Steven. Maybe even more than any of the other guys that have been in her life.

"I... I guess stuff like this happens when you... lie, ya know?" I say after. I'm not trying to sound mean. I just need her to understand that these lies can't go on. She's been lying to so many people her entire life, and it's what led to all of this. I'm not saying I entirely blame my mom for everything that happened, but... she *is* the cause of it. Her lies hurt people.

"Yeah, thanks, *Dad*." She rolls her eyes.

"Do you need to go to the hospital?" She still is so banged up from the accident. I can't believe Steven didn't take her.

"A doctor came to see me at Steven's," she answers. "I'm going to be okay. I'm just glad that *you're* all right. I'm sorry... Warner ..." She starts crying again. "I'm *so* sorry that I wasn't there for you. I wanted to be *so* badly. I was just so rushed trying to get to the school, and it was raining and..."

I sit down next to her and hug her, trapping her arms against her sides so she can't hug me back. Instead, she just sits there and sobs while I lean my head on her shoulder. "It's okay, Ma. You called the police. Ultimately, you *did* help us. If I didn't think that you would, I would've called somebody else."

She gives me a weak smile.

"And we're okay," I continue. "All of us are okay. And Carson is dead now. I'm still really confused about it all... and sometimes I think maybe Craig could have been lying when he said that... but... I don't know. Nothing has happened since that night."

"Yeah. Carson is dead," she agrees. "He can't hurt us anymore."

I nod. "Oh, uh...I've been staying with Dean."

"What do you mean? Like... at his *house*?"

"Yep. He wouldn't let me stay here alone."

She sighs. "I'm sorry. I just made everything harder on you."

"It wasn't that bad," I say. It could've been worse. Dean let me keep to myself in his guest room. He ordered takeout for dinner instead of trying to cook something for us. We watched some sports on TV.

"Still," she says, "I'm working on the lying, Warner. I am trying to be better. I... I've caused so much harm. And I've learned my lesson."

"Good." I get to my feet. "This probably isn't the time to talk about it, but we are really behind on a lot of bills. I know you haven't been working, and I don't have a job anymore, but I want another one now that this is all over and I can focus on other things. Maybe I can work at your salon? Can you get me a job? I'll be a receptionist. Or I'll clean, or whatever. Sweep up hair." I shudder at the thought. I just need the money.

"You wanna work at a hair salon?" she asks skeptically.

"I want to work anywhere I can make some money for us." I shrug.

"I'm gonna get myself back to work, you don't have to worry about that. No more callouts. And when it comes to getting you a job... I'll see what I can do."

Between football, school, and working a new job, my schedule will be packed. And the busier I make myself, the less I'll be thinking about Carson Price and wondering if he's still out there.

I try to go to bed. I *really* try. I look at part-time jobs on Indeed. I stuff my phone under my mattress and squeeze my eyes shut. I toss and turn. I turn the fan on. I turn it off. I try going with and then without covers. But nothing works. Nothing stops me from feeling restless.

I give up eventually. But I can't just sit around my room and do nothing.

I grab my tools and go out front. My Wrangler is from the 90s and needs a lot of upkeep, so there's plenty I can work on to keep busy. Then, when my eyes start drooping closed later— they have to eventually—I'll go back inside and finally get some shut-eye.

So, I work.

And I work.

And I work.

And the need for sleep still won't come.

But it's fine. I like working on my Jeep. It's a good distraction. In fact, I am so into what I'm doing that I don't register the sound of someone's footsteps until they are only a couple of feet away from me.

I look up from underneath my hood, and when I see one of the Bailey twins, I hit my head on it. I think the sound of it is going to make her head snap to look at me. But even when I cry out in pain, she doesn't seem to notice.

"Lyla?" I guess. It's dark out here, so it's hard to tell. But as I step closer, I know it's her. She's wearing a short-sleeved top, and I can see the scar on her arm.

She's not here to see me. She's walking in the direction of Jackson's. *Past* me. I don't think she even knows I'm here.

"Lyla," I try again. Still, she doesn't answer. I start to panic a little because she looks like a literal zombie. Like she's been hypnotized or something.

She's still walking to Jackson's house. She's in his front yard now.

I take a few more steps toward her. What is she doing? Does she have any idea what time it is? Does she plan on waking up his entire family *just* to talk to him? Why?

I have to stop this. She doesn't know what she's doing. "Lyla!"

I run over to her. She's still advancing toward Jackson's front door. She nearly gets a foot—a *bare* foot—on the first step to his porch, but I grab her arm and pull her back.

What I'm not prepared for is for her to start screaming so loudly I think the next town over can hear it. And then her arms flail everywhere. Her eyes see mine for only a moment. Then she lunges at me.

CHAPTER 14

LYLA

"Lyla, stop! *Stop!*"

I jolt awake, but my body feels like it's already *been* awake. My legs are like Jell-O. I'm out of breath. I'm... yelling at someone?

What is going on?

Warner is standing in front of me, his lip bleeding and his chest heaving rapidly. He's grabbing onto both of my hands tightly.

"Warner?"

He lets go of me. "Lyla! I think—were you *sleepwalking?*"

I look around. "I..."

Holy Crap. What the heck?

I walked all the way to Jackson's house? In my sleep? I don't even remember having a dream about coming here. I don't even know *why* I would come here.

"I was," I admit, my entire body beginning to tremble. I hate that I did this. It's so dangerous. Not to mention embarrassing. "Wh-what time is it?"

"Uh..." Warner pulls out his phone from his back pocket. "It's like, 2:30 in the morning."

"Oh no."

"Yeah... you... tried to go to Jackson's house. And I tried to stop you, and you beat the crap out of me."

I cover my face with my hands and shake my head, refusing to look up again.

"Hey, are you okay?" he asks.

"No. I'm so sorry, Warner."

His fingers pry my hands away from my face. "I'm here, Lyla. I got you."

I take a few deep breaths. He *does* have this calming presence about him that makes me feel better.

"Do you want to go sit on my porch steps and talk?" he asks, wiping the blood on his lip with his already filthy shirt. I didn't get him that badly. It's just a small scratch.

"What are you even doing out here?" I ask. "Did you hear me or something?"

He motions to his Jeep. "I've been working on tuning her up," he says.

"Oh. This late?"

He shrugs. "I couldn't sleep."

"I... get that."

We walk to his porch and sit down on the second step together. I'm still shaking. Not just because it's cold. I just feel so confused and overwhelmed. One moment, I was sound asleep in my bed. Now here I am.

"Uh...hey—how's your mom?" he asks.

"She's getting better. Have you heard from yours?"

He nods toward the house. "She's home. She made Steven think that Dean was behind all of this and Steven thought he was protecting her by hiding her at his house. Then he dumped her when he found out she was lying."

"Oh..."

I don't even know how to reply to that. Why couldn't Maddy just tell him the truth from the beginning?

Why didn't *anyone* tell the truth from the beginning?

"Yeah," he says.

We're silent. I stare ahead of me. I don't want to look at him.

"There's something I wanted to tell you," Warner says after a while, his tone soft.

"What?" I say, dread in my tone.

"Um..." He grabs the back of his neck. "When you were kidnapped... by Carson, he recorded you. He recorded you... screaming."

"H-how do you know?"

"He left the voice recorder in my locker as a nice little treat."

My face twists. "That's horrific."

"Yeah. And, do you remember at Wrigley's party? When you could hear what sounded like Sydney screaming for you? And people thought it was Trinity maybe? Now I'm pretty sure it *was* Sydney. And... someone recorded *her* getting tortured, too."

"Stop," I demand. I hold my hand out and shake my head frantically. "Just stop. *Please*. I don't want to talk about this."

"Lyla, I just don't think—"

"No." I get to my feet. "I just want to move on with my life, Warner. Carson is dead. It's all done now. What happened happened, and we can't change the past. So, let's just move forward, okay?"

He doesn't look like it's okay. He looks like he's going to keep talking about it. But before he can, I notice that something is buzzing in the pocket of my sweatpants. I brought my phone with me? I remembered by phone, but I couldn't remember to at least put on some *shoes*?

I pull it out. It's Mom.

"Crap," I say. Then I answer.

"Lyla?!" Mom's voice is high-pitched. Worried. "Lyla, *where* are you? Tell me right now!"

"I... I'm..." How do I tell her what happened without her getting mad? "I'm at Warner's."

"*What*?! Right now? Why?! I checked on you *two* hours ago and you were asleep! Get home now!"

I can't even say anything to explain myself. She hangs up on me before it's possible.

"You get caught?" Warner asks.

"I should have known I would. It's impossible to sneak out or go anywhere without them knowing now. Mom and Dad watch us like hawks."

"Well... Listen, Lyla—"

"She's freaking out, Warner. I have to go. Can you drive me home?"

"Yeah." He hangs his head. When he stands up, he looks disappointed that we're done having this conversation. But he has to know that it can't continue. I told him even before Carson was dead that I don't want to be a part of this. It's not on my list. I'm supposed to be the old Lyla.

I can't be the new Lyla anymore. She didn't do anybody any good.

CHAPTER 15

AMELIA

When Lyla gets home, I'm waiting for her on the sofa. Gentry is still asleep in the guestroom. I didn't wake him up to bother him with this. He's already handling so much.

"What exactly possessed you to go to Warner's in the middle of the night?" I ask when she sees me.

"Mom," she says, clearly not expecting me to be waiting for her like this.

"Hmm?"

"I... I just couldn't sleep. And he's a good friend to talk to."

"Well, talk to him in the daytime. When there are other people out in the world, and when you're not in danger, and when I know where you are at all times."

"You're right. It was dumb. I just wanted somebody to talk to."

"You can talk to your therapist."

She mumbles something under her breath, but it sounds a lot like, "So should you."

"Do I have to sleep outside of your bedroom door to make sure you don't go anywhere else tonight?" I ask her, ignoring the comment.

"No. I'm exhausted. I will lock myself in. I just want to sleep."

"Are you okay?"

"Yeah. Never better. Sneaking out was stupid. I'm really sorry, Mom."

I let out the breath I've been holding in. I put a hand on her shoulder. "It's okay. It's okay."

I think I'm saying it more to myself than to her.

When the girls leave for school in the morning—Lyla taking her own car again—it's just Joey, Gentry, and me. I've already told Gentry that I want some time alone with Joey to talk to him, so he's busying himself in his guestroom. He probably would normally go into the study, since that used to be his favorite room in the house, but no one has been in there since Carson died. It's still perfectly preserved from when I lost my marbles and went obsessive over my research about him.

Joey is at the kitchen table having a bowl of cereal since I've been too busy planning what I'm going to say to him to make breakfast.

I take my cup of coffee and sit across from him. "Joey, can I talk to you?"

He finishes chewing and swallowing before he answers. "Okay."

It's a good start—I kind of expected him to say that he was busy. That he didn't have time. That he didn't want to.

"I just wanted you to know how sorry I am for what I did, Joe. I know I've said it already, but I really, *really* want you to know how much I mean it. I never meant to scare you or worry you or put you in any sort of danger. I care about you so much."

He seems to carefully consider my words. Or maybe he's just considering what *he* wants to say. "It's okay," he eventually decides. But I can see the look on his face. It doesn't seem like it's okay. He hasn't been himself since the incident happened.

"Are you upset with me?" I ask.

"I was," he says. "I don't know. Everything is just really different and weird now."

"I know. And I'm sorry. But we're going to get things back on track really really fast, I promise."

"But they won't be the same," he says. "Not with you and Dad divorcing."

"I know." I need to find a way to cheer him up. "But your dad is doing everything he can to make sure that you get to stay with him *forever*. Isn't that cool?"

"What about you?"

Ouch. This is really killing me. "You'll still see me, too, of course."

And maybe he will at first. Maybe when Lyla and Audrey have their turn at my house, he will accompany them every so often. But

I know what will happen in the future. I will fade out. Joey will start coming less and less. He will stop seeing me as a mother figure. He will accept that he just has his father and that he's all he needs, and I will just be that woman who fostered him for three years.

But that's the way it should be. I'm not good for him.

"It's just... I don't know. It's still weird," Joey repeats.

I reach across the table and hold his hand, and I'm so scared that he's going to pull away. But he doesn't. Still, I can't shake the feeling that he wants to. "You're right," I agree. "It *is* weird. But it'll get better."

It has to get better.

CHAPTER 16

MADDY

Yesterday evening, I forced myself to reach out to everyone to let them know that I am home and that everything is fine, even though part of me wanted to just stay missing forever, hiding away and not having to deal with anything. Not having to have any responsibilities.

I even texted Mia to let her know, even though we got in a fight the last time we talked. So, I'm surprised when I wake up the next morning and see a message from her.

Mia: *I'm really glad you're safe. Can you come over and talk this morning?*

I'm supposed to go to work today. And I told Warner that I was done calling out. We need the money. But I'm still in a lot of pain. So maybe he can be a little understanding that I didn't mean I would go back *immediately*.

On top of the pain, I'm still super sad about Steven, feeling weird about Carson being dead, and wondering what's going to happen with Sydney's death investigation since the person who probably killed her isn't here to be questioned anymore. I'm also thinking about how I haven't really talked to Warner's father, who kissed me the last time we met up, and who had been keeping Warner at his house with him.

And I don't like that I got in a fight with Mia. She's my only friend. I text her back.

Me: *I'll be there in an hour.*

I get ready like I'm about to go to work because maybe I can just get by without even telling Warner that I didn't go. It's not lying, it's just omitting. That doesn't count.

Then, when I drop Warner off at school since we have to share a car again after I destroyed Steven's Audi, I go to Mia's instead of my job. When I park the Jeep outside of her house, I send my work a text to let them know that I was in an accident and can get a doctor's note if they need, but that I should be able to come back tomorrow.

When I knock on Mia's door, I wonder what kind of Mia I'm going to get today. The one who is prim and proper and incredibly fashionable and looking like a movie star? The one who flashes a gorgeous smile and makes you just want to know her from a simple look?

Or is it going to be the Mia I saw the last time we talked? The one who was mad at me for seemingly a million reasons even though in actuality, I hadn't even done anything wrong? Is it going to be the Mia who can hardly get herself ready anymore? Who doesn't even remember how to smile?

The door answers. And just based off of the look of her, I think I'm going to get something a little bit in between both of those versions. Mia got ready today, and she looks fantastic. But there's still a hollowness to her. And she doesn't give me that bright smile that tells me everything is fine between us.

"Hi," I say in a small voice.

"Thank you for coming," she says. She opens the door wide and lets me in. I still can't get over how nice her house is. She worked so hard to get where she is in her career. She could have done so much better than Toxey. She should have left a long time ago.

"I'm really glad that you asked me to," I say as we walk into her front room. I stop and take my shoes off first—it is *way* too clean in here for me to leave the black boots that I'm always wearing to work on.

She sits on her pristine white sofa, so I sit down in a leather armchair. She has the fireplace going. It's very cozy and relaxing in here. I'd stay all day if I could.

"I wanted to apologize to you," Mia tells me. She's pretty stubborn, so I'm surprised that she's *leading* the conversation with this. When we were kids, and she knew she did something wrong, she would always try to figure out if we could pretend like it never happened first before actually coming out with the apology. But I could be the same way. It was why we were always so feisty with each other.

"*I* should apologize to *you*," I say. "I know I had my doubts about whether it was Carson or not."

She nods. "But I didn't have to jump down your throat about it. And I was being nasty about Craig and Dean, and there was no need for it. I wasn't myself. I was obsessed with getting this all to stop."

"I'm just relieved that you don't hate me."

"Maddy. We've been through so much. I can't ever hate you." Finally, I get a little bit of that smile. It's not the full one, but it warms my heart regardless.

We dive into catching up on each other's lives. I learn all about her short time in the institute she was wrongly put in and what Carson did with her meds. And how it's going with Gentry and Joey and Joey's fostering situation. And how her girls seem to be handling things better than expected, and Lyla is even driving her own car.

I fill her in on my end. About the accident. About that night at the pool and how I had tried to save Audrey and Warner. About how Steven found me and how everything is going with that. I tear up a little, too, as I talk about Steve dumping me, which is so not like me. I don't cry over a guy, especially in front of anyone. And you think I'd be crying about much more important things rather than over losing him. I hate that I care about him so much.

Then the conversation circles back to Sydney.

"So, with Carson being dead, and Craig finally learning that he has been alive this whole time, how's the investigation with Sydney—or Megan—going to go now, do you think?" I ask.

"I still don't even get that," she says. "I don't get how this random girl who posed as a teenager tried to befriend our kids but got murdered. It's safe to say that Carson killed her, right? I just don't understand why."

"I have no idea." I lean closer. "But you know what else?"

She waits. Her legs are curled up underneath her on the sofa and her elbow is resting on the back of it as she holds her head in her hand and looks at me.

"Carson and Craig were best friends. What if, all this time, Craig had known Carson was alive? What if he's been helping him cover his tracks for everything he's been doing, and that's why he was so desperate to pin everything on us? I mean, what if Craig lied about Carson's suicide? And what if he's dangerous?"

"That's... a lot, Maddy."

"I know. But I can't stop thinking about it. There are still so many unanswered questions, aren't there? I just... I'm not satisfied with Carson being dead. Not just because I don't one-hundred-percent know if that's even true, but because... there's just so much we still don't know."

"You're right. We need to understand how Megan Young ties into all of this. I think the sooner we figure that out, the sooner we'll be able to get the answers to everything else, too."

"I agree."

I keep myself busy away from the house for a reasonable amount of time after Warner gets home from school, having gotten a ride from a friend. Then, the normal time I usually come home from work, I pull into the driveway and go inside.

"Hi, Warner," I say when I set my purse down. "You got a second?" He is working on his laptop on the sofa.

"Yeah, everything okay?" he asks, closing the computer and setting it down. I glance at all the unfolded laundry next to it, dread filling me as I realized I have so many chores I need to do, and take a seat with him. "I want to talk to you about Sydney."

I don't want to make him mad. I don't want him to think that I still think he killed her. So I wait to try to gauge what his expression is. He looks... surprised, maybe?

"Is that okay?" I ask.

"I... I guess. What about her?"

"Can you just... I don't know. Can you start at the beginning with her? When you met her. What she was like. Everything that happened between her and you. It's just still so weird how she ties into all of this, and if she even does. I know some things, and I guess

I just want to know how much *you* know, and I want to compare notes, or whatever."

"Okay." So, he fills me in. He tells me about how Sydney/Megan seemed really interested in getting to be his friend—or more—in the very beginning. He told me about how all the kids talked badly about her and made fun of her for her ratty clothes and style. How it seemed like she wanted to be friends with Audrey and Lyla, too. And how that night she died, she asked all three of them to meet with her.

So it has to be related to the Carson thing.

"That's... interesting," I say when he finishes.

"Yeah. We're pretty sure that she got in the middle of it somehow, whether she wanted to or not, and that's what led to her death," he says.

"We?"

"Audrey and I. Audrey's coming over shortly, actually."

I raise my eyebrows. "Audrey is?"

He nods.

"So, about that..."

"*Mom.*"

"Which one of those twins are you interested in? I sort of thought you liked Lyla. But you hang with Audrey a lot more. And what about Jessica? What ever happened with that?"

"We're not having this conversation," he says, getting up off the couch. He grabs his laptop like he's going to retreat into his room to hide from me. But then he turns back. "Hey, did you get me a job today?"

Um... no," I admit. He thinks I went to work today, and that I inquired about it. "I haven't yet, but don't freak out. I actually have something better in mind. And I'm going to go get you that job right now."

"Do you want to tell me what it is?" he asks.

"Don't worry about it. It will be good for you."

"All right... I'm trusting you..."

I stand. "Good. You should. I am taking your Jeep again."

I grab my purse again and go to the front door. He walks me outside. It's a thoughtful gesture. Maybe he is starting to enjoy spending time with me. Or maybe he just wants to make sure I don't fall over since I still walk with a little bit of a limp and make pained noises every so often. There is a lot of my body that still hurts.

As we reach the Jeep, we hear the noise of something heavy being dragged through gravel. It's Jackson, taking his dumpster to the curb for trash pickup. He glares over in our direction briefly but then ignores us.

"You know, when you were in the hospital after my car exploded, part of the reason I was worried about your involvement with Sydney is because of him," I admit. I'm talking quiet enough so that Jackson can't hear. Warner has his hand on the driver's side door handle of the Jeep.

He furrows his brows. "What do you mean?"

"He said that you said you wished Sydney was dead."

"Figures," he grumbles as I watch his jaw tighten. "It's not true. I never said that."

"I see."

"Jackson hates me. He's hated me for a while. We're definitely not friends anymore. He'll just do whatever he can to keep throwing me under the bus now. To get back at me for nearly trying to kiss his girlfriend."

"Nearly?"

He shakes his head and smirks. "Again. Not having this conversation. I'll see you later."

I kiss him on the cheek and then leave him alone.

CHAPTER 17

AUDREY

I'll admit, when Warner texted me and told me I should come over today, I was nervous about it. And I still am. I don't know what's going on between us. If I did, everything would feel much easier. Because hanging out with Warner *is* easy.

When I first get to his house, he's casual and friendly like always. We hang out in his bedroom and talk about nothing. It makes me think he didn't even have an agenda when he asked me here. That there was nothing he wanted to specifically say. It makes me think he just actually wanted to hang out and spend time with me.

But why? And what type of "spend time with me?" Does he want to hang out as a boyfriend and girlfriend would?

But that's not what Warner and I are.

"You good?" Warner asks.

Crap. I've just zoned out again. "Yeah, why?" I ask, smiling.

"You just seem a little... weird."

"*You're* weird."

"Ha ha. Sure."

I'm sitting on his bed, and he is casually kicking his soccer ball around his room. I pick up one of his pillows and throw it at him. He catches it and throws it back.

"So, where is your mom at now?" I ask.

"Somewhere getting me a job. She won't tell me where, but I don't even care. I am desperate at this point. Any second now, our power is going to turn off because we haven't paid the bill. I just know it."

"Wait, you help pay the bills?"

"I have to. Mom doesn't make enough. And she's been missing a lot of work."

"Warner, that... that sucks." I don't even need a job. Let alone would I ever have to give my parents any money.

"It is what it is," he says. This is the life he's lived for a long time, and he's used to it. "She was asking me about Sydney or Megan today. She wants to figure out how she's connected to everything, too."

I nod. "I think we still need to be on our guard about everything."

"Because you don't think Carson is really dead either?"

"I don't know what I think. My mind changes every other second. I'm just still scared. The feeling hasn't gone away. And I think I need to trust my instinct. We need to be careful."

"I agree with you."

"I've tried talking to Lyla about it, but—"

"But she wants to pretend like everything is over," Warner finishes for me.

"Yeah." I give him a puzzled look. "How did you know that?"

"I just figured she still doesn't want to be involved with any of it like she told us before."

"Right."

He comes and sits next to me. "She's not the only one who's been acting like she wants to just move on from the whole thing," he tells me. There's a mischievous look on his face, like he's teasing me a little bit.

"What do you mean? I still want to get to the bottom of it all."

"Yeah, but, at school, you sure seem unaffected. You have that new crowd you've been hanging out with."

He's referring to Ryan and the senior cheerleaders. How I have sort of become one of them.

I blush because it's weird he's talking about Ryan like this. Weird because... well... Ryan and I are still considered an item at school. but I have been kissing Warner in private.

"I'm just a good faker," I say, telling the complete truth. Warner is the only person I have said this to. To everyone else, I *am* unaffected.

"Are you faking that you like Ryan then?"

I open my mouth, but then I close it.

He makes a noise in the back of his throat and stands. "Never mind. Let's just... talk about something else."

But we can't just *not* talk about the fact that we like each other for forever. There is going to come a point where we have to figure out what is going on between us.

"Fine by me," I say anyway. That point is not going to happen tonight.

"Uh, you want a snack? We can raid the pantry. But I'll warn you—we might not have anything good. Maybe some stale saltine crackers and old protein bars."

I stand. "Mmm, count me in."

We leave his room and walk into the kitchen. Warner opens his cupboard, and I can't help but sort of check him out when he reaches the top shelf and I catch a glimpse of his six pack.

A car door slamming outside causes me to turn away. I walk out of the kitchen, to the window. The car suddenly parked outside on the street looks familiar.

My stomach lurches when I figure out why.

"Warner?" I ask.

"I al...most... got it!" he's saying, still reaching for a snack, straining his voice.

"That's great and all, but I don't think I am going to be able to eat it."

Finally, he gives up and drops his arms by his side. "Huh?"

"My dad just pulled up."

His eyes turn huge. There's a banging noise on the screen door. It sounds aggressive.

"What do we do?!" I whine, panicking and looking for a place to hide even though I know my dad already knows I am here. My car is outside, for one.

"I don't know!" Warner screeches. "He's *your* dad!"

I groan and throw his front door open. Dad still has his fist raised like he's about to keep knocking.

"Uh, Dad, what are you doing here?" I ask. This is so embarrassing. And awkward! And why does he look so mad?

"Audrey, let's go," Dad says. "Right now."

"What?" I leave the screen door closed. "But I—"

"*Audrey*!"

I jump.

"*Now*," he demands. "Do not even *think* about arguing with me."

"*Okay*!" I cry out. I turn back to Warner, who still looks scared, like he thinks my dad is going to come in here and beat him up. "I'll, uh, see you later."

He nods and doesn't speak.

I open the screen door and walk down the steps with my fuming father.

"I just don't get what the problem is," I say when we reach the middle of where our two vehicles are parked. "What's your problem with me hanging with Warner? He's my friend!"

"He's also a person of interest in a murder investigation," Dad hisses, stepping closer to me. "I've told you this before. I don't want you anywhere near anyone in that family. Get in your car and follow me back ho—to your moms. And then pack your things, because it's my week with you guys and you're coming back to my place."

"Warner didn't do anything," I snap. "Carson killed Syd—"

"The Carpenters are not to be trusted, Audrey. Okay? Mia's involvement with Maddy accounts for some of the reasons we're getting a divorce in the first place, and the situation regarding Warner and that girl is dangerous. I'm done talking about this. I am your father and I don't have to explain myself to you. Get in your car."

"*Ugh*!" I shoot him a nasty look and then begrudgingly obey him.

Sure. I'll go home. But I am not going to stop seeing Warner. I guess I will just have to be more creative about how I do it.

LYLA

I told Mom and Dad that I am going to Wrigley's after school to work on a project and hang out. Dad doesn't have a tracker on my car yet because he hadn't expected me to start driving anytime soon. I know it's only a matter of time before I have to stop lying about where I am going or figure out other ways to sneak around, but for now, at least I have the 4Runner—and I'm only a *little* bit terrified of it still.

I don't go to Wrigley's. And when Wrigley asks what I am up to tonight—we're together pretty much every day now, so he probably expected me to say, *Your place or mine?*—I tell him I am at my Dad's tonight, a place Wrigley hasn't been yet. Wrigley doesn't ask if he can come over, which is good. I'm not going to invite him.

I'm going to see Aunt Nora. She's begged me over text repeatedly the entire day at school asking me to. So, when school ends, I call her and ask her if I should go to her rental home. But she tells me to go to Craig Fritz's house instead. Apparently, she's been staying there ever since Carson attacked me at her rental.

I tell her I don't want to go to Freaky Fritz's place—ever again, if I can help it—but she insists he won't be home and I don't have to worry about having to talk to him.

So, when I ring the doorbell, I almost prepare myself for Craig to answer, for Nora to have lied to me. But she's the one who opens the door and lets me in, smiling at me. Her long dark hair is flowing down her shoulders and her frame is looking thinner than usual.

"You made it!" she cries, beaming at me before giving me a hug. "Ugh, I've missed you."

"I like, *just* saw you," I say awkwardly into her hair before she lets me go.

"I know, but when I was staying at your house, I got to see you all the time. I miss that."

"Why don't you come back then?" I ask.

"Uh... that's just not going to happen. Long story. Anyway... sit, sit, sit! Tell me about your day."

We go over to the sofas in the living room, and I sit down, even though I am acutely aware of how it's Craig's sofa and I hate sitting somewhere he's been. I know maybe I should start to like Craig a little more because he *did* save Warner's life and my aunt *does* seem happy, but I can't get past how he's treated my family and the Carpenters in the past.

"Aunt Nora, why did you want me to come over?" I ask. I don't want to make small talk with her. I would rather she just get to the point.

"I just like spending time with you, Ly," she says. "I know you're my niece, but you're also pretty much my only friend right now."

I feel a little bad. "Oh. How are you doing? You know—with everything that happened?"

"I can't talk to Craig about this because it would be weird, but I am having a hard time with Carson's death."

"You are?"

"Yeah. I don't know. I know I should be relieved—and don't get me wrong, part of me is—but so much of my life has been dedicated to him. It just feels so strange. I don't know how to explain it. He sucked."

"Yeah," I agree. My hands are on my knees and I am rigid in my spot. "I can't believe he's really dead. And that he would kill himself after all of that." I'm fishing or information here. Maybe Aunt Nora will tell me something Craig told her in secret about Carson's death. Like, that he didn't really kill himself.

"It doesn't make a whole lot of sense," she says.

"I think it makes him a coward," I say. For a second, I am back in that shed. I see him in that mask. I see his eyes. They had looked worried. Anxious. Desperate. "He hardly even got to pay for what he did to me. To all of us."

"I'm so sorry." She squeezed my arm. "It's all my fault. Ly, I am never going to forgive myself."

"It's not your fault. You didn't control him. You weren't responsible for how he decided to behave. How could you have known when you were my age that the boy you fell in love with would turn out to be like...that?"

"You're right," she says before eventually smiling a bit. "If I didn't have you and Craig, I—"

A loud banging noise makes us both jump, and Aunt Nora's eyes are wide as she stares behind me. I look over my shoulder, my heart feeling like it's about to fly out of my mouth, and see Freaky Fritz stumbling inside clumsily, his limbs flailing about like he's just tripped over the threshold.

I jump to my feet. This is more than I bargained for. Aunt Nora said I wouldn't be seeing him.

"Craig, what are you doing back already?" Aunt Nora asks, staying planted on the couch. I look back and forth between the two of them.

He only looks at me, his bloodshot eyes closed to slits, his body waving from side to side. He slowly lifts a finger, like it weighs a ton, and points it at me. "What is she doing here?" he asks Aunt Nora while still only looking at me.

I'm pretty sure Detective Fritz is drunk.

"I—she's just visiting me," Aunt Nora says. "She's not staying long."

"Good," he replies, slurring the word. *Gooooduh*. He takes a couple of steps toward me, and I feel frozen in place. It's completely bizarre to see him, a man of the law, like this.

"Actually," I start, grabbing my opposite elbow with my hand and clearing my throat, "I think maybe I should just leave now."

"Lyla, no," Aunt Nora says, sounding disappointed.

"I think she has the right idea, Nor," Fritz says, still swaying. I wouldn't be surprised if he fell over. And I bet he wouldn't be able to get up by himself if he did. Then he addresses me again. "I'm about sick of dealing with you people, ya know that?"

"Um, you people?" I ask, turning to look at Aunt Nora. She's part of my family, so wouldn't she be considered part of "you people"?

Nora just shrugs at me. I find it strange how she doesn't seem to be surprised or appalled by Craig's current state.

When I look back to Craig, he is nodding his head slowly, his mouth hanging open slightly, his eyes glazed over. It's giving me serious zombie-in-a-horror-movie vibes. "I don't want you in my house, Miss *Bayyyy-leeeee*."

"Craig," Aunt Nora says, talking as if she's addressing a toddler, or maybe an elderly person with dementia. "Lyla is my niece. I want her here."

"Uh, I think it's better if I go..." I try, my cheeks turning pink because of how uncomfortable I am, trapped between the two of them.

Fritz's hand goes to his belt, and my mouth drops open when I see the gun in its holster even though he's not wearing his police uniform. How can he even be allowed a weapon right now? And what is he planning to do, pull it out and shoot me?

"You're *tressspassin'*," he tells me. His eyes seem vacant, and I'm wondering if he even really knows where he is or who he is talking to right now.

"Craig! What are you doing?" Aunt Nora screeches, lurching to her feet when she sees where Craig has placed his hand. She takes me by the elbow, and at first, I'm horrified because she is pushing me toward him, but then I quickly realize she is just taking me outside.

Thank God.

He moves aside as Nora passes by with me, and he stumbles and bumps his hip into his credenza noisily as he does.

I can't get out of there fast enough.

"What the heck was that?!" I yell, my voice strangely high-pitched as we stand in his front lawn, the door closed and Craig out of sight—although I wouldn't be surprised if he was watching us through his window—if he can even see that far right now.

"You...weren't supposed to see that," Aunt Nora tells me. "He's going through a lot right now, too."

"Aunt Nora, that guy is crazy!"

"He's really not," she tries to assure me. "I mean—what he did just now was not okay, and I'll talk to him when he's... feeling better. He's not in his right mind. He probably won't even remember any of this in the morning."

"Is he like this a lot?" I ask.

Nora shrugs and lets out a long breath. "Lately, yes. But we're working on it."

"What does that mean?" I think back to the previous interactions I've had with Detective Fritz, all the way to when I first met him. I guess I hadn't really paid much attention to it over time, but now I recognize his mental decline. How each time I saw him, he looked scruffier, more tired, and worse for wear. Did he start having a drinking problem when he started dealing with all of us?

"Just—please ignore that, okay?" Aunt Nora says. "I promise it won't happen again."

Yeah, because I am never coming back here.

"I still think you and Craig being together is weird," I say, looking behind me, toward his house, worried that he's going to open the door up and start firing his gun at me for still being on his property.

"I know," she says, looking slightly embarrassed. "I actually never had feelings for him in high school. Sure, he was cute. And believe it or not, he was popular and liked by everyone, and for whatever reason, that kinda thing turned me off. I didn't want the guy that everyone else wanted. Except for Dean, apparently."

My eyes turn to saucers. "You mean, because of him and Maddy?"

"Um...yeah."

"Huh. So... why Craig now? How did that even start, anyway?"

"When I first came back to town to visit, he found out from Mia that I was here, and he reached out to catch up. He was Carson's best friend in high school, and since we were the two people closest to him back then, I think he just wanted to talk to someone who understood what it felt like to lose him. Even though I technically never lost him. Still. Craig didn't know that."

"He didn't?"

She shakes her head. "Still doesn't. You're the only one who does, Ly. I want to keep it that way. For now."

When I get home, I pull into my spot in the four-car garage and see that Dad's and Audrey's cars aren't here.

Crap. I forgot—I'm supposed to stay at Dad's tonight.

I go inside anyway and find Mom sitting on the sofa, her feet kicked up on the coffee table as she types on her laptop.

"Who's there?" she calls, not sounding the slightest bit worried that I could be some killer who just walked in. She sounds distracted.

"It's Lyla," I say. At this, she turns to look at me. "Oh, hey, hon. You were supposed to go to your Dad's after Wrigley's."

"I don't want to," I say, going to the couch to sit next to her. "I want to stay here and make sure you're okay. I don't like the thought of you being here all by yourself."

She smiles. I notice that she's starting to look more like the Mom I recognize. She's getting some of her color back. Her skin and eyes look brighter. "I'm okay, sweetheart. It's not your job to worry about me."

"Still," I say, leaning back and making myself comfortable. "I'm staying."

CHAPTER 19

MADDY

I purposefully don't even take the time to stop and carefully think about what it is I am doing before I park my car outside of The Viper, which is an upscale restaurant located in a super cute part of Toxey. I just get out, walk inside, and immediately ask the host if the owner is available to speak.

"Um," says the twenty-something-year-old with bubblegum pink hair and bad posture. "Did you have an appointment? I can grab the GM, but the owner doesn't usually talk to the guests..."

"I am not a guest. I am his girlfriend."

Okay, so *what* if I am not his girlfriend anymore? I am sure he wouldn't have told this chick that.

"Oh!" she cries, looking apologetic. "Okay, I'll be right back."

She takes her sweet time going to find Steven, first seating an older couple at a table on her way to him. I stand in the waiting area with my arms crossed, impatiently and anxiously tapping one foot.

I try to think about other things rather than what Steven is going to do when he sees me here. I stare around the restaurant and think about how he really did a good job with this place. I wonder who his interior designer was, and if Mia would know her. I love how dramatic and dark it is in here. The bar lit up with blue lights and the black laced pattern over it. The colorful painted tile flooring in a floral pattern. The dark, moody lighting. The incredible modern, angular light fixtures with the globe lightbulbs on them.

I stare at the bar and remember where I first met Steven, not all that long ago. We had shared an instant connection. It was as if we had both known right away that something was going to happen between us.

And then I went and ruined it.

"Maddy?"

I snap my head to the voice, and there Steven is, in a flattering button down and black slacks.

Ugh. It hurts to look at him. I just want to throw my arms around him and kiss him.

The host eyes the two of us.

"Can I talk to you?" I ask him.

He shakes his head in disbelief that I am here, then he motions for me to slip into a quiet booth, away from anyone listening, like the host. I sit down, and he sits across from me.

"Wh-what are you doing here?" he asks.

"I know you hate me. I know you don't want me here. But just hear me out?"

He doesn't say anything. I take it as a sign he's willing to listen, so I continue.

"Would it be possible for you to give Warner a job here? He can host. Buss tables. Wash dishes. It doesn't matter."

"You want me to employ your son here? *That's* why you came?"

"Well, he asked for a job at the salon, but he'd hate it there. And, I need to pay you back for your car somehow, and I can't do that on just my income. Please?"

"You don't need to pay me back for the car, Maddy—it wasn't your fault, and I had you insured on it."

I shake my head furiously. "I've messed up so much between us already, Steven. I have to pay you back."

"I..." he trails off, and I wait. I stare directly into his beautiful hazel eyes as they do everything but look back at mine. "Sure," he finally says. "Fine. I guess."

"Thank you, Steven."

"He can start tomorrow. I'll work out the details with the managers."

I nod, and then the silence that follows between us is heavy.

"Mads." His voice gets softer. He finally looks at me.

"Yeah?" My stomach rides a rollercoaster at the way he says my name.

"I...How are you doing? With your injuries."

"Oh..." I look at my lap. "I'm fine. Please don't worry about me."

"It's impossible not to."

I look up at him under my lashes. "Steven... I miss you."

Crap. I told myself I wasn't going to do this! That I was strictly here on business matters. Steven hates me and he has every right to. He doesn't want to be with me, and I don't blame him.

He sighs. "I miss you, too. But, the lies, Maddy. I can't—I just don't know how I feel right now."

"I am so sorry for not being honest from the beginning."

He nods. "Look. I'm heading out of town soon to check up on the other restaurants. I'll be gone for a bit. I think it will be good for me. To clear my head and think about...us."

Hope lights me up in an instant, and my entire posture perks up. "Okay. That's—that sounds good. Really good." He's going to think about us! That's all I can ask for.

Steven slides out of the booth and gets to his feet. "Don't get your hopes up. I'm still very angry with you and not sure this relationship is anything I want to keep pursuing. Not after everything."

My shoulders sag. I don't stand up with him. "Sure."

He puts his hands on his hips like he's about to kick me out for being a rowdy customer. Then the sigh he lets out can be heard from the other side of the restaurant. He seems like he wants to say something else. I *want* him to say something else.

Please don't leave it like this.

But he does. After one last look at me, he shakes his head again and gets back to work.

CHAPTER 20

AMELIA

It's really sweet of Lyla to want to stay with me tonight, but as she struggles to keep her eyes open while we watch TV together, I pat her on the knee and tell her she should get some sleep.

"Are you going to go to bed, too?" she asks like she isn't going to sleep if she knows I will still be out here, awake and by myself. I think my getting sent away like that really messed with her.

"Yep, in a few. I just have two more work emails to send," I say. She gives me a one-armed hug, yawns, and then drags her feet up the stairs to her bedroom.

I don't have any more work emails to send. And I am not going to bed. It's only nine. And with Lyla falling asleep early, I can still continue with the plans I had initially, before I knew she wasn't going to be going to her dad's with Audrey and Joey.

I wait about an hour before it's safe to have Dean come inside. When I answer the front door, the smile on my face is huge and genuine, and it feels foreign. I feel like a teenager, sneaking a guy into my house. Only, I am not hiding Dean from my parents—I am hiding him from my kid. How weird is that?

Dean kisses me on the cheek, his chin smooth. He smells like a fancy aftershave. Gentry always has some sort of stubble on his face. It's always scratchy when he kisses me. Dean likes to be clean shaven.

"Hi," I say quietly. "Let's go to the kitchen."

He nods and follows me, knowing he has to be quiet, too, because I texted him and filled him in on Lyla being here. We'd rather she not wake up and find us together. Not when everything is still so confusing.

I get out a bottle of white wine from the fridge and pour us each a glass.

"How are you holding up?" he asks, his tone casual and low. I love it.

"Really good," I say as we clink glasses.

"That's good to hear. I haven't been keeping up with the news as much as I should—has anything else come up about Carson?"

We're both sitting at the counter on barstools. Our bodies are angled toward each other.

I set my glass down on the marble countertop. "Nothing really. Just repeats of the same old information and speculation."

"Have you seen that TikTok page?" he asks.

I roll my eyes. "Yes. My poor girls. Their lives, and mine and Maddy's, exploited for entertainment. What we've been through is horrific. I'm worried they're going to want to turn this all into a made-for-TV movie."

He cringes. "Oh my, that would be awful. I wonder who would play me."

"Oh, you think *you're* significant enough to be in it, do you?" I tease.

He smiles and shrugs. "I *am* your daughters' teacher. And, well, Warner's dad..."

I bite the inside of my cheek and then take another sip of wine. There is still weirdness between Dean and me about that. He has a kid with my best friend. And my sister used to be hopelessly in love with him. For so many reasons, I thought it would never work with Dean. But I guess I never really let myself consider all the reasons that it *could* work. Not until now.

"Right," I say.

He places a hand on my knee. It's a gesture that's both comforting and romantic, but it also feels simple. Natural. "I'm really happy you let me see you tonight," he tells me. "I haven't been able to get you out of my mind. Ever, in fact."

I giggle and swat at him. "Stop."

"It's true. And you know it."

I sort of do. I read the letter he sent to Nora about me. I remember when we were kids, and how he wanted so badly to see where things could go with us, and how I told him no. For Nora.

Nora ended up hating me anyway. So, I figure I can finally try having what I've always wanted. "I feel the same way," I whisper.

"It only took...thirty years."

I raise an eyebrow. "When you were five and I was six?"

He laughs. "What can I say? I knew it the moment I met you."

"No, you didn't! We weren't even friends. You and my sister spent every second together."

"Oh, *come* on, haven't you ever seen a chick flick before? I was in love with my best friend's sister."

The smile freezes on both of our faces when we register what he's just said.

In love.

He clears his throat and grabs for the wine. "I... can't believe I just said that. Ignore it. It just slipped out."

I can tell by the redness on his face, which is usually very tan, that he's genuinely embarrassed.

But I can't stop hearing it.

I was in love with my best friend's sister.

I'm never going to forget this moment.

"Dean...I..."

How can I convey how I feel about him in return? I want to tell him I love him, too. And that I always have. But it feels wrong to say it now. Here, in this house where Gentry and I raised our family. And Gentry and I aren't even divorced yet.

"It's okay, Mia. Seriously," he says after a couple of sips—more like gulps. "I know. What's happening with me and you, its new and confusing and..."

"Has to be a secret," I finish. "For now."

"For now."

I take his hand and hold it. "It feels so good to talk to you like this."

He nods.

"I'm sorry I was so crazy before," I say.

"There's an explanation for it, though," he says, not disagreeing with me. The drug-switch.

"Right." But even before that happened, when Dean and I reconnected during the upperclassman camping trip, I had gone a little crazy. Straight away, my feelings for him came flooding back All the years of hard work I had put in to repressing them—undone in an instant.

Dean shakes his head. "Who knew all of this would happen the day Carson-the-new-kid showed up at Blackfell High back in 1998?"

"Definitely not me," I say. "You know, I tried to tell the police about when I found Carson the first time."

"You did?"

"Mhm. But I wasn't myself. As you saw. Of course, Craig was already not going to believe a word out of my mouth, but even Officer Wilde didn't believe me. Not that I blame them. I still don't even remember that day fully. I had taken...more than one of the pills because it was a really tough day. Everything about my confrontation with him is hazy."

"I wonder why he would do that to you," Dean says. "And how."

"Beats me."

Dean shakes his head like I am not understanding. "I'm talking about switching your medication. I know Carson did a lot of horrible stuff, Mia. But are you sure it was him who did that?"

I'm a bit taken aback. "Yes."

Where is he going with this?

"What about...?" He's afraid to say it.

"What, Dean?" My voice is a lot more serious than it was moments ago.

"What about Gentry?" Dean sees the crazed look on my face, I'm sure, so he keeps going, the words spilling out so fast I almost can't understand him. "What if he wanted to find a way to guarantee he got to keep Joey? What if he knew it would come down to some sort of legal battle, and he wanted to make sure he could use this against you?"

I'm shaking my head before he's even finished. "Dean," I say. "I don't think you really get Gentry's and my... relationship. We used to be best friends. Even after we figured out we weren't in love anymore. He wouldn't do that to me." I am one hundred percent certain of it.

"What changed, then?" he asks. "Because you two don't seem like best friends anymore."

"I don't know," I say. But the more I consider it, I suppose I *can* pinpoint the exact moment it changed. For me, anyway.

I was on a lunch with my clients, a lovely couple named Evan and Carrie Dobson. We were at a restaurant outside of Toxey, near where their house was located. I had just finished a site visit walk-through with them, and I was treating them to lunch so we could go over my ideas and their suggestions.

Even though Evan and Carrie lived outside of Toxey, they had spent their childhood in it, and they attended Blackfell High four years before I started. They had just graduated when I was a freshman. So, even after they moved to the house I was now renovating, they still knew who everyone in Toxey was, as well as about everything in everyone's lives, too. It was always impossible to stop the spread of gossip in Toxey.

I was midsentence with the Dobsons when Evan interrupted me.

"Wait a second, Amelia," he said, pointing to something over my shoulder. "Isn't that your husband over there?"

I turned around, and the breath left me. Gentry was there.

And he was with another woman.

"Oh, it is!" I said quickly, turning back to my clients and smiling at them. "He told me he was having a business lunch today, too. I just can't believe we both picked the same place!"

We all laughed.

"What are the chances?" Carrie cried.

"Too funny." I smoothed my skirt. "I better go swing by and say hello. Excuse me for just a moment." Then I slid out of the booth and walked straight over to him.

My husband.

"Hi." I said with a forced smile when I reached their table.

Gentry looked caught red-handed. The woman looked startled.

"Mia," Gentry said, coughing. "Uh, this is Heather."

I looked at her. She was beautiful. But prettier than me? Definitely not. At least I had that going for me.

I was still so stunned at what I was seeing that I could hardly think straight. "Nice to meet you," I said to her. "I'm Amelia."

"Oh," Heather said, shifting in her seat and looking away from both of us. She was uncomfortable. Good. So was I.

"My clients noticed you over here," I said, turning back to Gentry. "So, I thought I'd come say hi."

"Right," Gentry said.

The thing was, this had happened after we agreed to date other people. We said we'd keep it on the down-low. We wouldn't date them in Toxey, where people could catch us. But we also agreed that we would tell each other if and when we met someone we wanted to go on a date with.

And Gentry hadn't said a word to me about Heather.

"Anyway," I said, flinging some hair over my shoulder. "You two enjoy your lunch."

"You, too," Gentry said. We still lived together. He knew he had some huge explaining to do when we were both home later. But right then and there, I realized I didn't want to hear any of it.

"I hope I don't upset you by asking this, Mia," Dean says, "and I swear I am not trying to start anything here, I just feel like I *do* need to know. I mean—you *married* the guy. You clearly loved him. You have children with him."

"Okay?" I'm still half-thinking about that memory. I couldn't believe Gentry didn't tell me about Heather. We promised we would tell each other if we met someone. So why hadn't he? Had he been lying before when he said he was going on all those business trips? How long had Heather been in the picture? What if it was before Gentry and I even decided we weren't working?

The thought of him cheating makes me sick to my stomach.

Dean studies me carefully before asking. "Do you see yourself ever working things out with him?"

I think about Dean.

"No," I say.

I am not that innocent either. Part of the reason I knew it couldn't work out with Gentry forever was because of this man sitting here with me.

"No?" Dean looks relieved.

"Dean," I tell him, completely disregarding everything I had told myself earlier about keeping my feelings to myself. "As long as you're in the picture, it will never work between Gentry and me."

"I see." I can tell he's trying not to smile. It warms my heart, so I smile.

"I've loved you since we were kids," I say. "And I don't think I ever really stopped."

There's a moment's pause, as if he's considering if what he's about to do is okay, and then once his mind is made up, it's as if there is no stopping him. He cups my cheeks in his hands. He gets up out of his seat. It all happens in an instant, and then he is kissing me. It's deep and passionate and final. For the first time in the thirty years we've known each other, I have finally admitted I love him, too.

When he pulls away, we're both breathless. He presses his forehead to mine, and I close my eyes, enjoying the closeness with him. It's so new, but also feels so familiar.

His hands slide down and gently rest on my shoulders, and then he tells me, "Good. Because I am not letting you go this time, Mia. Ever again."

I don't know if anyone has ever said anything so wonderful to me. "I..." I am so woozy, so love-drunk, I hardly even know how to reply.

But then a knock sounds on the front door, and I don't have to.

Dean and I both turn toward the noise. Then I look at the clock. It's late. Who would be coming to the house right now?

"Invite over any other late-night gentleman callers?" he jokes.

I wordlessly shake my head, and Dean's expression quickly changes. He can tell I'm worried. Scared. I try to tell myself if it was someone dangerous, someone here to hurt me or my daughter, they wouldn't waste time knocking, but it doesn't make me feel much better.

"You stay here," Dean instructs bravely. "Let me get it."

He starts to walk toward it.

"Dean, no," I whisper, following behind him. I can't let him protect me. But as we reach the door together, he blocks any way of me stepping around to get in front of him.

He looks through the peephole. "What the...?"

"Who is it?" I whisper. He doesn't answer me. Instead, he unlocks and opens the door.

It's Craig Fritz.

"Craig?" I ask incredulously.

Craig looks at Dean, seeming almost as if he thinks maybe he went to the wrong place. Then he looks at me. And then back to Dean again.

This isn't good.

I wait for the questions to start about the two of us being here together, but instead, Craig choses to ignore it. "Amelia, is Lyla here? I need to ask her a couple of questions."

"Regarding what?" I ask, Dean finally stepping to the side so I can appear in front of our former classmate. He looks strange, in regular old clothes. His hair is damp, and he smells like Old Spice. I'm guessing he came here just after showering.

"Is she here or not?" he asks. He sounds like he doesn't have any time for nonsense.

"She's asleep, Craig. Because it's a school night. And it's late."

Craig eyes Dean again. "Uh huh" Then he looks back to me. "Look, I'm not here on the job. I'm here as a...as a friend. I just need to talk to her about something."

"Um, whatever you have to say to my daughter can be discussed at the police station, with me and her father present, during normal hours."

He glares at me a long while, all three of us silent. Then he shakes his head and sighs the words, "Just forget it, then."

"Why are you—?"

"Have a good night." Craig doesn't let me get another word in before he turns around and walks down the path to where his car is parked on the street.

Dean softly closes the door and looks at me. "What was that about?"

"I have no idea," I tell him, staring at the door and biting on my manicured thumb nail. "But I didn't like it one bit."

CHAPTER 21

LYLA

I'm surrounded by fire. The smoke is thick and choking me. I pound on the wooden, splintery door, but no one is coming to my aid. I can't even yell out for help. The smoke makes it impossible. No one is going to know I am in here. Will they even know it was me who died when my remains are found?

I don't want to die.

"*NO!*" I yell out as I sit up and jolt myself awake from the nightmare. I cough and clutch my throat. It had felt so real. But of course it had. I actually knew what it felt like to be trapped in a burning shed.

But I didn't die. I am okay.

I turn off the alarm on my phone and lay back down for a second. I try to forget about the nightmare and think about what I have to do today instead. I have a therapy appointment this morning, so I have to miss the first couple periods of school.

Dreading it, but knowing that by going, I will be making Mom and Dad happy, I shower and get ready. When I see Mom downstairs after, she's sipping coffee and yawning, but she looks ready for the day. Her outfit is adorable in flare-leg black pants and a dressy work blouse. And I love her Steve Madden boots.

"You look like you're going to work," I comment. I want to seem chipper and bright. I am not thinking about the nightmare. I am not a miserable human being. Everything is fine. I am moving on.

"I'm going to take you to your appointment," she says as if to remind me.

"Oh, actually, I am going to drive myself, if that's okay."

Her eyes widen like I knew they would. "Are you sure?"

"Yeah." I smile. "I'm getting used to being back behind the wheel." Because I am the old Lyla and the old Lyla loves driving her car.

"All right then." She smiles back. "School straight after?"

"Of course."

I stuff my face with a bowl of cereal and then hug her goodbye.

I find that when I do drive to my appointment, it's getting easier. I'm more comfortable with my Toyota each time I'm in it. Soon enough, I'll forget why I was so scared to drive again in the first place!

Ha. I wish.

Dr. Gloria Morton greets me with a polite smile. She's dressed in a formal business suit, as usual, and looks like she has a lot of money and prefers to spend it on making herself look younger. How else could a woman in her sixties almost appear twenty years younger than that?

"Hi, Lyla, welcome back," she says, motioning for me to sit on the sofa. I sit on my hands.

"Hi."

We go over the initial pleasantries, and I catch her up on the events that have transpired since I last saw her.

"I did hear about some of it on the news," she tells me after. "You've been in my thoughts."

"Thank you?"

She writes something down. I never get to see these notes. I wish I could.

"So, how do *you* think you're handling everything?" she asks.

"I don't know. Fine. I think. I am just moving forward, ya know? Which I think is good. I keep busy. I am getting caught up in school. Hanging with Wrigley a lot. Spending time with my Mom. Driving. I actually drove my car here today." She knows I'm afraid to drive. She'll be so proud to hear it.

"What persuaded you to do that?" she asks.

"Um, I guess it just felt like it was finally time."

"Because you felt ready?"

No.

"I don't know."

She nods. "It's great that you want to move on from all of this, but remember that it is okay—and important, actually—for you to take the time to process what happened, too."

"That sounds...horrible," I admit.

She chuckles. "It might feel horrible, too. But it's necessary to heal."

I don't think she's right. I think I'll heal better if I just don't think about it. Ever. Any of it.

I stay silent.

"You say you've been spending a lot of time with Wrigley," she continues, moving on. "He's who you were texting when you got into your accident."

"Yes."

"Do you enjoy being around him?"

"He's practically my best friend."

"He doesn't add on to your anxiety and stress?"

"Why would he? He's really helpful, actually. He tries to find ways to make me smile all the time. He's a good guy."

"While that may be so, Lyla, it might not be a good idea for you two to be together right now, while you're healing from all your trauma."

"Why not?"

"Whether he meant to be or not, Wrigley is part of the *cause* of your trauma. He's tied to the night you lost your best friend. It might help you to see things clearer if you stepped back from that relationship. At least for a while."

"I...I guess I didn't really think about that," I say. But in my head, I disagree with her. She's old, what does she know about being a teenager anymore? I like Wrigley. A lot. And dating is part of being a normal teenager.

And all I want, is to *be* a normal teenager.

CHAPTER 22

AUDREY

Since Warner brought it up, that he thinks Carson might not really be dead after all, it has only made me start considering it more seriously as well.

When I go to school, instead of paying attention like I should be, I find myself thinking more about it—I remember how Eric passed me in his car when I had confronted Jackson. I still think it's weird that he hasn't left town yet at the news that Carson is dead. But maybe there is a reason why. Maybe he still needs to talk to me about it. It's not like he has my number, and I doubt he's bold enough to just show up at Mom's house like that again after his run-in with Dad the last time he tried. Maybe he *wanted* me to see him driving past in his car. Maybe he wanted me to see him that day in the school parking lot. Because he wants to talk.

And I think I need to talk to him.

I can't wait until after cheer practice after school today. Dad will wonder where I am if I don't come immediately home. And then he'll be able to track my car.

At lunchtime, I come up with a plan to sneak off campus and walk a few blocks to the nicest hotel we have in Toxey. I don't know if Eric is staying there, but if he has any taste at all, or a desire for cleanliness, Hotel Monte Vista would be the one he would choose.

I don't tell anybody what I'm doing, and when I successfully sneak away, I get a text from Ryan shortly after asking where I'm at. I reply:

Me: *I'm so sorry! Completely forgot to tell you, I have to finish an assignment that's due next hour.*

I feel bad about lying. And not just about where I am.

Ryan: *Bummer. I'll miss you.*

It doesn't feel right to say I'll miss him back. Not with what's happening with me and Warner. So, I don't say anything. Hopefully he doesn't get mad.

Just focus on the task at hand, Audrey.

I make it to the hotel in ten minutes and enter the lobby. The Hotel Monte Vista has been remodeled multiple times, so everything looks new even if the outside appears a bit dated. The lobby is furnished and painted in shades of gray, all of the counters are white, and all of the flooring is redone.

It's not the busiest hotel in the world, but why would it be? There is literally no point in coming to Toxey. Usually.

I look around the place anyway, walking around the bottom floor to see if maybe Eric is hanging out somewhere. But as I figured would happen, I don't find him, so I sit in a chair in the lobby and think about my next plan. The receptionist, a middle-aged man with a buzz cut and heavy build, types on his computer but also continuously glances at me. I'm sure he's wondering what I'm doing here on a school day. It crosses my mind that he might call the school and tell them one of their students is missing.

I stand up and go over to him.

"How can I help you?" he asks. There's something about his voice that makes me think he's suspicious. Or maybe I'm just overthinking.

"Yes, I was wondering if you could call up to Eric Price's room and let him know that he has a visitor? Audrey Bailey? I am a friend."

I want to sound positive that Eric is staying here so that I don't seem like some creeper that is trying to figure out his whereabouts in case this guy doesn't let me talk to him.

"Let me see." He does some searching on his computer. I cross my fingers behind my back. Then the man smiles at me. "I'll let him know you're here."

I grin. "Thank you!"

I walk back over to my chair and sit down. As I eavesdrop on the receptionist, it sounds like Eric Price answered the call and he's on his way.

I can't believe I'm doing this. I am meeting with the father of the man who ruined my life. Who tried to kill me. Who tried to kill my sister.

When Eric Price comes down and steps out of the elevator, I get the chills. I don't really see any resemblance between Carson and him. But just knowing that this is the man who raised him has me wondering so much. What had happened to Carson that led him to being fostered? What kind of father was Eric? Not a good one, clearly. I think that villains aren't just born. They are made.

And this man created a monster.

Eric sits across from me. He is on the edge of his chair, his elbows on his knees and his hands clasped together.

"What brings you here?" he asks in a low voice.

"I'm sorry about the news of Carson," I say. "I'm sure you heard."

He nods. "I did."

"I... noticed that you were still in town, so I guess I am just wondering why."

"I'm just trying to understand," he explains. "After so many years of him missing, he turns up dead, in the last town he was seen in twenty years ago?"

He doesn't buy Carson's death either?

I shrug. I wonder how hurt Eric is by his son's death. "Maybe all of his guilt finally caught up with him and it was too much?" I try. "I don't know how much you know, but Carson did a lot of really horrible things to me and my family and a good friend of mine."

"I am aware that he might have gotten himself into a great deal of trouble," Eric says.

"He wasn't a good person," I say. I don't care if it hurts him to hear it. I don't care if it makes him mad.

"I understand," he says, much to my surprise. "I wasn't looking to reconnect with Carson because he's my long-lost son and I thought we could fix what was broken and have an amazing future as father and son together. I wanted to find him so that I could get him help. I heard about all of the terrorizing he did. I came across that TikTok page in a news article, so I downloaded the app and watched every single video. I know it was all speculation, but it seems that it's all likely true."

I cross my arms.

He continues. "It's not the first time he's done something like this. And you're not the only people he's done horrible things to."

"No?"

He shakes his head. "No. You see, Audrey, not long before I met Carson's mother, Lucy, I was married and had a daughter, Harley, with a woman named Felicity. Unfortunately, my ex-wife passed away. And when I married Lucy, she'd already had Carson. So, technically, I am his stepdad. But I came into his life when he was so young, and his father was never in the picture, that I raised him like he was my own. That's why he even uses my last name.

"Then one day, when Carson was a preteen, I got a call while I was at work. There was a fire at our house. And... Lucy died in it."

"I am so sorry," I say.

He waves dismissive hand. "I immediately left work and even though I was destroyed, I had two kids that I needed to get to. And when I finally talked to Carson, he admitted to me that he started the fire. That's all he would give me. He couldn't even so much as bother to offer me an explanation. And, since I wasn't his legal guardian, and Lucy was dead, Carson had to go into the system. It didn't matter if I wanted to keep being responsible for him or not. As much as it hurt me, I told him to just keep it to himself. The fire was an accident. Carson had nobody, and I didn't want him sent to Juvie.

"It took a little time, but eventually I realized that Carson still was my son, no matter what happened, and I needed to find him. But by the time I finally figured out that he was staying with a family in Toxey, I arrived here just to learn that he had gone missing. I don't understand why I have such horrible timing. Cuz now, I hear talks of him being alive, so I come back, just to find that he really is dead." He shakes his head and doesn't look at me.

This is a man who has been through a lot. Two dead wives, *and* a dead son?

I don't know what to say. But luckily, he keeps talking so I don't have to say anything.

"I know Carson had his demons. But I was hoping I could find him so that I could get him the help he so clearly needed. I guess I only wish I found him in time."

I don't exactly understand why Carson would start a fire that killed his own mother, and I don't understand why Eric would want to have anything to do with him after such a horrible thing, but it makes me see Eric in a new light. He's the good guy in this situation.

"Carson's best friend was a man named Craig fritz," I find myself telling him. "Craig Fritz is a detective. This detective claims to have been the one to find Carson. I guess... what I'm trying to say is that I don't exactly believe that Carson is really dead. Maybe... maybe you should stick around for a bit longer, because lots of people are trying to figure it out."

Eric seems relieved by what I have to say about it.

We talk for a little bit longer, and I answer some of his questions without getting into too much detail about everything Carson did to us and why Craig would maybe be protecting him. Then we exchange contact information in case either of us comes upon any other information that could be helpful and getting to the bottom of it.

As I'm walking back to school, five minutes before the bell signaling the end of lunch rings, I get another text message. I assume it's from Ryan again, wondering why I never texted him back.

Instead, it's from a number I don't recognize:

Unknown: *You're going to regret doing that.*

CHAPTER 23

AMELIA

I don't know what to do with myself after Lyla ends up not needing a ride to her appointment. I had been debating all morning whether or not I should tell her during our drive to Dr. Morton's that Craig stopped by for her last night. Then the opportunity slipped away completely. I still feel uneasy about Craig's appearance last night, and my manicure is now completely ruined from how much I bit my nails over it.

Forcing myself to occupy my time another way, I turn my thoughts to my incredible night with Dean, before Craig had shown up to ruin it.

I told Dean I loved him.

It still feels so strange to me. But wonderful.

It's a little cold out, but I don't want to waste my day alone in my house, so I decide to catch up on some much needed errand-running. And while I am out and about, I get a phone call from an unknown number, which makes my heart skip a beat as I stare at the number on the dash of my car.

Still driving, I answer the call over the Bluetooth system. "Amelia Bailey," I say, using my professional voice in case it's a potential client.

"Don't *you* sound fancy."

I don't recognize the voice. It's male, and their tone is playful.

"I'm sorry?" I ask, tightening my grip on the steering wheel.

"Mia. It's Parker."

I nearly slam on my brakes because I'm so shocked. "*Fritz?*"

"Know any other Parkers?" he jokes.

Parker Fritz is Craig's younger, Wall Street hot-shot brother. And also my only ex of high school.

"Definitely not," I say, not hiding my surprise in my voice. "I can't believe you're calling me right now."

"I can't believe *you* still have the same phone number from high school."

"Um... what's...up?" This is crazy. I haven't talked to Parker *since* high school. He went to college in California after he graduated and then went on to be some sort of businessman in New York. I don't know exactly what he does. We're friends on social media, but he never posts life updates. And I don't think he's ever come back to Toxey for a visit, not that I blame him.

"Well, as it turns out," he says, "I am going to be in town for a couple of days. I figure it's been a long time since I've seen...*anyone* from high school. And I wanted to see if you would like to catch up. It would be nice to talk."

"I..." This can't be weirder timing. "Sorry—*why* are you coming to town?"

"Eh. I've been talking to Craig, and with everything going on, I figure I should pay a visit."

"Oh." So, he's up to date on everything with Carson, I assume.

"What do ya say?" he asks.

"Um, yeah," I answer, unable to find an excuse to tell him no. "That would be great."

"*Ah*, awesome," he growls. "Oh, I can't wait to see you. I'll reach out when I get there, and we'll figure out details, yeah?"

"All right."

We hang up, and all I can do is shake my head in disbelief. I wonder what Craig told him. I wonder whose side Parker is really on. What if Craig is just having him get information out of me? I don't think I trust it.

Maddy and I decided to try and get to the bottom of the Megan Young thing. I'm not going back to work yet, and all of my errands are mostly done for the day.

I think it's time I resume my research.

The first place I decide I want to check out, is the last place I saw Carson alive. It's somewhere in the middle of the woods, so I know it won't be an easy search. I go back home first and change into appropriate hiking gear. I am not going to have a repeat of the last time I was there.

I pull over on the side of the road where it looks somewhere vaguely familiar, and then I begin my trek. It takes me about an hour of walking in different directions and somehow continuously circling back to the same places I've already been, but eventually, I spot the rusty orange color of what can only be Carson's old truck. When I had been here last, it seemed like Carson had been living out of it. And since it is unmoved from the spot it had been in, I think it's safe to assume he was.

It looks untouched. There is still cloth covering the windows to hide the interior. There is a fire pit that he made. A clothesline with a couple T-shirts and pairs of jeans tossed over it. Some food wrappers and empty cans and water bottles.

Carson kept his truck parked here and only traveled back into town on foot. I wonder why that is.

I step into the clearing of his little "home." Everything about my meeting with him feels a lot clearer now. How he told me about his father wanting him dead. How he pointed an actual gun at me and told me to run.

I take a step toward the truck. Maybe I'll find something inside of it to shed light on the situation.

Another footstep crunches on the ground behind the truck, and I jump back as a figure appears. It's a woman, somewhere around my age.

I cry out, scared half to death.

"Who the heck are you?" the woman asks me, her eyes darkening.

"Who are *you*?" I ask back.

She has long blonde hair, but her roots are showing. I think she's naturally a brunette. She doesn't look like some homeless person who found Carson's truck and took it over for herself. She's dressed in jeans and a flannel. She has somewhat clean Converse on.

She puts her hands on her hips and looks me over. Then recognition hits her. "Wait a minute. I know you." She points an unmanicured finger at me. "You're Amelia."

I swallow. "Well, I don't know you," I snap. What is happening right now?

She laughs. But I don't get why she finds this funny. "Of course you don't," she says.

"So...? Why don't you tell me then?" My hands are on my hips now, too.

"I'm Harley, Carson's stepsister."

My jaw drops. "Stepsister?"

She nods. "Yep. So, I know why *I* am here, going through my poor brother's things, but tell me, Amelia: why are *you* here?"

"I...I'm looking for answers."

"Huh. Funny that you'd run into me here, of all places."

"Is it?"

"Yeah." She takes a step toward me. "You have questions about what happened to my brother. And I happen to be the person who probably knew him better than anyone."

CHAPTER 24

WARNER

It's not exactly close, and I have to order a Lyft to get there, but hopefully I'll make enough money to balance it out—or more. My mom got me a job at her boyfriend's—or *ex*-boyfriend's—restaurant, The Viper. I am going to be a busboy.

I'll admit, it definitely sounds better than working at a salon full of middle-aged women with all of that "frying hair" smell.

When I get to The Viper, I tell a pink-haired host that my name is Warner and it's my first day.

"Oh my goodness, aren't you adorable?" she says with a grin. "I'm Katie."

I smile sheepishly. "Nice to meet you."

"So, you're the owner's girlfriend's son?" Her voice is slow like she doesn't want anyone overhearing what my status is.

I shrug. "I don't really know if my mom is Steven's girlfriend. And I don't know Steven that well."

"Still. Remind me not to get on your bad side." She winks at me. "Let me take you to Cassius. He's training you."

"Cassius?" It sounds like a name a vampire would have.

"Yeah. He's around your age. What high school do you go to?"

I begin following her. "Wait, how old are *you*?"

"Twenty-two."

I guess I'm sort of bummed that she can tell I'm just a teenager. But then again, if I were older, would I be taking a job as a busboy? Maybe that was my giveaway. I'd like to think I can pass for older than seventeen.

"Oh," I say before going back to her question. "I go to Blackfell High. I'm a senior."

"There is some seriously crazy stuff happening there. I went there, too. You're a senior? I just finished college last year. We just missed each other." She gives me another smile over her shoulder.

"That's a bummer."

"Totally."

We go into the kitchen. I've never been in a restaurant kitchen before. She introduces me to various workers as we pass by them, then I go to the office, where I have to do a bunch of initial paperwork. When that is done, I'm given my apron and told that the next time I come back I have to wear nonslip tennis shoes, but the rest of my outfit can be whatever I want.

"Is Steven here?" I ask Katie, who has been my guide the entire time I've been here so far.

"No," she says. "His visits are always so random and out of nowhere, and they're not that often. He has two other restaurants in different states that he's always flying to. I think he wants to open up several more in the future, too."

Steven is clearly a guy with a lot of money. I've been to Wrigley's house before. No wonder my mom likes his dad.

I keep the comments to myself.

Finally, Katie takes me to Cassius. The first thing I notice about him is how tall he is. Incredibly tall. Like six-foot-five at least. Maybe six-foot-seven. He has jet-black hair that's gelled high on his head. He's got a gangly build, like he's all elbows. He's pale, too, like he never leaves this restaurant. Never steps out into the sun. Like a real vampire.

"Sup?" He nods at us, not offering a smile.

"Hey," I say back.

Katie looks back and forth between the two of us. "All right. You two have fun. I've got guests to seat and an old man to tell to stop hitting on me." She flips her hair over her shoulder and then walks out of the kitchen.

Cassius gets started on training me. My first impression is that he's some goth kid that's not going to be interested in making friendly conversation or in being friends. But I quickly learn he's actually pretty cool. He tells me about how there's the "right way" to do my job responsibilities, and the "easy way" to do them, so I can pick for myself what I'd rather. He shows me how to get free food from the kitchen. We joke about similar dumb TV shows that we both like. I watch as he talks to an older lady who is a waitress but also acts like his mother. She has a hard look about her, but I get the feeling that she's going to try to act like some mother to me, too, really soon.

Cassius and I are busing a large table that sat twenty; he's down at one end and I'm at the other. He's saying something to me about his high school, Ridgefield, which is in the next town over, but I stop listening because a familiar person has caught my eye and caused me to stop dead in my tracks. It's like I'm frozen, my hand clutching a plate while my body leans over the table.

In one of the booths along the wall, I see a girl who looks like Sydney. They have the same sharp jawline. The same deep-set eyes and thick eyebrows. They also have the same messy dishwater-blonde hair. But it's not Sydney. This girl is far older. She is reaching across the table and holding hands with a guy who looks like he's in his thirties.

I get a painful feeling in my stomach. It sucks that Sydney is dead. I can't help but feel like I'm the cause of it. I shouldn't have let her out of my sight that night.

What if she had been trying to warn me about Carson?

But how would she have known about him? And how long did she know about him if she did?

I think back to the first time we ever hung out. Sydney was pretty incessant about it, getting my phone number and texting me nonstop. I felt like I didn't have a choice—I told her she could come to my house and we could hang out outside sometime.

I was in the middle of fighting with mom. Then someone knocked on the front door, and we both jumped and stopped arguing.

"Looks like one of your boyfriends is here," I muttered under my breath. I was still fuming, so I started heading to my room. I wanted to get away from her. However, I froze when I heard the tone of my mom's voice when she answered the door.

"Oh," she said. "Hello."

I waited. *Who could it be?*

I couldn't hear what the person was saying, but then Mom spoke again. "*Yes*, actually, he is."

Who is?

"Warner!" Mom called to me. I turned around and came back out of the hallway. The door was for me?

Mom pointed at it. She had closed it to a tiny crack, hiding whoever it was so that I couldn't see them. "There's a *girl* out there to see you," she said in a whisper.

It was then that I knew who it was. I had told Sydney that she could come over, but I never said *when*. I had figured she would ask if it was a good time to come, or that she'd at least let me know when she was on her way. Instead, she just decided to take it upon herself to show up out of the blue.

Still, I checked the window, peeking out of the blinds to see who it was anyway.

Yep. Definitely Sydney.

I looked at Mom. "I...um—I'm going to go. I'll see you later."

I didn't want Sydney coming inside. It would just give Mom the chance to ask her a ton of questions. So, without waiting for Mom to say anything, I opened the door, gave Sydney a nod, and then went outside with her.

"Sorry," I told Sydney as we walked down the porch steps. "I didn't realize you were coming right... now. How did you find out where I lived?" I hadn't even given her my address. But I wasn't that suspicious about it; Toxey is a small town. She probably had to just ask somebody.

"Is now a bad time?" Sydney asked instead of answering me.

I thought about the fight I was having with Mom. "Um, no. It's actually good timing," I decided.

"Oh yeah?" She raised an eyebrow as we continued walking down my street. I don't think we had a destination in mind. We were just walking.

"Yeah. My mom is insufferable sometimes."

She barked out a laugh. "I know that all too well."

"What is your mom like?" I asked. I knew she was a foster kid. I wondered if it was okay for me to even be asking that question.

She shrugged and kicked some loose pebbles as we walked along the road. "Sort of the worst," she said. "Evil. Strict. Controlling. You know, your typical mom."

I wouldn't say that my mom is evil. Or controlling, really.

"Mine's just more... irresponsible," I said.

"Moms suck."

"Yeah."

Even though I was mad at Mom, I already felt guilty the second I agreed with what Sydney said.

Sydney had her hair up high in a messy, tangled ponytail. She was wearing baggy clothes. Her eyes had dark circles under them.

"Do you like it at your foster home?" I asked, assuming based on her appearance that maybe it wasn't that great.

"It's fine," she said. "I don't wanna talk about it."

Her face clouded over, but only for a moment. Then she looked at me and smiled as we walked.

"So, rumor has it that your mom got around Toxey and there's, like, thirty possibilities of who your father could be. Any ideas?"

I stopped walking and glared at her.

She shrugged simply. "What? Is that not true?"

"That's kind of messed up," I said. Who was this chick? And why did she think she could just show up and start asking these insulting questions?

"It's not like I am the one who thought it. It's literally what I was told," she says.

I shake my head. "She doesn't 'get around.'" But still—how could my mom just *not* know who my dad was?

"What if she does know, and she's just been keeping him a secret?"

I couldn't quite pinpoint the look on her face when she said it. She wiggled her eyebrows. Put her hands on her hips. She looked mysterious.

She looked like a girl who knew too much.

But Sydney couldn't have known about Dean. She wasn't from Toxey. She didn't know anything about anyone. It would have been impossible for her to arrive in town and learn everything about everyone's secrets that quickly.

"Uh, dude?"

I snap my head up, and Cassius is suddenly next to me, raising one of his eyebrows and looking at me like I just had a stroke.

"What? Sorry," I say. I hadn't been listening to anything he just told me.

"Are you good?" he asks.

"Yeah," I say, grabbing the last few dishes on the table since he got the rest. "Sorry."

I glance at the girl who looks like Sydney again.

What was Sydney's role in all of this?

As we walk back to the dish pit, I am having uncontrollable flashbacks about every moment I had spent with her. All the times she talked to me in the hallway. Tried to get me to hang out with her after school. Texted me nonstop. I remember how Jackson gave me so much crap for it, and so did a bunch of other people. Just because I was nice to her. No one else wanted to be nice to her because they thought she was weird. And in a way, she *was* weird. But she wasn't that bad. Not as bad as everyone made her out to be.

Then again, I would've agreed with everyone else a lot more if I had known Sydney was nineteen years old posing as a student.

I just wish I knew why she did it.

Cassius and I drop our bus tubs and start unloading them for the dishwasher, an old man who is blasting 80s music from his phone and dancing while he sprays dishes down in the sink.

When my bus tub is unloaded, before we head back out to keep working, I pull my cell phone out and go to my old text message thread with Sydney. I go to that night she asked me to meet her.

Sydney: *Sneak out of your tent and meet me on the trail to the lake. After everyone is asleep.*

Me: *I'm not going to do that.*

Sydney: *Please? I just need to talk to you about something. It's important.*

I was so focused on being mad at her for being so obsessed with me and not leaving me alone, I hadn't even thought about what it was she had wanted to talk to me about. She had said it was important.

The whole trek to getting to her that night, I was huffing and puffing and rolling my eyes as I tried not to get caught sneaking out of my tent because I didn't think Sydney was worth getting in trouble for and I was mad at myself for doing this.

When she finally grabbed me in the practically pitch-black darkness, I had been annoyed. So annoyed, that I didn't exactly recognize how she wasn't smiling like she usually was. How she looked serious. I was only thinking about myself and how mad I was at her. How this was my chance to get her to leave me the heck alone.

"I can't believe you actually came," she told me. Then she looked like she was about to keep talking. Like she was about to tell me something, probably the thing she wanted to tell me in the first place.

But I talked first.

"I need to talk to you," I said. I just wanted to get the words out quickly before I changed my mind. Sydney had basically taken over my entire upperclassman trip. It had turned into being all about her, and I hardly even liked her.

"Okay then, shoot," she said. Then... she was looking at something over my shoulder. When I turned around, I didn't see anything. But I didn't stop to ask her what she was looking at. I didn't think to ask her what it was she wanted to talk to me about. All I cared about was telling her to leave me alone. I argued with her. Told her that I don't like her.

I had expected to get more of a reaction out of her. For her to insist that she liked me and that I liked her and that we would be good together. For her to be really apologetic about getting me in trouble or saying whatever she could so that we could keep being friends. Instead, she hardly seemed like she was even paying any attention to me. She was distracted. Fumbling with her hands and shuffling her feet.

Then I said, "I only came to meet you to tell you that I don't want to talk to you anymore."

I didn't understand her expression. But I'm wondering if maybe I get it now—she looked at me like I had far bigger problems than trying to rid myself of her crush on me.

But that's ridiculous. How could she have known anything?

But if Carson killed her, it had to be because somehow, she knew too much. It's the only explanation.

"We're done here," I said to Sydney that night before I started walking away. Her grip on the back of my shirt was tight as she pulled me back.

"Warner, wait!"

There it was. The desperation. That thing she needed to tell me. That thing I wouldn't listen to.

"No, Sydney!" I yelled, yanking myself away from her.

"But I meant what I said in that text, I do have something to tell you!"

Standing inside The Viper's dish pit, I feel sick to my stomach. Why didn't I just listen to her? Why did I leave her there?

"I..." I trail off. My head is spinning. I feel like I can't breathe. "I have to go to the bathroom," I tell Cassius.

I run away from him before he can even say anything. I dash into the men's bathroom and slam the stall door shut. Then I spend the next three minutes dry heaving over the toilet. But nothing comes out. I'm shaking and sweating, but I feel cold.

I am sick with my own guilt.

I didn't kill Sydney. But I might as well have.

CHAPTER 25

MADDY

I n the early evening, I am invited back over to Mia's again.

When I knock on the front door, I hear Mia call, "Come in!"

I let myself inside, and the gesture takes me back to high school, when I would show up unannounced at her house all the time, just walking in through the front door like I was part of the family. Her parents never seemed like they minded. And I preferred them so much more than my own.

I can hear Mia talking to someone in the kitchen. It surprises me because I expected her to be alone. But then I remember that everyone knows about our friendship now and we don't have to keep sneaking around.

"Hi, Maddy," Audrey says when she sees me. She, Mia, and Lyla are all sitting at the table, Audrey with what looks like homework out, Mia with her laptop in front of her, and Lyla just sitting with her feet up on the chair and her hands wrapped around her shins.

"Um... hi," I say as I tuck some hair behind my ear.

"Sit," Mia says with a smile. I pull a chair out and sit across from her.

I look at Lyla, and she gives me a faint smile.

I like Mia's daughters so much more now. I only ever disliked them because I was so mad at Mia for so long and since they were her spawn, I decided they were horrible. And then when Audrey found out my biggest secret, Dean being Warner's father, I didn't like her because I was just so scared of what she could do to my life.

But I owe Audrey so much. Warner told me everything: Carson told her he would kill me if she didn't go to the pool at Blackfell High. So she went.

Would Carson have actually killed me? Did he even know where I was? I heard that he had a video of me, which definitely creeps me out, and I did not ask Warner to see it. But was it an empty threat? And if Carson wanted to kill me, why didn't he just do it?

Why did he want Audrey dead instead?

"We're just all hanging out," Mia says with a pleasant smile. She looks happier than I think I've seen her since we started being friends again. It's similar to the look I wear on my face when I spend some good quality time with my own son.

"It's a party," I say, smiling back.

"I am actually not staying long," Lyla says. She side-eyes her mom. "I'm gonna go hang out with Wrigley."

"Am I ever going to get to finally meet this boy that you spend every waking second with?" her mom asks.

"I'm sure you will," she says, slowly getting up from her seat. "I won't stay out too late, okay?"

"Ten o'clock," Mia tells her.

Lyla nods. "Bye, Maddy."

"Have fun," I say.

So, Lyla and Wrigley. I wonder how Warner feels about it. I wonder if that's why he's been hanging out with Audrey more.

Lyla leaves, and I hear the unmistakable sound of car keys jingling before she goes into the garage.

I look at Mia. "She's driving?"

Mia nods happily. "I don't know what changed her opinion about it," she says. "Maybe she was just too anxious about constantly having to ask someone to give her a ride to Wrigley's house. Those two, I swear."

"I never see her anymore," Audrey says.

"They're that serious?" I ask.

"I don't really know," Mia says. She looks at Audrey.

Audrey shrugs. "They definitely like each other?"

"Well, I'd like to meet him," Mia tells her, as if Audrey is going to make that happen for her. "It would be nice to know what he's like, and if he's good for her."

"He's a good kid," I say. "He's Steven Hall's son. I've gotten to spend a little bit of time with him." Mia knows about Steven. I blabber to her about him all the time. I've been texting her nonstop about how sad I've been since I left his house.

"Are you sure?" Mia asks, smirking. "Is he the type of guy I would've dated in high school, or the type of guy my sister would've dated in high school?"

I know what she's referring to. Nora dated Carson, who was known as Blackfell's bad boy. And she dated Parker Fritz, who was the class clown, popular, and athletic—but not as good as his older brother, Craig. Parker always hated that he never lived up to him.

"Definitely more your type of guy," I say, even though I'm not entirely sure. We're older now. We don't know what it's like to be a teenager anymore. Therefore, I can't exactly gauge the kind of kid that Wrigley is. But Steven has never had anything bad to say about him.

Mia gets up and grabs snacks and drinks for everyone. We make small talk, but once she is back in her seat, I can tell the small talk is over.

"So," Mia begins. "I wish Lyla would've stayed, because what I want to talk to Maddy about is important, Audrey. And I think that since, whether we like it or not, we are all involved in it, you should stay and we should hear your input. Because right now, I think we all need to put our heads together and figure out what is going on. And I think the only way we can get to the bottom of this is if everybody comes clean about their secrets and lays it all out on the table."

"Warner doesn't think Carson is really dead," Audrey says.

"It's understandable as to why," I say, agreeing with my son. Craig is the one who "found" Carson. But they're best friends.

"It's crossed my mind that maybe Craig did find Carson dead, but that he blames it on us and our past," Mia says. "Craig has been going haywire lately. What if Carson's death pushed him over the edge, and he wants to retaliate somehow? I don't think we can trust the cops. I don't even know if we can really trust Officer Wilde, even though I do like him."

I am so busy racking my brain that I miss the look on Audrey's face until I notice the way Mia has begun to stare at her. I turn my head and see that Audrey is shifting in her seat. She has something to admit.

"What's on your mind?" Mia asks her.

"I think you're right," she says. "We all need to start being honest about things. I don't like all these secrets. It feels like everybody has them. And that's why all of this started in the first place."

My stomach dips. She's so, so right.

"Is there a secret that you have?" Mia asks her.

"Sort of."

"No judgment," I tell her, trying to sound reassuring. "Not after what Mia and I caused."

"Okay." She sits up straighter. "I know who Carson Price's father is. Stepfather. And I have... sorta...met up to talk with him."

"When?" Amelia asks, her voice shrill. I give her a look to remind her, "No judgment," and she relaxes.

"Today," Audrey says.

"Audrey!"

"Mia, it's okay," I say.

"No, I don't think you understand just how not okay it is," Mia tells me.

Audrey continues. "I met him once when he showed up here before Carson was found. Then I snuck out of school to talk to him. And I shouldn't have, and I'm sorry. But he told me all about how Carson started a fire that killed his mother, Eric's wife. And how he has been looking for him to get him help. I haven't told anyone this."

Mia's face is scrunched up like she's in pain. "Audrey, do not do that again. You need to stay far, far away from that man."

"What's the big deal?" she asks. "I don't think he's dangerous."

"He is dangerous," she snaps. "I just so happened to meet Carson's stepsister today when I was out looking for answers."

"Harley?" Audrey asks.

I'm stunned. They both know way more than I do.

"Yes," Mia says. "And we had a long talk. I even got her phone number in case I had any more questions. Audrey, Carson's father is dangerous. He's been looking for Carson so that he can get his vengeance for him killing his one true love. He could've been the one who killed Carson, and it wasn't suicide after all! And that's probably why he's still sticking around. To make sure all gets covered up!"

Audrey's eyes widen. "I... I didn't even think..."

Mia puts her head in her hands. "Seriously, Audrey! He could've killed you too!"

I reach across the table and take one of Mia's hands in mine. "It's okay, Mia."

She nods.

"I'm sorry," Audrey says.

Mia doesn't say anything. So I keep the conversation going. "You don't happen to have a picture of either of them, do you?" I ask Mia. "It might be good to know what they both look like in case I see them around town."

"Why would she have a picture?" Audrey asks.

Mia's face reddens slightly. "Actually, I do." She stands and walks away from us, leaving us alone together.

I don't know what to say to Audrey. She doesn't seem like she knows what to say to me. So we're silent until Mia returns.

"I haven't taken everything down in there yet," she says. "In my office, I was doing a lot of research about Carson, to try and get enough proof that he was alive. And I found pictures of Eric and Harley Price. I didn't know anything about them yet, though. I just found out who they were. I was going to dig deeper into the both of them, but then I found Carson, and it didn't feel necessary anymore." She slides the pictures to me.

One is of Eric Price. He looks like he's spent the majority of his life in prison. I can't believe Audrey didn't think he was dangerous. He looks like a killer.

"Wait, this is his stepdad?" I verify.

Audrey nods. "I don't know what happened with Carson's real dad."

Then I look at the picture of Harley. "That's weird," I say as I squint at it.

"What?" Mia and Audrey ask at the same time.

"I don't know. She just looks familiar for some reason."

"Harley knew Carson was running from his father. She thinks he's scary, too," Mia says.

"I don't know why I trusted his story," Audrey says. "He had seemed so genuine..."

"I can't believe you didn't tell me about meeting him in the first place," Mia snaps. "I can't believe you just kept it to yourself."

"Dad's the one who made me lie," Audrey barks back. "I didn't want to. But he said you were already going through so much and it wasn't another thing we needed to add to your stress."

Mia purses her lips.

"Do either of you have anything you'd like to tell me?" Audrey asks. "Or do I know it all already?"

"I don't really have anything new," I say. "Just what Warner told me about Megan. Which I'm sure he's told you."

Audrey nods and then turns to her mother. "Mom?"

"Nope, I've said what I learned."

"Okay," she says. "I'm going to go finish my homework in my room and let you two have your girls' night, or whatever."

She picks up her stuff and leaves us to it.

"You know, she's right about us needing to be more honest and open about things," I tell Mia now that we're alone.

"What do you mean?" she asks.

I feel awkward because it feels so... high school. "I have to tell you something."

She raises an eyebrow.

"The other night, Dean came over to my house and was talking to me about how he wants all of us to be a family and... he kissed me. Can you believe that?"

"He...what?"

I scoff. "Yeah!"

She looks just as repulsed as I am.

"I shoved him off of me immediately," I continue, "because, you know, I really like Steven, and I don't want to have a relationship with Dean. Ever. Seriously, ever."

"What happened after?"

"He left," I say simply.

"Wow."

I nod.

"When did you say this was?" she asks.

"Halloween."

Her lips turn downward.

"It was so weird," I say. "He came over to talk about you, actually. He was really worried about you. And then, he kissed me. I don't get it. It was a crazy night. Nora also came over, and she had a run-in with Dean as he was leaving. I don't know how long it had been since they last saw each other. Ugh, and then I guess Steven was also trying to come see me, because he kinda…saw Dean kiss me. It was this whole… thing."

While Mia knows Steven and I aren't together right now, I didn't tell her the full story as to why. I just told her I did something stupid. So I decide now to fill her in on everything fully. It takes hours for us to talk it all over and for her to make me feel a little bit better, and it's late when I finally leave to go back home to Warner. It was his first day at The Viper today, and I hope he's still awake because I want to hear all about it.

I'm driving, cautiously because I don't need to nearly kill myself again in another accident, when my mind flashes back to a memory: the reason why that photo Mia showed me of Harley Price looked so familiar.

I was a junior in high school. I was newly into my relationship with Dean. We were at some music store that's long gone now in downtown Toxey. We went to pick out CDs for each other we each thought the other would like. We had similar music tastes. Dean and I actually used to have a lot in common.

I think Dean gave me a Stone Temple Pilots CD and I had given him The Cranberries. He went to go pay for them, and I wandered over to the window, where I saw Carson outside. He was across the street, leaning up against his ugly old car, and he was arguing with a girl.

Now I know who that girl was.

Harley Price, his stepsister.

She was yelling at him. And Carson was yelling back, flinging his hands in the air and looking at her darkly. And I remember the way he clutched her wrist and yanked her back to him when she tried to walk away.

Carson had looked like a monster. But Harley hadn't looked afraid of him.

What were they fighting about?

I remember being worried about Nora when I saw that scene all those years ago. I thought Carson was maybe cheating on her with Harley. I tried to look into it, but I didn't get very far before everything went so, so wrong.

I immediately call Mia and fill her in on the memory. I think Harley might turn out to be the perfect person to give us more of the answers we've been searching for.

Chapter 26

LYLA

Wrigley and I are hanging out in his game room, where I am getting better and better at air hockey. We've played three games and I've won two of them.

"I just let you have that last one," he says to me as we set up to start a new game.

"You're full of it," I tease. "You just can't believe you're getting beaten when you've had all this time to practice."

He rolls his eyes, but the smile doesn't leave his face.

There's a knock behind me, and I turn to see Wrigley's dad, Steven, popping his head into the room.

I like his dad. He's always been nice to me. He lets Wrigley and me have our space. He doesn't seem to want to interrogate me. I've noticed that he and Wrigley kind of just keep to themselves. In this giant mansion, they could probably go days without seeing each other.

"Just wanted to say goodbye," Steven says, noticing that I am here and waving at me. "Good to see you again, Lyla."

"Hi, Mr. Hall. Where are you going?"

"Oh, just another work trip to check on the other restaurants."

"See ya," Wrigley says, his voice flattening.

"Be good. I'll Venmo you money for food."

Wrigley nods. Steven gives me one more smile and then leaves. Did he not see it? Can he not tell that it clearly bothers Wrigley That his dad leaves so much?

"Another trip, huh?" I ask a still glowering Wrigley.

He shrugs, and then suddenly, he's grinning at me in a way that is jarring. I shake my head to make sure I'm seeing him clearly.

"All right, this time, I'm not going to take it easy on you." He hovers over the air hockey table, gearing up to play and looking excited about it.

"Are you okay?" I ask. I saw the look on his face before his dad left. I heard his tone of voice when he told his dad goodbye.

"You're here," Wrigley says. "Why wouldn't I be?"

I smile, but I can tell he's trying to change the subject. "You can talk to me, you know," I say, not ready to. "I talk to you."

"What is there to talk about?" he asks. He genuinely sounds confused. "I'm good."

It saddens me a little that Wrigley won't open up. But maybe I just need to keep trying.

We keep playing air hockey.

He's playing even worse than before, now. I win pretty quickly, and he wipes the sweat off his forehead and tosses the puck carelessly down on the table. "All right, I'm calling it." He walks over and hugs me tightly. "Good game."

I hug him back, enjoying the warmth that envelops me and the feeling of his arms around me.

I look up at him, and he kisses me on the lips. It's soft and quick.

"I'm gonna throw a party."

I do a double-take. "Wait, what?"

"Yeah. I haven't had one in a while. It'll be fun."

"Wrigley, are you sure? With everything going on..."

"Even more reason to. You could use a distraction. It'll be good for you. You can feel like a normal teenager."

"I don't need to go to one of your parties to feel like a normal teenager. What if you get caught? Won't your dad get mad?"

"Has it ever stopped me before?"

I almost forgot that Wrigley is such a party boy. I never questioned it before. But now it's so clear why he does it.

"Wrig, do you throw parties to get back at him? Do you want to get caught?"

"Jeez, Ly, no. It has nothing to do with my dad. Can we just... stop talking about him, please? I really could care less about what he does."

I want to tell him I don't buy it. But he's clearly annoyed with me. I'm kind of annoyed with him, too. He has a huge issue with his dad and he needs to be better at communicating how he feels.

"Yes, sorry," I say. "I won't bring it up again."

But I don't know if I mean that.

"Thank you."

We're still standing with our arms awkwardly around each other. So I step away and clear my throat.

"Hey, I have to go bowling with my dad and his new girlfriend tomorrow, believe it or not. You should come. You'll make it so much more bearable."

"You want me to meet your dad?" He looks stunned. I start mentally panicking. Does he not think we're at that point in our relationship yet?

"I just thought it could be fun," I say with a shrug. "But I get it if you don't want to. If you're not ready to meet my parents. There's no pressure."

"It's not that I am not ready," he says slowly. He picks up his air hockey peg and fiddles with it, not looking at me.

"Then what is it?" I ask.

"I guess I'm just not really interested in meeting the people responsible for all of the horrible stuff you've had to go through."

What is with him today?

"Wow," I say, unable to find other words.

"What? It is their fault, isn't it?"

"I... I don't think there's anyone to blame except for the person who did all of this."

He gives me a look.

"What?" There's an edge to my voice.

"Come on," he says.

"I'm serious," I tell him. "My parents are going through a lot, too. I'm not mad at them."

Maybe Wrigley just hates all parents.

"Well, I am," he says. "I'm sorry, Lyla. You were kidnapped. And I think you are trying way too hard to pretend like that never happened."

"Is that so?"

He shrugs.

"Honestly, Wrigley? You seem like you're in a bad mood today. Maybe I should just go."

I make the move to leave. He's making me in a bad mood, too. His bringing up my parents and kidnapping is making me want to start crying.

He drops the peg and hurries to me to take my hand and stop me from going. "I'm sorry. Please don't go, Lyla."

I stare at him expectantly. I want him to give me something. I want him to open up to me about something.

"I'm a little... on edge," he admits. "I just have a lot on my mind. And every time I think about what happened to you, I just get so mad. I don't want to fight with you. I'm being an idiot."

"No, you're not," I say. It is sweet how much he seems to care about me—I guess being mad at my parents is maybe his way of showing me that.

I hug him, to show him I accept his apology.

He hugs me back, resting his chin on the top of my head. Hopefully the mood has turned around and we can go back to making each other laugh.

But as I breathe in the scent of Wrigley, I think about Dr. Gloria Morton's words. She warned me to take a step back from my relationship with Wrigley.

I am right to not listen to her. Wrigley is so good to me. I'd probably be a mess if I didn't have him to distract me and make me feel better. Dr. Morton doesn't know what she's talking about.

CHAPTER 27

WARNER

I'm in second period, my weight training class, the next day, watching Wrigley Hall fool around with the workout equipment, not taking the class seriously, when I get a text. I pull my phone out of my sweats after I finish my set of deadlifts, my hamstrings aching, and see that it's from a number I don't have saved. Given everything that has happened to me so far, I immediately get suspicious.

Unknown: *Hi Warner.*

My first thought is Carson. But starting off the conversation with a "Hi" like that doesn't really seem like his style.
I reply.

Me: *Who is this?*

There is a loud banging noise, and I snap my head back up, my heart skipping a beat, to see that Wrigley has dropped a heavy barbell on a bumper plate. He laughs with another junior, Orion Potts, and some of the other guys shoot them a dirty look. Wrigley's acting a little different today. Like he's in the mood to get in trouble. It makes me wonder how things are going with him and Lyla. If something happened between them. I've also been hearing talks of him having a party at his house this weekend. His last one, where Lyla had been tormented by the noises of Sydney screaming with the voice recorder, hadn't been too successful. But Wrigley Hall throwing a party makes things sound like they're getting back to normal, whether I want them to or not.

"You have one more set," Ryan Copeland says to me. He asked if we could be partners today so that he could get some tips from me about being the new football captain. The last thing I wanted to do was say yes, because it's incredibly awkward since he and Audrey have a thing, and Audrey and I also have a thing.

A thing I can't exactly figure out, but still.

I don't want to seem like a sore loser about losing football captain to him by telling him to stay away from me. So, I agreed.

I put my phone away and do my last set. Then we switch.

"How is Audrey?" he asks me, grunting as he lifts the barbell.

"What?"

He finishes his set and then drops the barbell to the mat, too concentrated to be able to talk during it. "You were with her when she nearly died at the pool. Is everything okay with all of that stuff?"

"Oh." My chest feels tight. My stomach is in knots. But Ryan and Audrey are not in a serious relationship and he does not have a claim over her. Still, I'm that guy—the guy who keeps stealing everyone's girlfriends.

She's not his girlfriend.

"I-I think she's doing oh...kay," I stammer. "I don't really know."

"That TikTok page is crazy," Ryan says quickly moving on. "I feel like I hardly talk to you, but I know your whole life."

"You and the rest of the world," I tell him. The TikTok page is still huge, getting more and more followers every minute. People love to watch others suffer. "I thought you wanted to talk to me about football stuff."

"Yeah, sure," he says. "You're just, like, basically famous, so how could I not ask, you know? Is Mr. Reeves really your dad? And you didn't know? "

"Yup."

"Crazy."

Does he know any other words?

I repeatedly check my phone throughout the day, but the person who texted me never replies. However, when the bell rings at the end of my last class, I head to the locker room to change for football practice, and the number calls me instead.

"Hello?" I answer, stopping in my tracks.

"Warner?" It's a woman's voice. I don't recognize it.

"Yes?"

"Sorry, I am really no good with texting. I just wanted to make sure it was you before I called. You're out of school now, right?"

"The bell just rang and I have football practice...Uh, who is this?"

"Oh, I apologize, I thought I texted it to you. This is your grandma, Cathy."

"My...huh?"

"Does your school have bad reception?"

"Uh, no..."

I've never talked to my grandma before. She's never once reached out to me. When my mom stopped talking to her parents after high school, they never tried to talk to her either.

"Grandma?" I ask. It feels foreign, like I should just call her Cathy.

"Yes! Hi!" she cries. "Oh my goodness, I can't believe it's really you."

"Yeah... I..." I trail off because I don't know what to say.

What is happening right now?

"I'm sorry to just call you out of the blue like this, sweetie, but you have no idea how long I've wanted to talk to you."

"Wait, you have?" I start pushing past people in the hallway so I can get outside and hear her better.

"Yes," she says. "But I should have known you wouldn't know this."

"Did Mom give you my number?"

"No. I had to get it from other *'sources.'*"

"Oh. Does she know that you're calling me?"

"Heavens no," she says. "Warner, your grandfather and I have tried to reach out to you your whole life. But your mom never let us. She always got in the way and forbade it. I was going to wait until you were eighteen and she didn't have a say anymore, but with everything I've been hearing, I changed my mind. So I'm doing this behind her back."

"I'm sorry," I say. "My mom just never told me any of this."

"I'm sure she didn't. I'm sure she has her reasons for not wanting us to get to know each other, but you're my only grandson."

"Why would she want to stop you guys from getting in contact with me?" I ask. "Is my grandpa with you?"

"Oh no," she says with a laugh. "We divorced a long, long time ago. I don't think your mother ever really recovered from it. It's why she turned into a little rebel and decided to run away from us and ruin her life."

"Ruin her life?"

"Before she had you!" she clarifies. "Warner, I'm sure your mother has tried to paint your grandparents as the bad guys, but we tried our hardest to set up a good future for her. She had that trust fund. And she made the decision to waste it all and be irresponsible."

"Trust fund?" I'm so confused. It's impossible to word anything not like a question. My head is pounding.

"Warner, what are you doing bro?" Cody Lawson says as he passes me. "We got practice!"

"See, there's much you don't know about her," my grandma Kathy tells me in my ear.

"Um, Grandma? Kathy?" I say. She is yet another family member of mine I have no idea how to address. "I am really happy to hear from you and it's so crazy that you called, but I have football practice. I really have to go." I'd also like to get off the phone so I can process what the heck is happening to me right now.

"Of course. of course, I'm sorry for disturbing you like this. You'll call me back, right?"

"Of course," I say. I'm sure I'm going to have more questions for her. A lot more.

We hang up, and my mood turns sour as I get changed in the locker room.

I'm going to have a lot of questions for my mother, too.

CHAPTER 28

AUDREY

Something is up with Lyla. I am her twin. I just know.

We're at Dad's with Joey, preparing to leave and go bowling with Dad's girlfriend, Heather.

"So, what are you girls going to say to her when you see her again?" Dad asks as he checks out his appearance in a mirror by the door while Lyla and I sit on the couch.

"That we're sorry," Lyla and I say together.

"I hadn't meant to be rude or disrespectful when I snuck out," Lyla adds innocently. "It wasn't anything to do with her. But I shouldn't have done it."

"Oh, barf," I say, rolling my eyes. "Dad, it was an emergency situation."

He glares at me. "I don't want to hear it. If you had stayed with Heather like you were supposed to, you wouldn't have nearly died. I wouldn't have nearly lost my kid."

I fall silent. We're in a little bit of trouble with Dad for various reasons. I think he's just very angry about the entire situation regarding Carson. No wonder he and Mom are getting a divorce. Mom's past simply has become too much for him to handle.

But they've been together for so long. I find it hard to believe they just "fell out of love." Something had to have caused it. Something is causing a rift between them, and I bet if they could just figure that out and solve it, they could be happy together. And I wouldn't have to be going to this stupid bowling date with his stupid girlfriend.

"Joey," Dad calls up the stairs to Joey's room. "We're leaving soon!"

Next to me on the sofa, Lyla is typing away furiously on her phone.

"Are you okay over there?" I ask when I see it.

She finishes a text, sends it, and then she looks at me. A sigh escapes her. "So, I invited Wrigley to come tonight," she tells me. "And he didn't want to. He just... didn't want to meet my dad. And he doesn't want to meet Mom, either. And he's throwing that party because his dad is out of town, but he won't admit that he's just mad at him. He won't ever tell me what he's really feeling. I just... I don't know."

"Do you not want him to throw the party?" I ask.

"No. I don't."

"But... he's Wrigley. He's always thrown parties. "

"I know. You're right. It's just, he's a lot different than Jackson. I try not to compare, but I can't help it."

"I get it. Jackson was basically best friends with Mom and Dad."

"Exactly. Always trying to be in their good graces. Wrigley could care less."

"Just give him some time," I suggest.

"Yeah."

"All right, let's go," Dad says upon the arrival of Joey in the stairway. We all shuffle out the door and into Dad's car, the three kids in the backseat to save room for Heather, who gets into the passenger seat after we pick her up at her small cottage-style house.

"Hi," Lyla says when Heather buckles in.

Joey and I look at each other and don't say hi to her. But then I see the dirty look on Dad's face through the rearview mirror.

"Hi," I add.

"Thanks for inviting me," Heather says, turning in her seat to smile at all of us. "I'm looking forward to getting to know you guys."

"Yeah, same here," Lyla says, sounding chipper. "I'm really sorry about the other day. We shouldn't have snuck out while you were just trying to help my dad."

Oh, so we're doing this right now.

"Yeah," I throw in. "I'm sorry, too. It was wrong."

But what feels wrong, is saying the apology. I don't mean it. I don't care that I ditched her. I don't even like her. She's not my mom. She's not supposed to be dating my dad. This is all just too much to even process.

I don't want to be here.

Heather looks a little embarrassed as Dad resumes driving. "Oh, I appreciate your apology," she says. "It's okay. We'll just start over. Sound good?"

I look at Lyla, but she's not looking at me. She nods at Heather and smiles. "That would be great."

Ugh, someone kill me.

We get to the bowling alley, put on disgusting, overly used bowling shoes, pick out our balls, and get our names punched in on the TV screen. It smells just as old in here as it is. Even though there's no smoking allowed inside anymore, it lingers, the smell of cigarettes stuck to the walls and forever inside the carpet. There's a mixture in here of teams in their bowling league shirts, little kids running screaming while their parents and older children are trying to actually bowl, and older couples enjoying a date with their longtime significant other. There are no other teenagers here.

"Ready to get your butt beat by me?" I ask Joey playfully as he sits beside me, his eyes downcast and his facial expression glum.

He doesn't look at me. He doesn't change his body posture. "Yeah right," he mumbles. I can tell he's still upset about everything, but that he's also exerting energy into not letting himself get into a good mood.

I go to tell him it's okay if he wants to smile, but Heather's high-pitched giggling as Dad says something to her I can't hear on the other side of the ball collector thingy distracts me from doing it.

Dad is grinning from ear to ear. Heather is looking at him adoringly, her hand on his forearm. It looks so strange. So off. I'm so tempted to run over there and smack her hand away and yell, "Stay away from my dad!"

But I guess I can't.

Lyla returns from taking her turn. She got two pins down. Now it's Dad's turn.

"That was nice, Ly," Dad says as he picks up his ball and looks at us, "but let me show you ladies—and Joey—how it's done."

I squint at him, not recognizing his weird, showy behavior, but when I sneak a glance at my sister, she's smiling like she's having a blast.

I don't get it.

Dad goes to take his turn and Heather cheers and claps proudly.

"This is weird," Joey says, quiet enough that she can't hear.

"Thank you," I am quick to chime in, glad he's bringing it up.

Lyla shrugs. "Yeah, but you have to remember it's not weird for them. Mom and dad knew it was over a long time ago. We're just playing catch-up now."

"I don't even know why I think it's weird," Joey says. "I feel like nothing should surprise me anymore."

"What do you mean?" Lyla asks, concern growing in her eyes.

"Just with everything. What mom—Amelia—did when she took me out of school and tried to bring me to a hotel far away, I get that it was wrong, but it really wasn't that bad. And it's not like she pushed me out in front of a car or anything. I've dealt with way worse. It's more just weird that they had all these secrets that we didn't know about. Or at least I didn't. It makes me feel like a complete outsider, like I don't belong."

"Aw, Joey!" I wrap my arms around him, and Lyla does, too. He's sandwiched between us, getting smothered by his foster sisters' love. "You'll always belong! If there's one clear thing, it's that you belong with us."

"Yeah," Lyla agrees. "There were only so many secrets because they just wanted to protect you."

"And they probably didn't want to risk you getting taken away from them, so they were trying to keep everything as quiet as possible," I say.

With us hugging him and with the reassuring words, he finally gets a hint of a smile on his face.

"I guess," he says. "But, you know, it's kind of no wonder that Carson dude was such a bad guy."

Lyla pulls away first and gets a little more serious. I let go of him, too.

"What do you mean?" Lyla asks. The sound of bowling pins flying thunders behind her as dad makes a spare. Then Heather loudly cheers, so we pause and all cheer, too.

"He was in foster care, too, right?" Joey resumes asking after.

"Yeah?" Lyla and I say at the same time, both wording it like a question.

"Well, he has a bad past. Most foster kids do. I have a bad past, too."

"Yeah, but..." I half-smile at him. "Joey, you're not going to be anything like Carson when you get older."

Joey shrugs. "I know. But I've heard a lot of stuff. A lot of stuff about people in foster homes turning bad when they aged out."

"Joe, what were your parents like?" Lyla asks, shifting gears. Maybe she doesn't like Joey discussing Carson. Maybe she doesn't like anyone discussing him. She still wants to just move on like it never happened.

"They are still alive," he says. "They're married. But they hardly ever live in the same house. Sometimes they do. It was always really confusing and I would never know when Dad was coming home. Or how long he'd stay. They both did bad things. They were alcoholics. And they got in really crazy, scary fights with each other when they were drunk. And my dad would... He's gotten really mad at me when he drinks, too."

"Oh my God," Lyla whispers. But I'm too shocked to say anything. I can't bear to hear any of this. Mom and Dad have always been so vague with me about what Joey's past life was like. And we were never really sure if Joey wanted to talk about it, so we never pressured him to tell us anything.

Joey shrugs. "It was a long time ago. Even though Amelia and Gentry are getting a divorce, and even though Amelia did what she did, I still prefer this life so much more compared to my other one."

"You're up, Joe!" Dad calls when Heather returns from her second attempt. Both of her turns were gutters. How lame.

"You'll get it next time, Heather!" Lyla tells her with a bright smile.

Joey stands and takes his turn.

Right now, there's too much spinning in my head and I can't fake that I am having a good time as well as Lyla can. My thoughts are back on Carson. All those evil things he did. Did his stepdad turn him into the monster he was? Does that mean Harley is right? Or is there still any chance that maybe Eric was telling me the truth?

CHAPTER 29

AMELIA

Dean has been trying to get ahold of me all day, but I have been avoiding him. I haven't figured out what it is I want to say to him. How I want to bring it up. But I know I *have* to bring it up. He kissed Maddy. Recently. And yet he claims to be in love with me?

But he *kissed* her! He dated her! He had a *kid* with her! What if I am just a second choice? I know that I am good enough to not be anybody's second choice.

When I finally muster up the courage to face him, I decide I'd rather do it in person rather than reply to his calls and texts. So I make the drive to his house. And sure, maybe a part of me is a bit paranoid that when I pull up, I'm going to see Maddy and him together through his living room window, curled up cozily on the couch, having hot cocoa and—I don't know—kissing, maybe?

When I pull up to his moderately sized two-story, with the neatly trimmed yard and the tidy, swept porch, I don't see any other cars in the driveway. Relief floods me. I'm being silly. I'm sure Dean has a good reason for the kiss.

I swallow audibly and make my way to his front door.

I knock timidly.

Dean is quick to answer, and when he does, he is wearing workout gear and his shirt is drenched. His chest is rising and falling like he's a bit out of breath.

"Mia, hey," he says.

"Can I come in?" I ask.

He seems to be a bit taken aback. "I... Yeah, of course. I've been trying to reach you all day." He steps aside so I can come in. Then he closes the door behind me and wipes his face with the hem of his T-shirt. "Sorry, I just got back from a run."

I don't think Gentry has ever worked out a day in his life. He likes golf and playing some other sports with Joey or friends, and that keeps him in pretty good shape. And he's always eaten generally healthy and had a really fast metabolism.

Why am I comparing them?

Well, at least I do know *one* thing they have in common right now. I'm mad at both of them.

"It's fine," I say, my posture stiff as we stand in the foyer.

"Oh—sorry, why don't you come sit down?" he offers, leading the way into the living room. "Are you okay? Can I get you a drink?" I don't like the way he's looking at me. It makes me think he's worrying that I've reverted back to being the crazy Mia. Maybe that's what I get for showing up like this. And maybe I *am* a little crazy still. Crazy for jumping into this with him. Crazy for falling right into his trap.

"I don't want a drink," I say, having a hard time looking at him. I sit down on the edge of his leather sofa, and he stands across from me on the other side of the coffee table. He probably doesn't want to sit down because he's too sweaty from the run. He puts his hands on his hips and tries to control his breathing. He must have *just* made it back before I pulled up in my car. "Oh," he says.

"Dean, you kissed Maddy?"

His lips part and he blinks slowly. "Mia," he says, his voice slow. "Please let me explain."

I can tell he's expecting me to run for it. Or to yell at him and tell him that I'm never speaking to him again. That's always sort of been the Mia and Dean way.

But I'm going to surprise him. I sit back on his sofa, getting myself more comfortable, and I cross my legs and then cross my arms. "Okay. Explain."

"Oh—okay. I... I know I messed up. It was stupid. And I promise you I regret it. I was just... To be honest with you, Mia, I was so mad at you."

"Okay..." I'm surprising even myself with how calm I'm being. I let him continue.

"I was crazy about you—still am, clearly—and I had spent *so* many years waiting for you, Mia. Feeling guilty for *so* many things. You know what I mean. I've said all this to you before. But... after I found you in the woods, when you went searching for Carson? Seriously, I had never been so scared. So afraid that something terrible was going to happen to you and I was going to lose you forever. It just made me angrier. It made me think that I shouldn't have this... *attachment* to you. Because I knew I would just be ruined if I lost you. Completely ruined. So, I don't know. I tried telling myself that maybe I should just try and move on and be the responsible father and try to have a family with Maddy, for Warner. That maybe it was a safer choice. The less scary one. It's stupid. And Maddy's right; we're just never going to happen. We're not meant for each other. And I knew that even when I kissed her. I swear to you, Mia, I don't have feelings for Maddy. I was just... a mess."

I let it all sink in for a moment, and for once, I am careful about using my words before I just go on and spit them out. "You... have a strange way of handling your feelings," I say slowly.

He smiles haphazardly. "I'm an idiot," he tells me. "A huge idiot. And I should've told you that it happened."

"Why didn't you?"

"Because I'm terrified of losing you, Mia. I'm always terrified of losing you."

I know he's being genuine. When you know somebody for as long as I've known Dean, their expressions become so easy to decipher.

"Maddy and I are friends again, Dean," I say. "I think the only way you're going to lose me is if anything like this ever happens again. I don't want to lose you to her anymore. I read that letter you wrote Nora when she was sent away. If it was always truly me, I'm going to need you to prove it."

His shoulders finally relax. "I've never been good at relationships. But I think it's because I've never been all the way in, not like I was when I was with you. I will gladly spend the rest of my life proving it to you."

"Good."

"So you, uh, read that letter, did you?" He smiles, but I know it's because he is embarrassed.

"The letter that destroyed the friendship you had with my sister for so long? Yep."

"I don't think it's an exaggeration when I say I might've been the dumbest teenager alive."

"We are all dumb when we are young."

"Not like I was. I know I should've been there more for Nora. I miss her all the time. But I am sure to her it felt like I used her all that time just to get to you. And then with me dating Maddy—which started just because I wanted to make you jealous, by the way."

"That's awful, Dean."

"It just *started* that way. But I ended up liking her. She was the first person that made me feel like maybe I could get over you. But let me emphasize how this was a *very* long time ago. Because when you and I finally got together in college, it just made it even clearer to me that getting over you was going to always be impossible. Even though you ended things with me."

"Because you got Maddy pregnant."

"I'm not saying you shouldn't have. You were completely right to break it off. Just like Maddy was completely right to write me that letter, telling me she didn't want me coming anywhere near her or Warner."

"I didn't know she wrote you a letter," I say. But there's a whole lot about Maddy that I don't know. We stopped being friends for so many years. And even when we were friends in high school—best friends—she still kept so much from me.

"Yeah," Dean says. "It's why I moved from Toxey and stayed away for so long. But as I grew older, I just knew if I didn't come back and try to make things right, and try to have a relationship with my son, I would regret it forever."

Dean and I have had to jump a lot of hurdles to get to where we are now. We've hurt a lot of people along the way. It feels a little toxic. A little wrong. But when two people really love each other, like I truly believe Dean and I do, is there anything we wouldn't do, anyone we wouldn't push down, just to be together?

"So, you came back to Toxey just for Warner?" I ask.

"I did. I truly, seriously did. I kept tabs on you on social media. I knew you were married and had kids. I had zero intention of coming here and ruining that. But you just *had* to come on the upperclassman trip."

I can't help but smile.

"What?" he asks.

"I think... we were always supposed to find our way back to each other."

CHAPTER 30

AMELIA

I don't stay long at Dean's after we make up because I know he has a ton of grading to do before tomorrow, and I want to be a responsible adult and make sure to get a good night's sleep myself. I get home before Gentry and the kids have even returned to his rental from bowling. I know this because I told Gentry to call me when he's home, after his new girlfriend—if you can even call her "new" anymore—leaves.

I am in bed when he finally gives me a call, and I had just been about to fall asleep. I almost don't even answer it because I'm too tired and don't know if I want to get into this with him. I already had one confrontation today. Did I have it in me to have a second one?

"Hello?" I ask, trying not to sound sleepy.

"Hey," Gentry says in a low voice like he doesn't want the kids to find out who he's talking to. Or maybe his girlfriend is still there and he's calling me in secret. "Sorry it took me so long to call."

I don't even want to picture the reason *why* it took him so long.

"It's okay," I say.

"Joey wanted to play a board game when we all got back. The kids just went to sleep."

"Cute."

"Yeah, so what's up? Why did you need me to call you, everything all right?"

"Um, not exactly. Before you freak out, I'm fine. But, I did have a talk with Audrey last night, and she told me something interesting."

"What?"

So, I guess Audrey didn't admit to him she came clean to me yet.

"Since when do we coerce our kids into keeping each other's secrets?" I ask.

"Wait..." Gentry trails off. But then it seems to hit him. "Audrey told you about Carson's father?"

"Bingo." I sit up and lean against the headboard. I have to admit I'm pretty proud of myself for not having flipped out on either man today. Granted, I think a big reason behind that is that I don't want anyone to have any reason to continue thinking that I am still a nutcase. I don't ever want to go back to that place I got sent.

"You were dealing with a lot," Gentry tries. "I didn't want to overwhelm you or stress you out. That's all it was."

"Maybe you had good intentions, Gentry, but it led to Audrey putting herself in danger. I don't think you fully understand every-thing that's going on."

"Well of course not," he hisses. "When have I ever?"

"That man happens to be very dangerous. He's the reason that Carson was on the run for so long."

"I thought he just wanted to stay hidden so that when he got his revenge against you and Maddy by taking it out on our kids you wouldn't see it coming."

So, it's a little bit of both. But that's neither here nor there. "Audrey decided to take it upon herself to have a 'secret meeting' with him, Gentry. And it could've been avoided if you would have just been upfront with me."

"She shouldn't have done that," he says. "But you're being a hyp-ocrite right now, Mia. There is *so* much that could've been avoided if *you* had just been upfront with *me*. From the very beginning."

Gentry harbors a lot of resentment for my past. Sometimes I think it stems all the way from high school. He hadn't exactly been the most popular. He was kind of a recluse. But even though I was more social, we were both drawn to each other because we were both smart. I always liked when I was partnered with him for stuff. And I always had a casual, light friendship with him. Not one where we called each other on the phone or ever hung out outside of school, but I was always friendly toward him. I knew even when I was young that he would grow up to be so much better than a lot of the people we went to high school with. And I had been right. But there was always gossip circling that seemed to have my name involved in it, and I think it bothers him that I never showed him any romantic interest until after we graduated. I think he thinks it's because I didn't find him cool enough to date, but in all truth, it was because after Parker first dumped me when he somehow found out Dean and I kissed a few years before, there was just too much going on in my life and I just wanted to finish my senior year without any more drama. And that meant swearing off boys.

When Gentry and I went to the same college, he began making it a lot clearer that he saw me as more than a friend. I began to see him the same way, but, Dean was still in the picture then. So, while Gentry and I had gone on a couple of dates, I held back from agreeing to officially be his girlfriend because I felt there was still so much potential for something huge to transpire between Dean and me, and I wanted to see where things went with him first.

But then I found out that Dean got Maddy pregnant.

There was no way I could be with him after that. It was too complicated and too messy. And I was too hurt.

And who was there waiting to treat me right and cause me minimal stress and make me feel like the only girl in the world? Gentry.

While Gentry and I had gone to the same high school, I felt that he was so much easier to start fresh with. He was somebody who knew me but didn't know *everything*. Toxey may be a town that is good at exposing everyone's secrets, but the one Maddy and I shared about what we did to Carson seemed to be the only one we had managed to keep hidden.

I did have a lot of skeletons in my closet when I married Gentry. And he didn't have any in his.

"You're right," I finally say back to Gentry. "But I can't control anything that happened in the past. All I can control is what's happening now, and you didn't have to do that."

"Spare me the lecture, Mia. I don't want to do this with you right now. You know how early I have to be up for work. I have to go."

He doesn't even wait for me to say anything back. When the call ends, I sit there with the phone held to my ear and my jaw hanging open. I can't believe he just hung up on me.

Somewhere throughout our marriage, I stopped keeping any secrets from Gentry. But that is probably around the same time when things shifted, and *he* started being the one who kept secrets from *me*. We don't need to hurt each other anymore. Gentry and I getting a divorce really is the best thing for everyone.

CHAPTER 31

MADDY

Between clients at work, I accept a phone call from Warner. But I never would have answered if I had known what I was going to get an earful of.

"Why is Grandma Kathy calling me and telling me how she's wanted to talk to me my entire life?"

I nearly drop my phone from the shock of it. My *mother* called him?

"Wait, wait, wait—rewind and back up a second," I say.

"No!" Warner is heated. "I won't! You've been lying to me. Again! My whole life! You kept me from Dean. You kept me from my grandparents. What is *wrong* with you? Why am I not allowed to have any other family except for you?!"

"What did she say to you?" I demand.

"Not a whole lot, but I guarantee you she was more truthful with me that entire two-minute-long phone call than you've been my entire life."

"Warner," I say with warning in my voice.

"Just tell me why," he demands. "I wanna know. Right now."

"You know I'm at work," I whisper-hiss at my station. There are other customers in the salon and I don't want them to overhear how I'm getting in trouble with my own son. "I cannot have this discussion with you right now, it will have to wait."

"Go outside or something! Take a break! I don't want to wait. I want answers."

"Goodbye, Warner." I hang up on him and turn my phone off. I'd love nothing more than to be able to run back home to him and explain everything. I would love nothing more than to know exactly what ridiculous lies my mother told him to get him on her side. After all these years... What was wrong with that woman?

I know Warner is furious with me. But I can't just leave work. I already got a talking to today by my boss, Louisa. She's not happy with my performance. I think she's mad at me for getting in a car accident and being unable to work. Granted, I could have kept her more informed on why I disappeared and maybe given her a doctor's note, but I've been a little preoccupied trying to keep my life held together to remember little nuances like keeping Louisa in the loop.

I resume work and start on my next client, but I am so distracted by my thoughts of my parents and Warner and everything else, that I butcher my client's haircut. I had gotten her confused with my last client, combining what they both wanted done to their hair into one bad, *bad* hairstyle. Naturally, my client gets furious, and Louisa gets involved, and in the end, my client gets a full refund and I get nothing.

Before Louisa turns back to her office, I get that look. The one that says, "You are pushing your luck here, Maddy."

Would I really get fired?

Feeling horrible, I force myself to focus more on my next client and then I stay late to take a walk-in and to help clean up. I'm trying to redeem myself a little bit.

But when I finally leave for the night, I can tell Louisa is still unhappy.

I stand on the curb, crossing my arms and shivering from the cold misty air as I wait for an Uber to accept my pick-up request.

"Come on," I say to my phone. No one is accepting.

Can this day get any worse?

"Maddy?"

I snap my head up at the voice. A man is walking toward me. I don't immediately recognize him. He's average height, average build, but he has a handsome face with a five o'clock shadow.

He looks a lot like Craig Fritz, and *that's* when I put it all together.

"Oh my God," I say when it clicks. "Parker Fritz?"

He grins at me, and I am transported back to high school, when he would chase Mia around like a puppy, dying to get her to date him.

I remember him being the class clown, maybe overcompensating for how everyone always seemed to prefer his older brother.

I can't believe he's here.

"Guilty," Parker says as he reaches me. He has a grocery bag in his hand, having just left the store in the same plaza that my hair salon is in.

"What—this is crazy," I say.

"You look incredible," he says.

"Oh, thank you," I reply, feeling embarrassed. I am a freaking hairstylist in the same city I went to high school, and here is Parker, who is filthy rich and making a name for himself in New York City. I've never even been to New York City. Then again, I'm from Seattle, and I've always told everyone I've talked to that I love my city and New York could never compare.

But I've never been back to Seattle, either.

"What are you doing here?" I ask.

"Just felt the need to check in on everyone," he says.

I wonder if Toxey ever really left him, because he isn't exactly dressed like a businessman. He's casual in jeans and a T-shirt.

"I'm sorry," I say. He's probably seen the TikTok videos. He probably keeps up with the news. I wonder how much Craig has filled him in on, too. And I wonder what kind of light Craig painted Mia and me in if he did.

"It's crazy to run into you like this," Parker says. "I was just grabbing the toiletries I forgot to pack with me. I was going to go to my hotel, order room service, and probably fall asleep before eight."

"Doesn't sound half bad," I reply.

"Maybe not, but if you're not busy, I would love to go grab a drink with you instead."

I know that what I should be doing is going home to Warner to clear the air between us. But a drink and catching up with an old friend sounds like something I could really use after such a lousy day.

I cancel my Uber.

"Let's do it."

He walks me to his car, a rental that isn't too flashy, and I have him drive us to The Mix. I say hi to the bartenders and regulars that I have acquainted myself with over the years, and Parker sees a few people he used to know, and he says hi to them briefly, too. Then we grab ourselves some cold ones and have a seat at a high-top in the corner.

"This is so weird," I say.

"*Being* here is weird. I've always wanted to come to this place."

"Is it everything you hoped and dreamed?" I joke. The Mix is a total hole-in-the-wall.

He laughs. "Oh yeah. There *definitely* aren't any decent dive bars in New York City."

"Gosh, do you just love it there?" I ask, knowing he was being sarcastic about his last answer. "I bet you love it there."

He grins. "I do."

Then we both laugh. I don't know why we're so giggly. I don't know why I'm smiling so much.

"So, Maddy, tell me about your life."

"I'm pretty sure you probably know a lot about it," I say.

"I'm not on social media," he informs me. "However, oddly enough, a *colleague* was talking about this crazy TikTok account from this small town where all of this bizarre stuff was happening. That's how I came to learn about a lot of it."

"What are the chances?" I ask.

"That's what I said!"

We laugh some more.

When it dies down, he shakes his head. "I thought Craig would have told me about all of this, but I guess we have kind of drifted over the years. So, after Frank of all people filled me in on everything going down in my own hometown, I reached back out to Craig. I got to town yesterday. And I got to talk to him in person a bit. Work is pretty hard for him right now."

"Why, because his friend is dead?" I don't mean to sound bitter. But I'm definitely bitter. It's hard for me to pity Craig. "Did he tell you that we dated briefly?"

"You and *Craig?*"

"I know. Me and a cop? It doesn't make any sense." None of the guys I get with usually ever makes sense. Like Steven. What would he want with a poor single mother like me?

"Well... it makes a bit of sense." Parker winks at me.

What is he insinuating? I don't say anything.

He elaborates. "I get why my brother would want to date you."

Oh. He's flirting with me.

"I don't think you do," I say. "He only dated me to get information out of me. How much has he told you about everything that's happened?"

"I don't know. A lot."

"I bet he didn't tell you about how back in high school, Mia and I pushed Carson over a balcony and thought we killed him."

Parker chokes on his beer. "You what?"

Shrugging, I dive into telling Parker everything. Everything that I should have been honest with Steven about from the beginning. I don't care about Parker knowing. I don't care what he tells Craig. And I guess I'm just now realizing it. Maybe it's because, by the time I finish filling Parker in, we're no longer on the first beer.

"Yikes," Parker says, slowly nodding his head after he officially knows everything. "I can't say I'm sad that I left this place."

"But I can say that I'm sad I didn't," I say.

"You'd love New York, I bet," he tells me. "It seems like much more your style."

"Oh, I don't think I could ever move," I tell him, surprising myself.

"Why not?" Parker asks. He motions to the bartender to get another round started for us. "What's keeping you here?"

"The same reason I always manage to get sucked in. A guy."

He doesn't hide his surprise. "Oh, you're seeing someone?"

"I was. I screwed it all up."

Man, I am *really* just letting Parker know everything about me. In high school, we weren't even that close. I don't know why I am being so open and vulnerable. Maybe it's the way Parker seems so casual about it all. He's not overwhelmed by the information I've given him. He isn't mad at me. He doesn't seem to judge me about any of it. That go-with-the-flow attitude never really left him, I guess. It's nice.

As more drinks come, I vent to Parker about all my problems with Steven, and about how I messed it all up.

And Parker is so nice about it after. He doesn't seem annoyed like he no longer wants to talk to me after finding out I am interested in somebody else.

"Hey, Maddy," he says, "you did what you could. You put it all out there on the table. You acknowledged your mistakes and you apologized. What more can you do, ya know? It's not like you can change the past. My advice to you is just to let the chips fall where they may. Try not to overthink it. Overthinking can take *years* off your life."

"Parker, have you ever met another woman before?" I tease.

"Funny. But I'm serious. The Maddy I knew in high school never really struck me as an overthinker. Not like Mia was, anyway."

I sit back in my seat. As I stare at him, all I can think is that he's so right. When I was in high school, I never cared this much. I never really cared about *anything*, and I just did what I wanted without worrying about any consequences.

But then the Carson thing happened. And that's when it all changed.

But, if it's really true, and Carson is really dead now, maybe I can actually listen to Parker's advice.

"All right, Parker Fritz." I say. Then I clink my glass to his. "Here's to not overthinking it."

He clinks his glass against mine, and then we fall into another fit of laughter.

CHAPTER 32

WARNER

Mom informed me that she was going to be out late, and I'm sure she thinks that means I'll just go to bed and table this topic of discussion for another day, but that's where she's wrong.

I wait for her on the couch like some parent waiting for their misbehaving child to come home from sneaking out. The roles of the responsible person in this family have always been so twisted.

When Mom walks in, she's a little unsteady on her feet and smiling.

But then she sees me.

"Oh, you're still up. Don't you have school tomorrow?"

"Nice try," I say.

"What?" she asks with a shrug as she goes into the kitchen and opens the pantry to find something to snack on.

"Mom, you know what I want," I say, getting to my feet and following her.

"Then why don't you just ask your *grandmother*, since you trust her so much more than you trust me." Mom gives up on trying to find something to snack on—probably because we don't have anything good, or anything at all—and rolls her eyes as she closes the pantry door.

"Because I'd like to give *you* the chance to be honest with me first," I say through my teeth. I am tired. I would rather be in bed asleep. But instead, I have to do this with her. It's a bit infuriating.

She's always hiding something.

"You're going to get mad at me when I say it, but I only wanted to protect you. And I was only doing what I thought was best."

I fling my hands in the air. "Oh, come on! For once in your life, why can't you let me make my own decisions?!"

"I do!" she argues.

"Oh really?" I snap. "Like when you knew Dean was my dad so you told me all about that and let me decide for myself if I wanted to have a relationship with him? Or like how you told me about everything that happened with you and Mia and Carson in the very beginning and let me decide how to handle it?"

"Warner, I—"

"You never letting me make my own choices has only caused further implications in our relationship. Don't you get that?"

She chews on her bottom lip. "*Ugh*, why do you have to be so right?"

"What?"

"Great," Mom says. "It's always been my *dream* to have this conversation with you."

"What conversation?"

"According to my parents, Warner, they are not the bad guy. According to them, they have never done anything but try and make me happy and give me a good life. The reality is that, for some reason, it is impossible to make them understand how much they messed me up."

"What do you mean?"

Already, I feel my anger sort of dissipating. I was so mad about catching her in yet another lie that I hadn't even stopped to consider why she might have felt the need to do so in the first place. Why has she never wanted to talk to me about them?

Mom groans dramatically and then hops up on the counter and sits facing me as I stand in the arch. "My parents fought like crazy when I was a kid. They drove each other mad. They were loud and they threw stuff. And then my dad started drinking heavily. And my mom was never around because she was starting this huge hair salon empire, so she never had time for me. And I was left alone with my drunken father. And then before long, Mom met someone and left my dad for him. And when my dad moved out, got a job in Toxey, and relocated, even though he was an alcoholic, my mother decided it would be best that I went with him since she was so busy traveling all the time for work.

They divorced, and my father ended up getting a lot of money out of it, and his decent job here also afforded him the luxury of thinking he could just keep me happy by buying me stuff and giving me money to do things. I think he had his mindset that he could keep being a drunk as long as I was distracted by shiny things. He sucked. And my mom sucked. She hardly ever came to visit, and when she did, it was to see Dad, because she was still in love with him even though she had left him for someone else. It wasn't even ever to see me, and I knew it. She doesn't think I know, but I always did. She would greet me with a hug and some cash. And that was that."

"Whoa." That's all I can really think to say. I am still processing everything she just admitted. Still trying to picture her being a kid once and having to deal with that.

She gives me a sarcastic smile. "But wait—there's more," she says.

I'm a little nervous, but I still want to hear it.

"When I got pregnant, my mother and father wanted me to give you up for adoption. They didn't want me to keep you. When we had that conversation, it was the last time I ever really talked to them."

"Wow," I mutter.

"Right? Kind of funny how I went against their wishes and had you anyway, and they *still* felt entitled to be able to have a relationship with you."

If my mom *had* put me up for adoption, how different would my life be now?

I shake my head. I know I've been through a lot, and I know Mom has put me through a lot, but I wouldn't change any of it for the world. I don't wish I had been given up for adoption. I am full of relief and appreciation for my mom. She was a teenager, and yet she wanted to keep me.

"They do kind of suck," I agree.

She beams at me like a proud mom would. Feeling not at all mad at her anymore, and instead really bad for her, I open the pantry and go to the hiding spot where I have been keeping a stash of chocolate bars I bought after being embarrassed I didn't have anything to offer Audrey when she came over. Feeling like Mom is more than deserving of it now, I give one to her.

"Sneaky," she says, gladly accepting it and tearing it open.

"Mom?" I ask.

"Yeah?"

"What was your relationship with Dean like?"

"Oh…" She pauses right before she's about to take a bite. "Um… well, we started dating when I was a junior and he was a sophomore. We had a lot in common. I was kinda the new girl at school and friends with his best friend, who was Nora. He was always such a nice guy. He was *good*. In a way that was almost boring. But, like I said, he and Nora were best friends, so they were always together. And, I was a young, jealous teenager. I ended it with Dean because I was certain he and Nora were going to end up together. But they didn't. And after I graduated, when Dean was still a senior, he wanted to try again. Nora was institutionalized over the death of Carson. Dean told me he stopped talking to her for some reason. And I thought since she was no longer in the picture that maybe things would work between us. Mia had left Toxey for college, not that she was very far. And even then, I had no idea that either of them had feelings for each other, and Mia and I weren't friends, so I never even considered the two of them. Never.

"Dean and I got back together. And it was good for a while. But I always had this sense about him, that he always had one foot out the door. I chalked it up to us being young. Nobody wants to settle down when they're still in high school. And even after he graduated, he still seemed not really willing to put in the effort to make the relationship work. We started fighting a lot. And I had a feeling things weren't going to work out between us, but then… I got pregnant. It was truly an accident. Without getting into specifics. It wasn't like I did it on purpose so that I could force him to stay with me. And I didn't keep you to torture him, either. I truly wanted you, Warner. I know I was young, but I also knew the second I found out I was pregnant that I wanted to be your mother. No matter what. I told Dean that I was pregnant with you, and he flipped out. The always-good Dean, who listened to his strict parents and never got into any trouble, had finally made a pretty substantial mistake. And he couldn't deal. He dumped me and he left. It hurt, but more because you weren't going to get to have a dad and less because he broke my heart. And it took him a really long time to come around, and by then, too much damage had already been done. And I didn't think he deserved to go anywhere near you."

It's information overload. But I needed to hear it.

I just talk with my mom has given me the clarity I've been looking for. So much more makes sense about her decisions. About what makes mom the person she is today. She hasn't had it easy. And she basically walked away from a life that would have been easy if she had decided to put me up for adoption. She changed everything about her future just for me.

"So... Yeah." Mom seems a little apprehensive like she needs to fill the silence with more words since I am unable to say anything.

I'm still unable to say anything. How am I supposed to respond to any of that?

I know one thing I can do.

I cross the kitchen as she hops off the counter, and I throw my arms around her. As I hug my mom this time, it's tighter than I ever have before.

CHAPTER 33

AMELIA

I have one other senior designer at my office along with a couple of junior designers, the receptionist, and an intern. While I've been going through my mental health crisis, and everything going on with my family, they've been running Amelia Bailey Designs.

But today is the day that I go back to the office.

It gets off to a good start when I get up on time and get ready for the day like I used to, doing my hair and makeup completely and picking out a trendy outfit. I spent a good part of the day yesterday before my confrontations with Dean and Gentry, at some boutiques around town getting myself some new clothes. I felt that a wardrobe refresh was truly necessary in order to feel good about getting back on the grind.

I start the workday off with a meeting with my other designers, the receptionist Ivy taking notes. That's when things start to go a little downhill. Apparently, no one has wanted to send me any emergency messages because they've known what I've been going through, but that also has meant that problems were not getting solved in a timely manner with issues with things like the contractors, tile selections, and furniture mark-ups. So, I spend a majority of the first half of the day putting out fires and feeling slightly panicked. It's only when I sit down at my desk and take a sip from my water bottle that I have a second to realize what has me feeling so worked-up about all of these new problems when I used to handle them with such ease.

For one, I would've never let things get this bad if all of the horrible stuff hadn't happened with my family. But two, this all feels so similar to the job I had before I decided to start my own firm. I had a situation with one client once, where it didn't matter what I did, I wasn't good enough. No matter how I tried to help, she wasn't satisfied.

Her name was Lindsay Fuller.

I worked at a high-end boutique firm outside of Toxey. I had an apartment with Gentry then. The job offer had felt like it was our chance to not get sucked back into our hometown. But Gentry didn't have a job of his own that was set in stone yet. Still, he had a lot of internships out of college and a lot of part-time gigs to help pay for the bills while he did the internships.

I was happy. I was basically living out my dream. How many girls in my graduating class landed a job right after they graduated? *In* their field? I felt special. Important. Like I was accomplishing my goals. No more working at places like Delilah's, where I worked in high school, or Cuppa, the coffee shop I worked at to put myself through college—and to help my parents pay for Nora-related bills.

The college I ended up going to wasn't that expensive because I didn't go to the one of my dreams—I no longer could after everything happened with Nora. My parents needed help paying for her institutionalization, and I, feeling guilty for thinking I was the reason she was there, wanted to put all the money I could into that.

The school I ended up at still had a good interior design program, and the job I landed afterward was at a reputable place. So, it all seemed like it was working out.

Until Lindsay.

Lindsay hired us and specifically wanted to work with me after she got to look through my portfolio and see the work I had done for my first three clients as well as some of that work I had completed in college. It was the first time I had a client that had requested me personally, so I worked harder than I ever had, often taking my work home with me and staying up late at night drafting drawings on my computer on AutoCAD.

But she was never satisfied.

And it didn't take long for me to realize that no matter what I tried, she was going to find something to complain about. So eventually, I had to give up. But giving up only led to her leaving the company a bad review, and then she called my boss and complained about me. I'll never know what was said in that conversation, but all I do know is that it was the reason I ended up getting fired. Me. Fired. From my first important job.

I thought I was done for. I thought I'd never find work ever again.

Gentry and I ultimately came back to Toxey after that, mainly because we had run out of money; I refused to get another job if it wasn't going to be in the interior design field, and Gentry hadn't landed his big-boy job position yet, so money was always tight.

Eventually, I started doing interior design as a freelancer. And I was able to build my empire from the ground up that way.

I'm jolted out of the memories of my past by a phone call from my mother, Susan Flynn.

"Mom?" I say when I answer. My mother and I don't talk much. But lately, I've been hearing from her more. I don't ever hear from my father, but I'm not offended by it; he's gotten grumpier with his old age and doesn't much like to talk to anyone.

"Have you heard from your sister?" my mom asks immediately. It's a little irritating because doesn't she want to check on me? I haven't heard a word from her since I was released from the institution she had a part in sending me to. Not even a "Sorry I didn't realize you were being drugged"?

"Nora?" I stupidly ask because I am just so shocked that this is why she called.

"Do you have *another* sister?"

I roll my eyes. "No, I haven't talked to her. Why, is everything okay?" I have no idea how Nora is taking the news about Carson's death. But I haven't really given it much thought. In a way, it's been a bit refreshing because I used to be filled with so much guilt over thinking I killed Carson, but that turned out to not be true.

However, now my guilt is replaced entirely by everything *else* the Carson situation led to with my own kids.

"I guess she's just out of contact with everyone again then," Mom says.

"Including you?" I ask.

"Yep. Haven't heard from her since the news came out about Carson Price."

When I tried to explain to Nora shortly before Carson's death that he was still out there, alive, after she spent years thinking otherwise, she reacted by slapping me in the face.

"I'm sure she's just processing," I tell my mother.

"I'm just worried," she says with a heavy sigh.

"She's Nora. She does this." Nora pushed herself away from my family when she was finally released from the hospital when she became a legal adult. She'd disappear for months, sometimes *years*, at a time. She went off and started a new life without any of us, only calling to fill Mom in every so often. When she stayed with my family recently, it was the longest amount of time I had spent with her in years.

"I suppose..." Mom trails off uncertainly. "But you know how thinking he was dead the first time nearly destroyed her, Mia. What's going to happen to her now?"

I don't want to worry about Nora. We're not close, and I'd rather focus on the family that I built. "She is a big girl and can take care of herself."

"Easy for you to say. You're not her mother. Ugh, I haven't felt this worried about her since..."

"Since she was in high school?" I guess.

"*No*, since she told me a while ago that she found out she can't conceive. Nora doesn't reach out to me for much, but when she called me to tell me that... Oh, it was so sad."

How bad of a sister do I have to be to not remember if I was ever told that Nora can't have kids? I'm not sure if my mom saying this to me now is the first time it's ever been mentioned, or if she's just simply trying to converse with me like I should already know this pretty significant bit of information.

Not wanting to get found out by asking anything about it, I simply say, "It *is*... sad."

"Yes. And with Carson, she was just so hurt about what she *thought* she saw when she was younger... I don't think she ever fully came around to believing that he could still be alive in the first place. So, I wonder if she's even believing what's on the news right now."

"Considering that he's the one responsible for everything that's been happening to us, I would *hope* that she understands and is maybe a little relieved that he's finally out of the picture for real, like I sure am."

Maybe part of the reason Nora and I were never as close as we could've been, like Lyla and Audrey are, is because I've always thought my mom had a favorite.

And it's not me.

"I'm sorry, Mia," she says. "I'm not trying to sound insensitive. You have just always... known how to take care of yourself. You've always had such a good head on your shoulders. Of course, we can pretend like that incident of yours the other day never even happened. And you go back to being my perfect, normal daughter."

Oh, so I just have to be mentally unstable to get more attention from her?

"Um, right," I say through my teeth, clenching my phone harder. "Hey, Mom, I'm at work right now, actually. I'll let you know if I hear from Nora, okay?"

When we hang up, I try to get back into focusing on my job, and how to get the Bartons—the clients I really wanted because their project seems awesome—to *un*fire me, but the conversation with my mom has only made me feel extra tense.

I decide to call the person that I bet will make me feel better.

"Hey, you," Dean says when he answers my call on the second ring.

"Hey, you're on your lunch break, right?" I ask. "Can you talk?"

"Yes, and yes."

I begin my rant. "You know, *only* Susan would have the audacity to talk to me about how worried about my sister she is when she knows about everything going on with me," I say. I lean back in my chair and put my feet up on my desk. I glance around my office and think about how exceptionally girly it is. Even Maddy said something about it when she visited for the first time. I used to love it, but I know neutral palettes are coming back in style, and maybe my clients would prefer to see an office that reflects current design trends.

"Your mom has always been very protective of Nora, hasn't she?" Dean asks with a slight chuckle.

"She's insufferable."

"Aren't most moms?"

Dean didn't have the easiest childhood either. His parents had always been super strict. He never told me what happened when they found out he got Maddy pregnant, but I can only imagine the shame they made him feel.

"It's good to hear your voice," I say, wanting to change the topic.

"I take it you're not having the easiest first day back at work?"

"You'd be correct. On top of an annoying phone call from my mother, all of my clients hate us, and my girls here haven't exactly done the best job of keeping me in the loop. I don't blame them, but it's causing a lot of issues."

"Do you want to vent to me about them? I can offer some words of encouragement. But don't ask for design advice."

I laugh. "Your house isn't half bad, actually. You might have *some* decent taste."

He laughs, too. "If I ever have a desire to switch careers..."

"I'd have you start off the job by trying to get me my clients back. The Bartons. Don't ever tell Lyla this, but with the news of her texting and driving during her car accident—and probably other rumors they've been hearing—they've decided to fire me as their designer. But I *really* liked their house."

"The Bartons? Do you mean Bryan and Rebecca?"

"Those would be the ones."

"You know I teach their son, Finley?"

"That's *right*—I forgot they had kids similar to mine in age."

"You know what, Mia? I might be able to actually help you with that."

"Dean, I wasn't being serious," I feel the need to remind him.

"Too late."

"But I—"

"Sorry, gorgeous, lunch is about to end and I've got to prep for next period."

"Dean, wait!"

He ends the call, and all I can do is stare at my phone screen and laugh in disbelief. I guess now there's nothing for me to do but wait and see.

CHAPTER 34

MADDY

Normally, I would've called out of work or gotten somebody to cover my shift so that I could go to Warner's football game tonight, but since I am hanging by a thread at the salon, I have to miss his game and work late. I expect him to be gone when I get home, having gone out with his friends afterward like every other normal teenager would have done; Steven apparently was pretty cool about Warner's work schedule and had the general manager give him three shifts a week, never on Fridays, and only sometimes on the weekends. Tonight, however, when I walk through the front door of my house, Warner is grabbing a slice of pizza out of a box on the counter and plopping it on a paper plate. He smiles when he sees me.

"Did you win?" I ask as a way of greeting. My stomach growls at the smell of greasy cheese and salty toppings.

"We did. As much as I hate to admit it, Ryan Copeland actually makes a pretty good captain."

I set my stuff down, kick my shoes off, and join him in grabbing some pizza.

"I can't believe your own father removed you from that position," I say. But Warner just shrugs.

"Since everyone knows now that he's my dad, he couldn't have a nepotism scandal on his hands."

I roll my eyes.

He changes the subject. "What about you?" he asks. "No plans for you tonight either? You were out pretty late last night. New guy?"

I raise an eyebrow. "Since when do *you* ask me about the guys I'm seeing? Don't we have a rule?"

He shrugs again and shovels pizza in his mouth so he can't answer me.

"I *was* out with a guy last night, actually. But not like that," I say. "Crazy enough, I was with Detective Craig Fritz's younger brother."

He chokes on a particularly stringy part of cheese. I hit him on the back a couple of times, and after he gets the bite down all the way, he drops the slice to his plate. "Freaky Fritz has a *brother*?"

"Yes. But we like him better."

"Who is he? Does he live here? Why haven't I ever heard about him?"

"He's visiting from New York. He's not a cop, either. Just a regular guy. He used to date Mia, actually."

Now Warner is the one rolling his eyes. "Of *course* he did."

"It's a small town," I say. "It was even smaller when we were in high school. Not a lot of options when it came to dating."

"So, why is he visiting?"

"Just to check in on Craig, I guess. After the Carson thing."

"Interesting..." He gets a faraway look in his eyes, and it's as if the pizza is completely forgotten about.

"What?" I ask.

"A brother...It just sort of changes things a bit. I think—I want to meet this guy. Can you set it up?"

"You want to meet Parker Fritz?"

"I just have questions. And he might be the only one besides Craig himself who has the answers, since Craig's been talking to him. Would that be too weird of a favor for you to ask?"

"It might sound a little strange when I bring it up, but I will ask him anyway."

Warner looks over my shoulder at the clock on the microwave in the kitchen. "It's still early," he says. "Could you set it up for tonight?"

CHAPTER 35

AUDREY

The win of the football game only makes everyone that much more excited for the party at Wrigley Hall's house. I go with Ryan, straight from the game, and we're standing next to each other in the living room when Danielle strolls up to me and hands me a Red Solo cup. I take it from her cautiously, eyeing the clear liquid inside of it.

"It's lavender blueberry soda water," Danielle says with a smile. "I raided Wrigley's fridge. I must say, he and his father's taste has upgraded."

I smile and think of Maddy, who must have been the one to stock the fridge with it. "Thanks," I say, then I look at Ryan. "This is Danielle."

He smiles at Danielle as he snakes an arm around my shoulder. "Yeah, I know you," he tells her. "You're the one who cleared the air with all that drama about Sophia."

Danielle shrugs. "I am," she says.

I look over her shoulder and see Sophia and Olive not far away talking to some guys in our grade.

"Are you still not talking to either of them?" I ask Danielle.

"Nope," she says, sipping from her own cup. "Olive will message me on Instagram and TikTok sometimes, but I told her that when she's ready to stand up to Sophia as well, that's when she can come to me."

"Good for you," I say. "I hope she takes you up on that offer soon."

"I didn't realize that Sophia so conniving," Ryan says. "She makes herself look really likable."

"It's okay," I tease playfully. "You didn't know better when you were hanging out with her."

He gives me a sheepish smile, and I know he's really embarrassed for hanging out with her to get back at me. "Is it cool if I go get a drink and say hi to some friends?" he asks, removing his arm from around me.

"Yeah, totally."

He kisses my cheek and disappears into the thick crowd of our classmates standing in front of the kitchen island.

As much as the senior cheerleaders kept talking to me and trying to include me in their clique during tonight's game, I found myself sticking more and more by Danielle's side instead. Since she was no longer friends with Olive or Sophia, she didn't really have anyone else on the squad to talk to, and I guess I feel partially responsible for that. Danielle is way too nice to feel isolated. She's a lot more real than the senior cheerleaders, too.

As the party goes on, Danielle and I stick together, and I lose sight of Ryan completely. We find Lyla and see that she's without Wrigley and looking slightly irritated, but Danielle and her bubbly personality are so quick to engage her in conversation that her look washes off pretty quickly and is replaced by a friendly one. I can see Lyla becoming friends with Danielle again, too. Yes, Ly was always closer to Trinity, but now she has the opportunity to get to know the *real* Danielle. The one who exists without Sophia clouding her sunshine.

"You two keep chatting," I eventually say as I grab both of their shoulders. "I suppose I should go find my date."

When I leave them, I can't help but find myself scanning the crowd of partygoers looking for Warner's face. It's silly because I know he's not here. He texted me that he had no plans to come and that the idea of going to a party right now didn't feel right to him. And it makes me wonder if it's because he just doesn't want to see Ryan and me together.

But if Warner would just tell me how he felt about me, maybe there wouldn't *be* a Ryan and me.

It strikes me as a crazy coincidence that I'm having these thoughts right as I walk into the game room and find Ryan, because not only is Kiley among the people he's talking and laughing with, but Kylie is sitting perched on his lap, and they look like a total couple.

I turn, wanting to get out of there as soon as I can, hoping he doesn't spot me and wishing that I could just ghost him and leave him always wondering what it was he did wrong. But there's a huge crowd of people in the doorway now, and it's hard for me to make my escape.

"Audrey!"

Ryan says my name so loudly that there's no way I can pretend I didn't hear him.

I turn back around slowly and see that Kylie is quick to get off of his lap and smooth her hair. She doesn't look guilty—she hardly even looks like she cares at all that I caught her. But Ryan does.

I'm too angry to hear Ryan's excuse. So, I turn around again, and this time, I *push* my way through everyone so that I can get out into the hall.

It's fine, I tell myself as I descend the staircase. It's probably for the best. *You cannot live that fantasy of having a normal life with Ryan forever.*

I decide I want to find Danielle again. I'll spend the rest of the party avoiding Ryan and hanging out with her. At least *she* seems to actually care about me.

CHAPTER 36

WARNER

Sure, people hated Lyla for a while after they learned about her causing Trinity's accident. But that lasted all of what? Five minutes? Because then she was kidnapped, and all everyone wanted was to find her again.

And when it came to Audrey, she was nothing more than a victim in this entire situation. The only thing she got accused of being was a boyfriend stealer, which turned out to not even be true.

Even though I have been a victim, too—ya know, when I was nearly killed in the pool room for one example—I still don't fit in at Blackfell High School. People still talk about me. Ever since I lost my position as football captain, and since Jackson has always been more likable than me, I've basically been shunned by my own team. It wouldn't make sense for me to go to Wrigley's party. Nobody wants me there.

"So, what kind of teenager are you anyway?" Parker Fritz asks me as we sit across from each other in a booth inside Delilah's. To my amazement, when Mom called him up a little while ago for me and asked if he was free, he agreed to meet with me.

"What do you mean?" I ask him as a server hands me a sundae and Parker a brownie a la mode.

He digs right into the brownie with his spoon. "Oh *man*, I've missed this place!" he cries before wiping his mouth on a napkin and then looking back at me. "Sorry. I just mean, it's a Friday night, and you're sitting here with me wanting to ask me questions about my detective brother."

"Right. Uh, well I guess, partially *because* of your brother, I'm *not* exactly a normal teenager."

"Why not?"

I figure it's good for him to hear *our* side of the story, in case he's gotten all of his information so far from Craig and Craig only. So I tell him everything, from the very beginning, with the upper classmen trip and Sydney Hutton, to now.

When I'm done, he has practically finished his brownie and I haven't even taken a bite of my sundae. The whip cream has fallen flat and is dripping down the edge of my glass.

"Seems like a lot for one kid to handle," Parker says to me.

"It is."

"I'm not exactly sure why you think I can help you."

"I guess I just want to know about Craig. The real Craig. The one that *you* know. I want to know what he's told you. How it compares."

"And why is that?"

"He was friends with Carson in high school, wasn't he?"

"Yeah, for some strange reason, he was. No one else wanted to be Carson's friend. Apparently, everyone except for Craig—and Nora —had been able to see that something wasn't right about him. And I don't mean to speak ill of the dead, especially since Carson killed himself and all..."

"What if he didn't?" I ask, leaning forward.

I see a little more of the resemblance between Parker and Craig when Parker raises his eyebrows and looks at me like I've been wandering the streets naked and babbling about the end of days.

"Do you think my brother is part of some cover-up?" he asks. I can't tell if he's offended or intrigued by the idea. I don't know how he and Craig are. But Mom told me Parker hardly visits, so they can't be *too* buddy-buddy.

"I don't know *what* I think," I say. "I'm just trying to explore all the possibilities. And sure, go ahead and say I just can't accept that Carson is dead because I've been through so much, and maybe that's partially true. But I just want to feel satisfied with this conclusion, and I'm not yet. Because there are still a lot of questions unanswered."

"Well—" he pauses to lick his spoon "—*whatever* went down with Carson Price recently, it's definitely been affecting Craig."

"What do you mean?"

"He's kind of a wreck. He hasn't been doing well. And I suspect he hadn't been doing well even before I got the news about Carson. He doesn't tell me a whole lot, but I...I think his attachment to the case and to the people involved hasn't boded well for him."

"Do you think he's in trouble at work?"

"It's just a theory," he answers. Then he points at my sundae. "You gonna eat that?"

I push it toward him. He gives me a pointed look before diving into it. "I'll have you know, I don't normally eat like this." He pats his stomach, and I can tell he's in good shape. "Feels like I can't find anywhere in New York that is as homey as Delilah's. What happened to just simple desserts like this? Why do they all have to be so big and extravagant?"

"Uh huh," I say, only half-listening because I'm still thinking about Craig.

"You know, your mom really hasn't changed a bit since high school," he tells me out of the blue.

"Oh yeah?" My attention snaps back to him.

He nods and takes another bite. "I never saw her as someone that would stay in Toxey, but other than that, she's still the same spunky, sassy Maddy she was back then."

"Yeah, I heard that she and Mia were pretty much opposites. That's why they always fought so much."

"You got that right. Maddy was always trying to get Mia to loosen up. And Mia was always trying to get Maddy to take life more seriously. Those two were something else. Mia's sister Nora was a nut job, too."

"Why?"

"What do you mean *why*? I'm sure you know all about how she 'claimed' Carson was dead. That's when everyone *else* started seeing her as crazy, though—*I* thought she was crazy the second she decided to date Carson Price. I'll never forget the first time I saw them together. I always thought it was so weird because she spent most of her time with Dean Reeves—who is your father, I guess. Wild. Anyway; I always thought that Dean and Nora were secretly together or something. But then one day, Nora was suddenly the girlfriend of the creepy new kid. Mia *hated* it." He laughs a little.

"Well, she was right to," I say.

Parker looks down at his Apple watch. "Yeah, hey—I didn't realize how late it was, I really should take off." He pulls his wallet out and throws some cash down on the table, more than enough to cover the entire bill and probably even the next table's. I can't tell if things are just more expensive in New York and he's used to having to cash out more for two small desserts, or if he's trying to be a little bit showy with how much money he makes. But I like Parker. Much more than I've ever liked Craig.

"Oh, uh, yeah—sure. Thank you for meeting with me," I say.

"No problem, kid. And, hey,"—he stands—"I know a lot of people in New York. If you ever need help with your Sydney, Megan investigation, I might be able to connect you with someone who can get you some information. You just let me know."

I grin up at him. "I might just take you up on that."

CHAPTER 37

LYLA

Me: *Are you not coming to Wrigley's party?*

Warner: *Nah. I actually just had an interesting meeting with Freaky Fritz's brother.*
Me: *Wait.*
Me: *His BROTHER?*

I stare at my phone intensely waiting for Warner to reply to me. So intensely, in fact, that I'm hardly paying attention to anything else around me. Not until I feel breathing in my ear from behind me, and I turn my head to see that Wrigley is suddenly there, glancing over my shoulder down at the phone in my hand.

I click the screen off.

"You're texting Warner," he comments.

"You didn't seriously just read over my shoulder, did you?" I ask, taken aback because I never thought Wrigley would be the type of person to invade my privacy like that.

"His name was just kind of... there... on the screen," he says coolly. "I came to ask you if you wanted to go into the game room and show off our air hockey skills. It's not like I *meant* to see that you're texting some other guy."

"Except he's not just 'some other guy,' Wrigley. We've been over this before. He's my *friend*. I'm allowed to text my friend."

"Yeah, and your 'friend' is in love with you."

My words get caught in my throat. I don't immediately have a smart reply back to that. I don't think what Wrigley just told me is true, but the possibility of Warner actually being in love with me is enough to make me stop and think about it. Although I'm not exactly sure why that is.

"You know what, Wrigley?" I ask, vivacity rising in my town. "Why didn't you want to come bowling? It would've been fun. And why don't you want to meet my parents? They're not that bad. They're not *completely* responsible for everything that happened to me. There have just been some... bad circumstances. You don't really know everything; you can't blame them for all of this. I don't."

"Whoa."

He just stares at me, his eyes slowly getting bigger. And I don't get it. What is it that I did, other than try to voice my feelings?

"What?" I snap. He looks like he wishes he could just back away and pretend like he never approached me in the first place.

Like I'm being some sort of crazy, clingy girlfriend.

"Where is this even coming from?" he asks. He puts a hand on my shoulder, but it's more in a "buddy" type of way than in the way that a boyfriend would. "Lyla," he says, giving it a little bit of a shake. "It's a *party*. Just relax and have fun."

I didn't even want to come *to the stupid party,* I think to myself as I try not to glare at him. I'm not going to glare at him, but I'm not going to give him a smile either.

"I have to go to the bathroom," I lie, simply because I don't have the energy to continue fighting with him.

I turn and walk in the direction of the guest bathroom that is furthest away from him in the back of his giant house.

It's late. I'm tired. This party is stupid. I don't like the way Wrigley is behaving. All I really want is to just go home. But I can't leave Audrey, so I have to wait until she's ready.

I find the tucked-away guest bathroom inside one of the guest rooms, shut myself inside of it, and send Audrey a text:

Me: *I'm over it. Ready to leave when you are.*

I anxiously jiggle my leg as I sit on top of the closed toilet seat and wait for her to reply. But neither she nor Warner says anything back.

I look up from my phone and notice the window with the curtains closed over it. It's very strange to have a full-size window in a bathroom like this. Shouldn't the glass at least be frosted so there doesn't have to be curtains that probably always have to stay shut for privacy?

I stand up and put my phone in my back pocket. It's quieter on this side of the house. The music isn't making my chest vibrate with the bass. I can actually hear myself think. And I can hear that rustling noise outside the window.

I freeze, catching my reflection in the mirror, which looks startled.

That rustling noise outside the window?

Slowly, I turn my head to the left, back to the window, the curtains still closed around it.

Could somebody really be out there? Who? And why?

A shudder rippling down my spine propels me to put my hand on the doorknob. *It's time to get the heck out of here.*

Before I can even turn the knob, there's a great crashing noise, and I scream at the top of my lungs. The window has been shattered. By what or how, I have no idea. I fling the door open just as a massive figure in all-black clambers inside the small bathroom, emerging from behind the curtain.

I scream louder and dash into the guestroom to get away from them. Glancing over my shoulder, my feet feel like they've turned to lead, making it harder to move.

They're wearing the mask. *Carson's* mask.

What does this mean?

I don't have much time to think about it because I need to run.

I leave the bedroom, glancing behind me again to see that they're still right on my tail. Are they really going to do this right now? In front of all of these people?

"Help me!" I scream as I re-join the partygoers. I run and shove and push my way through everyone. They all look at me weird at first, but then when they look over my shoulder, I know I'm not crazy because they see him, too. More screams erupt. Instead of anyone trying to help me, everyone is just scrambling to go in their own direction.

Everyone just wants to save themselves.

"Audrey!" I shout, desperate to get to her. If I'm with her, we'll be safe together. And I *need* to know that she is safe. That he didn't already get to her.

"Help!" I cry. I scramble behind a bunch of people who are trying to pile out the front door, and I get stuck behind them.

"Move!" I shout. *He's not here for anyone else but me and Audrey!*

I can't bury myself in the crowd, everyone is pushing and crowding too tightly to break through them.

I look over my shoulder again, and the masked figure is close enough to touch me. Everything about this feels wrong. Yes, the man who's supposedly behind this is supposed to be dead. But that doesn't feel like the right reason. To attack at a high school party like this... I just don't understand it.

I give up trying to push through the crowd and instead lunge to the right to go at the staircase—maybe I can hide in a closet somewhere. I get halfway up before a hand grabs my ankle, and I clutch the railing for dear life as they try to pull me down.

"*No!*" I scream.

At the top of the stairs, someone descends quickly to where I am, and all I see is a foot wearing some Vans kicking the masked figure in the stomach, and my leg is freed as they fall back. I straighten myself up, whimpering in fear. I look up and see that my savior is Jackson.

"Lyla, come on!" Jackson yells to me, holding out his hand as around us, everyone else at the party is still freaking out and trying to get away from the intruder. I don't even think twice. Feeling overwhelmed with gratefulness, thankful that somebody does care after all, I take Jackson's hand and let him lead me up the stairs.

"Don't look back, just run!" Jackson advises, pulling me along. We dive into the upstairs bathroom, and he closes the door and locks it once we are inside.

"Call 911!" I screech. My heart is hammering in my chest. I can barely breathe.

"And get all of us arrested for being at this house party?"

Crap. I didn't think about that.

I tug my hair and pace in front of the vanity. I don't take my eyes off the door, afraid that my attacker is going to burst through it any second.

What would they have done to me if Jackson didn't rescue me? What if they had gotten a good enough hold on my leg, dragged me down the staircase, and then had me at their mercy? What would've happened then? Would they have killed me in front of everyone? Chloroformed me again and stuffed me in the trunk while everyone sighed with relief and felt grateful that it wasn't them?

Nobody seems to care about me—where is Wrigley, anyway?—so why should I care if I get all of them in trouble by calling the cops? I could've just been killed!

"Lyla, are you all right?" Jackson asks, taking my arm gently and stopping me from pacing.

I look at the door again. I stop tugging on my hair and take a deep breath.

"I'm fine," I bite out. "I just... How did that even happen? What is going on right now? I just don't understand... "

"You're safe, "Jackson says. "I got you. You're safe here, okay?"

His eyes are genuine. For a moment, he's not just Jackson. He's *my* Jackson. My first boyfriend. My first real relationship. He's that cute, sweet, caring guy who stayed on the phone with me all night up until it was time to get ready for school the next day even though he was exhausted just because I wanted to keep chatting. He was the Jackson who held my hand in public and showed me off, proud that I was his girlfriend. He was the Jackson who asked me to school dances in obnoxious ways and goofed around with me the entire time we were at them. The Jackson who was always taking random videos of us, and not even always for his social media. Sometimes he just liked to record the two of us together, claiming, *You'll be happy when you have these to look back on someday.*

"Thank you," I tell him. A flood of different emotions swims through me and I can't process any of it because they're all so different and confusing. Tears fall from both of my eyes out of nowhere.

Jackson is quick to brush them away. As he does, as his pointer finger grazes my skin, it's so familiar. Like I am re-watching an old movie.

"Lyla..."

For once, I want to know what it is Jackson wants to say to me.

But he doesn't get the chance to tell me.

"Lyla! Where are you?!" a voice yells from outside the door. They sound like they're at the bottom of the staircase. "Get out of my way!"

"That's Audrey," I say to Jackson.

"Lyla!" Audrey yells again. Then at somebody else, she yells, "No! You're not going *anywhere*!"

"Oh my God," I gasp, turning from Jackson and unlocking the door so fast that he can't even call out to me in time before I'm already running to the staircase again and looking down into the foyer over the railing.

My thoughts are confirmed when I see it. People are staring wildly, including Wrigley, as Audrey wrestles with the person in the mask right in the middle of everyone as they try to get out of her way, creating a circle with just Audrey and the attacker inside of it.

What am I even seeing? How is this possible? The way Audrey is easily handling the masked intruder, it makes them seem... smaller.

"Audrey, what are you doing?!" I yell down. "He could kill you!" But the words don't feel true as I say them. How could someone who she's overpowering that easily be capable of murdering someone?

"It's not what you think!" Audrey yells up to me. Then she turns her head to yell at somebody else. "You! Stand in front of the door and don't let anyone out of here."

When it seems like the door is well guarded, and the circle that has formed around the masked figure is tightly woven so that they can't make an escape, Audrey shoves the wriggling tormentor away from her, slightly into the crowd. Our peers cry out and shrink into each other, clearly scared, but not scared enough to shy away from the scene unfolding before them all.

"Go ahead!" Audrey yells at the attacker as Jackson comes to stand beside me at the railing. "Take the disguise off. Show everyone who you *really* are."

They have nowhere to run. Nowhere to hide.

Could this person really be the one who was truly tormenting us all along? Is it Carson, still alive after all? Or is it someone else entirely?

The person in the mask looks around as if they're trying to find an exit. No one wants to let them through. I'm worried he's going to pull out a knife and kill his way through.

But instead, I watch their shoulders sag and their feet become still.

"Are you going to take the mask off, or you want me to do it for you?" Audrey snaps, the venom in her tongue shocking. I don't think I would be able to be that brave if I were in her shoes right now. To face our tormentor like that...

"Lyla, wait," Jackson says beside me. But I ignore him. *Can't you see that what's going on down below is much more important than whatever it is you want to tell me?*

Audrey growls, apparently fed up with the waiting, and then she lunges at the masked figure and rips the mask from their face.

"W-what?" I whisper. Terror, shock, and confusion make the room start to spin. Everyone gasps and takes photos and yells in outrage.

Suddenly, no one's afraid anymore.

Because the person who just attacked me is Sophia Key.

Audrey glances at the mask and then drops it to the floor and looks at her. "You have some *serious* issues."

"What is this?" I ask, taking a few steps down the stairs. "Sophia?"

Sophia rolls her eyes as people continue to record and snap their pictures of it all.

"She's not the real one, Ly," Audrey tells me. "She and Jackson planned this whole thing."

I freeze in the middle of the staircase. I turn around, thinking Jackson is right behind me, but he's still at the top of the stairs. I can't read his expression. He's glaring at Audrey. He won't even look at me.

"What?" I ask, looking at my ex-boyfriend. "Jackson, what is she talking about?"

He had just saved me from her.

He *saved* me from her.

Wait. No. It all makes sense now.

"Oh, you've *got* to be joking!" I yell at Jackson.

"It's not the only time they've done this either," Audrey says. "That attack at the school carnival? That was Jackson wearing the mask that time. And I'm willing to bet it was *also* him who was wearing it at homecoming."

"This is like a wild episode of *Scooby Doo*!" someone in the crowd yells. Some people laugh. Other people are too shocked to say anything.

I can't believe I have to have this confrontation in front of all of our peers like this.

"Wh-why? "I stutter, unsure who to address. I feel hot. My mouth is dry. I hear a weird *whomp-whomp* sound in my ears.

"You don't know what you're talking about," Sophia says to Audrey, crossing her arms like she's about to throw a tantrum, in true Sophia fashion.

"Oh, I don't?" Audrey asks, matching her stance. "So, you're *not* the owners of the Toxeydramaenthusiast account?"

This revelation from my sister drives our peers wild. They act like we're on an episode of *The Maury Show*.

"How do you know this?" I ask Audrey the same time Sophia says, "No, we're not!"

Audrey's never said anything about this to me before.

"I've had a hunch," Audrey explains to me. "But I wasn't sure about it until now. I was outside with Danielle when Sophia came running out the front door. She purposely ran in our direction, and instead of doing anything to *me*, she just shoulder-checked Danielle. So, I ran after her."

"It was just a *joke*," Sophia says with an eye roll. "Tell them, Jackson. We aren't the owners of that account. We have nothing to do with that part."

Jackson holds his hands up in the air in surrender and backs away slightly from the railing. "I have nothing to do with any of this," he says.

"Yeah *right*!" Sophia yells, stomping a foot. "The only reason we set this whole thing up was so that he could be the one to save Lyla and look like a hero so he could try and get her back!"

Everyone's eyes are on me again.

I know deep in my gut that Sophia is telling the truth. That it's *all* true. Jackson and Sophia both love and crave attention. Of course they'd team up and do something like this. They're not the real person who's been harming us, but they've been anonymously running a famous TikTok account over it.

"Sophia, stop making stuff up," Jackson says. But then loudly, people start booing him. No one believes that he doesn't have a part in this.

"Throw them out of here!" a voice yells. Everyone cheers in agreement. It's all happening so fast. I stand frozen in my spot on the staircase as people rush up the steps to grab Jackson, who's yelling in protest that none of it is true. Sophia is yelling, too, as the crowd shoves her out the front door. *Everyone* is booing them and putting them on their social media, calling them out.

It hurts. It stings and feels like a hard punch at the same time. It's all I can think about—that it hurts. The pain. The betrayal. And everyone gets to watch me hurting.

I don't even look at Jackson as he is dragged past me back down the stairs by some of our classmates.

"Lyla, it's not true!" he yells to me. "Let me go—Lyla, come on!"

I bite down on the inside of my cheek until I taste blood.

At least that's a pain I can control.

CHAPTER 38

Maddy

I've been sitting in my chair, absentmindedly folding laundry for the hundredth time while I stare at my front door and wish for Steven to appear. I'm pathetically imagining a scenario where he shows up unannounced, and I answer the door, my eyes with fresh tears from crying over missing him, to find out it's him there, and he has rushed back across the country, leaving his busy restaurants behind, just to tell me that he loves me, and that he's sorry, and that he's not going anywhere ever again.

Ugh, when did I get so pathetic?

When a knock *does* sound at my door, I let out a scream and my pile of folded clothes are knocked over as my hands fly up in the air in fright.

"Maddy?" a voice calls through the door. "Are you okay in there? It's, uh... me, Parker. Parker Fritz."

I sit in my chair with my hand over my heart for a solid five seconds before I'm able to find my voice again.

"Uh, I—coming!" I yell, and then I finally get up and go to answer the door. For the shortest of moments there after the knock sounded, I thought maybe my daydream had come true. But then Parker's voice served as a cool reminder that that is likely never going to happen. Steven is likely never going to forgive me, and my relationship with him is over. There's probably not a lot of men out there that can handle my craziness anyway. I'm destined to be alone.

"Parker, what are you doing here?" I ask when I fling the door open and see him on the other side of the screen. "How do you know where I live?" My voice is a little snappy, but I'm trying to disguise it.

"I didn't mean to scare you," Parker says with a chuckle. "Warner hinted that you were probably home, and doesn't everyone know where everyone lives on the town?"

"If you *live* here," I protest.

"Oh, come on. I lived here once. I still know people in town. It's not hard to figure things out."

He probably asked his stupid brother.

"What are you doing here?" I ask. "What are you carrying?"

"I wondered if maybe you were hungry and wanted to share this Thai food with me."

I eye it wearily. "First off... where is that even from?"

"Or, how about for 'first off,' you let me in instead?" he deadpans.

I roll my eyes and open the screen door for him. "Fine, come in. But there's no good Thai places in Toxey, so that food ya got there better come from outside of town."

"Of course it does," he says with a cocky smirk. "Like I said. I'm not a complete stranger."

When I check the time on the stove, I am surprised at how late it is. How long had I sat in my chair in my trance over Steven while folding the laundry—but I knocked it over, so now I'll have to re-fold it—before Parker arrived and scared the crap out of me?

My stomach growls at the smell of spicy noodles, and I am reminded that I never ate dinner.

"Weren't you just with Warner?" I ask. "Where is he?"

"We were both hanging out at Delilah's, and he said that he had to run because some stuff was going down at some party. I don't know. *Teen* stuff, I'd imagine."

Immediately, I'm concerned about him, so I go and get my phone from the coffee table. I'm about to call him, but before I can go to his name in my phone, I see I already have a text message from him.

Warner: *Parker is cool. Had to go to Wrigley's party. I won't be out too late.*

Knowing he's safe, I relax. But I wish he hadn't told me about Wrigley throwing a party. Now I feel like I have to either lie to Steven about knowing about it, or I need to report to him what his son is up to, which I know is probably the right thing to do. I just hate the idea of being a tattletale on Wrigley when it's important to me that he likes me. I remember being a teenager once. I threw a party or two. I would have flipped a lid if my dad's new girlfriend ratted me out.

"So," Parker says, jiggling the brown paper bag. "Are you hungry?"

Oh, right. I have to focus on the matter at hand.

I give him a skeptical look, still trying to gauge why he's here, and then I go to the kitchen to get us plates and silverware along with something to drink. We sit down at my little rickety table, and I am self-conscious because I know Parker probably has some fancy apartment in fancy New York City, and here I am in my shoebox, rundown home on the wrong side of the tracks.

But as Parker and I eat the Thai food—it's delicious—and talk, I feel less and less insecure about myself and my place. Parker is warm and friendly and does not seem the slightest bit like some elitist. He's still so... down to earth. New York hasn't really changed him much at all.

We talk about everything from memories of high school to the scary stuff that's been happening over the past few weeks. It's easy. I have fun. It kind of reminds me of chatting with Mia.

"Ya wanna know something?" I ask him as he helps me clear the table when we're all finished, the takeout boxes completely emptied by us even though the food he brought could have easily fed a family of four. "You have a very calming presence about you."

"I do?" His thick eyebrows, identical to Craig's, wrinkle and create lines above the bridge of his nose.

"What?" I ask.

"I don't think I've ever gotten that one before."

"Huh. Well, it's true. I'll admit, I wasn't sure at first, but I'm glad you came over." My back is to him as I scrape crumbs from our plates into the disposal and then rinse them off under the faucet. Then I turn the sink off, set the plates inside of it, and turn back around. When I do, I find Parker is suddenly a lot closer than I had been anticipating. Much, much closer.

He's smiling kindly at me. "Hey, thanks for letting me just drop by unannounced like this." His voice is different. Quieter. Softer. And he's looking directly at my lips. "I'm glad I came."

I put a hand on his chest and look into his eyes.

And then I giggle obnoxiously and push him back.

"You weren't seriously just trying to *kiss* me just now, were you?" I ask.

He immediately turns red, sticks his hands in his pockets, and steps away even further. He's practically not even in the kitchen anymore.

"What are you talking about?" he quickly asks, avoiding my incredulous gaze. "Wh-what would give you that impression? *Me*, kissing Madeline Carpenter? I don't think so."

I laugh some more because he's so clearly lying. "I'm sorry," I say, trying to calm myself. "I don't mean to laugh. It's just—that can't happen, Parker. I'm sorry if I gave you the wrong impression. I literally thought we were just two friends hanging out."

"We were," he says fast, shaking his head. "We are. I swear, that was my intention when I came in the first place."

"Uh huh."

"I'm serious. I don't know what came over me. It was stupid."

We stare at each other for a while. I laugh again. I can't help it.

"Parker. It's late," I say. "I need to call Warner and tell him to get his butt home, and then I need to go to sleep."

"Yes, Maddy, of course." He walks to the door, so I follow him. I hold it open as he shrugs on his coat.

"Thank you for dinner, Parker," I tell him, still shaking my head at how ridiculous he is. "Stay warm out there."

He smiles at me.

"What?" I ask. Although, I don't know if I even want to know.

He shakes his head and says, "Nothing." Then he steps outside. "I'll see you, Maddy."

I nod goodbye, and then I close the front door and fall with my back against it. I laugh again, this time a bit exasperated, and put a palm to my forehead. I can't *believe* I had misread that situation with him. After all, I had been venting to him about Steven and my relationship problems! Why would I do that if I was interested in him?

"Holy cow," I breathe, talking to myself. If there's one thing I never want to happen again, it's Mia and I getting involved with the same man.

CHAPTER 39

LYLA

The morning after the horrific party at Wrigley's, I go to that pond I like in a neighborhood close to mine and bring along a loaf of bread so that I can feed it to the ducks.

I don't know if I've ever been so mad at the world.

I walk there because I could use the fresh air, even though it's freezing out. I'm comfortable driving my car—or at least more comfortable than I used to be—but I still prefer to walk. I sort of think I wouldn't mind running, too. But I'm not really a runner.

I sit down in the dry, dying winter grass and smile when I see the ducks in their own little world. I love that the second I throw a piece of bread into the water, they all turn and rush over together, loudly quacking and fighting each other just to get a piece, even when there are plenty more pieces to come.

I feed them, ignoring the sign that says I'm not allowed to, but the smile quickly leaves. This isn't bringing me the same amount of happiness it used to. And I hate that it's not working to cheer me up. What else would make me happy? Accomplishing all those things on my list?

I cannot stop thinking about last night and what a disaster it was. After the bickering with Wrigley and the gigantic cluster-mess of everyone finding out at the same time that Jackson and Sophia were owners of the TikTok page and then kicking them out, I'd had about all of the partying I could take, and I left without even telling Wrigley goodbye. Now I don't know what's happening with us. He hasn't tried to reach out to me, even to comfort me about how I had been thinking I was about to die last night when Sophia chased after me in her disguise as my tormentor. I get the feeling he's mad at me, but I don't quite understand how I could be the bad guy in this situation.

"I'm just messing everything up, aren't I?" I ask the ducks as I throw in more bread. A brown, fat one quacks especially loud, and the noise sounds a little off, which reminds me of when I came here with Sydney once. We had come here together multiple times before, because it was where I liked us to hang out, since not many kids from school would run into us here. It's shallow, I know. I wish I could change the past, *desperately*, but I can't.

One of the times Sydney and I were here together, it was when I told her the truth about Wrigley.

"Look at that duck," Sydney said, cracking up and getting on her hands and knees to crawl closer to the edge of the pond as she pointed at the brown one that was making a weird quacking noise. It sounded almost as if it were a dog that was trying to pretend like it was a duck.

I laughed along with her a little, but I didn't find it as funny as I normally would have. I was in one of those "moods" because I had accidentally fallen into one of those pity parties I liked to throw myself earlier in the day; I scrolled nonstop through the album in my phone that was reserved for just photos and videos of Trinity and me. There were tons of them. Because we were always together. At Delilah's. At the swimming hole. Goofing around in her bedroom. Goofing around in mine. In the hallways at school. During cheer practice.

And in my car.

"You seem especially dull today," Sydney commented, looking back at me. I was sitting further away from the edge of the pond than she was, over on a blanket I brought.

"Sorry," I muttered.

"What's on your mind?" The annoying duck stopped it's crazy, strained quacking, so she turned to face me instead of them and sat crisscross in the grass.

"Just... had a rough physical therapy session after school," I lied. I'd had physical therapy that day, but it hadn't been that bad. In fact, my leg was doing quite well.

"Oh, you do physical therapy because of the accident, right?"

Her question immediately made me wish I had come up with a different lie. I should have known she would find the opening to ask more questions about what happened.

"Yeah," I answered.

"So, what really went down during that, anyway?"

"What are you talking about?" I asked, making a face.

"No—I know your friend died—I'm not asking for, like, the gory details or anything. But, like... it must have been so scary. Did you just, like, look up and see a flash of bright white lights, and then all of a sudden... everything changed?"

I shrugged. "Something like that."

But my response to her quickly ate at me. Because I had never told anyone what actually happened. The reason why I was so consumed with guilt. The reason why I felt ashamed to even be alive.

And out of everyone I knew, Sydney was the least judgmental person probably all of Toxey. She hadn't yet been plagued by the gossiping-curse that inevitably came for everyone. She didn't ask all her questions with accusation in her tone. She didn't seem calculated. She just seemed genuinely curious. And I thought maybe it would be good for me to get it out there. To finally say out loud. Just once. Maybe saying it to Sydney would make it easier to say it to my therapist. And then it would make it easier to say it to other people after that.

Or maybe it would still remain a secret forever.

But I had to try to find some way to ease the guilt. It hurt too much.

"Do you know who Wrigley Hall is?" I asked Sydney. She shook her head and then crawled back to me. I think she could sense that I was about to confess something bad.

And she was right. I did.

I did eventually end up telling Dr. Morton about texting and driving and being responsible for the accident, too. But that's as far as I could let myself go. And then, when Sydney died, I thought my secret died with her. But it still got out somehow. I just don't understand it.

The annoying duck quacks loudly again as if he's yelling at me to give him more bread. So I do, wondering if maybe the duck is really Sydney somehow, taunting me. Quacking loudly to say, *You'll never figure it all out.*

Quack quack quack.

You'll always have questions. For the rest of your life.

Quack quack quack.

Keep pretending like you don't care to know who I really was.

I practically throw the butt-end of the loaf at the stupid duck.

But the dang thing is right.

If I don't follow my list, I'll be breaking the promise that I made when I was locked in the shed. And if I break that promise, I feel something horrible is going to happen to me. So, while I'm terrified to do anything that strays from it, all of my questions about Sydney and how she ties in with Carson Price are going to plague me.

Maybe I need to take a pause from the list. Maybe I just need to get myself some answers first, and then I can get back to it. Get back on track. It's just a little detour. It's not like I would be abandoning the promise completely.

I crinkle the bread bag in my hands and stand up, ready to do what I know I need to.

But then a gray mustang pulls up to the curb and stops me in my step.

Jackson gets out of the driver's seat. He rounds the hood of the car and walks directly toward me.

I'm tempted to run.

I'm so mad at him. I feel so betrayed. This boy walking toward me right now—I don't even recognize him anymore. That Jackson I saw last night in that bathroom was a ghost. There's no getting him back.

"Stalking me for your TikTok page, Jackson?" I bite out when he's close enough. "Why aren't you recording right now? This is quality stuff. And the lighting is really great."

He took my private life and gave it to everyone. For his own personal gain. For fun.

My misery. Turned into a game.

He stops a few feet short of me. "Lyla," he starts, taking a deep breath. "I'm not even going to try and lie about it this time, okay? I'm just here to tell you the truth. I swear."

"Oh, you *swear*, do you?" I laugh because the idea of him thinking he can trick me again is just too ridiculous.

"I mean it," he tries anyway. "No more lies. What Sophia and I did was dumb."

"Nice apology."

I try to walk past him, but he grabs my wrist and barks, "Lyla, just wait."

I freeze and squeeze my eyes shut. Behind my eyelids, I see that masked figure again. I see them, the night I was kidnapped, tightening their grip on me no matter how desperately I struggled to free myself from them.

No wonder I have been having nightmares about Jackson. In a way, he *is* a part of my monster.

I shoot him the dirtiest look I can muster. "If you'd like to still have kids someday, I suggest you take your hand off of me." My tone is dark and icy. I don't think I've ever sounded so cold. So threatening. I like it. I feel strong.

He lets go of me quickly, like I've developed the superhuman ability to burn whoever touches me. "I'm sorry," he says. "I just... will you please listen to me?"

I look down at where his hand had just been. How could he possibly think it's okay to grab me like that? He knows what I've been through. He *should* know how scary it was for me. He should be treating me like fragile glass right now, but he doesn't care. He just takes what he wants. And if what he wants turns into something he doesn't, he'll just try to force it back to how it was.

All for himself.

"Would *you* listen to you right now if you were me?" I ask him.

He opens and closes his mouth.

"That's what I thought."

I try to walk again. He walks with me this time, but I guess it's better than him grabbing onto me to get me to stop turning away from him. Still, I do wish he would just leave me alone.

"I just wanted a way to get you back," he mutters. He sounds pathetic. Like a sad puppy trailing after me. I don't feel bad for him at all.

"You're a psycho!" I yell.

"Lyla, please!" His cry is so broken and loud that when he stops walking, I take a couple more steps but then stop, too. I slowly turn to look back at him. Tears are in his eyes. "You're all I know, Lyla. You are my whole future. I never pictured not having you in my life. So without you in it, I literally don't know what to do. I am a complete mess. If y-you can just tell me what I can do, h-how I can be the guy that you want, I'll do it. I'll d-do anything. Come on. You can't do this to me, Lyla. We can't have made it so far just for it to—to end. It can't be the end."

"Jackson."

"I don't know how to do anything other than this," he continues. "Every day that's passed since we broke up has been just...horrible. I never liked Sophia. And she knew that. All I did every time I was with her was talk about you. I'm sure it got really annoying, honestly. But she talked about you a lot, too. We just... miss you. I m-miss you."

He's not softening me. He's done too much damage for that.

"What you and Sophia did is *not* how you show someone you miss them," I say, my eyes narrowing. "That's how you show someone that you hate them."

"Lyla, I'm sorry. I'm so, *so* sorry."

I take a step toward him. He's still crying. And because I am still so angry, I begin to cry, too. I wish I was stronger.

"It's too late, Jackson."

He shakes his head repeatedly, sobbing now. "No, Lyla." He just keeps crying and saying no over and over again.

"I wish I wanted to hug you right now," I say, sniffling and trying not to burst into sobs with him. "But I'm not going to comfort you for the way you hurt me, Jackson. You're never going to get me back. I'm sorry that it's not what you want to hear. But it's done. And it will never be undone."

His shoulders shake with his sobs, and he hangs his head.

It's hard to leave him like this.

But I do it.

Because I don't need to *wish* to be stronger.

I need to show myself that I am.

CHAPTER 40

AUDREY

When I hear the sound of Lyla going into her bedroom, I race out of mine to go see her.

"Where were you?" I ask, letting myself in. "Thanks for ditching me last night, by the way."

"Thanks for filling me in about Jackson and Sophia," she snaps back.

"I know—I should have said something when I first suspected it. There has just been a lot going on and I wasn't even sure until last night, and—"

She interrupts my babbling. "Can you call Warner and put him on speaker?"

"Huh?"

"I have something I need to tell you guys."

"You call him then," I tell her. I've already bugged him enough. Last night, after that confrontation went down with Sophia and Jackson, Lyla left me at the party, so I called Warner, and he picked me up and gave me a ride home.

"Fine, I will," Lyla says, rolling her eyes and picking up her iPhone.

"Hello?" Warner asks when he answers the call.

"It's me and Audrey," Lyla says.

"Hi," I say, feeling awkward.

"Uh, good morning," he replies.

"So, I had a strange interaction with Freaky Fritz the other day," Lyla says, jumping right into it. "When I... ran into him."

"Where?" I ask the same time Warner asks, "What happened?"

She goes with Warner's question. "He was drunk. Like, completely wasted. And he still had his gun on him, can you believe that? I thought he was going to shoot me—anyway, I had never seen him that bad, but it got me thinking—"

"You thought he was going to shoot you?" Warner asks.

"*Yes*. But listen; I'm pretty sure he's had a drinking problem for a while. I'm talkin' *serious* drinking problem. Even drinking on the job. Tell me I am not the only one who has noticed how off he's been."

"Whoa," I say, considering it. "I could see it."

Lyla nods at me. Warner is silent.

"What do you think, Warner?" she asks him.

"Now that I think about it, I'll bet it isn't water he's always carrying around in those plastic bottles of his," he says. "It makes total sense. Especially after talking with his brother yesterday."

"Oh yeah," Lyla says, talking fast. "How'd that go?"

"Hang on!" I hold up my hand to stop her. To stop both of them. "You talked to his brother? Why does Lyla know this and I don't? And Ly, I thought you were stepping away from all of this. So, what exactly is happening right now? What does this mean, are you helping us again?"

"Yes," she says simply, offering no other explanation. "Warner met up with Freaky Fritz's brother last night."

"Yeah," Warner says before diving into how his conversation with Parker Fritz went. By the end of it, I've made myself comfy on Lyla's bed, and she's pacing around her room like she has too much pent-up energy.

"Okay," I say when we're all caught up. "I think I have an idea. Warner, are you busy at all this morning?"

"No, why?" he asks.

"I think you should follow up with Officer Wilde."

"You want me to talk to Officer Wilde?" he repeats. "Why?"

"To corroborate what Parker told you. To see if Wilde says anything about Freaky Fritz's strange, alcoholic behavior, too."

"Good idea," Lyla agrees, flashing me an impressed glance. "Are you up for it?" she asks Warner.

"What if FF is there?" he asks.

"FF?" Lyla asks.

"Freaky Fritz," I inform her. She gives me a silent "Oh."

"Just try and dodge him, if you can," she suggests.
"Alright," Warner says, sounding a bit apprehensive. "I'm on it."

CHAPTER 41

WARNER

I pull into the parking lot of the Toxey Police Department and put my Jeep in park. Then I go to the text thread on my phone that consists of me, Audrey, *and* Lyla. I got a message in it earlier from Audrey, who had initiated the group chat, saying, *I'm glad you came to your senses and are ready to help us again, Lyla!*

I smile, but I'm not sure what it is I am smiling about. Audrey's text? Or the fact that I'm glad Lyla is back on the case?

Last night, I got to Wrigley's party as soon as I could after I got a call from Audrey. When I got there, she filled me in on what horrible ex-best friends we both have and told me about how humiliated Lyla had been before she left, leaving Audrey behind. All around us, the party was still in full swing. There was an excitement hanging in the air still from what had recently transpired. Audrey seemed to be the only one who looked uncomfortable. Especially because people wouldn't stop staring at her. I felt bad. She clearly didn't want to be there anymore.

"Can I drive you home?" I decided to ask her.

"Ugh, would you?" She had never looked so grateful. Her big blue eyes were twice their size as she stared at me. "My ride options before were Lyla or Ryan, but now Lyla's gone, and I'm not exactly talking to Ryan at the moment..."

"You're not?" I asked. "What ha—?"

She was quick to interrupt, her face twisting into a scowl like she had known I was going to try and ask. "I do not want to get into that right now."

"Noted," I replied, leading the way out of the party and back to my car, not making eye contact with anyone the whole way there. I just wanted to lie low. I didn't want anyone to know I had shown up. No one wanted a potential murderer, their English teacher's long-lost son, at their party.

Outside my Jeep, I took off my jacket and handed it to her, since she was shivering and had her arms crossed.

She sheepishly accepted it, not saying a word, and then I held my car door open for her, and she tugged the jacket on and climbed inside.

"I really appreciate this," she muttered after several minutes of driving in silence.

"Don't worry about it."

"No, I mean it." She reached out and placed her hand on my forearm as I gripped the steering wheel tighter. Her voice was as soft as her hand. I wondered if my car would still smell like strawberries after she got out of it. "Thank you."

"I'll always look out for you, Audrey."

I meant it, too. After everything we had been through together, after nearly losing her forever, there was absolutely no chance of me not having her in my life.

What I told her last night also applies to Lyla. Why hadn't I told her that? *I'll always look out for you* and *Lyla*.

I do a full body shake, getting myself back to the present.

I am here, I type to the twins.

I'm a little nervous about going inside the police station since I was recently a person of interest in the murder investigation of Sydney Hutton/Megan Young, and I might even still be, but I have to do what makes me uncomfortable if I'm ever going to get what I want.

And I want to know what happened.

Why *all* of this happened.

As I walk through the cubicles behind the receptionist, my eyes scan the place for Fritz, but I don't see him anywhere. I'm relieved because surely he would try to intervene if he caught me trying to get Officer Wilde alone.

"Warner," Officer Wilde says when I arrive at his desk, not hiding the surprise in his tone.

"I'm sorry to disturb you," I say, licking my lips and talking in a rushed voice. "I just wanted to ask you some quick questions, if you have a sec."

"You wanna ask *me* some questions?" He chuckles. "Usually, it's the other way around."

I sit down in the metal folding chair outside his cubicle—the cubicles all have short walls that are about desk height, so Wilde can still see me—even though he hasn't exactly invited me to sit. "I know," I say. "I was just curious about Detective Fritz."

"Oh." The smile falls from his face.

"Oh?" I repeat, wondering what would cause him to have that reaction to my question.

"What do you want to know about Fritz, kid?" Wilde asks.

I open my mouth, but he stops me by pointing a large finger in my face.

"And *before* you continue, remember that he *did* save your life."

"Yeah," I remark bitterly. "And I don't understand why."

"You don't understand why a police officer would try to save a civilian's life?"

"Yeah. I mean—Fritz clearly hates me."

"Even if you think that's true, it's his duty as a police officer to rescue you, Warner."

I fight the urge to roll my eyes. "Officer Wilde, how certain are we that he told the truth about what happened to Carson Price that night?"

Officer Wilde leans back in his creaky rolling chair and makes a noise like he's ninety years old. "You're not the only one who has questions about it," he explains. "Lots of people are confused about that night."

"Where is he, anyway?" I ask, looking around again.

"Not here."

"Why not?"

"It's really none of your business, Warner."

"Did he call in sick because he's too hungover to work?" I ask, getting myself worked up. "Or is he maybe still drunk somewhere, unable to drive himself here?"

"Hey, kid," he scolds.

I lean in closer. "The guy's an alcoholic, Officer Wilde. It's obvious. Don't bother trying to tell me otherwise."

He opens and shuts his mouth.

I think about what Lyla told me. "He shouldn't be allowed to carry a gun—he shouldn't be allowed anywhere *near* one. He should be fired, don't you think? Or at least demoted to a mall cop or something. They don't get to have guns, right? But wait—I wouldn't trust him with a baton either. He needs a position with absolutely *zero* weapons. Put him on desk duty!"

Officer Wilde raises an eyebrow. "Desk duty?"

"I don't know how police stations run—you're the cop."

"And as 'the cop,' you need to let me do my job."

I look around. "So where is he then?"

"I'm sure it would be only a matter of time before you found out for yourself anyway. Detective Fritz is taking a leave of absence for some health-related reasons."

"Seriously?" I ask, thinking that it's too good to be true. So, he did get in trouble?

"There is a lot to it I don't think you understand. This case has been consuming him," Officer Wilde says, "because of his personal connection to it, which is why cops need to not take cases involving their personal lives. And I told him that again and again. But he didn't want to listen. And now his friend is dead. And he is a mess."

He is all but confirming it. Craig Fritz is on the fritz. How fitting.

"So," I say slowly as I register what his absence means. "Then...Frea—*Detective* Fritz..."

Officer Wilde finishes the sentence for me. "Yes, Warner. I don't think Craig Fritz will be giving you a hard time anymore. At least, not for a while."

CHAPTER 42

MADDY

I t's sometime in the afternoon when I get a phone call, and the name on the screen makes my jaw drop and my pulse race.

It's Steven! He's finally calling!

"H-hello?" I ask, tripping over my words when I answer. I ponder what it is he could have possibly called me for. To tell me he forgives me? To tell me he wants to get back together? To tell me he's sorry it took him so long to realize we're meant to be together?

"Maddy, sorry to bug you right now," he says, sounding oddly formal. Some of my excitement dies down at his tone. He doesn't sound like someone who is about to confess his love for me.

"Is everything okay?" I ask, hating that with every single phone call I have these days, I seem to have to ask that question.

"Not exactly," he replies. "Turns out, Wrigley decided to throw a party yesterday. I don't know if he thought he turned the cameras off, or if he just completely forgot that I had them installed after the break-in, but I guess it doesn't matter. That's not why I called."

Why *did* he call then? Did Warner do something when he went to the party? At least Steven doesn't seem to know that I know about it.

I grow tense, wishing I had told Warner to just come home last night when he texted me that he was going to the party.

What did he do?

Steven continues. "I'm calling because... well, I rushed home when I saw what was happening since the cameras are connected to my phone, and I've been reviewing the footage from his little soirée, just to see who made what mess."

"Okay?" I'm utterly confused about why I'm hearing about any of this. Did he just call me because he wants to vent, and he feels like I'm the only person he can talk to?

"The thing is... I'm not exactly sure how to say this, so I think it's better if I just show you. There's something weird about the footage. I—do you think you'd mind coming to my place so I can show it to you?"

"Oh, um, when?" I ask. I have to go into work a little later today.

"Now works, if you can. I think it's important that you see it. It has to do with all that stuff you and your friend have been dealing with."

"Mia? "

"Yeah."

I don't like the sound of this. "Uh, would it be all right if I brought her with?"

"Yeah, sure. I'll be here all day, lecturing Wrigley and supervising him as he cleans up his mess. Your son attended the party too for a bit, in case you wanted to know."

"I-I'm sorry, Steven. I'll talk to him." My cheeks heat up at the lie. *Ugh, why am I like this?*

"He's not the one who threw the party," Steven says. "So, you'll be here soon?"

We hang up and I immediately call Mia. When she answers, I tell her what Steven told me, and she says she's on her way to his place.

Warner has the Jeep, I don't even know where he is right now, and he hasn't returned my calls or texts. So, with a frustrated sigh, I quickly grab a Lyft and make my way to Steven's mansion. My stomach rolls and turns the entire ride there, because not only am I nervous about seeing Steven again, I'm nervous about what it is exactly he wants to show me on his security footage. I don't have any idea what could possibly be waiting.

I get a text shortly before I arrive from Mia saying that her daughters found out where she was going and invited themselves along. Then, when I pull up to Steven's house, I finally get a text from Warner telling me he heard Steven found something on his security footage and that he is going to be here soon, too.

I'm the first to arrive, but I'm too terrified to face Steven all by myself, so I stand outside and hope Steven doesn't see me. Then after a short while, Mia's car pulls up. She gets out, and we greet each other with a quick hug, then she takes charge, leading the way to Steven's front door.

I am so grateful for her. I truly don't think I could do this without her. We've both been through so much, yet she manages to still be so brave.

When Mia rings the doorbell, another car pulls up and Audrey and Lyla get out.

Steven answers the door, yelling over his shoulder at Wrigley, "Scrub that grout, too, it's all sticky from those sugary drinks you guys were having!" Then he gives Mia and me a closed-lip smile.

"Hi," I say, sounding weirdly shy. Even Mia gives me a funny look like she doesn't know who I am.

Steven nods his head in the direction of the twins. "Did you invite them, or did my son?"

"They're with us," Mia replies.

"Warner is coming, too," I add. Right as I say it, I hear the sound of more tires crunching on gravel and turn around to find the red Jeep pulling into the circular driveway.

"The more the merrier, I guess," Steven says. It's nerve-racking to even look him in the eye because I don't know what he's thinking, but I try to anyway. He doesn't look at me. His jaw is set. I'm sure he's angry with Wrigley, and maybe he's more focused on that right now than on the fact that his ex-girlfriend who is still madly in love with him is here at his house.

"Right this way," Steven says, once everyone's arrived on the porch. He leads the way into his house, looking over his shoulder at the kids and adds, "Although, I'm sure *you* three already know your way around here. Did you have fun at my son's party last night?"

I look over my shoulder as well to find them exchanging looks with each other. They all have guilty expressions on their faces.

"I'm so sorry," Lyla says quickly. "I can help clean."

Steven shrugs and we enter his study. "Something tells me you're not the one who suggested he throw it."

"Still."

"Don't worry about it. Although, you might not be able to hang out with your boyfriend for a while. He is grounded, and I haven't decided for how long yet. I took his phone, too."

Lyla falls silent. I look at my son and see he's busying himself staring at some books on the massive floor-to-ceiling bookcase in here. I know he's not actually interested in them because he's not a big reader. I wonder if he's just uncomfortable about Steven talking to Lyla about Wrigley. I wonder if my son still has a crush on her.

Or is he into Audrey now?

"I have the video paused and loaded up already," Steven tells us, motioning for everyone to surround his computer screen. All six of us crowd around it, and then Steven presses play.

The video is from one of the outside cameras, the one on the front porch. It shows the porch, but it also shows the front of his house several feet to the right of it. I don't know exactly what it is I'm supposed to be looking for, but I wonder if everyone's heart is pounding as hard as mine is. What is so bad in the video that Steven can't just explain it to us and needs to show us instead?

"That Carson Price guy is dead now, isn't he?" Steven asks as we all stare at the footage, not seeing anything. But then no one says anything to him because a figure has just stepped into view, in front of the house, creeping toward one of the windows next to the porch. They're wearing all black, their hoodie covering their face. The hoodie is so bulky that it's hard to even tell the build of the person wearing it. They crawl up to the window and duck underneath it. They fiddle with something in a small black drawstring bag, and it takes me a second to realize that they're putting on the mask—the cartoonish one that looks like a caricature of a male, human face.

"Oh, that's actually just Sophia," Audrey says, straightening up like she doesn't need to see any more of the footage. "Fun fact: she and Jackson have been pretending to be Carson because they are the ones behind the TikTok page and they needed more content."

"Wait, what?" Mia asks her daughter.

"No, see, that's the thing," Steven says, pausing the video. "I reviewed the rest of the footage. I watched the entire party, from beginning to end. And, this is happening the *same* time that everyone is chanting for Jackson and Sophia to leave. Here, listen."

He turns up the volume and presses play, and while the person wearing the mask on the screen is spying through the window, I can hear the voice of many teens inside the house, booing and yelling about how Sophia and Jackson need to leave the party.

Audrey bends back down and squints at the screen. I watch everyone's expression, trying to gauge what they're thinking. It's the first time I'm hearing about Jackson and Sophia being the owners of the TikTok account, but if this person spying on the party isn't either of them...

"Who is that?" Warner asks in a whisper. His expression tells me he's terrified. It's like I'm watching his worst fear being confirmed right in front of him. The person terrorizing him isn't gone. They're still out there. Watching. Waiting. But for what?

"And what are they doing?" Mia asks.

I look back to the video, and after a few more seconds, the front door opens, and it makes the figure turn and run away, leaving the frame.

Steven pauses it again. "So, yeah, that's all. I just thought you might want to see that."

Everyone scatters around the room, away from the computer screen. Lyla walks furthest away, over by the door, like she wants nothing more than to just get out of here. I stay by the desk, closest to Steven. I look for signs in his body language that he misses me and is worried about me and wants to talk to me about...things, but he is rigid, still strictly business.

"I don't understand," Audrey says. Her face is scrunched up like she's in physical pain. "What does this mean?"

"I bet that was Carson Price," Warner says. "I bet I was right, and Craig is covering for him. He is still alive, and he is still trying to mess with us."

"So then why didn't he mess with us?" Audrey asks. "He had the opportunity to, didn't he? Why come to the party to just stand there and spy on us, and then leave?"

"Maybe the fake tormentors scared him off somehow?" I offer. Could it really be Carson? Could Craig really be covering for him?

"I don't know, it's pretty hard to fake a death," Steven says, offering his two cents.

"Maybe," Warner says, "but it's a small town and people get away with so much here. Besides, I just talked to Officer Wilde a little bit ago, and Craig is taking a leave of absence. Maybe his captain was starting to suspect that he was covering something up? Maybe he's under investigation because other people are suspecting him of lying, too."

Mia looks at Steven. "Thank you for showing us the footage, Steven. We really appreciate it. And your home is lovely, by the way." Then she looks at us. "We shouldn't take up anymore of his time discussing this in his house. We should go."

The others mutter their thank-you's and goodbyes and then shuffle out of the study with Mia. I start to follow them, too, but I move slowly, hoping that Steven will call my name and tell me he wants one more second with me so that we can talk about us. But he says nothing, so I frown and leave.

CHAPTER 43

AUDREY

The eerie, ominous footage we all watched inside of Steven Hall's house has replayed in a loop over and over again in my mind ever since I saw it. It leaves me wanting to do nothing the next day but sulk in my bedroom, sad and confused, wishing that my life could be different. I don't want to sit around and continue discussing the possibilities with my mom and Lyla. I wanted this to all be over, but now it's not.

"Audrey!" Mom calls from downstairs. I sit up in my bed and groan out loud. I don't want to hear any more of their theories. I don't know who that was outside that window wearing that mask at Wrigley's party, and I'm not so sure I *want* to know.

I wait to see if maybe Mom will let me ignore her, but then she yells my name again. So, I drag my feet out of my room and creep over to the banister.

"What?" I curtly ask.

"You have a guest at the door."

Oh.

"Coming," I say, relieved that she's not just summoning me downstairs to discuss Carson-related topics.

I answer the door, and to my dismay, it's Ryan. I have ignored all of his attempts to contact me since Friday night. I'm still mad at him for what I saw transpire between him and Kiley. She was sitting on his lap, and he was totally okay with it. They looked like a freaking couple. The last thing I feel like doing is dealing with him.

"Hi," I say, peeking my head out through the crack in the door, hopefully signaling with my body language that I don't want to have some long conversation with him, nor do I want to invite him into my home.

"You have to let me explain, Audrey," he says, running a hand through his hair. He's antsy as he stands on my doorstep. It's weird to see Ryan Copeland looking nervous.

"I have to?" I challenge.

"No, that's not what I meant—of course you don't *have* to. But... I would really appreciate it if you could please hear me out. I know it looked bad at Wrigley's party."

"*Looked* bad? It *was* bad."

He nods quickly. "Yes. It *was* bad. But Audrey, I assure you, Kiley and I are just friends. I'll be honest, I know that she would be more with me if she could, but I'm not interested in her. I've never been interested in her, and I'm pretty sure she knows that."

"You're *pretty* sure?"

He pulls his phone out. "I will call her and tell her right now, if you need the confirmation. I'm sorry, Audrey. "

It feels like a genuine apology. He *did* come all the way to my house since I wouldn't text him back. That showed effort, right? If he was having some sort of secret fling with Kiley, would he really bother to go through all this trouble to get me to believe there was nothing going on?

Besides, it's not like I'm any better than him. It's sort of hypocritical for me to even be upset given the fact that all he did was let some girl he doesn't like sit on his lap. I'm the one who has been sneaking around and kissing Warner.

"You don't have to call her," I say, rolling my eyes and offering the smallest of smiles. "I believe you."

He sighs with relief and then grins at me. "It won't happen again. I'll be sure to set clear boundaries with her. I really like you, Audrey. And I really hope you'll keep letting me prove it to you."

My smile gets a little bigger, and I open the door wider. "I'm not one of those girls who is going to tell you you can't be friends with her. She was in your life before I was. I get it."

"Still. She needs to know she can't be doing stuff like that, especially if I'm going to stay friends with her."

I don't know what else to say, and as Ryan stands there on my doorstep, I don't know what to do, either. Say, *Okay, bye!?*

"Um..." I trail off, trying to decide what the right thing to do is. "Do you want to come in?"

When Mom comes to tell me she's about to start cooking dinner and sees Ryan and I hanging out together in the upstairs loft, she smiles at him and asks if he'll be joining us. I was just trying to be nice when I invited him in, especially since he came all the way to see me, but I didn't exactly want him over for dinner. Still, Ryan beams at my mother appreciatively and nods his head up and down over and over again, like an excited dog. "That would be wonderful," he says. "Thank you so much, Mrs.... Flynn?"

Mom looks at me, and I feel guilty because now she knows I've been talking to Ryan about the separation my parents have been going through. But her smile doesn't falter. "Why don't you just call me Amelia," she suggests.

Then, when dinner is ready, Mom, Lyla, Ryan, and I all sit at the table, and it feels weird because I've never had a guy over for dinner. It feels like the roles have been reversed and Ryan has taken Jackson's place as the guy who's trying to impress my parents. Only now, there's only *one* parent he hast to sweet-talk.

And Ryan is a *great* sweet-talker. He's super charismatic, even more so than Jackson had been. With Jackson, it seemed like he was *always* saying whatever he could to get Mom and Dad to like him, even after it had already been established that they did. With Ryan, he makes easy conversation with Mom like they are two friends. It feels very mature and adult. And dang it, I can tell that Mom likes him, and it makes me like him a little bit more, too, even though I *seriously* don't want to. It would almost have been easier if he *did* like Kiley. Then I wouldn't have to still feel so conflicted about my feelings for him and my feelings for Warner.

But, in my life, nothing can ever just be easy.

"So, how are you liking being football captain?" Mom asks, wiping her mouth on a napkin. She's made a healthy version of tater tot casserole with sweet potato tater tots and lean ground turkey.

"It's fine. But I don't know if I'll play football in college," he answers.

"No?" Mom asks. "Are there any other sports you like to play?"

"Weirdly enough, it's kind of like a secret hobby of mine, but I like to golf."

Mom sits back in her chair. "The girls' father likes to golf," she tells him, smirking slightly. But it's not a good smirk. She looks almost irritated. Like Ryan has said the wrong thing.

Ryan clearly doesn't know how to answer, so I'm quick to rescue him. "Speaking of Dad, have you talked to him? Filled him in on what happened yesterday?" I move my food around my plate because I'm not really that hungry.

"Oh, you mean since I learned that he had you lie to me about meeting Carson Price's stepfather?"

I cough loudly. When did she figure that out?

She continues. "No, I haven't, and I don't know when I will."

"Wait, so you guys are fighting again?" Lyla asks.

"It's not as if we were ever *not* fighting," Mom replies.

"But, you guys were talking on the phone, and he was coming over here, and... stuff." Lyla's shoulders sag.

"Don't be mad at Dad," I try, wanting to salvage their relationship. I don't want my parents to get a divorce. And it's so clearly obvious that they still care about each other. They're unhappy with each other again because of a situation involving me, and it makes me feel like complete garbage.

I can't do anything right.

"He had no right to make you do that," Mom says to me. "But I don't want to discuss it further. Especially with the guest at the table."

"But he just thought he was doing the right thing," I try.

"Audrey, enough."

I fall silent and put my head down. Thankfully, Ryan is quick to bring up the subject of my mom's job, asking her about the kind of houses she remodels and if she has any interesting projects going on, and Mom's pleasant mood returns, even if she's just faking it for him.

All throughout the rest of dinner, I can't stop feeling helpless. Like everything in my life is a complete mess. I feel overwhelmed. I have this urge building up inside me to just run outside and let out the loudest scream I can.

When the meal ends, I walk Ryan out, and he kisses me on the lips goodbye, making me feel even crummier. Even though we haven't established anything, I'm pretty certain Ryan sees me as his girlfriend. And he deserves to know the truth. But since I am a coward, I simply smile at him and tell him goodnight. Then I race upstairs to my bedroom so I can finally be alone.

I shut the door and collapse onto my bed, and the tears start coming hot and fast.

But then there's a knock on my door, and my alone time is interrupted. Again.

I sniff quickly and wipe my eyes. "What?" I ask whoever it is.

"Let me in," Lyla says, jiggling the locked door handle.

"I don't feel like talking, Ly. I'm tired," I call.

"But I need help with homework. I literally have no idea what I'm doing. And it feels impossible to catch up."

You can do it, Audrey. It's just homework help. Lyla needs you.

"Fine, coming," I say, getting out of bed yet again and going to unlock the door. I can help my sister with her homework. Because everything is fine. I am completely fine.

CHAPTER 44

MADDY

I send Mia a text telling her to wish me luck. I made it very clear with her already that I have invited Dean over for dinner tonight, and that it is only for Warner-related purposes. I figure it's better to keep her informed rather than have her accidentally find out from who knows who—Carson, maybe—and risk her getting upset and taking it the wrong way. None of my secrets are safe, *nothing* I do is safe, so I have to just be honest about every decision I make. Nothing is as it seems here in Toxey, and there are people that do a really good job keeping things twisted.

We're having an incredibly late Sunday dinner because I didn't get off until eight. And Warner is not even home yet. He had a swing shift over at The Viper, and he dropped me off at my work before going to his.

I hear the sound of the screen door opening, and then somebody knocks. I assume it's Dean, since Warner would have just let himself in. I think to stop and check my reflection in the mirror to make sure I look okay, but then I force myself to remember that I shouldn't care what I look like in front of Dean. He's not here to see me. He's here for his son.

Dean is smiling and holding a bottle of wine when I answer the door.

"That was nice of you," I say, trying to be friendly and casual. I open the door wide and step aside to let him in, and he shrugs and takes his coat off. "I didn't want to arrive empty-handed. I hope you're okay with a Merlot."

"I like it all," I say, waving my hand. "Um, Warner isn't back yet. But he should be any moment."

He hangs his jacket by the door and looks around. "Something is different about this place."

"I cleaned, for once," I joke. But it's true. When Dean texted me asking when a good time to get together with Warner would be—and if he was even *allowed* to—I was the one who suggested tonight. And then before my shift, after the whole debacle at Steven's, cleaning was the best way to keep myself busy.

Dean chuckles. "It looks lovely."

"Have a seat," I say, going back in the kitchen to continue dinner. I've made lasagna and a Caesar salad. The lasagna may have been premade from the grocers I go to, but I didn't exactly have the time to make anything from scratch.

Dean opts to take a seat at the kitchen table, on the side where he can look into the kitchen at me.

"So, is Warner liking his job?" he asks.

"I think so," I say with a shrug as I mix the dry salad. I'm not going to put the dressing on until the very last minute.

"Does he work with Steven much?"

"Not really. Steven's out of town a lot."

"I see."

I sense the awkwardness hanging in the air. And I'm pretty sure he does, too.

I might as well just get this over with.

"Listen, Dean, since we have a second before Warner gets back, there's something I wanted to talk to you about."

"I think I know what it is," he says, straightening up in his chair. "Maddy, I shouldn't have kissed you."

A grin escapes me. "I have a literally never been so happy to hear someone say that to me."

He smiles back. "It was stupid. I was... misplacing my feelings. My head has been a mess lately. But you should know, I don't have feelings for you...like that...anymore. And I'm really sorry."

"I appreciate you telling me. And it's completely fine. It's been a very long time since we were together."

"Yes, it has."

"Dean, I'm really honestly ready to just let the past go. All of it."

"Oh yeah?"

"Yes. That includes when it comes to... Warner."

I watch his face light up. "So...what are you saying, exactly?"

"Keep in mind, he doesn't have long before he's eighteen. But until then, when he is making all of his own decisions, you can be in his life as much as you'd like."

CHAPTER 45

WARNER

I have to bring in a chair from the back porch that's covered in dust and cobwebs so that I can have dinner at the table with my mom and my... father.

And it feels incredibly weird.

This whole set up is strange. Mom cooking dinner... the house clean without me having done a single thing to make it that way...*candles* are even lit. It actually smells good in here for once.

And I am having dinner with my parents like we are some normal American family.

But I know we're far from it, and I think that is what makes it so odd.

"So, Dean," I say to my dad as I stab at my salad, "have you heard the latest?"

"Has anything new come out since he died?" Dean asks.

"Warner, this isn't really suitable dinner talk," Mom warns. The color starts to drain from her face. I can tell she's uncomfortable. When I tried to talk to her about that video Steven showed us after we got home today, she didn't have much to say. She told me she was too confused, and then she said she was busy, and that's when she started going nuts cleaning the house. I'm not sure I've ever seen her do anything like that. So, she *must* be really freaked about it. And if she's freaked, then it makes me feel *I* should be freaked, too. Because what does it mean? Who was that person in the video?

"I just want to know if you've heard anything," I tell Dean. "Has my mom told you the news? Or maybe Mia?"

"Mia, as in, Amelia Bailey?" Dean asks, coughing and taking a sip of his wine. I notice the tips of his ears turning red.

What do you have to feel embarrassed about, Dean?

What is he hiding? What is he trying to do by having dinner with us tonight? Does he want to be with my mom, or does he want to be with Audrey and Lyla's?

"That'd be the one," I say.

He puts his wine glass down and wipes his mouth with his napkin. Mom had me set the table when I got home from work, placing cloth napkins from the way back end of one of the cupboards at everyone's seat. I didn't even know we had these.

"No, I—I guess I haven't heard anything lately," he says.

I look at Mom to see if she's noticing the way he's reacting to my mentioning of Mia, but she seems completely unaffected. Almost like she's trying to think of another topic we can talk about instead of this.

"I'm sure you'll hear all about it at school tomorrow, but Jackson Mullens and Sophia Key have been going around dressing up like Carson to scare us so that they have new content for the famous TikTok page they're running. And so that Jackson could fake-rescue Lyla in an attempt to win her back."

"I have seen the TikTok account, but I had no idea they were the ones behind it." His shoulders stiffen.

I nod. "Yeah. They've just recently been outed. And on top of that, there's still somebody else wearing that freaking mask following us. Spying on us. And we have no idea who it could be. Maybe Carson isn't really dead after all. Who knows? And then on top of *that*, Detective Craig Fritz is taking a leave of absence for his mental health from his job."

Dean nods slowly, like he's trying to process it all, but I wonder how much he already knew. If he is still seeing Mia often, and she's keeping him informed, is it possible that his reaction right now is fake?

"There are just a couple more messes that need to be cleaned up," my mom says, sounding just as calm as if we were discussing the weather. "Let's change the subject, please. *Now*."

"Um, the food is delicious, Mads. Thank you for having me," Dean says, picking his fork back up.

"You're welcome, Dean." She gives him a smile, and I'm creeped out. It's weird to see her being nice to him. It's as if she's completely accepted that he wants to be a part of our life. As if suddenly, she sees him as family.

But how will she feel about it when she finds out the truth about him and her best friend?

CHAPTER 46

MADDY

I t's late when Dean finally leaves. But I think that means it was a successful dinner. Once I got Warner to change the subject from all of the craziness in our lives, we all ended up having a nice time. It was kind of sweet to watch Dean and Warner bond with each other. And it was surreal to have them seated next to each other, where I could look back-and-forth between them and really put together all the ways that they look similar. Warner does have a lot of the same characteristics as his father. It kind of makes me wonder how he didn't figure it out sooner, or how none of the kids at his school pointed out the suggestion.

It's well after ten pm when I lock myself in my room, certain that Warner has gone to bed. I pull out my phone and dial the phone number off of the business card from my wallet.

"Officer Wilde, Toxey PD," Officer Wilde says when he answers my call. There's obvious grogginess in his voice, and I'm certain I've just woke him up.

"Officer Wilde, this is Madeline Carpenter."

"Maddy?" he asks. "It's late."

"I know. And I am so sorry to bother you. But you did say to call you *anytime* if I had questions."

"Yes, but I—oh, I suppose you're right." He makes a noise like he's getting himself out of bed. "How can I help you this evening?"

"I heard that my son talked to you."

"He did swing by to have a chat. Is everything okay?"

"I guess I just wanted to hear it for myself about Craig. What exactly happened?"

"It's not really my place to say, Maddy. He is going through some stuff. Like I told your son, his personal life was getting in the way of his work. Ya know somethin'—I kinda got the vibe that you didn't much care for him anyhow. I thought you'd be pleased to learn of his leave, but you sound the opposite of that."

"I... I don't know *what* I am," I admit. I don't know how to feel because I don't know what Craig is up to. He saved Warner's life at that pool inside Blackfell High. But he could also be lying to the public about Carson's death. I can't figure him out.

"I'm worried we're still in danger," I tell Officer Wilde.

"We're trying our best to get answers. At least *I* am."

"Do you...?" I want to ask him if he thinks Carson is really dead. But I'm too afraid of the answer. I'm too afraid he's going to tell me that that's *why* Craig was suspended. Because he lied. And I'm not sure I'm ready for that truth yet. I like it here where I think Carson can never hurt us ever again.

"Never mind," I say instead. "I should let you go. I am sorry for calling so late."

"Actually, while I have you, I *do* have a bit of news. I was going to probably let you know sometime this week, but—you know—during *normal* business hours."

I freeze in my spot on my bed. My posture is rigid and tense. "What is it?"

Please let it be something good.

"I have uncovered new information about Megan Young."

"Y-you have?"

"I found her parents. They're in New Jersey."

"New Jersey?" It's a long way from Toxey.

"I was able to inform them of her passing."

For a moment, I imagine somebody breaking that news to me. Then I decide I hate that idea and force myself to shake the horrible mental image from my mind. "How did they take the news?"

"It's hard to say," Officer Wilde replies. "Since I couldn't talk to them in person, and it's very difficult to gauge reactions over the phone. And... everyone grieves so differently."

"Right," I say. "Were they able to give you any information about why she came here? And changed her name and all of that?"

"I haven't done too much research on the parents yet. But they haven't heard from their daughter in a long, long time. She evidently went missing when she was fifteen years old, but that hadn't been her first time running away."

"So, she was clearly unhappy at home."

"Maybe. Or maybe she was having trouble at school and was unhappy there. I still don't know the full story. But I'm working to get more answers. Because I, too, would like to know what she was doing in our town. Was she simply trying to escape her old life and start over here? Get the high school experience she never got? Or does it really tie back to Carson price?"

"What are your thoughts leaning toward?"

"I can tell you this much, Maddy. Toxey is a small town. It's not the kind of place you just find yourself ending up at unless there's a reason for it."

The word sends chills down my spine. Officer Wilde is absolutely right.

CHAPTER 47

Audrey

The treatment of Sophia and Jackson at school today is a cruel reminder of how quickly your peers can turn on you. They're bullied and shunned by everyone. And I watch it firsthand as I stand by my locker with Lyla and Danielle as Sophia and Jackson walk past together, keeping their heads down, Sophia looking tearful as people whisper about them and yell cruel things right to their faces.

I don't know what to think as I stare at my former best friend. I've known Sophia my entire life. We weren't immediate best friends or anything. We only had play dates here and there and went to each other's birthday parties because the whole class was invited. We didn't really form our clique until we were in middle school. Sophia was popular, and she decided she liked us, so we became popular, too.

When her eyes meet mine, she gives me a cruel stare, and I know she hates me for outing her. I know that she'll never forgive me. That she thinks I am solely responsible for completely ruining her life.

But what about my life? What about Lyla's and Warner's? Does she really not see the harm she's caused with that stupid TikTok account?

I think it's completely unfair for her to look at me like that. She's not the victim here. She is not the one crumbling at the seams, fighting every single moment of every single day to hold herself together. She's Sophia Key. Holding herself together comes effortlessly. I, on the other hand, am beginning to crack.

"I really try not to see the worst in people," Danielle says, standing on one side of me, Lyla on the other. "But I should've known she was capable of doing something like this. I'm so sorry, you guys."

"It's whatever," I snap, shutting my locker rather harshly, warranting a look from Lyla.

"What?" I bark.

"Are you good, sis?"

"I just…"

No! I want to scream. *I am not good!*

I'm causing our family to divorce. I'm sneaking around behind Ryan's back with a boy that I am not even certain really wants to be with me. My sister is dealing with the trauma of being kidnapped and locked in a shed when it was supposed to be *me* who was kidnapped. My former *best* friend betrayed me in an absolutely horrific way. Carson Price might not really be dead. Or, Craig Fritz, a cop who we are supposed to be able to trust, is possibly finishing what Carson started. I can't sleep. I can *never* freaking sleep. I can't concentrate on school. I can't stop looking over my shoulder everywhere I go. I'm afraid to be left alone, even though being by myself is all I really want to do right now.

Why can't everything just stop?

"I gotta go," I tell my sister and Danielle. Then I offer zero explanation before I ditch them and hide out in the bathroom until first period.

I go through the first half of the day feeling like a zombie. I don't think I've paid attention to a single word anyone has said to me. I didn't take any notes in any of my classes. Did I even go to second hour?

I'm beginning to wonder if this is how my mom was feeling before she had her breakdown after seeing Carson in the woods. I'm wondering how she's doing now, after seeing that footage yesterday. Is she spiraling, too? Is Lyla? I need to be brave in case they are. Somebody has to hold us all together.

But it's just too hard.

"Hey," a voice says behind me at my locker before the last period of the day. I jump, startled out of my skin, and see that Kiley has approached me. "What did you say to Ryan?"

She doesn't look angry, per se. Right now, she just looks confused. But girls like Kylie and Sophia are the same. They're able to put on whatever face they want everyone else to see. Kylie might *appear* calm and casual about her inquiry to my face, but inside, she's probably screaming her head off and calling me every name in the book.

"What do you mean?" I ask, not in any type of mood to deal with this right now.

Can't you see I'm losing my mind?!

Her perfect, thick, fluffy eyebrows bunch together as she stares into my eyes. "He came up to me today and started talking to me about how he only likes me as a friend and that we don't have a future together because he's only interested in you. And I'm assuming he said that because of whatever *you* told him after you saw us together at Wrigley's party on Friday."

"I didn't *make* him say anything to you," I say with a huge sigh as I slowly close my locker door, trying very hard not to slam it again like I did earlier. "Look, I really can't talk right now."

"Why not?" she jeers. "Can't handle a little confrontation?"

"What? No?" I say, getting defensive. Kylie has officially turned on her snottiness.

Poor little Kiley. So concerned about something *so* insignificant compared to everything else that she could be having to deal with. She has no idea how easy she has it. And because she's probably only thinking of herself, she has no idea how *I'm* feeling right now. What I might do.

"Ryan and I have a history, okay?" she informs me.

"You do?" This is news to me.

"Oh, you mean he didn't tell you? It's probably because he doesn't want you to know that he has feelings for me so you won't get suspicious when we keep hanging out together. I don't know why he's wasting his time with you, you little *freak* show, but I assure you, Ryan is going to end up with me. So, if you think—"

"Oh my *God*, Kylie, will you *shut up*?!" I get louder and louder with every word until I am practically screaming at her. And I am well aware that I am being loud enough to be heard across the school, but there is absolutely nothing I can do to stop myself now that I have started.

I think it's been a long time coming.

"I don't *care* about your stupid crush on Ryan *freaking* Copeland!" I continue.

Kiley looks to her right and her left, half-smiling at our peers, probably trying to get them to think she has no idea why I'm suddenly having an outburst. She's probably trying to play it off like she never even said anything about Ryan in the first place.

"If you want him *so* badly," I say, still screaming. "Then you can *have* him! I don't care anymore! I don't have time for this stupid, petty, *childish* drama!" I stomp my foot.

Speaking of childish...

"I don't—that's not what I am—" Kiley begins stuttering and backing away, and I feel as if I am an angry, feral beast that has just been accidentally let out of their cage. I think she's afraid of me.

I turn from her and face everybody who stopped in their tracks to stare at me. "I am so sick of this! Of all of this!"

A hand is gently placed on my shoulder, and I turn around wildly to shrug it off. It's Lyla.

"Audrey, let's go," she tries, speaking gently.

"*No!*" I scream, backing away from her as she tries to grab for me again. "Don't touch me, Lyla!"

"Ree... it's okay."

"Are you *kidding* me?! It's not, '*okay*,' Ly! None of it is! I can't take this! I can't freaking take it!"

"Hey, I get it." She's still holding her hand out to me, but I refuse to take it. I just back further away from her instead, making myself more the center of everyone's attention.

"No, you don't get it! I have tried, for *so* long, to pretend to be fine! But guess what, I am not fine! I don't think I'll ever be fine!" When did I start crying? I don't even remember. "I shouldn't even *be* here right now!"

Warner appears by Lyla's side. But even his presence doesn't calm me down.

"What are you talking about?" Lyla asks me. "Audrey, come on. Can we please just get out of here?"

"I'm supposed to be dead! Lyla, why did you go, huh?" I'm full-on sobbing and screaming at the same time. "Why did you do that?!"

"I'm not going anywhere. I didn't..." She's flabbergasted along with everybody else.

"You did!" I screech. I'm a snotty, blubbering mess. And I can't calm down. It feels like I'll never calm down again. "You snuck into my phone and you went behind my back! It was supposed to be *me* in that shed! Me!"

I can't say anything else because my crying has overtaken me. Lyla rushes forward and throws her arms around me even as I try to wiggle away. She overpowers me, hanging on tight. Eventually, I give up and sob onto her shoulder, and together, she and Warner start pulling me through the crowd.

CHAPTER 48

LYLA

"She'll be all right," Principal Mathers says to Warner and me inside the front office, talking about Audrey.

Warner and I didn't get very far down the hallway with my sobbing mess of a sister before Principal Mathers intercepted, having heard the commotion. He escorted us here, even though it isn't where I wanted to take Audrey; I had planned on ditching school and getting her out of here, somewhere she could be away from everybody.

Principal Mathers' bald head looks especially shiny in this lighting. "She's in with a counselor," he informs us. "Are *you* two all right?"

"Yeah, fine," Warner says. Beside him, I'm silent.

"Lyla?" Principal Mathers presses.

"Uh..." I trail off because I don't know what to say. I'm definitely shaken up. Not once have I ever seen my sister meltdown like that. I wish I was with her right now, but maybe talking to a counselor is what she needs. Maybe talking to a *therapist* is what she needs. Maybe she should start seeing Dr. Morton.

Still, all of this is stuff I don't want to say to Principal Mathers, or else I might end up having to go speak with the counselor next.

"I'm fine," I say.

"All right," he says, nodding his head as if he's completely satisfied with our answers even though after what we've all been through, he has to know none of us are *all right*. "Hang tight. I'll go get you two some passes back to class."

He leaves us by the receptionist desk. I walk away from it and go and sit down on a bench. Warner follows and takes a seat next to me. I notice how close he decides to sit. There's enough room for a whole other person to sit on the other side of him.

"I always thought she was so much more put together than me," I tell him. "That she was just way better at handling things." Now I know the truth. She kept everything bottled up until it made her explode.

"You can tell she feels really guilty over you getting kidnapped instead of her," he says.

"Thanks for the reminder."

He ignores my sarcasm. "So... why did you do it, anyway?"

When I look at him, I can see not only confusion, but also a little bit of hurt. Like he's mad at me for doing it, too. *Everyone's* mad at me for it.

I sigh and look at my lap. "I wanted answers. And I wanted to protect her. I don't know. I guess I thought, up until that point, this person was just trying to mess with us. I guess I just wasn't expecting a kidnapping. I was expecting a confrontation. So, I thought maybe I would be brave and learn who the person contacting her was. I thought I could finally get some answers for everybody. I know now how stupid it had been. But, the thing is, my wig fell off when he was... trying to get me to come with him. And even after he found out that it was me and not Audrey, he still carried on with it. It wasn't like he realized the mistake and that he had the wrong twin and let me go. It was almost like he didn't care which one of us he got, as long as he got one."

"Maybe it would make her feel better if she knew that," he offers.

"Yeah. Maybe."

We're silent for a beat. I hope Principal Mathers takes his time getting back to us with those hall passes. I know I'm supposed to be getting my grades back on track, but I have no desire to go and learn right now. Not when my sister is in distress like this.

"So," Warner eventually says in a casual tone. I can tell he's about to change the subject. "How is Wrigley?"

"What?" It's such a bizarre question. Almost like something a jealous person would ask me.

"You know, after getting caught throwing that party. Is he grounded for life or what?"

Oh. He's not asking about mine and Wrigley's relationship. I take it back then. He's not jealous.

"I don't really know, honestly," I reply. "I didn't really see him today. That's weird, right?" I'm more talking to myself than to him. "I mean he's—we're—I don't know what we are. But if we were boyfriend and girlfriend, wouldn't it be kind of weird to just go all day without talking? I know he doesn't have his phone, but even in the hallways…" I trail off and think back to earlier.

When Wrigley and I first became friends, back before Trinity's accident, the only relationship we had was over Snapchat. We didn't talk at school. We would eye each other down in the hallway when we passed by one another, but that was it. Today was only a little bit more than that—Wrigley gave me a head nod when he passed me. But he didn't hang out with me in the morning, or at lunch, or at all in between classes. I hardly even saw him.

I look at Warner. Does Wrigley know that Warner and I are in here together right now? Would that make him even more angry and annoyed about Warner's and my relationship?

My stomach churns. I don't even *have* a relationship with Warner. Yes, he's super cute, and yes, I think he's a great guy, and yes, we did almost kiss once…

"Is he mad at you or something?" Warner asks.

"I don't—I don't know."

I don't think it would be wise to tell Warner that Wrigley is jealous of him.

"You don't know?" he asks.

"I…" *It's not wise to tell him, Lyla.* "What about you and Jessica?" I blurt out, just as a way to change the topic. But now I realize *I'm* the one sounding like a jealous person. But I'm not.

Okay, fine. Maybe a little.

"Oh, I ruined that," Warner says. "Or should I say—Jackson ruined that. Long story. It doesn't matter."

"What do you mean?" I ask.

"Uh…she's just…changed her mind about me."

"Because of the rumors about Sydney's death? I ask. "That's so stupid. Hasn't everyone figured it out yet? Carson's responsible for everything."

"Yeah…yeah, I know," he tells me. "Oh well. I wasn't really into her anyway."

"Oh." I hate that I feel satisfied by that. I shouldn't care.

He loudly clears his throat. "So... Wrigley *is* sorta your boyfriend?"

"Um... it hasn't been established. I don't know."

"Well, he definitely cares a lot about you. I'm pretty sure he hates *me*, though."

"He doesn't hate you. He's just jealous of you."

Dang it, Lyla!

"Jealous?"

"I..." I trail off again. There's no way for me to *not* explain it now. So, I sigh. "Yeah. He doesn't like you and me talking."

"That's weird. We're friends."

"That's what I said" I cry, flinging my hands in the air. "You and I were friends before me and him were anything. It wouldn't be right to stop talking to you for him. Especially not when we're going through this...*thing* together."

"Exactly."

He shoots me a quick smile, and I smile back. But on the inside, there's a feeling nagging at me.

We're friends.

The feeling is disappointment.

The cemetery's gate creeks when I open it. I approach Trinity's gravestone and place a fresh bundle of flowers down even though the ones most recently left aren't anywhere close to dying. I wonder who left them.

The grass looks damp and slightly muddy, so I don't sit this time. I just place the flowers at the base of the stone and rest my hand on top of it. "Hi, Trin," I say to her. "I miss you."

I wonder what kind of things she'd like to talk about. I'm a little too exhausted to go into everything with Carson. And I'm sure she would be *so* sick of hearing about it, were she really here. I'm sure she'd want to talk about something different for a change. And maybe *I* want to talk about something different for a change, too. I want to talk about something that I don't think I can tell anyone else.

"Wrigley being mad at me about the whole Warner thing is so ridiculous," I say, rolling my eyes. "I bet he'd be furious if he knew I spent the whole afternoon with him. But it's not like Wrig has directly asked me to be his girlfriend. And It's not like Warner and I have some sort of secret fling. And it's not fair for Wrigley to be jealous. But at the same time... maybe he's onto something?" I wince slightly as I stare at her stone. "Cuz he's not *completely* wrong to be jealous. I don't know, Trinity. I like Warner. A lot. And maybe Wrigley can tell. I like Wrigley, too. And I chose being with him over going after Warner, after all... but I guess maybe now I am wondering if I made the wrong choice.

Wrigley is different than I thought. Or different than what I was used to with Jackson. And Dr. Morton even said that I shouldn't be associating with him right now. Maybe she's right. Maybe I'm not supposed to be with him anyway. Would you be mad at me if you were still here, if you had survived the accident, and you learned that it only happened because I was texting *him*? It's messed up of me to even go and date him when my texting him is the reason you're not here anymore, isn't it? Ugh, it is. I know it is. But, I told Wrigley already that Warner and I are just friends and that he can't stop me from talking to him. So, wouldn't I just look like a huge jerk if I ended things with Wrigley and then was seen dating Warner like a week later? Besides, Warner even said it himself today that we're friends. *Just* friends. So, he probably wouldn't even go for me."

I take my phone out and scroll to Warner's text thread. "Warner texted me a lot while I was... gone." I don't want to say *kidnapped* out loud. I don't want to say *locked in a shed* out loud. *Gone* is better. Like I was on a nice little vacation.

"Maybe you can help me with this. Help me decipher what all these mean," I tell Trinity.

I scroll back up in the thread of messages until I get to those days.

"*You have to be okay, Lyla,*" I recite. "*You have to be.*"

I scroll to the next.

"Here's another. *Where are you, Lyla? What happened to you? Please just come back or let us know you're safe.*"

Then to the next.

"This is crazy, Lyla. You can't really be gone. Everyone's looking for you. I am looking for you. We're going to find you and we're going to bring you home."

Then to the next.

"How does anyone expect me to keep going when I don't know where you are, or what happened to you? How does the world keep spinning? I don't understand it."

I start to get a little choked up as I look back up at her gravestone. "Wrigley texted me a bunch, too. But he didn't say anything like this. He just said that he missed me and that he was looking for me and that he hoped I was still alive. He sent me some jokes, like if I did have my phone and was allowed to get on it, I would get cheered up by them or something. I don't know."

I go back to reciting more of Warner's text messages.

"People think I did this. Go figure. Wrigley Hall got pretty aggressive with me today. Do you two have a thing or something? I don't think I've even seen you guys really talk to each other. When did that start?" I laugh a little bit. "And then he texted me again pretty much immediately saying, *That was stupid. None of my business. It's just been a really crappy day and I really wish you were here."*

There are more, but I don't want to read them all. I might start sobbing like Audrey did earlier. So I click my phone off and put it back in my pocket.

"So, what do you think?" I ask Trinity. "Are those texts you'd send a *friend*? Or do you think that maybe it—we did almost kiss... but who had initiated that? Me or him?"

I groan and look up at the sky. The sun has fully set already, and some stars are shining in the parts of it that aren't covered by clouds. I forgot that it's starting to get darker much earlier now that we're heading into the colder seasons.

"I'm *way* too into my head about all of this. But hey, it's a normal, teenage problem to like two guys at once and to wonder if one of them likes you back. If this was the only thing I was dealing with right now, I'd honestly be happy."

I think back to school again today. How Wrigley had hardly said a word to me. He didn't have his phone, which meant he couldn't text me to ask me where to meet up with him, and maybe he had been waiting for me in the library at lunch when I went to the cafeteria instead. And maybe I had hidden away in the bathroom between all my classes instead of lingering by my locker or making my way over to his.

"Crap," I say, my stomach dipping. "Maybe Wrigley isn't the one doing the avoiding."

I think maybe it's me.

CHAPTER 49

MADDY

I am on my phone at work, going through my search results for social media profiles of people named Megan Young. Searching for her before did me no good because there's about a million Megan Young's on Facebook, and I knew nothing about her location back then. Now that I can fine-tune it to New Jersey, it has lowered the number of search results.

"I think your fifteen-minute break was up like, ten minutes ago," Rochelle says to me as I sit in the break room, popping her head in through the doorway. "And I *swear*, I'm not trying to be that person—I'm just trying to save your butt from getting in more trouble with you-know-who."

I hop up with a quick gasp. "Crap, does she know?"

"I don't think so. But just grab a bunch of stuff from the supply room on your way out here so it looks like you were busy looking for things and that's why you were back here for so long."

"Good call." I smile at her and then go to the supply closet. I grab a couple of things, but then I sneak another peek at my phone.

In this next search result, the profile picture is in black and white and is definitely old, but it looks promising.

I press on the photo to make it bigger and then and scroll through more of them.

Bingo.

I finally found Megan Young's old Facebook.

I grab some more random stuff off the shelves and then take it all to my workstation. I check the time and see that my next client is coming in in ten minutes.

"Oh crap, I forgot something," I say loudly as I turn back to go into the supply room once more. How am I supposed to work when I have just found something so huge?

Once inside, out of sight from everyone, I open Facebook back up on my phone. Sydney/Megan hasn't posted anything in years. *Go figure*. But, what I *do* find is that back when she had been posting, there was consistently one girl with Sydney/Megan in a lot of her photos, who also commented on all of her posts and liked all of her uploads.

Her name is Paisley.

"Where did Maddy go *now*?" I can hear my boss asking out by my workstation. I have to hurry.

"I think she forgot something in the supply room," I hear my coworker say.

I go to Paisley's profile and compose a message:

Me: *You don't know me, but I would love to speak to you about your old friend, Megan Young. I know what happened to her.*

There. That's going to make her interested in replying to a complete stranger, right?

I stand there for a second to see if maybe this Paisley chick will read my message while I'm still on my phone. But the message still only shows as delivered, so I have no choice but to put my phone away and get back to work.

Chapter 50

Amelia

I am inside a tile store looking at options for one of our client's bathroom showers when my phone rings. I pull my phone from my purse and see the girls' school calling.

"Amelia Bailey," I say when I answer, even though I'm curious to know if perhaps Dean just called me from a school line.

"Hi, Amelia," a female voice says, sounding polite and friendly. "This is Jenifer Nunez from your daughters' school. I am the counselor here."

"Counselor?" I ask. I've never met her.

"Yes. Do you have a moment to chat?"

This can't be good.

I step over to the window, away from the store's employees. Then I talk in a quiet voice. "Yes, I'm available."

"Oh, great. I actually had a really good talk with your daughter, Audrey, today. And I asked her if it would be all right if I called you to discuss this with you, and she gave me her permission."

"Audrey?" I suppose since Lyla is the one who sees a therapist outside of school, I just assumed *she* would be the one who the counselor had talked to.

"Yes, Audrey," Jennifer Nunez says. "Without getting into too much detail, Mrs. Bailey, I know that Audrey is going through a great deal right now."

"Yes," I say. "Our whole family is."

"Right. And, there was a bit of an incident today at school, which led to her coming to see me. And when we talked—"

"An incident?" I interrupt. "What kind of an incident?"

"I'm sorry, what we discussed exactly is confidential. I'm only calling to discuss the thing with you that she gave me permission to."

That's annoying.

"Okay…"

"I don't think I am fully qualified to give your daughter all of the help and resources that she requires right now. I suggested her seeking therapy outside of school, and she didn't seem super interested in it, but when I asked her if I could call you about it, she said it was fine."

"Audrey needs therapy," I say out loud. *Audrey.* My daughter, who has always seemed so brave throughout all of this. Who has kept a smile on her face and made me think she was completely fine.

"It's something you two can discuss together," Jennifer says, "but I do think it is in her best interest."

"I'll—I'll talk to her. Thank you."

When I get off the phone, I quickly finish up at the tile store, drop some samples off at my office, and then I hurried to get back home to my daughters.

Audrey is in her room, the door open so I can see her propped up on her bed watching TV. Since she's alone in there, I seize my opportunity.

"May I come in?" I ask, knocking on her door frame.

"Sure," she says. She doesn't perk-up at my arrival. She doesn't even look away from the TV.

"So…" I trail off.

I don't exactly know how to start. All I know is I feel horrible.

"You're a pretty good little faker," I say with a gentle smile, trying to ease into it. I stand by her bed, not sure if she wants me to sit with her.

"I'm guessing you talked to Miss Nunez," she says, still only looking at the TV.

"Yes. And I am *so* sorry, Audrey."

Now, she looks at me. "Sorry for what?"

"I don't have any idea how much you were struggling."

She shrugs. "No one did. Because I didn't want anyone to know."

"Why not?"

She shrugs again and doesn't answer me.

I try something else. "Miss Nunez said there was an incident today, but she didn't tell me what it was."

"It's probably on Sophia and Jackson's famous TikTok page by now. I'm sure tons of people took videos and sent it into them."

"I already checked it," I tell her. I was looking for some sort of insight as to what the *incident* might have been before I had this talk with her, and I had the same thought that she'd had: since Sophia and Jackson want the world to know about everything in all of our lives, surely they would have something about an *incident* of Audrey's on their page. "The account has been deactivated."

"It has?"

"Yep."

This seems to make her feel a little bit better. "Finally. I bet all of their adoring fans are going to throw a fit."

"We'll see. But, do you want to tell me what happened?"

"Not really. It's embarrassing. Can I say that I just couldn't hide how I was really feeling any longer and leave it at that?"

I sit down next to her. "Okay. If you do want to talk about it, I'm here whenever you're ready."

She nods.

"You don't have to pretend around me, okay? I'm your mom. It's not your job to look out for me. It's the other way around. Besides, we're telling each other the truth now, right?"

"I guess."

"It might be a hard habit to change, but I want you to try. That's why I'm going to have you start seeing Dr. Morton as well."

"I'll *try* therapy," she agrees. She is a lot more willing than Lyla had been when her father and I first brought it up. "But if I don't like it, I do not want to be forced to go."

"I'll only *not* force you if I think you're doing okay without it. Deal?"

"Deal." She still doesn't sound thrilled, and I am also not too excited about the idea of having to tell Gentry about all of this. But when she offers me a hint of a smile, I take it as an invite, and I practically drag her into my lap and give her a ginormous hug.

Dean's text, *Have fun with your ex-boyfriend tonight,* makes me giggle. I know he's only joking about the text, but I also know part of him is secretly jealous that I'm meeting up with Parker Fritz downtown.

I text him back that I will swing by his place afterward, and then I go inside the little Italian restaurant Parker and I agreed to meet at.

Parker is already seated at a table, waving me over. I can't help but smile. He hardly looks any different than high school. He has the same gelled hair he did back then. And I feel like maybe he had that same flannel back then, too. He doesn't exactly look like he works on Wall Street. I had been expecting some clean-cut guy who only wears business suits and silk pajamas and expensive athletic wear.

He stands when I arrive at the table and hugs me tightly. He doesn't smell like I remember, so at least he's changed his taste in that aspect. Instead of all over body spray, he smells of an Armani cologne.

"You have no idea how good it is to see you," Parker says with his arms still wrapped around me. He leans back, not immediately letting me go. Instead, he stands there for a second, beaming at me. "Mia Flynn."

"Bailey," I correct. *Or does he already know about the separation?*

"Right," he says with a smile. He doesn't *look* like he knows, which is good. I do not feel like discussing my separation with him tonight. In catching up with Parker, all I want to know is what he's been up to all these years. I don't really care to divulge too much about what's going on with me. Especially since it's been so messy.

"This is the strangest blast from the past," I say to him as we finally sit. A server comes to take my drink order, and I get a soda water with lemon. Parker already has a pint of beer in front of him. I don't want to drink because I don't want to be tempted to overshare.

"I hope I wasn't keeping you waiting for too long," I say when the server walks away.

"I got here early to have a drink and calm my nerves."

"Oh *stop.*"

He chuckles. "No. This is my first one, I assure you."

"I'm surprised you even wanted to meet up with me. I guess your brother hasn't *completely* transformed your opinion of Maddy and me." I eye him skeptically. "Or has he?"

"No," Parker says, shaking his head. "Craig has never had influence on me."

"You did always march to the beat of your own drum."

"Sort of what you have to do if you want to get out of this place."

"I wish *I* had made it out."

"You had a lot of things keeping you here."

"I guess."

"And you can still get out, if you want."

"Maybe once the girls graduate. I would hate to make them start somewhere new now. They just have one more year after this."

My drink comes, and so we clink our glasses together and each take a long sip. Then we dive into catching each other up on our lives, Parker talking all about how he got to where he is in his job, inadvertently making it *very* clear that he has a lot of money but isn't showy about it.

I talk a lot about my job—having started my own business is one thing I'm always proud to brag about—and I talk a lot about my daughters and Joey, which I'm even *more* proud to brag about.

"And you and Maddy became friends again, right?" he asks when we're talking about people from high school.

I smile. "She just can't stay away from me."

He laughs. "You two are something else. What do you think about her having a kid with Dean?"

My face heats up and I take a drink, hoping that he doesn't notice it. "It's quite the scandal," I say after.

"Huh."

Ut oh. I don't like that look on his face. The slight side-eye. The way his head is tilted back. The way he's staring me down like he's calculating something in his mind.

"I'm afraid to even ask what you're thinking right now," I tell him.

He leans back in his chair and crosses his arms, still appraising me. "You and Dean... whatever happened with that?"

And now the conversation has officially turned awkward.

The reason Parker broke up with me in high school was because he found out Dean and I had once shared a kiss, and he refused to believe that I no longer had feelings for him. It hurt, but at the same time, Parker had been right.

"I really am sorry that I never told you about our kiss," I say to him, feeling like it would be wrong not to. "But if it makes you feel better, we didn't tell *anyone*."

He smiles at me. His smile and his goofiness are the things that I liked about him most when we were together. He never took life too seriously. And as someone who *only* took it seriously, I always appreciated that about him.

"I should be the one apologizing," he says. "It's not like you guys even kissed while we were together. I was an idiot in high school."

"No, you weren't."

"Yeah, I didn't need to attack him like that. Make a scene."

The server comes back, and Parker and I laugh and apologize to her and tell her we haven't even looked at the menu yet. She leaves some bread and olive oil to dip it in, and then we're alone again.

And there's something I have been wanting to ask him. "While we're still on the topic, I don't think you ever told me how you found out that Dean and I kissed in the first place. Or did you?"

"I don't know. It was so long ago, and even just *saying* that makes me feel incredibly old."

We laugh some more. He grabs a piece of bread and dips in the oil. So I do, too.

But before he takes a bite of his, he says—in a casual, simple voice like his answer isn't going to completely shock me— "but, yeah. I guess one of you *did* tell someone else. Because it was your sister, Nora, who told me you two kissed."

CHAPTER 51

WARNER

Lyla and Audrey tell me that since their mom isn't home, and their dad doesn't live there anymore, that it's okay for me to go to their house. I'm mostly here so I can make sure Audrey is doing okay, and also since they're really my only friends these days. But, like it always does, the conversation turns to Carson and Craig pretty much right after I get there. Audrey doesn't even want to bring up her 'incident' that happened earlier today.

"Ly," Audrey says as we all lounge on the large L-shaped sectional in their family room. I'm on the part that's under their windows into the backyard, Audrey is curled up in the corner, and Lyla is lying with her head on the armrest, her feet toward Audrey, on the part that backs to their massive, white, and shiny kitchen. "Have you talked to Wrigley? Has he mentioned anything about there being more footage of that masked person lurking around their house?"

Lyla looks up at the ceiling. "I haven't heard from him."

"Like... at all?" Audrey asks.

Lyla shrugs and doesn't reply.

Audrey looks at me. "Have any new strange occurrences happened to you or Maddy?"

"Nothing to report," I say. "Did you guys see that the TikTok account was deactivated?"

"I heard Jackson and Sophia are in trouble with the principal—they might get suspended. Or expelled. *That* would be cool." Lyla sounds almost bored as she stares at her nailbeds. I wonder how she's taking the news of not only her ex-best friend, but also her ex-boyfriend, being the owners of the account. I wonder if Jackson has been trying to reach out to her about it. *I* haven't heard anything from him. We've pretty much cut each other entirely out of our lives. It sucks, but I know it's for the best. No one likes how Jackson has changed.

Or maybe we all changed, and he stayed the same, and that was the problem.

"I wonder what Carson is doing right now," Audrey says. "Do you think he's outside right this moment, trying to find a window to watch us through, or a door to sneak in through?"

The hairs on the back of my neck stand up at the thought. I look around, and thankfully, anything with a clear windowpane has curtains drawn over it. "So, we all think he's alive then?"

"Who else would be doing this, besides maybe Craig?" Lyla asks.

Audrey sighs so loudly that it causes Lyla and I to both look at her. Lyla has to lift her head up from the armrest to see her.

"What?" Lyla asks.

"Did either of you know that I have been talking to Carson's stepdad?"

This makes Lyla sit up fully, her eyes bulging. Mine are, too.

"What?" we simultaneously say.

"I guess not," Audrey says. "Mom and Maddy know about it, but...whatever."

"What do you mean?" Lyla asks. "Wh-who is his stepdad? How? *Why?* Why didn't you say anything before?"

Audrey and I have been hanging out and texting nonstop lately, and I think it's odd she didn't tell us until now.

She fills us in on her first encounter with this Eric guy, and on how her father made her keep it to herself, and after that, she tells us about when she met up with Eric in the hotel. Then she explains Mia meeting Carson's stepsister, Harley, and how both of Carson's former relatives had completely opposing stories.

"And if Harley is telling the truth," Audrey says after we're caught up, "then I probably should have stayed far away from Eric."

"You think?" I ask, annoyed with her. *Eric and Harley*—new names to add to the massive, confusing, twisted puzzle.

"Okay." Lyla twists her face in concentration. "I'm so confused."

"About what?" Audrey asks.

"I—well..." She gives us guilty looks.

"What?" I ask, still feeling tense because of the new info from Audrey. Now it looks like Lyla has something she's been refraining from telling us about, too.

What else could there be?

"Okay—let me just start from the beginning and try and put all of this together," she says. She gets to her feet and begins pacing in front of the TV. "Aunt Nora dated Carson. He was abusing her. So, Mom and Maddy followed him to some random lake house to confront him, and they end up killing him—or so they thought. They pull him out of the pool, he's injured. He seems dead. Maddy and Mom run away and keep it a secret. Aunt Nora finds him next, and as it turns out, he's not dead after all. But he uses it as the perfect opportunity to *pretend* to be dead. So, he makes Nora go along with it and let him continue to play dead, leaving Aunt Nora to be known as this girl no one believed, a girl who went 'crazy,' and Aunt Nora let it all happen because she was afraid of what Carson would do to her otherwise.

"So, at this point, it's a mystery. Some people believe Nora about Carson being dead. Others speculate that he ran away. And Nora was never told the reason why Carson needed to stay 'dead'. She just helped him blindly because while she was also scared of him, she was in love with him.

"But on the other side of the thing, this Eric person had already been trying to find Carson after Carson's mother died in a fire and Carson was put into the foster system. And Eric claims he's been looking for Carson because he raised him and sees him as his son, and doesn't hate him for accidentally killing his mother—if it *was* an accident. But Eric's daughter, Harley, says he's looking for Carson to kill him to avenge the love of his life.

"Going back to Aunt Nora. She said she started getting therapy and realized Carson was horrible—*finally*, and after years of help-ing him hide and giving him money. And she decides to try and cut him off. But he doesn't let her. He threatens her. Blackmails her. Then that stops working, so Aunt Nora believes that is his reason for going after us now—her family, which to Carson, includes Maddy and Warner because Aunt Nora had never lost touch with Maddy. But—another possible motive that Aunt Nora doesn't know about, is that Carson wanted to get his revenge on Mom and Maddy for trying to kill him."

"But maybe not," I say, leaning forward in my seat. "Maybe the motive about Nora is more likely. Yeah, my mom and Mia thought they killed him and tried—and succeeded in—getting away with keeping it a secret, and that's kind of messed up, but Carson didn't really die. And he needed an excuse to stay on the run anyway because of his Dad."

"Unless he wanted to stay 'dead' so that he could plan his revenge on Mom and Maddy," Audrey says.

"But why would it take him this long to finally act out on that revenge?" I ask.

She shrugs.

"Whatever his motive, Carson begins his tormenting," Lyla continues, still pacing. "And it gets out on the news that our families are being messed with. It's all over the media—and TikTok. People—probably those amateur sleuths—do their own research, and it starts being theorized that Carson Price has something to do with it. Eric gets wind of this, and he heads to Toxey to find his son."

"But then Carson is found dead in the woods by Freaky Fritz," I say. "Weird timing for Carson to die as his stepdad comes to town."

"So, are you saying *Eric* could have killed Carson, and he really is dead?" Audrey asks me. "Mom had that theory, too. But, if that's the case, does that mean we're pretty sure it's Craig who is now wearing the mask?"

"Maybe that's why he didn't attack us that night," Lyla says. "At the party. Maybe he's wearing the disguise, pretending to be Carson, just to get himself spotted, so that we all stop thinking Carson was the one behind it all."

Audrey groans. "Where does Sydney play into all of this?"

My stomach dips. "I think she was killed for accidentally finding out something she wasn't supposed to."

Lyla stops walking and frowns. "I don't know. There's gotta be more to it."

"Maybe Sydney didn't really die and she's actually Harley in disguise?" Audrey suggests.

"Okay—don't even go there," I tell her, my head beginning to spin.

"Mom says Harley had been in contact with Carson while he was in hiding," Audrey says. "Do you guys think Aunt Nora knows this, and maybe knows who she is?"

"Speaking of Aunt Nora." Lyla has that guilty look on her face again. "There's something I haven't told you guys. She asked me not to. But I don't think I should keep it to myself."

"What?" I ask.

She entwines her fingers with each other, avoiding our stares. "Aunt Nora has been staying at Freaky Fritz's house—because they're in a relationship."

At this, I get to my feet. "Are you kidding me?"

I'm mad. How could I not be? This feels like huge information. I can't believe she withheld it. I look at Audrey, expecting to see her looking just as worked up over the new revelation as I am. Instead, she just has her thinking face on.

"She says they caught up when she first came to town to visit, and they hit it off," Lyla says.

"Why would she want to keep it a secret?" Audrey wonders aloud.

"I don't know. Fritz didn't seem to want anyone to know either."

"Why would she even *want* to be with him if he has a major drinking problem and hates the rest of her family?" Audrey asks.

"Again—I don't know," Lyla says.

I shake my head. "So much for keeping each other in the loop about stuff."

"I'm sorry!" Lyla whines. "She asked me not to tell, just like Dad asked Audrey not to say anything about Eric."

"We're trying to figure out who's been trying to *kill* us, and if there is *still* someone out there trying to kill us!" *How are they not getting that?* "Who cares what everyone else is asking us to keep hidden?! *We're* the ones being chased and attacked and kidnapped. We need to tell each other everything! Or we're never going to figure this out!"

"Warner, we're sorry," Audrey says defensively. She's the only one still sitting. "We told you now."

"Yeah," I say sarcastically. "I'm sure that's *all* you're hiding. I bet next week, when someone ends up dead, you'll suddenly have more important info to share. I haven't been keeping secrets. I can't believe I am alone in that."

"Ha!" Audrey barks.

I glare at her. "What? I haven't been!"

"Oh really?" she asks me. "What about the fact that you and I kissed? Why have you wanted to keep quiet about *that*?"

My mouth opens, but my brain has lost any capability to form more words. *Come on, Warner, say something.*

I am too afraid to look at Lyla.

"W-what?" Lyla asks, her voice barely audible.

"There," Audrey says, sounding heated. "*Now* we're all in the loop."

"You..." Lyla still sounds completely stunned. "You two kissed?"

Finally, I look at her. It makes my heart crack when I see the sadness and betrayal plain on her face.

"Lyla..." I begin.

"No." She shakes her head.

"Ly—" Audrey tries, but Lyla is quick to interrupt her.

"No. Stop. I—I just..." Instead of saying anything else, she sharply turns and leaves the room.

"What is *that* about?" Audrey asks me. But I don't answer her. I don't even look at her. I am still staring at the spot where Lyla had just given me that look.

Lyla doesn't want to be with me. She is with Wrigley.

So why the heck did she just react that way?

CHAPTER 52

AMELIA

After catching up with Parker, I go to Dean's house. I text the girls when I park to make sure they go to their dad's tonight, and they reply that they're there now, hanging with Joey. My heart swells with sadness when I see Joey's name on the screen. I miss him so much. I wonder if he misses me, too. If he wants to still be in my life. If he's really forgiven me.

"I have to tell you something," I say a little while later to Dean in his kitchen. He's eating my leftover Chicken Parmesan straight from the box while I sip on some hot cocoa he made me.

He stops eating, his fork mid-stab. "What?"

Just say it, I tell myself. *Get it over with.* "Nora knew about our first kiss."

He sets the box of food on the table we're sitting at. It's as if he's lost his appetite, which is exactly what happened to me after *I* was told this.

"Um... w-when did she find out?" he asks.

"Apparently, pretty shortly after it happened."

"Wait... did Parker tell you this?"

I nod. "That's how he knew. Nora told him. And that's why he punched you."

"I always wondered how he found out," Dean said. "I thought maybe you told him, not expecting that he'd get so... mad about it."

"I never told a soul. Did you?"

"No."

"Hm."

"I wonder why Nora never said anything to me about it," Dean says. "She gave me no signs that she knew—and we were together *all* the time. Or, maybe she did hint at it, but I was just clueless."

"I didn't think she knew either," I say. "At least not then."

Dean gets up suddenly, his chair jerking back against the tile flooring, the loud noise making me jump.

"HEY!" he shouts, looking behind me. I turn around, and outside his back window, all I see is darkness.

"Dean?" I squeak as he rushes to his back door, flinging it open, his face red.

"Mia, stay here," he demands. "Lock the doors!"

"Dean!" I get up as he goes outside.

"WHAT DO YOU THINK YOU'RE DOING?!" I hear him yelling as he disappears out of sight.

I know what's happened.

He saw someone in his backyard. And I have a feeling that someone is wearing a cartoonish mask.

And Dean is out there, alone and unprotected, with them.

My heart pounds as I hurry to the foyer to get my phone out of my purse. With shaking hands, I take it to the back porch, my fingers hovering over the screen, getting ready to dial 911.

"Dean!" I shout, unsure where he went. He has no lights on out here, but from the light in the kitchen, I can faintly see that his yard is empty. Where did they go?

I don't know what to do. Should I call 911? I don't even know exactly what's happening.

"Dean!" I cry again, feeling like my chest is going to explode.

I hear the noise of a gate opening and jump. *Who is that? Is Dean okay?*

When a figure rounds the corner to the back porch, I cry out. It's Dean. He's out of breath and still red in the face.

"I told you to stay inside," he snaps, taking my wrist and pulling me into the house.

"What *was* that?" I ask as he closes and locks the back door. Then he goes around and begins closing all the blinds and making sure everything else is locked. "Who was out there?"

"Some freak in a mask," he says. He's fuming. "It's Craig."

"*What?*" My stomach drops. Did Dean see his face? What happened out there?

I follow him into his living room, where he checks those windows next before he turns to me. "It has to be. They're buddies. Craig is loyal. Always has been. He's mad that Carson offed himself, and he blames you and Maddy for it."

"Dean, calm down," I try. "Let's just...sit down, okay?"

"What was he planning on doing?" Dean asks. "He snuck *right* up to the window. I don't know if he thought I wouldn't be able to see him or something..." He runs a hand through his hair. I step close to him and place my hands on his shoulders.

"It's okay. He's—he's gone now, right?"

"I chased him off, but he might come back," Dean says. "Who knows? He could have hurt you, Mia."

"He didn't."

Dean sighs and pulls me into his arms.

"Not this time, he didn't," he says into my hair. "But what about next time?"

CHAPTER 53

LYLA

When Audrey comes into the bathroom the next morning to start washing her face as I put my hair up in two small buns at the base of my neck, I don't say a word to her. I don't even look at her, even though I can feel her eyes on me.

"Ly, are you mad at me or something?" she asks. We're at Dad's now, because we told Mom last night that we'd go stay with him, so Audrey drove us here shortly after Warner left last night. I hadn't said a word to her then, and I still don't want to say anything to her now.

I ignore her question and finish my hair.

"Is it because Warner and I kissed? I guess I am just confused," she says, running the tap. "I honestly did not think you'd be mad about it."

I scoff because *yeah right*, but I still don't say anything.

"I'm serious!" she whines. "If you like him like that, that's news to me."

I can't hold in the outburst as I turn to her. "I specifically asked you if you liked him, Audrey. Remember? In the woods? You told me you didn't!"

"Why are you yelling at me?! You're with Wrigley!"

"And *you're* with Ryan!" I picture Warner and my sister kissing, and it's like getting stabbed. In the gut. In the heart. In the stomach. I picture the two of them exchanging their secret, flirty, knowing looks when the three of us are in the same room. I'm so mad. At both of them.

"I'm not, actually," Audrey says.

"Since when? He just came to Moms for dinner!"

"But we aren't official. I—I don't even know why I am explaining myself to you. I didn't know, Lyla. You can't be mad at me when I didn't know. Warner told me he didn't know either."

"That's a load of crap!" I screech, only getting angrier.

"How? You're with Wrigley!"

I want to palm her on the forehead. How could she have not known how crazy about Warner I am? How could Warner lie to her and say he didn't know either? "Because I couldn't be with Warner! Because of Jackson, you idiot!"

"Hey!" Dad's voice calls from the kitchen. I hear him thud up the stairs, and in seconds, he's in the doorway of the bathroom. "What's going on in here?" He's getting ready for work, adjusting his bright blue tie, his blazer draped over his arm.

We're not little kids anymore. It's not like I can tattle on Audrey for stealing the boy I like and have Dad fix the issue.

"Nothing," I snap to him, shouldering my way past him. I don't even want a ride from Audrey to school. I don't want to be near her. I'll walk to school. I'll avoid Warner, too.

Tears threaten to spill because I am not just mad, I am sad. Warner and Audrey had to have known that their secret kiss would hurt me.

Or else why would they keep it a secret in the first place?

CHAPTER 54

AMELIA

So what if Dean and I are in the same coffee shop? To everyone else, we could have just simply run into each other in the parking lot and decided to catch up.

That's what I tell myself as Dean orders my favorite drink without me having to remind him what it is. Last night, after he chased off...the intruder, Dean refused to let me be alone, so he followed me home in his car with an overnight bag and stayed over. He was a complete gentleman about it and slept on the couch, reminding me that he was only there to keep me safe. I told him several times he didn't have to stay, but I was secretly very grateful; I didn't want to be alone in my big house either. Dean's question kept replaying in my mind, and it was hard for me to think about anything else.

What was he planning on doing?

If Dean was right, and Craig was the new man behind the mask, what exactly was it he wanted? Craig saved Warner and Audrey's life at the pool when they were attacked. I don't want to believe he's doing this to us now. But what if after he found Carson's body in the woods, he regretted saving the kids? What if he thought he was doing Carson some sort of favor by finishing what he started? What if it was his way of making it up to him?

Dean pays for the coffees, and I thank him as we stand off to the side and wait for them to be made.

It feels weird to be in a public place in Toxey with Dean. But at the same time, it also feels nice. I want to be able to go places with him. I wish I could, without the town seeing it as some huge scandal. People would think I left Gentry for Dean, and I bet rumors would even start that I cheated on Gentry with him. People would think Dean was the reason Maddy and I killed our friendship back in high school. In all truth, there were a lot of reasons Maddy and I stopped being friends. Thinking we killed someone definitely played a big part in it—us staying friends after that would be too much of a reminder of the awful thing we had done—but even before then, we had been fighting a lot. Over everything and anything. And *fine*—I was mad at her for being with Dean. But as far as she knew, it was only because I didn't think it was fair to Nora.

If people found out about Dean and me, I bet I'd start to lose more clients, too. People would side with Gentry.

But Gentry has a girlfriend, too. He's the one everyone should be suspicious of, but since Dean and I already have a complicated past, I just *know* people would prefer to blame us for tearing our family apart.

"You okay this morning?" Dean asks. I realize I've completely zoned-out.

"Yes," I say, shooting him a smile.

"Are you thinking about last night?" he guesses.

"Sort of."

He looks like he wants to touch me. Hold my hand or put his arm around me and bring me closer to him. But he knows we're still keeping our relationship a secret.

"I'm going to get my proof that it's Craig," he says. "I can promise you that."

His name is called for our order, and he hands me my latte and leads the way to the door.

"Dean," I say in a low voice, walking closely behind him—probably closer than I should be. "It's not your job to catch him."

"Oh, I don't *believe* this."

I look up, taken aback that he's suddenly so annoyed by me, but I quickly realize as he opens one of the glass doors to the parking lot that he hadn't been talking to me.

Craig is approaching the coffee shop.

"Dean, don't," I try warning him.

Dean completely ignores me, his jaw clenching. "Craig," he barks. Craig pauses, his hand on the handle of the second door.

"Dean," Craig says, pursing his lips. He's a mess as usual, his eyes bloodshot and his face unshaven. "Mia. I—"

Craig doesn't get to finish his sentence because Dean throws a sudden punch, and his fist slams into Craig's face.

I scream and drop my coffee, worried that a fight has started and I am going to have to jump in the middle and try and keep the two off of each other.

"Stay away from Mia!" Dean shouts at Craig. "Stay away from all of them!" Thankfully, Craig, with his nose bleeding, doesn't look like he's about to hit him back.

"Dean!" I grab Dean and try to pull him away from Craig anyway, just in case Dean is thinking about hitting him again. "Dean—come on!"

Craig stands there, holding his bleeding nose as he looks in through the coffee shop window. Inside the coffee shop, there are *tons* of people who just saw the whole thing.

CHAPTER 55

WARNER

I could text and call Lyla a million times and try and explain myself. But I don't because I know she's not going to respond. I know she's mad at me. And at school, I can tell she's avoiding me.

I also don't try and talk to her because I am trying to sort out how I am feeling myself. I hadn't been expecting her to get so upset when she found out about Audrey and me kissing. Is that stupid on my part? Should I have somehow known—even though it looked very much like she moved on with Wrigley—that she's had feelings for me all of this time?

If I *had* known that, I would have tried harder to win her over. If I *had* known that, the confusing feelings I started to develop for her twin would have never happened. I still don't even know exactly how I feel about Audrey. Kissing her had been nice. Thinking about her makes me happy. I like being around her. At the start of this year, she was barely even a friend. Audrey was just my best friend's girlfriend's sister. But now, Audrey sort of is my best friend.

But is she more?

I shove my schoolbooks into my locker at the end of the day with aggressive force. I'm mad. Mad at myself for getting into this situation. And honestly? I'm mad at Lyla, too.

And I get madder and madder at her as I close my locker and head to the parking lot. It builds up so much that when I spot her unlocking her bike, I decide I don't want to keep letting her ignore me.

"Hey," I say when I reach her.

"What?" she mumbles.

"I—why'd you ride your bike here?" I ask, momentarily distracted. Then I shake my head—this isn't why I approached her. "Can we just talk?"

She holds the handlebars like she's debating whether or not to climb on.

I don't want to say it, but it might be the only way to get her to agree, so reluctantly, I tack on, "*Please?*" and wonder if she can tell that I am annoyed.

She rolls her eyes, but then she relocks her bike to the rack and starts walking.

I guess I am supposed to follow her.

We go around the perimeter of the school, toward the orange grove behind the sports fields. It's not exactly a short walk, but she is silent the whole way there.

When we're underneath the shade of one of the orange trees, where it has to be at least twenty degrees colder, she finally turns around to me, her arms crossed, her eyes distrusting.

"Just—tell me straight, Warner. Do you have feelings for my sister?"

"No." *Why are you lying to her?* "I—I don't."

"Warner," she scolds.

"What?" I snap. "What would be so bad about it if I did? You and I are just friends. You don't...like me...like that."

I want her to admit it. I want her to tell me she lied. I want the truth. I always just want the truth. And rarely do I ever get it from anyone.

I can see her jaw twitching. Her lips are pursed shut tight as she attempts to figure out what to say to me.

Come on, Lyla. How do you feel about me?

"You both made me feel stupid," she says. "I don't like being kept in the dark. Especially not about that kind of a thing."

"*That's* why you're mad? Because we didn't tell you sooner?"

She stares at me for a long while. I stare back, silently begging her to tell me what she really wants to. I can see it on her face. I can see it on the edge of her tongue. Part of her is screaming to let it out. But she's holding back.

"Yes," she finally says.

"Really?"

"I…"

"Lyla. I'm sorry. I really, truly am."

She turns her head away from me. She doesn't want to hear it.

But I continue anyway. "I thought you wanted to just be friends. I thought you wanted to be with Wrigley. I've been spending a lot of time with Audrey lately. After I watched her drown and thought Carson killed her—right in front of me—I don't know. I was just messed up about it, and it made me confused about how I felt about her."

She starts shaking her head and backing away from me. "Warner, I don't want to stand here and listen to how you fell for my sister instead of me."

"Oh, what—you preferred it back when you knew I was crazy about you and were telling me we couldn't be together?"

When I see the look she gives me, I know I messed up. That had been the wrong thing to say.

"I'm leaving," she tells me, brushing past me.

"Wait, that came out wrong!" I say to her, "Lyla, please!"

When it's clear she's not even going to so much as glance back at me over her shoulder, I yell out in frustration and kick a tree, jamming my big toe through my shoes.

"OW!" I shout, hopping up and down on one foot.

Maybe I should have stayed far away from *both* Bailey twins.

CHAPTER 56

MADDY

I only agree to hang out with Parker Fritz again when he texts me, *If I promise not to try to kiss you again, or even look at you, would you be open to meeting up again?*

And even then, I'm still a little wary when I drive to his hotel because I don't trust him to keep his promise. Still, I could use some company. Mia said she got caught up at work tonight. Nora isn't speaking to me. And the love of my life never wants to see me again.

But Parker makes me laugh. It's easy to have a good time with him and forget about all of the ridiculousness of my life.

"Thank you for giving me another chance," he says when he greets me in the lobby. He's staying at the nicest hotel in Toxey, Hotel Monte Vista, but that's not really saying much. It's still not all that fancy, especially compared to the other places he's probably stayed at before.

I chuckle and give him a hug in greeting. "Don't make me regret it," I tease. I'm glad he can be so casual about the whole try-ing-to-kiss-me thing.

When we pull away and I catch sight of the handsome grin on his face, part of me wonders why I *don't* just go for Parker. Mia doesn't have any interest in him anymore. He's good looking. *And* he has lots of money. I should just settle and find someone to support me. Be a trophy wife.

Who am I kidding?

That's never been my style. People don't normally guess this about me because I seem like a pretty cynical person on the outside, but I am nothing but a huge romantic. All I want is to be loved by somebody that I love in return. I just want my own special man, so I can live a happy and fulfilling life with him, and with Warner.

And Parker may have the makings of a perfect husband, but I just don't see myself getting feelings for him in that way. And I know it's because I am still so hung up on Steven.

"Want to go to my room and order room service?" Parker asks. "I got a suite, so there's a whole living room and kitchenette."

"Fancy."

"I am not trying to brag, I just don't want you thinking I want us to hang out in some small. dingy hotel room with a queen-sized bed and a wobbly desk and basic cable TV."

"*Sure* thing, Parker. Whatever you say." We argue about it as we walk to the elevator.

"I'm serious!" he cries.

"You have money, I *get* it."

We playfully bicker the entire ride up to the top floor, and I am surprisingly impressed when we enter his hotel room. I didn't think this place would have something this nice. It's remodeled and looks nothing like the rest of the hotel's decor. Everything is sleek and gray with dark wood. The sectional looks deep and comfy. There's even an electric fireplace that's turned on. Real heat is coming out of it.

"This is nice," I say when I sit down on the sectional.

He walks over to the counter and picks up a room service menu and hands it to me. I skim through it, also surprised at how decent the options look.

"Ooh, lobster bisque."

"Oh, I had that—delicious."

We both pick out a random assortment of items, and he calls in the order. We put a comedy on the TV and sit the way two friends would sit on the sectional—with plenty of space between us.

"Did you have fun at your dinner with Mia?" I ask.

"I did," he says. "It was really good to catch up with her. She's... different."

"How do you mean?"

"Different than what I remember."

This surprises me because I feel that Mia and I practically picked up our friendship right where we left off. But I wasn't ever once her boyfriend. So, maybe Parker had just seen a completely different side of her.

"Is it a good or bad thing?" I ask.

"I don't know," he says, throwing an arm over the back cushion. "I can't really figure it out. She seemed kind of... closed off. She was kinda that way before, but back in high school, it had been easy to get her to crack. It's not so easy anymore."

"She's been through a lot. She still is going through a lot now."

"Yeah. Totally."

"Speaking of people who are going through a lot," I say, "how is Craig taking his 'leave of absence' from work?"

"How did you know about that?"

"Have you forgotten where we are?"

"Ha. True. So, does this mean everybody knows? Everyone's talking about it? Poor Craig."

"Poor *Craig*?" I scrunch my nose up.

"Oh, come on. You really think he's that bad?"

"Sort of."

"From the sounds of it, he's just been trying to do his job. Figuring out who killed that girl and why you're being harassed."

I think about arguing with him. But I don't want to get too deep into the topic of Craig and Carson.

There's a knock on the door a short while after we table our discussion, but Parker is in the kitchenette, pouring us some sparkling water and slicing up some lemon.

"I can get it," I offer, getting off the couch and walking over to the door. I'm assuming it's our room service delivery. I even have some cash on hand to tip them with the money I got from cutting hair earlier.

I open the door, and no one is there.

"That's weird," I say, stepping out into the hall and looking both directions. To my right, there is nothing. To my left, I can see a hotel worker pushing a cart of food in our direction. They're still far away from reaching Parker's hotel room, though. No one else seems to be around. But I could've *sworn* I heard somebody knocking.

"Everything okay out there?" Parker asks from the kitchenette.

"Excuse me, ma'am?" the hotel worker, a short and plump guy with a bit of an accent says. "Are you looking for the person who just knocked on your door?"

"Did you see who it was?" I ask, growing a bit uneasy.

"Yes. It was very odd. There was a person in a mask. Once I stepped off the elevator with your tray, they ran toward the stairwell." He points to my right, and at the other end of the hall, I see the door to the staircase.

"A-a mask?" I ask stupidly.

Parker appears at the door, holding both of our glasses of water. He comes into the hall when he sees me out here and looks at the worker, who has finally arrived at the door. "What's going on?" he asks. I don't even want the stupid water anymore, but he hands it to me, so I accept it.

"Some weird guy in a mask knocked on your door and ran to the stairs when they saw me," the worker repeats. "Were you expecting anyone?"

"No," I say. "We weren't."

What? Did the worker think we had ordered some sort of scary telegram delivery?

"Ma'am, you look frightened. Would you like me to notify security?"

"Yes, immediately," Parker says for me. He gently places a hand on the small of my back. "Hey, are you okay?"

"Wh-who was that?" I ask as he steers me inside. The worker follows us in with the rolling cart. Parker gives him cash, then the worker says he'll call security straight away, and then he leaves.

Parker locks the deadbolt. "How did they know you were here?" Parker asks. Neither of us move to get the food off of the cart.

"I... He must've followed me."

What if the hotel worker hadn't gotten off of the elevator at that exact moment? What would've happened when I opened the door?

"Who, though?" Parker asks.

"I..."

"So, does this mean Carson *isn't* the one that was harassing you? Craig's been telling me that he's not so sure. This has to prove that it wasn't him, since Carson is dead, right?"

"*Or*," I say, my eyes narrowing, "it was your brother in that mask, finishing what Carson started because he hates us."

"You're joking, right?"

Something about Parker has changed. He doesn't seem so funny anymore. He seems apprehensive, as if the fact that I am still a targeted woman has made him have second thoughts about getting involved with me. He's gripping his glass tightly.

"I'm not, actually," I say to him. "Parker, you said so yourself that Craig hasn't been well lately. Do you know where he is tonight? Or where he said he was going to be? Do you think there's a chance that it could've been him? Wouldn't it make sense?"

"No, it *wouldn't*," he replies. "Maddy, why on Earth would *Craig* try to kill you and your family?"

"Because!" I can feel my face heating up. "He hates us! And his best friend, who hated us, committed suicide. Maybe Craig feels like he owes it to him to finish us off? Maybe he feels like Carson's suicide is our fault, and wants to avenge him."

I know I sound crazy. And this is mainly because Parker is now looking at me like I *am* crazy.

"Craig and Carson were hardly friends," Parker says. "Yeah, Craig hung out with him in high school, but he said he felt bad for the kid. I don't know, most of the time, Craig was complaining to me about him, saying a bunch of stuff about how he didn't think he could trust him, how he has a shady past, and that he had a violent streak."

"Still, I think—"

Parker interrupts. "And then when Carson went missing—or died the first time, according to Nora—Craig never knew where he went, Maddy. He never contacted him. And that was like, twenty years ago! Craig had no idea Carson was even *alive* until he found him in the woods that night."

"I see. And you believe that."

"Of course I do. And you should, too. My brother's not behind any of this, Maddy."

"I think you're wrong. And maybe because he's your brother, you just can't see the situation for what it really is, but—"

"No, Maddy, you're the one who's wrong."

Parker is *past* apprehensive. Now he's just plain angry.

I set my glass of water down on the coffee table. "I think maybe coming here tonight was a mistake."

"Yeah," he agrees, nodding his head vigorously. "Ya know what? I think I agree with you there."

"Okay... Thank you for this—but I'm going to go."

I start walking to the door.

"You need to get the idea of my brother being the bad guy out of your head. You don't know him."

"Oh, and you do, Parker? When's the last time you came back to town? When was the last time you talked to Craig before finally paying him a visit? Huh?"

He glares at me as I unlock the deadbolt. I've definitely struck a nerve. I wonder if maybe it's a topic he and Craig have fought about before.

"See you later, Maddy," he says, giving me the feeling that he has no intention of actually seeing me ever again.

I go to leave, but not before he calls out one last thing.

"My brother was right about you."

CHAPTER 57

AUDREY

I had my first appointment with Dr. Morton yesterday. It was after school, and even though I drove myself to her office, Mom was waiting for me once we got there. She was being supportive, looking out for me, which I appreciated. But the fact that I knew my mom was just outside the door, waiting for me the whole appointment, I think it made me want to hold back from being completely honest with the therapist. Dr. Morton even promised me that no one could hear anything through the walls. But I still felt weird about it.

And I still feel weird right now—I don't want to go back to school today. Yesterday had been horrible enough. Everyone was talking about my meltdown. Everyone was whispering about me. It wasn't really anything new, since I had gotten used to that when Carson started harassing us. But I just don't know how I'm supposed to act anymore. I am clearly not okay, and since everyone now knew it, when I saw all the stares and heard all the whispers, I couldn't put the façade on anymore. But who am I *without* the façade? Who am I when my sister, who is my best friend, isn't speaking to me?

Needless to say, it was a hard day.

Lyla is still not speaking to me this morning, and I can't stand it. I can't stand that I've hurt her when all I've been trying to do is repay her for risking her life to protect me. I wish I hadn't been too blinded by my own feelings for Warner to realize how much Lyla liked him, too.

I get out of my bed in Lyla's and my shared room at Dad's. Lyla's in the bathroom getting ready. Joey is still eating his cereal in the kitchen—I know because I can hear him gabbing away at Dad.

I need to use the bathroom to get ready, too, but I know Lyla doesn't want to see me, so I don't want to bug her by going in there.

Everything seems to be even harder now that I can't hide how I really feel. All I want to do is cry. And now, what's stopping me?

Negative thought after negative thought starts flashing through my mind. It gets harder to breathe. I dig around in our closet to try to find the jacket I want to wear today. I realize I'm not even looking at the clothes as I go through them. I am too focused on how everything in my life is going wrong.

I drop my arms from the clothes and turn away from the closet. I put a hand to my chest and begin to *really* panic. It hurts. I can't get a full breath in. My vision is blurring. Am I having a heart attack?

I gasp, hyperventilating and choking on nothing, and then I fall to my knees.

What is happening?

I hear footsteps running, and Lyla shoots into the room, dropping to her knees in front of me and grabbing my shoulders.

"Audrey?" she asks. She puts her face close to mine, so we're nearly nose to nose. "Audrey, it's okay. "

I try to tell her I can't breathe. That I am in pain.

That I am sorry.

But I can't get it out. Should she call 911? Am I dying right now?

What kind of teenager dies of a heart attack like this?

I grab onto her forearms, and she presses her forehead to mine.

"You're having a panic attack," she says. I continue to hyperventilate. *That's* what this is? "But I am here, Ree. It's okay. It will pass. I know it doesn't seem like it will, but I promise it will. I'm right here with you."

I manage to nod, and I clutch her arms tighter, trying to signal that I don't want her to move away for me. She doesn't. She keeps her forehead pressed against mine, her hands gripping my shoulders, until finally, the pain has faded and I can breathe easier.

"I thought I was dying," I say.

She laughs lightly and falls back to the floor on her butt. I do the same.

"Yeah," she says. "They suck."

"You get them?" I ask. "I've never seen it."

"I know. They're rare."

"Lyla." I still feel a bit out of breath. "I'm sorry. I really need you to forgive me. I can't... I can't take it when you're mad. The last thing I wanted to do was hurt you."

She swallows audibly and nods. "I was wrong to react that way," she says. I can tell she's embarrassed, and it's always been hard for Lyla to admit when she is wrong. "You and Warner are both right. How could you have known I had feelings for him? It's not like I ever told you. Either of you."

"I still feel terrible."

"Well... don't."

She gives me a half smile, so I chuckle.

"I'm sorry, too, Audrey," she says.

"You know, I'm honestly surprised we made it this long without a boy coming between us."

"Oh, *please*. You were *always* trying to steal Jackson from me."

I know she's joking, so I roll my eyes and pretend to barf. Lyla joking around is a good thing.

It means we're going to be okay.

But I need to ensure it. I need to redeem myself.

And I think, suddenly, I know exactly how I can do that.

I pull up next to Warner's red Jeep Wrangler in the overgrown, practically nonexistent parking lot. I am in Lyla's Toyota—I had to borrow it so that Dad couldn't see where I was going, not only because he would get mad at me if he knew I was with Warner, but also because this is Warner's spot, and I would hate to accidentally reveal this secret location to a parental figure who might, in turn, inform *his* parental figure about it.

Warner is not in his Jeep, which means he's probably on the bench at the abandoned train station. I get out of the car and take slow, deep breaths as I make my way over to him.

This is not going to be easy.

I quickly see that I was right—Warner is sitting on the bench, hunched over with his elbows on his knees. When he hears me approaching, he looks over his shoulder.

"Hey," he says. He sounds kind of glum.

I sit right next to him. It's cloudy out as usual, but it's also windy tonight. I didn't put my hair up, so it's blowing wildly, and I keep having to re-tuck it behind my ear so that it's not in my face while I'm talking to him.

"You know, I don't normally come here as often when it starts to get colder out," he says in a lame attempt at a joke. "We could have met up somewhere else."

I try to smile, but when he gives me a funny look, I know I failed miserably.

"What's wrong with you?" he asks. Earlier, I had only simply asked if he wanted to meet at his spot tonight. I hadn't given him a reason why. So, he probably thinks we're just here to hang out like normal.

And I wish that were the case.

But I need to do this.

"I'm sorry for creating that whole mess with Lyla," I tell him. "I should've handled that much differently."

He shrugs. "We probably shouldn't have hidden it from her in the first place. It was stupid. I don't know why we did."

But I *do* know why.

I nod along anyway. "When you came over last night, you were pretty mad at me and her for the things we hadn't told you."

"I know."

I move my hair out of my face again. *This dang wind!* "And you said that we need to be more honest with each other."

"I've *been* saying that."

"Right. Warner—there's something else I think you should know. Something I should have told you a long time ago."

"A long time ago?"

I nod. "It's something that happened during the upperclassman camping trip."

I'm really doing this.

There's no going back now.

"Something with Sydney?" he asks.

"Not exactly."

"What happened then?"

"I accidentally overheard Mr. Reeves talking to your mom in one of the chaperone cabins. Warner, I knew that Mr. Reeves was your dad. I found out during that trip."

Already, it feels better now that I got it out. But still, I'm terrified of the repercussion.

Warner doesn't know quite how to respond. Which makes it all the more agonizing to wait.

"You..."

It's all he's managed to get out so far.

"Your mom found out I overheard and confronted me about it, telling me I needed to keep it a secret. And I figured it wasn't my secret to tell. But then you and I started... getting closer... and it got harder to not tell you."

"But you kept it from me anyway," Warner says. "It must've not been *that* hard."

"I wanted to tell you so many times."

"But you didn't."

Oh great. He hates me. "I—I know. And I'm really, really sorry."

"That's nice," he says. Then he gets to his feet. "But I don't really *care* that you're sorry, Audrey. I... I don't believe this. I... I found out about Dean from *Freaky Fritz*. Do you know how much it sucked to find out that way?"

"No," I say quietly. I'm not trying to defend myself. Whatever he wants to say to me right now, I fully and completely accept it. Not only do I accept it, I deserve it.

And he lets me have it, all right.

"Of course you don't. You've had a perfect family most of your life. And that must've been *real* nice for you." He walks away from the bench, toward the tracks, pausing at the edge of the concrete platform. "Too bad your parents are divorcing and your mom is dating my dad now."

"*What?*"

My mom? Dating Mr. Reeves? How does he know? Did he just make it up because he's mad?

He ignores me and continues with his rant. "Why even bother admitting to me that you knew?" he asks with his back to me. "To ease your own conscience? You should've just kept it to yourself. Because now... now..."

Now you'll never look at me the same.

"I understand if you never want to talk to me again," I say, getting to my feet.

And that's exactly why I told you.

CHAPTER 58

MADDY

"Warner?"

I stare at my son in confusion when he bursts through the front door drenched in sweat and out of breath.

"Oh, hi, Ma."

"What... what happened?" I ask. "What's wrong?"

"What do you mean?" he asks, his hands on his hips as he struggles to breathe normally. "I just went for a run."

"But... you're not wearing workout clothes."

He looks down at his outfit like he's just realized this.

"Yeah. So?"

"And where is your Jeep?" I ask. "Didn't you take it somewhere?"

"Geez, Ma. What's with the twenty questions? I need a shower."

He disappears down the hall with a shake of his head.

What was that about?

I resume stirring the pot of water on the stove, waiting for it to boil so I can throw in some noodles and Warner and I can have a lame spaghetti dinner.

My phone dings with a notification. I pick it up off the counter and completely forget about the water altogether when I see who I have a Facebook message from.

Megan Young's friend replied to me. Paisley.

I can't open up the message quick enough.

Paisley: *What happened to Megan?*

It's a start.

I reply, seeing the little green dot that signifies she is still online. I type up as quickly as I can all about how I feel horrible breaking the news to her but want her to know that Megan was murdered. I try to be as caring and gentle as possible about it, even though what I really want to do is ask *my* questions. I have to be patient. I don't want her to ghost me before I've learned anything.

It takes her so long to reply that the pot of water bubbles over. I turn off the stove completely—I see the three dots on my screen that show she is typing a reply, and I don't want to miss it. Dinner will have to wait.

Finally, she responds.

Paisley: *Thank you for telling me. I am a little surprised her parents haven't made plans for a funeral or anything. But I'm not really surprised that Megan got herself into trouble like that.*
Me: *You're not?*
Paisley: *I knew that she didn't get along with her parents, but I didn't know it was bad enough to where they wouldn't even announce that she died, or invite any of her friends to a funeral for her.*
Me: *That's awful.*

I have to say something else so that she doesn't think it's the end of the discussion. I need my questions answered.

So I type again.

Me: *Why doesn't it surprise you that she ran into trouble?*
Paisley: *Because she was always getting into trouble. She ran away from home before she even finished high school. I didn't go over to her house much, but she was always complaining about her parents. About how horrible it was living with them. I tried to tell her that it couldn't be worse than being a homeless teenager without a high school diploma, but I guess maybe I was wrong about that.*
Me: *So, she was rebellious?*
Paisley: *That's what I thought. I thought it was just a stunt she pulled for attention and that she would come back. It took me a good six months to realize that she was 100% really never going to return home. And by then, I didn't blame her because even though it had been announced that she had gone missing, her parents did*

not put in much effort to find her. She reached out to me here and there. She told me she was sure her parents were glad to be rid of her. She knew they had stopped looking.

Me: *When was the last time you got an update from her?*

Paisley: *I'm not sure. About a year ago?*

Me: *What was she up to then?*

Paisley: *She didn't say much, she was mainly just excited that she had a phone again. I asked her where she got it and she said she was being paid and given food and a place to live to do work for somebody.*

Me: *Did she say what kind of work?*

Paisley: *She didn't get into specifics. All she told me was that she was doing somebody's dirty work.*

Oh my God.

Me: *Did she say where she found this person?*

Paisley: *She said THEY found HER. They picked her up off the street. She was in New York City at the time, I think.*

I can't believe it. Thanks to Megan's friend, I finally have an answer. I finally know how Megan ties into all of this.

Warner was right about one part of it: Carson *did* kill her for knowing too much.

But only after he hired her to learn it all first.

CHAPTER 59

MIA

I open my front door to Dean.

"Hey there, cop-assaulter," I greet him with a smirk.

"Are you ready to go?" he asks, rolling his eyes at my comment. I haven't been able to let it go that he punched Craig in the face. He got an earful of it from me while I iced his hand outside his car in the parking lot of the coffee shop after. I yelled at him for being so reckless. He's lucky he's not sitting in jail right now. This isn't high school anymore. He can't just go around punching people. Even *if* he is convinced they're trying to kill me.

But it didn't matter how much I argued with Dean about it. How much I yelled at him for getting in the middle of it like that. He still says he doesn't regret it one bit, and that Craig had it coming.

"I really don't know if we should do this," I tell him, not making the move to leave my house.

Dean had spent all of his free time yesterday in between classes and on his breaks pestering me to tell him everything I know about everything that has happened to Maddy's and my family. Eventually, it came up about Harley and Eric, and Dean decided he wanted to meet Harley and ask her some questions himself.

"We need to," he says, jiggling his keys. "Come on."

We walk his car together, and he holds the passenger door open for me. As we drive, he keeps tapping the edge of his iPhone to his chin, deep in thought.

"What's troubling you?" I ask. "Harley seemed more than fine with meeting us to answer more questions, so doesn't that right there make you feel any better?"

"I don't know," he says. "There's just something strange about how all this time, she knew Carson was alive, she talked to him, and his stepdad never found out about it. *Nobody* ever found out about it. I don't know. I don't like it."

"She made it sound as though she's been trying to protect Carson from her dad."

"How did Carson *accidentally* burn his house down and kill his own mother?"

"I don't know, Dean, I didn't ask her to walk me through exactly how that night went down."

"Maybe we should."

"But that doesn't have anything to do with us."

"Are you sure?"

"I—I'm pretty sure."

But now you have me questioning everything, not that that is anything new.

Harley has agreed to meet us at some dive bar in a slightly shady part of town. She had been the one to suggest the location. I was just grateful that she was willing to meet me again, so I wasn't about to try and convince her to go somewhere else. Maybe it's close to where she is staying.

Dean and I go inside and get comfortable at a high-top table, and it doesn't take long at all for Harley to join us.

"Do you want to get a drink first before we dive into things?" Dean asks her after I make the introductions.

"I'm fine, thank you," she says.

"Thank you for meeting with us," I say.

"Sure. You caught me at a good time because I am going to be heading back home soon."

"Why *are* you still in town?" Dean asks. "If you don't mind me asking."

"My brother killed himself. And I wanted answers. Just like I know you guys do."

"I'm sorry about that," Dean says. I know he doesn't mean it.

"Thank you," she says, even though I'm sure *she* knows he doesn't mean it either.

"Why do you think he did it?" Dean asks.

He's much bolder than I am. I wouldn't have been brave enough to ask Carson's sister that.

"I don't know. Maybe all of his guilt caught up with him," Harley says.

"Guilt about what?" Dean asks.

"About what he's been doing. Messing with your families. Kidnapping that girl. Your daughter, right? Killing that other one."

"Wait," Dean holds up a hand, his eyes bulging. "Killing *what* girl?"

Harley shrugs. "That Megan Young girl. I suppose it's fine that I tell you now, since my brother is no longer around. But...he told me how he killed her. And how he hadn't meant to. How he doesn't even remember doing it. He was really worked up about it."

"So, you mean to say that he *confessed* to being a murderer to you, and you did *nothing* about it?" Dean asks.

I've been stunned into complete silence.

"I'm sure if *you* had a brother who killed someone, you'd keep their secret," she says.

Maddy is not my sister, but she watched me hit Carson with that shovel. And even when she thought he was dead, she never told a soul. So, I get why Harley didn't, either.

"Uh huh," Dean continues. "And even when he was going around harassing and attacking and kidnapping the Baileys and the Carpenters, you just stood by his side?"

"I didn't know he was doing all of that. He never told me. Or—he never told me *directly*."

"What the heck does that even mean?" Dean demands. I can tell he doesn't like this girl one bit.

"He *did* mention that he'd been coercing Nora into being with him and helping him out several times over the years. I think he felt bad about that."

"I'm sorry," I finally say. "Are you—are you telling me that *Nora* has also known this whole time he was alive?"

"Yeah."

I look at Dean. "All this time..." I trail off, trying to comprehend it. Trying to make sense of it. "Dean, when I told her that Carson was still alive, she freaked out on me. She slapped me, even. She said I was crazy. Because he was dead."

"You're absolutely sure she knew?" Dean asks Harley.

"Positive."

All these years, my sister has been lying to me. All these years, she's been involved with somebody who tried to hurt us.

She told everyone he was dead. She had been a wreck over it. Her mental health disintegrated. She went into an *institution* for crying out loud! And all of it was an act?

CHAPTER 60

WARNER

This can't be happening. Not again.

I read the text message I received from an unknown number over again as I stand in my bathroom with a towel wrapped around me. I only got out of the shower when the hot water had finally done its job of calming me down after my confrontation with Audrey, who isn't who I thought she was. And now I have to deal with this?

Unknown: *You might think it's over, but I assure you it's far from it.*

Normally, Audrey would be the first person I call about this kind of thing. Or I'd mention it in the group text between her, Lyla, and me. But I'm still furious with her.

Things are still pretty rough with Lyla right now, too. But I need to tell one of them. This is bigger than our stupid little spat.

To my surprise, Lyla answers when I call.

"I thought I was going to have to leave you a voicemail," I say.

"I answered because it could be an emergency," she says. "Is it not?"

"Not exactly, but it is about Carson."

"Great. What happened?" She sounds devoid of emotion. Which means she's still furious.

"I...I just got a text from an unknown number."

"Did it say some crap about how we're stupid for thinking that everything is over?"

"So, you got it, too?"

"Yeah. I was just about to send a screenshot to you and Ree."

"Who do you think it's from?"

"I don't know anymore."

"Do you think Audrey got it too, then? Our moms even?"

"Whoever it is really should just have us all in one big group chat. It'd be much more efficient, don't you think?"

"Ha."

"Where are you right now?" she asks.

"I'm at home. Why?"

"Is your mom there with you?"

"Yes?"

"Okay. Just making sure. Keep an eye on her, okay? And make sure all your doors and windows are locked. I don't know if that message was a threat or a warning. I'm afraid something... bad is going to happen."

I swallow. "Well, what about you?"

"Huh?"

"Are *you* somewhere safe?"

"Yeah. I'm at my dad's. Everyone's here. Even his lovely girlfriend."

"Okay, good."

We're both silent. I wonder if I should continue trying to apologize to her about the Audrey situation. I also wonder if she's debating on saying anything to me about it, too. I want to ask her if she's talked to Wrigley. If she's still going to be with him.

But it's none of my business.

"Okay then..." Lyla says when it's been quiet for too long. "I'm gonna go."

"All right. Call me if anything happens."

"You too."

We hang up, and the second I do, I wish I hadn't. I wish we could just clear the air.

I go back to the text again. How is whoever it is even able to text us from an unknown number? Whether it's Carson or Craig, what are they using to send the messages? A burner phone? A certain app? Did they contact their carrier and ask for a way to make their number show up as UNKNOWN whenever they contact someone?

My mind quickly flashes back to when I had that meeting with Parker inside Delilah's.

I think I have an idea.

CHAPTER 61

LYLA

I jump when loud, sudden thunder rattles the window inside my bedroom at my dad's. I've just spent an annoying forty-five minutes hanging out in the living room with Joey, Dad, and his girlfriend, Heather. It's not necessarily that I find Heather annoying, because if she were anyone except for my father's girl-friend, I think I would kinda like her. But since she *is* my father's girlfriend, and I don't want my father to be with anyone except for Mom, it's impossible for me to like her. And it got even harder to pretend to be nice, to pretend that I was enjoying myself after I got that creepy text message from the unknown number. but I didn't want any of them to know that it had happened. I didn't want Dad to get all worried again. So, I kept the fake smile plastered on my face, and I was finally able to escape them when Warner called me just now, and I snuck away to my bedroom.

I jump again when I see my sister standing in the doorway.

"Jeez, Ree!" I cry.

"It's crazy out there," she says, setting her car keys on the dresser and taking her jacket off.

"Where were you?" I ask. Her hair is windswept. She was clearly outside somewhere.

"Oh," she says in a casual voice as she walks over to her bed and flops down on her butt, tucking her feet under her, "ya know... just telling Warner that I knew Dean was his dad before he found out."

I gape at her. "Um... I'm sorry, *what?*"

She nods and shrugs. "He's furious, go figure. But... I didn't want to keep that secret anymore. He's so sick of everyone lying to him, Ly. You saw him at Mom's. He's been lied to his whole life. By the people he cares about most. I needed to tell him the truth. No more secrets, remember?"

"But... I was just on the phone with him... We both got creepy texts. He didn't say anything..." I trail off, trying to think how he sounded when we were on the phone. Trying to figure out why he didn't tell me about Audrey knowing about Dean. Or about how he had just been with her. But then I shake my head because I need to focus on what it is I *actually* want to ask Audrey. "Did *you* get a text?"

"I did. And I had Siri read it to me while I was driving. Wasn't the best idea."

"Because it said that it's not over?"

"Exactly. So, yours said the same thing? So did Warner's?"

"Yep."

"Oh Joy," she says sarcastically. "I'm not surprised Warner only talked to *you* about it. Honestly, I wouldn't be surprised if he never talks to me again. But that's okay."

"You don't mean that," I say, shaking my head at her.

"Not really," she admits. "It would suck if he wanted to stop being friends over it. But...Lyla. I want you to know that it's okay if you want to be with him. I'm serious."

"Oh." This is weird. Awkward. "Audrey, I—"

"He liked you first. A long time ago. Who am I to get in the way of that? I just want you to be happy, Sis."

"But... I want you to be happy, too."

"Don't worry about me, okay? I'll be fine."

Before I can say anything else about it, she changes the subject.

"Do you know what he said to me before he... ran off?"

"Ran off?"

"That's beside the point," she says. "He said something crazy, and I don't know if he made it up to make me mad or if it's true. But my gut's telling me it *is* true. And it kinda makes a lot of sense."

"What?"

"He told me that Mom and Mr. Reeves are dating."

"*Dating*?!"

"Yeah. They're like... *together.*"

"I..."

"Weird, right?"

"Yeah..."

Again, this shouldn't be what I'm focusing on right now. "Do you think Mom *also* got a text?"

"Does she usually get creepy texts like we do?"

"I don't know."

"Let's call her. I want to ask her about Mr. Reeves anyway." She pulls her phone out and puts it on speaker.

"Hey, sweetie," Mom says.

"Did you get a creepy text?" Audrey automatically asks. Then she throws in, almost as if it's an afterthought, "and are you dating Mr. Reeves?"

I slap a palm to my forehead at her directness.

"Uh...um..." Mom stutters uncomfortably. Which can only mean one thing.

She is.

"I-I *did* get a message, yes," she answers, only to the first question. "Maddy did, too."

"And my other question?" Audrey asks.

"I...um—you know what? Can you tell your dad that I need you two to come over? I'm going to have Maddy and Warner come over, too. I think we all need to have a meeting."

"Right *now*?" Audrey looks at me with an eyebrow raised.

"Yes."

We try to explain to her that Dad is going to be angry if we leave, but she half-jokingly says he's more than welcome to come, too. That he, Joey, and Heather all can join. She won't take no for an answer.

We get off the phone with her and hesitantly try to explain to Dad without giving away too much information that it's important we go back to Mom's. Just like we guessed, he gets angry and annoyed, but when we tell him that he, Heather, and Joey can come along, he caves and lets us leave. But he doesn't come with.

When we get to Mom's, I see a Lyft driver dropping off Maddy and Warner.

"Where is your Jeep?" I ask Warner, automatically thinking something bad happened to it. That he was in an accident. That Carson or Craig tried to run him off the road again.

"Oh…" Warner carefully avoids Audrey's eye contact, which gives me the answer. Now it makes sense why Audrey said he "ran off" earlier. He must have left it wherever he and Audrey met up.

We go inside together. I lead the way, hearing Mom say, "We're in here," from the living room.

We?

When I turn the corner with everyone, we see Mom and Mr. Reeves sitting next to each other—their knees touching—on our sectional.

"Oh boy," I say with a sigh. "This is… neat."

Dean and my mom look apologetic.

"Dean?" Maddy asks with an eyebrow raised. If Maddy didn't know Dean and my mom were dating, then how did Warner find out?

"So…" Mom says, slowly getting to her feet. The rest of us remain standing, eyeing them. "I think we have a lot to discuss."

"Yeah, *I'd* say," Maddy says, not hiding her surprise. "Why are *you* here?" she asks Mr. Reeves.

"Uh…" Mr. Reeves gets to his feet as well. He probably doesn't want to be the only one sitting. "The thing is…"

"You and my mom are dating," Audrey says for him. "Warner told us already."

Mr. Reeves looks at Warner. I can tell he didn't know Warner knew.

"How *did* you know?" I ask Warner.

"I…" Warner clears his throat. "I followed him. He went to go see Amelia when she was at that… place. It was just a hunch."

"You *followed* me?" Dean's eyes narrow. "Why—why didn't you say anything?"

"Hang on," Maddy says, interrupting. "You're *dating*?"

Mom bites her bottom lip and nods. "Yes."

"Since… since when?" Maddy asks.

"Oh, it's very recent," Mom explains, looking at all of us. "And I know it may come as a bit of a shock to all of you—minus Warner, apparently."

"I *knew* he liked you," Audrey says, a hand on her hip.

Mr. Reeves blushes slightly.

"But there are also other things I want to discuss tonight, so let's move on before we're up until three in the morning getting this all sorted out." She motions for everyone to sit. We all take our places, but the tension is heavy in the air.

First, Mom tells us about how she and Dean just met with Harley. About how Harley knows Carson killed Sydney. And then she tells us about how Aunt Nora knew Carson was alive this whole time, thinking that she's breaking some big news to us. Then we have to tell her how we actually already knew, and I have to explain how Aunt Nora is dating Detective Fritz. And that I've been seeing her in secret. And then I fill them in on everything Aunt Nora told me in the car after we were attacked at her rental.

Once they get over the shock of what I've admitted, Maddy tells us what she learned from Sydney's former best friend. And finally, I understand Sydney's role in all of this. She ran away from home. She needed money and food and shelter. A stranger approached her and offered her all of it. She accepted, thinking she would just play this role as some random teenager in some random high school and learn information about some random kids to pass along to Carson. And in exchange, she'd make some quick cash. She'd have a place to temporarily live. But what she *didn't* know was that once Carson no longer needed her, he was going to kill her.

It's horrific. And it only confirms our suspicions. Carson really is a murderer. He murdered his mother. He murdered Sydney. Craig is covering for him, probably manipulated into thinking that he's doing the right thing for his "buddy." Carson is still alive, and he's still trying to end all of us.

AUDREY

I t's still incredibly windy and stormy out the next morning. It rained all night, and it's been raining on and off since I woke up. It's an especially cold and dreary day. I feel dread the second I roll out of bed. I tossed and turned all night, trying to sort everything out in my head. Trying not to feel that ache in my stomach every time I thought about Warner. He didn't look at me once last night. He basically pretended as if I didn't even exist. But I deserve it. I should have told him the truth about his dad a long time ago. Warner is totally right, it wasn't fair for him to have to learn it from Freaky Fritz.

When Lyla and I get to school, I stay close by her side, as if she can hide me from all of the stares. But the two of us together is like a circus act for everyone. We are these poor, tortured souls, and we're on display for everyone's amusement.

"Do you guys want me to say something?" Danielle asks us as we all huddle by Lyla's and my locker. The halls are extra full this morning before the first bell because no one wants to stand outside in the rain. It smells disgustingly like wet dog in here. Danielle is referring to everyone who is talking about us and snapping pictures, not even trying to be discreet.

"You could try, but it wouldn't stop them," Lyla says flatly.

Danielle pouts. "Are you guys okay?"

"Not exactly," I admit.

Look at me, being honest and stuff.

"Because of all the people talking about you guys?" Danielle asks. "Or is it something else?"

"It's a million things," I say. "For example, you know I've been hanging out with Warner a lot lately, right?"

Danielle nods. Next to her, Lyla busies herself inside her locker.

No more secrets.

Danielle is our friend. And she has been for a long time. And she chose me and Lyla over Sophia.

"Well, I sorta had a small crush on him," I continue, "which is weird because I really do have a crush on Ryan, too. Needless to say, it's been really confusing. Um...anyway, Warner and I kissed."

Lyla peeks at me from her locker. I can see the surprise on her face. She probably wasn't expecting me to admit my wrongdoings to Danielle like this.

But oh, am I doing it.

"And I know it's wrong because I have that thing with Ryan... but it was also wrong because, even though I didn't know it, Lyla has—or had—feelings for him."

"Oh my God," Danielle says, looking back-and-forth between me and my twin.

"But I've forgiven her," Lyla says. "And Warner is an idiot."

"Do you still like him?" Danielle asks her.

"I..." She trails off. Does that mean yes?

"I thought you were with Wrigley," Danielle says.

"I know. I *know*," Lyla groans. "I made it impossible for anyone to realize my feelings for Warner. I get it. But I *had* to keep them to myself because of Jackson. He was his *best* friend. I didn't want to be that person who came between them. But their friendship ended anyway. I don't know...I was stupid. I should've just been more honest from the beginning."

"So... does Warner *know* you like him?" Danielle asks.

Lyla blushes a little bit. "I think I made it pretty obvious when I found out they kissed."

"And you haven't talked to him about it?"

"What am I supposed to say?"

"That you...like him?" Danielle asks back. She then addresses me again. "Or is she not allowed to?"

"I-I never said that," I stammer. "Warner and I are totally done. I sort of burned that bridge."

"How?" Danielle asks.

"Long story." I don't feel like getting into how I already knew Dean was his dad. Because then I'd have to *really* tell Danielle everything, and there isn't much time before the bell rings.

"Okay..." Danielle is a deep thought.

"I feel sick to my stomach," Lyla says.

"Why?" I ask. Danielle tilts her head at her.

"I just have this impending doom feeling. My anxiety is, like, through the roof."

"That's exactly how I feel," I say.

"So, who does *Warner* like?" Danielle asks, still stuck on that.

Lyla and I look at each other. Deep down, I know the truth. I know how Warner feels about my sister. I know that I was just a blip in the matrix.

"I *thought* he liked... me," Lyla says, "stupidly. Because then he kissed my sister instead."

"What if he just kissed Audrey to make you jealous?" Danielle asks.

"Ouch," I say.

"Sorry, Audrey. Just trying to explore the possibilities."

"It honestly doesn't even matter," Lyla says. "There is so much other stuff we have to deal with."

Danielle nods slowly, looking down the hall. I follow her eyes and see that she is staring at Sophia, who is with Jackson. But she's not with Olive.

"Do you think Jackson is her only friend now?" I ask about Sophia.

"Where is Olive?" Lyla asks. Could it be that Olive finally saw Sophia's cruel ways?

"Who cares about them?" Danielle says. "Jackson and Warner aren't friends anymore."

"So?" Lyla and I say.

"And you burned the bridge with him, Audrey, right?" she asks.

"Yes."

"And *you* like Warner, Lyla, right?"

"No. I hate him."

Danielle rolls her eyes. She doesn't believe it for a second. "I don't know ... Ly, pretty much everyone already sees you and Warner as a couple, did you know that?"

"What are you talking about?" she asks.

"People talk about it all the time. Ever since it got out that he sent Jackson that text message about being in love with you."

"He didn't *actually* send that," she clarifies.

"*Sure.*"

"He didn't!"

"Anyway. Then you started hanging around Wrigley. Everyone thinks it's super weird."

"Why? Wrigley is so much less... complicated," Lyla tries.

"Ooh!" Danielle's face lights up as if she's just had an epiphany. "I bet Warner was heartbroken that you picked Wrigley over him. I bet when you got kidnapped, he thought he lost you, and then you were saved, and he thought, 'Here's my chance!' But then you picked Wrigley. And being all sad about it, Warner turned to Audrey. Sorry again, Audrey, to make you sound like a total rebound."

"Honestly, I probably *was* a rebound," I say.

Lyla winces.

"It's okay," I reassure her.

The bell rings.

"I... I'm going to go to class," Lyla says. "Where I have to deal with Jackson *and* Wrigley."

"Good luck," I say. Danielle gives her shoulder a squeeze.

I walk to Precalc, thinking over what Danielle said. It's a crummy feeling to be used like that by Warner. But I'm the idiot for letting it happen. Danielle said it herself—the whole school thinks that Lyla and Warner should be together. That their love makes the most sense. I should have realized that much sooner. I just want my sister to be happy. It doesn't matter how I feel.

"Do you know where Mr. Reeves is?" Lyla asks me at lunch. We're the only ones at this table. Danielle is still in the lunch line, but she'll be joining us shortly.

"What do you mean?" I ask.

"He's not here today. We had a sub in English."

"Huh. He seemed fine last night."

"Exactly."

"And where is Warner?" I ask, looking around the cafeteria again. *Are they both gone?*

"I haven't heard from him."

"Me neither."

Not that I would.

There's more thunder outside. I can see through the window that the trees are nearly falling over from how strong the wind is. Sneakers are squeaking repeatedly on the wet tile flooring. The lunchroom is extra loud because again, no one is outside. I still feel anxious. I don't like not knowing where Warner is. And usually, I wouldn't care about Mr. Reeves being gone, but with him learning so much about everything last night, it feels weird that he suddenly wouldn't be here today.

Something just doesn't feel right.

All throughout lunch, I look around for signs for Warner, but still, he's doesn't show. I think about texting him to check in, but he doesn't want to talk to me. I think about suggesting Lyla check in, but I don't want to make things awkward. It's still weird to talk to her about him. It's almost nice that Danielle is here to change the subject to mundane, typical high school talk so that there's no room to even discuss anything about last night. Anything about Carson.

When I go to English after lunch and see if the random sub sitting at his desk, it feels weird. Where is Mr. Reeves? Where is Warner? What is happening? What did Carson mean when he sent that text?

How come this Harley chick just seemed to appear out of nowhere? Is Eric still in town? Why is Harley still in town?

I text Mom to ask about Mr. Reeves, but she doesn't reply. And that makes me feel even worse. I should be able to rely on my mom texting me back so I can always know that she's okay.

When the bell rings at the end of class and I go into the hall, I call Lyla. "Meet me before fifth hour," I tell her.

We get to our lockers at the same time.

"What's up?" she asks.

"I think I need to meet with Eric again." It makes me nauseated to think about it, but I still have his contact information, and I want to know if he's still in town. And if he is, then I feel like I need to talk to him again.

"No," Lyla says. "Audrey, *no*. That's a bad idea."

"But why are we trusting his Harley chick?" I ask. "She let Carson get away with *killing* Sydney. She claims she had no idea Carson was torturing us, but I don't believe it. I don't know. She could be telling the truth. But I think I need to confront Eric about it. I want to get the truth from him. I want to know if he lied to me. And why."

"Audrey, I—" someone taps on my shoulder, interrupting my sister.

I turn around and see Ryan.

Okay, I am literally *going to throw up. I can't take any more of this*.

"Ryan," I say uneasily. I haven't talked to him since my breakdown, but it's not for lack of trying on his part.

"Hey, is it cool if I talk to you for a sec?" he asks.

"It's fine," Lyla answers for me, getting a book out of her locker. "I'll see you later." Then she abandons me.

That brat.

"Hi," I say to Ryan, tucking some hair behind my ear.

Thunder rumbles, and we both look up at the noise.

"Hey. You've been avoiding me," he says.

"Um, yeah, I..." *No more secrets.* "I have," I admit. It feels kind of nice, just being honest instead of trying to find an excuse.

"And you told Kiley she can 'have' me."

"I'm sorry about that," I say. "I... I didn't mean it. I was just angry. She really likes you. And she hates you talking to me."

"I tried talking to her about that," he says, "but I think it just made things worse. I'm sorry. I—I didn't know she was so upset about it. But it still holds true, what I told you; I don't have feelings for her. And I'm sorry she's making it difficult for you to be with me."

"Honestly, Ryan?"

He purses his lips. I can see the dread on his face.

I continue. "There are a lot of things that are making it difficult for me to be with you. And it's not *all* because of you. Or Kylie. It's everything I'm dealing with. I don't think I can be with anyone right now."

"I had a feeling this was coming."

"I'm really sorry."

He hangs his head and shoves his hand into his pockets. "Yeah."

"You are a really good guy," I say, meaning it. "And I had the biggest crush on you earlier this year. Probably even *before* this year. So, trust me when I say that it's *not* you."

"I guess clichés are clichés because they happen so often, right?"

I attempt a smile.

The bell rings. I realize that we are the only two people out here. I am late to class. But it's fine because it's good that Ryan and I are having this talk. I know I'm not still sneaking around with Warner, so technically, I *could* still be with Ryan. But I meant everything I just told him. It's just not the right time. I am hurt about Warner, and it wouldn't be fair to be with somebody else when my heart is aching over him.

"All right, Audrey," Ryan says, nodding slowly. "I get it. But I really like you."

My stomach knots. I don't know what to say.

So, he continues. "I can't really picture myself moving on. And I get that you're going through a lot. That you need some time. But I just want you to know—I'll still be here. Okay?"

I'm surprised to hear it. From somebody like Ryan Copeland, who all the girls drool over, who is going to be graduating soon and going away to college and meeting all kinds of other girls, I figured he would tell me off and be dating somebody else by tomorrow. I can't believe it. I've actually won his heart. I don't think I truly realized how much he likes me until right this moment. Because my head has been too clouded by my feelings for Warner.

I smile bigger now. "Thank you," I say.

Who knows? Maybe Ryan and I *could* still have something in the future. I guess only time will tell.

Chapter 63

Lyla

Wrigley wasn't in first hour, but I know he ditched class because I saw him in the hallways earlier. And it annoys me because he's already in trouble with his dad, so why is he risking getting into *more* trouble? To avoid me?

Jackson *was* in first hour. But he was on the other side of the room and behind me, so I just faced forward the entire period.

But now, in Algebra II, I have both Wrigley and Jackson in my class again. And Wrigley decided to show up to this one. Jackson is within my line of sight in this class, and I can tell with my peripherals that he keeps staring at me.

So does Wrigley.

I hate it.

Just to give myself something to do, and not because I like Warner and am worried about him, I take out my phone and text him under the table, ignoring the lesson our teacher is giving even though we're about to have a practice test on it.

Me: *Are you OK? Where are you? Where is your dad?*
Warner: *No idea where DEAN is at. Don't call him that.*
Me: *LOL*
Warner: *ANYWAY, I'm fine. Wasn't at lunch because I am trying to work out something. I got an idea after we talked last night.*
Me: *What's the idea?*

I wait, but I don't hear back from him. Then the practice test gets passed out. The whole time I work on it, I'm distracted because of stupid Wrigley and Jackson. I don't ever want to talk to Jackson again. And Wrigley... I don't even know what's going on with him. With us.

I'm half-tempted to snap my head to him and ask him what he wants. Why he's been ignoring me. Why things have been weird. Is it still because of Warner?

Maybe I should just tell Wrigley the truth—that he was right to be suspicious.

Because I do have feelings for Warner.

I have feelings for Warner.

The thought makes me both lightheaded and nauseated. It's like I'm finally letting myself accept the truth.

I am doing horrible with my list. When I was in the shed, it was on my list of promises to leave things with Warner alone. That I would go after Wrigley because he was a safer, easier choice. It's just yet another promise I don't think I can keep.

When the practice test is over, my teacher tells us that we need to pair up to grade each other's work, and I *try* to pair with the person to my left, but Wrigley, to my right, nudges my elbow with his. "Partners?"

"*Me?*" I ask sarcastically.

"Oh, come *on*," he says like I'm being ridiculous. But I *know* I'm not being ridiculous. He's been ignoring me all week.

He moves his desk closer to mine, like everyone else is doing with their partners. I stay rooted in my seat.

He hands me his test. I hand him mine. I try to stay focused on the grading, but how am I supposed to know if he got anything right when I have no idea how to do any of this?

"So, how are you doing?" Wrigley asks.

Oh, now *you want to know?*

"Fine," I say.

"What?" he asks.

"Uh... I just haven't really... talked to you much ... like... all week."

"That's not true. We've talked."

"Hardly." *And if you're basically my boyfriend, wouldn't you think it was weird how little we've communicated?*

I don't get him.

"It's just been a weird week, right?" he asks.

"I guess."

I continue failing at grading his paper, but when I see something black and shiny and lit up on Wrigley's desk, I snap my head back to him. He has his phone out, and he's texting someone.

"You got your *phone* back?"

I'm seething. Heat creeps into my cheeks. His dad gave him back his phone, and he never called me or texted me to tell me so?

"Oh." He puts it back in his pocket. "Yeah. Got it back yesterday."

"Are you kidding me?"

"What?"

"Why are you playing dumb?"

"What are you talking about? Lyla, I *just* got it back. I've had a long week. My dad is furious at me. He won't leave me alone. I got it back last night and went to bed. And then this morning, I was running late for school, and something came up first hour..."

"I'm just hearing excuse after excuse after excuse."

He nods his head toward my pocket. "You seemed to be pretty busy texting someone else anyway."

I just want to scream at him. "You know *what?*" I snap without thinking. "I *am*." I slap his test back on his desk and rip mine from him. "Grade your own paper."

I pick up my desk and move it away from him even though technically my desk is already in the spot it's supposed to be.

When I side-glance at Wrigley, I can see he's just as mad as I am. Good. My response worked. He thinks I'm busy texting Warner. Which is true.

I'm done with Wrigley. I'm done with his vague answers and jealous tendencies. I really liked him at first. But now, as I think it over, I think I just liked that he was someone new. Someone different. Somebody who liked the new Lyla. I don't really think I even stopped to consider if I actually, truly liked him back.

Maybe Audrey was Warner's rebound.

And maybe Wrigley was mine.

CHAPTER 64

AMELIA

"Any answer?"

I sigh and shake my head at Dean. "But we figured this, didn't we?" I ask him. "She hates me. She doesn't want to speak to me."

We are at my house. Dean took the day off so that he could help me get this all figured out. We decided late last night after the girls went to bed, after our long talk getting everything sorted out, that it would be worth it to talk to Nora and Craig and confront them about knowing about their relationship. But naturally, my sister won't answer my calls. And neither will Craig. Dean has tried them as well, but he hasn't gotten any answers either.

"But it doesn't make any sense that she would hate you," Dean shakes his head, looking a bit exasperated, and then he stands up from the counter and starts pacing through the kitchen. I'm still sitting at the counter, wanting to pull my hair out. We've been at this for a while now.

"I don't know," I say. "I just don't understand it."

"Nora knew Carson was alive but then slapped you when you tried to tell her so. "

"Maybe she wanted me to get that idea out of my head so that I would leave it alone because she was worried Carson would find out I knew and blame her."

"If she was scared of him, if she was *really* in trouble, why didn't she say anything? To anyone?"

"You know Nora... Even when we were younger, when she first started dating Carson. She wouldn't tell anyone what he was doing to her. Not until that night, when it got really, really bad."

"So, okay—Nora was supposed to meet Carson at that cabin the night of prom. And even after their fight, she still went. And this was well after you and Maddy already disappeared." He's not wording anything like a question, but I nod my head anyway.

"Nora was still so in love with him even though he was hurting her," I say. "And that's why she never told anyone what he was doing. She probably had immediate regrets that she even told us about it that night, when we found her in the bathroom with the broken nose. I just—she was willing to ruin her *whole* life... *just* to keep his secret. Part of me thinks that she *did* belong in that place she was sent, because she was so willing to go there for him in the first place. Does that make sense?"

He nods. Then we just stare at each other for a while. I think we're both thinking the same thing.

"We have to go to Craig's house, don't we?" I ask.

He bites his thumb nail. "I think so."

We grab a quick bite to eat somewhere on the way; Dean insists since I haven't eaten anything in nearly twenty-four hours. I manage to scarf down half of a sub and a few bites of a salad, and then we get back in Dean's car and make our way to Craig's house.

"I could have figured this out a lot sooner if I had just driven past here before," I point out as we pull up to the curb and I see Nora's car in his driveway—that beat up, old jalopy that used to be parked out front of our house when she was staying in my guestroom.

Dean doesn't say anything. I move to get out of the car, but I stop when I notice Dean isn't doing the same.

I touch his forearm. "Hey, are you okay?"

"I—yeah. Sorry."

"What's on your mind?"

"Nora. We went from being best friends, to not speaking for years. We used to tell each other everything, ya know? And then suddenly, she was keeping all of these secrets even though I never gave her any reason not to trust me. I just don't know when that changed."

"Are you nervous about seeing her again?" I ask.

"Not... *nervous*, really. More just... confused? I don't know."

"Do you want to wait in the car? You don't have to do any of this, Dean. I'm serious. You don't have to be involved in all of my drama."

He offers me a smile. "Yes, I do," he says. "I have to be there for you. Always."

He's so thoughtful. So considerate. So helpful. And so dang sweet. I lean over the console and kiss him softly on the lips. His fingers weave through my hair before landing gently on the back of my neck. The kiss deepens, and for a minute, we both fall completely away from this wretched world. We land in one that is all our own. And I like it here. I like it when it is just Dean and Mia, and nothing else matters.

But then the kiss ends. And we have to go knock on that door.

"Are you ready?" I ask him.

"Are you?"

I swallow and look at Craig's screened-in front door. "No idea," I admit. But I get out of the car anyway. And so does Dean.

We cross his yard, step onto the porch, and ring the doorbell. Feeling antsy, I tap my foot and stare at Dean as we wait.

To reassure me, he gives my hand a squeeze. And then he doesn't let it go.

A couple minutes go by. No one answers.

He rings the doorbell again. I knock on the screen door.

Still, no one comes.

"Craig?" I call. "Nora? Are you there?"

Still, no one comes.

"Where do you think they went?" Dean asks.

I shrug, looking at the window, where the blinds are closed. But... did they just move slightly?

"Nora? It's me, Mia," I say, stepping closer to the door. I am riddled with apprehension. I am nauseated. Clammy. Something just doesn't feel right. "I just want to talk." My voice is quiet. I think I sound a little sad. Dean squeezes my hand even tighter.

Tears spring to my eyes, and I quickly turn from the door, and from Dean, and start down his lawn toward the sidewalk.

"Mia?" Dean calls after me.

When I reach his car, I turn around to him. "What if she's in there, Dean?" I ask as the tears fall. "What if Craig has her? What if he's not letting her answer the door? I can't shake the feeling that something is wrong. Like really, *really* wrong."

He hugs me, but I really don't feel like getting the physical attention right now, so I'm stiff in his arms, still crying. Still feeling panicked and sick. "All I ever did was try and protect her," I say. "What if she doesn't want to see me? What if Craig and Carson have turned her against me?"

Even though now is not the time for it, it feels like all of these years of pent-up feelings toward my sister are overflowing and I can't keep my thoughts—or my tears—about it to myself any longer.

"I rearranged my *entire* life to cater to her. To help my parents with my paychecks that afforded to keep her in that place. And she didn't even *have* to be there! I just don't understand it!"

I feel him nodding his head on top of mine. "I know," he says, brushing my hair with his hand. "I know."

"And she was *with* Carson when he was doing all of this stuff to my daughters. To me. How did it take her so long to realize Carson was behind the attacks?"

"I don't know." His voice is practically a whisper. I slowly melt into him, realizing that maybe I *do* need the hug after all.

"I'm so confused."

"Well, hey, we're not done yet," he says.

I sniff, wipe my eyes, and pull away so I can look up at him.

He continues. "So, we're not gonna get answers from Nora or Craig—at least not right now. Who else can we talk to? I think... maybe we should try and meet up with Harley again. If she's still around. Ask her some more questions about Sydney. What do you think?"

"I... I guess. Yeah."

"We're going to figure this out, Mia. Today. I promise."

Thunder cracks overhead. It's loud and dark and foreboding. I wonder if it is sealing Dean's promise.

Or if it's a warning.

CHAPTER 65

AUDREY

Because of the bad weather, cheer is held in the gym again. After I get changed in the locker room, I meet up with Danielle and we walk there together. We start stretching, like usual, and then the doors open loudly, and the sound of two people cackling together echoes through the gym. Danielle and I turn to the sound.

"Oh, would you look at that," Danielle mutters, her tone full of disgust.

"*Lovely*," I say sarcastically. The two girls laughing are Kiley and Sophia. They have their arms linked together as they find a spot to start stretching, not too far away from Danielle and me. They look like they've been best friends forever. But I've never seen them talk before in my life. Not unless it was something cheer-related

"I wonder when *that* became a thing," Danielle says.

"I don't know, but do you see the way they're looking at me?"

I watch Danielle sneak another peek. Surely, she can see the way Kylie and Sophia keep shooting dirty looks over in our direction.

"Oh, I get it now," Danielle says as she turns back to me. "They started an 'I hate Audrey' club. That must be it."

Danielle and I giggle, which I'm sure ticks Sophia off. Heaven forbid I be happy about something. Heaven forbid I'm not shaking at the knees because of the sight of the two of them together. I don't care. I have bigger problems than them.

"I know lots of people who would like to join that club," I say to Danielle.

"Oh, *stop*. People love you."

"Oh yeah—especially the one who's trying to kill me."

She winces. "H-how are you doing with all of that, by the way?"

I shrug. Miss Green, our coach, has just walked in, and it's time to get practice started. But I want to run something by Danielle, just to get a second opinion.

"So, you know that Eric guy?" I ask her. She's been filled in pretty thoroughly now about everything that's happened. Everything that is *still* happening. Lyla and I have taken turns filling her in and answering all of her questions.

"That's... Carson Price's former... stepdad?" she confirms.

"Yes."

"The one who might have killed Carson?"

"Maybe. But I don't think Carson is really dead. So, Eric is the one who supposedly *wants* him dead."

"Okay... What about him?"

"I've been thinking about it all day. And I know that my sister, and my mom, and... Warner... probably wouldn't want me to, but I think I want to talk to him again."

"Really?"

"Is it really that crazy? I don't know... I just feel like I want to confront him, I guess. I want him to know that I know the other side of the story. That I know what Harley told us. And I want to see if that changes anything. Eric might not even know that she's been around."

Danielle stands and tightens her ponytail. She appears to be in deep thought about it.

I get up, too. Then I bend over and touch my toes.

"I think it might be worth it," she finally says. It makes me snap back up so I can look at her. I was expecting her to tell me all the reasons why it was too dangerous or a bad idea. Instead, she just shrugs. "Sure, Eric may have killed someone, or he *wants* to kill someone, but it's not you. And you deserve answers, right?"

"I...I *do* deserve answers."

Practice begins, but the second I have a chance, I sneak away into the locker room so I can take my phone out of my locker and send Eric a message. Danielle's words replay in my mind the entire time. I deserve to know who's doing this to all of us. I deserve to know the truth.

Me: *Can we meet again? I have more questions.*

My hands are surprisingly steady as I hold my phone and wait for his reply. I expected myself to feel a lot more nervous about this. Scared. But I'm not. I just feel determined. Even the thunder outside isn't sending chills down my spine.

Eric: *I can do that. Do you want to come to my hotel again?*
Me: *No. I don't want to risk being followed. And I don't want you followed either. So you have to make sure you're not.*
Eric: *Just tell me where to go.*
Me: *There's a place called The Swimming Hole. I bet you could look it up on Google. It's closed down until the summer. Let's meet there. After it's dark.*
Eric: *"Thumbs Up" emoji*

"I'm really doing this," I whisper to myself, looking around the locker room. I know I promised no more lies. But just one more might ensure that all of the answers we've been looking for are finally brought to light.

CHAPTER 66

WARNER

We still have a full football practice even though Dean isn't here, and the lightning is bad. The rain has been on and off, creating a muddy field, and all of my teammates and I are filthy when we head into the locker room after.

Ryan had been off his game this practice. Maybe it was because Dean wasn't there to coach him along. Or maybe it was something else. He doesn't seem to be paying me much attention, so I don't think that Audrey told him anything about us.

Thinking about Audrey, my stomach twists. Anger pulses through my body. I'm still so mad at her. And I'm annoyed. Because I think she *wanted* me to be mad. Or else why would she tell me? I think she wanted me to have a reason to stop talking to her.

I clench my jaw and sit down on a bench after I get change out of my wet, muddy, disgusting football uniform. Then I send Lyla a text:

Me: *Delilah's?*
Lyla: *It's going to be a bit hard to sneak out. I am at my dad's. And he doesn't want me near you.*

I don't know what to say back to that. I don't get why Gentry still hates me so much. I'm pretty sure Amelia's come around to me. Can't she tell her almost-ex-husband that I'm not a threat? That I am a good kid?

Before I can say anything back, Lyla texts me again.

Lyla: *Audrey is going to cover for me.*
Me: *Great. See you there.*

Lyla and I park on the street at the same time outside of Delilah's and walk in together. We move at a bit of a run because it's starting to rain a little harder again.

"Thanks," she says when I hold the door open for her. She flashes me the brightest of smiles, and I am quick to smile back.

We slide into a booth.

"What's up?" she asks, putting her elbows on the table and tilting her head to the side. Dots of water from the rain freckle her face. There are a couple tiny, misty drops on her eyelashes, and as she blinks, she doesn't seem to notice that they're there.

"I think I worked out a plan," I tell her, trying not to get distracted.

"What kind of a plan?"

A waiter comes to take our order. I get a hot fudge sundae. Lyla gets a strawberry milkshake. It's not super busy inside Delilah's right now. Only two other tables are taken, and only one worker is behind the counter. Old, 50s music is playing on the jukebox. The ancient linoleum flooring is filthy from everyone's muddy footprints trailing in from the rain. Everyone in here still has their jackets on. Everyone is in dark colors.

"You know how I spoke to Craig's brother the other day? Parker Fritz?" I ask.

"Yeah?"

"He told me he has connections, if I ever needed help. I thought it was a longshot, but I reached out to him anyway. The unknown number that texted all of us—I asked if he knew anybody that could track it. And he gave me some guy's information. And I've been texting him and working with him all day long."

"Holy crap," she says. "Did he figure it out yet?"

"Not yet," I say. "But he said he'd have an answer for me by tonight."

She is mystified. Her lips part slightly, but she doesn't know what to say.

I lean a little closer to her over the table top. "Lyla, I really think this guy is legit. I really think he's going to be able to tell us who that phone belongs to. Or at least where they're located."

"That's..."

"Huge," I finish for her. "I know."

Our desserts arrive. She slowly inserts her straw into the milkshake glass. I dive into my Sunday. I am ravenous from practice. I should probably eat something a little healthier than this, but the local organic sandwich shop isn't a very popular high school hang out.

"Do you think it will lead us right to Carson?" she asks.

"I hope so."

"So then... what happens when you get your answer from Parker's friend?"

I tell her my idea, as ridiculous as I know it sounds. By some miracle, she agrees to do it with me.

We finish our desserts, pay, and leave Delilah's.

"Wanna know a fun fact?" she asks me as we walk across the street toward my Jeep. We've decided to ride together back to my house, where we'll hang out until we get an answer from Parker's friend.

"Yes," I say.

"My mom named me after this place."

"After Delilah's?" I ask. "Is your full name *Delilah*?"

She giggles and shakes her head. "Just Lyla. But I guess she's loved this place since she was a little girl. Even *after* she had to work here. She told me she always knew if she had a girl that she would name her Lyla. She didn't have a second name picked out when she first found out she was having twins. She started scrolling through a baby name book. She didn't even make it through the A's."

The rain has slowed to a slight sprinkle, for now, and the lightning and thunder are distant. We're standing by the passenger door of my Jeep. Together, we look back at the front entrance of Delilah's. While it looks rundown and not at all charming enough of a place to want to name someone after it, I try to imagine what it looked like all those years ago, when Amelia and my mom were younger. I suppose that in such a dark, dreary town like Toxey, a brightly lit, sugary treat-filled place like this was seen as a haven for everyone. A place for them to escape. A place where they could pretend they lived somewhere more magical.

"Maybe she gave the name Lyla to the wrong twin," Lyla says, sounding a bit melancholy.

I turn to her. The corners of her lips have angled downward. She's no longer looking at Delilah's with me. She is looking at her feet, where she's tapping at a puddle with her Converse, and she's not worried about getting them dirty because they've already been dirty for a while. She wears them a lot.

"Why would you say that?" I ask her.

She shrugs. "I don't know. I don't feel like Lyla. Maybe I used to. And I've been trying really hard to get there again, but... I've honestly been doing a horrible job. I want to be the old me *so* bad, Warner. Everyone preferred her."

I shake my head repeatedly. "What are you talking about?"

"You know it's true," she says, rolling her eyes. "I—it's dumb, but when I was... kidnapped... I made this list that I promised I would follow if I made it out of there alive. And I ended up getting out, so I've been trying to stick to the list. I'm doing an awful job. And it eats me up because I made a *promise*, ya know? So, what happens if I don't follow through? What will happen to me?"

"Well... what kind of stuff is on that list?"

"Just..." she trails off.

"What?" I ask again.

"It was a list of way I could hopefully get back to being the old Lyla."

"You can't be serious."

"What?" she snaps, suddenly defensive.

But I'm not trying to offend her. "Lyla, you can't expect, after everything you've gone through, to still be the same person you were a year ago."

She folds her arms. She doesn't agree with what I'm saying.

I chuckle softly, and before I can stop myself, I grab her hands and make her unfold her arms. "I'm serious," I say. "The old Lyla? You can just forget about her. She's long gone, and she's not coming back. And no one expects her to."

Begrudgingly, she lets me untangle her, and even after I have, our hands stay linked together.

I step closer to her.

She gently gives my hands a squeeze.

"Wanna know what I think?" I ask, my voice turning into a whisper as we move nearer to each other.

"What?" she breathes.

"You don't need to try to be the old Lyla. And you don't have to be this new Lyla, either. You could just be... *Lyla*, and... well... I'd still be just as crazy about you."

I smile softly and watch her light up. It's as if she's realizing she needed somebody to tell her that a long time ago.

In perfect unison, we bend our heads together and go in for the kiss at the same time. Finally, it happens. Finally, our lips touch. And it feels so different than any other kiss I've ever had. For so long, I built up what this moment would be like. And, anything I had imagined—well, *this* blows it out of the water.

It took several bumps in the road to finally get here, but I've known it all along. I'm supposed to be with Lyla. She's the girl of my dreams.

And finally, I think I might have won her over.

CHAPTER 67

MADDY

When I get off the phone with Mia, I'm just as annoyed as she is. She's just filled me in on the day she and Dean have had. Yes, it's still completely bizarre to me and a little bit off-putting that Mia and Dean are together, and I am a little annoyed that she didn't tell me about it sooner, but for the most part, I'm okay with it. I always knew they were supposed to be together. I always felt that her relationship with Gentry wasn't fulfilling. Especially when I saw the way Mia and Dean interacted during the upperclassman trip. They were completely gaga over each other.

Mia also just told me on the phone that she and Dean are meeting up with Harley again soon. And she asked me to try getting a hold of Craig. *And* she wants me to go to his house to try to get Nora to come out if Craig doesn't answer me.

It's around 7:30 now, so it's not too late in the evening to try and bug Craig some more. I give him a call, expecting to have to try multiple times before giving up and going to his house like Mia requested.

But to my surprise, he answers.

"Hey there, Mads."

He doesn't sound good.

"Craig?" Why ignore Dean and Mia all day but answer when *I* call?

"Who else would be answering my phone?" he asks.

"I don't know," I snap. I want to say, *Maybe Nora?*

But maybe right now is not the time to admit that I know about them.

"Are you home? I want to talk. In person."

"I have no doubt that whatever you have to say is going to be *ridiculously* exciting."

Something tells me Craig hasn't been doing a good job using his leave of absence from work to get his wellness back on track. Not based on the way his words are slurring.

"I could do without the sarcasm," I say. "Are you home or not? I can be there in ten minutes."

"I'm not there," he says. "I am in the alleyway between that sporting goods store and law office downtown."

"The *alleyway?*"

"Yep."

Oh God.

"Okay... just... stay there. I'll be there soon. Don't make me chase you all around Toxey, Craig."

"I ain't going anywhere."

I end the call and text Mia the update. Then I grab my purse and step outside. I lock up and start down the porch steps while ordering myself a Lyft. I hear thunder in the distance. I feel small, light rain droplets on my skin.

The sound of a car door shutting makes me look up.

I freeze in my step. My heart nearly flies right out of my chest. I've forgotten how to breathe. How to think. How to do anything other than stare at Steven Hall as he crosses my unkempt front yard to reach me.

He's in a suit. But it's wrinkled. His hair is slightly askew. His eyes look tired. His face is slightly unshaven. If I didn't know any better, I would've guessed he came straight here from a long flight.

"Maddy," he begins, slowing to a stop a few feet away from me. Hearing my name leave his lips makes me shiver. I still can't get myself to say anything back. Did I fall asleep? Am I dreaming?

Stop having stupid, cliché thoughts, Maddy. You're not freaking dreaming. This is real life.

Steven smiles sheepishly and drops his hands to his sides in a way that looks like he's surrendering. It's like he saying, "I don't know what the heck I'm doing anymore."

"I..." he trails off, unable to finish his sentence.

"Steven," I say. "What are you doing here?"

"I'm so sorry, Maddy," he tells me. "I've been so caught up in everything going on with Wrigley. He's... he's not who I thought he was. And we've had to have a lot of long talks and lectures. Or else I would've come to you much sooner. It's not an excuse. I messed up."

"Oh... I don—"

He interrupts. "I don't even really *need* you to say anything back. I'm serious. I just came here because I wanted you to know how sorry I am for being so mad about it all. I understand why you kept everything hidden and didn't want to come to me with the truth. How the heck are you supposed to know who to trust? I get it. And you don't have to trust me. You don't have to even like me back anymore. But I just really need you to know that I am still so in love with you. You've been on my mind every moment of every day."

Suddenly, as if somebody flipped a switch, the rain starts coming down harder. But with the way Steven and I are looking at each other, you would think neither of us have even noticed it. Not until eventually, when I crack a smile and then laugh at how soaked we're both getting.

He laughs a little, too, still several feet away from me.

Sometimes, you *can* have everything you want. Sometimes, it all just works out.

I close the distance between us. And then out here in the rain, where we can hardly even see because there's so much water in our eyes, where it's freezing cold, nothing else matters because Steven is here, and he forgives me. And I finally got him back.

He wraps his arm around me as I practically jump into his. And then I kiss him.

"I don't know if I like this."

Steven is a little overly cautious about dropping me off in an alleyway in downtown Toxey, which is understandable.

"It's going to be okay," I reassure him, putting a hand on his wet shoulder. It's still raining pretty heavily out. "If anything happens to me, you will know where I was last seen and who I was last with."

"Yeah," he says, nodding, "That's *really* reassuring. Thanks."

I chuckle, and then I turn his face to mine so I can kiss him on the lips again. One last time. Just to confirm that this is all real. To confirm that Steven forgave me. That he still loves me. That he's finally accepted me after how much I wronged him.

"How about I come straight to you afterward?" I ask.

"Yeah, I'd like that. Or at least give me a call and update me. Okay?"

"I will. I promise."

"Good. I trust you."

It's like music to my ears.

I get out of the car, back into the rain. I really should've brought an umbrella, but what is the point anymore? I'm already drenched. I don't even want to know what my makeup looks like.

Craig is parked in his car in the alleyway. I know it's him because he flashes his headlights at me. In the glow from the streetlights on the other side of the alley, I see the steam from his exhaust rising through the cold air.

I run and open his passenger door and crawl inside. At first, I hear a lot of voices. A lot of static. Craig is in the driver's seat, drinking from a plastic water bottle.

"Mia and Dean have been trying to get a hold of you," I say instead of any sort of greeting. I realize when I see the device on his dash that he's listening to a police scanner. That's what all of the voices are. I pause and redirect the conversation before he says anything. "What are we doing in here? What are *you* doing?"

"I juss like tuh keep tabsson things."

Whoa.

Craig's voice is slurring so much I can hardly understand him.

He goes to drink out of the water bottle again.

I snatch it out of his hand.

"Dangit, Maddy," he growls. "Givat back."

I sniff it.

Vodka. The cheap stuff.

"I'll do you one better," I say. I unroll his window and dump the vodka out.

"You're geddin' mahseats wet!" he grumbles.

"You've had this car since high school. I think me getting the seats wet is the *least* of your concerns."

I close the window and toss the empty water bottle to the floor by my feet. I shoot him a dirty look.

"What are you doing, Craig?" I ask. "What's with you? Were you seriously driving around like this?"

"I'm not driving anywhere."

"But you drove *here*, didn't you?"

"Thas before I started drinking."

"I don't understand, Craig. When did this start? What happened? And where is Nora? Your secret's out. We all know you two are together."

He doesn't even look surprised. He just shrugs. The police chatter on the speaker is slightly annoying because of how static-ey it all sounds. But I try to ignore it.

"Figures," he utters.

"Where is she?" I ask again.

"Prolly at muh'house."

"Mia went there. Nobody answered."

"You really think Nora wantsta talkta Mia?"

"I don't know. Why wouldn't she?"

He barks out a sarcastic laugh.

"*Craig*. This isn't you. Before all of this started, before Sydney Hutton—or Megan Young—died, you were a good detective. You were respected. Everyone trusted you. And I... I really liked you."

Then I realized you were using me.

"Things change." He sighs heavily. "Whaddaya want, Maddy? I'm not here tuh discuss my prob'ems withyew. So'f thas the only reason you wanted tuh meet up..." He points to the door.

"Why are you still listening to the police scanner, huh?" I ask. "You clearly still care about your job. You clearly miss it. Don't you want to take the steps to get back on track so that you can get your job back? And what about Nora? Does *she* know that you're drinking like this? Does she even know where you are right now?"

He shrugs again. "Nora's been really helpful, actually," he says. "I wanna be better. Only for her. An' I guess... sometimes that ain't enough."

"Craig. Did you hear me? I know who Sydney Hutton really was. I know that Carson paid Megan Young to pose as a teenager and come to Blackfell High School to learn all about my son, about Mia's daughters, and about us. I know that Carson was looking for ways he could ruin our lives. I know he wanted to learn all of our secrets to use them against us. And I know that he killed Megan."

Craig doesn't even react. And it's infuriating.

"Did you hear me?" I bark. "I said I *know* he killed Megan. He *killed* someone, Craig."

"Yeah. An' now he's dead."

"Is that really true?"

He won't look at me. He hasn't looked at me the entire time I've been in here.

"*Craig.*"

Still, I don't get a response.

"Carson did some really horrible things, Craig. You and I both know it. Think about Nora. Think about what Carson did to Lyla. I get that he's your buddy or whatever. That you've looked out for him. But this has to stop. This has to be over now, okay? You need to come clean, Craig. You need to tell us where Carson is. Before he can hurt anyone else. He just needs to be put away. For good. You know it's time."

At least look at me. Acknowledge that you even heard anything I just told you.

He says nothing.

I want to cry. I want to scream and hit him. I want to smack the sense right into him. I just want him to understand, to finally see, that he's protecting the wrong person. And it's ruining his life. It's ruining so many lives.

How can I have gone from so over the moon happy just thirty minutes ago, when I was standing out in the rain with Steven, to miserable, and fed up, and so, *so* angry now?

"It's time, Craig."

Slowly, he turns his head, and for the first time since I got in his car, he looks me in the eyes.

"Maddy. What y—"

He stops short when he hears something on the scanner. I listen in, too and catch what it is they're saying this time.

I don't understand all the codes or numbers or anything, but I do hear "Swimming Hole," and "Trespassing."

"Huh," Craig says. "Eh, no one's gonna bother withatt call—too cold and too far to get tuh."

I take my phone out. Where is my son tonight? Why do I have this sinking, awful feeling that this call might be about him?

I go to view his location on an app on my phone. The sinking feeling worsens. His location isn't showing up as exactly at the swimming hole, but with this storm, my phone probably just hasn't given me an accurate update yet.

'Oh no," I groan.

"What?" Craig asks.

"It's Warner. He's the trespasser at the Swimming Hole."

CHAPTER 68

AUDREY

The parking lot in front of the hiking trail to the swimming hole is completely empty when I arrive. Eric must not be here yet.

Walking through the forest, in the rain, by myself, has my heart pounding in my chest. I am hyperaware of every noise around me. Of the fact that I am completely alone. I might be meeting up with either a murderer or a *potential* murderer. And I came *alone*?

What is the matter with you, Audrey?

The only thing that keeps me going is my quest for answers. My desperation for them.

Someone has to figure all of this out. Someone has to get to the bottom of this. For my family. For Warner's family.

For me.

Maybe it was always *supposed* to be me who figured it out. I know I'm the glue that holds everyone together. But I don't want to be the glue-stick kind of glue—that's the kind that lasts thirty seconds and hardly holds anything together. I want to be the rubber cement kind. The kind that once you put stuff together with it, it's held together permanently.

I use the flashlight app on my phone, but I am a little nervous that all of the rain is going to break it.

A tree branch snaps somewhere nearby. I jump in fright. I shine my phone around, but I see nothing. Maybe the water made the leaves on the trees too heavy, and it bent their branches. Maybe it was a squirrel climbing to higher ground.

I keep going.

Last summer, when I went to the swimming hole with my friends, feels like a lifetime ago. Last summer, Trinity's death brought me, Danielle, Olive, and Sophia closer together. Never before had we all cried together. Never before had we checked in on each other so often. Never before had we had so many sleepovers. So many late night phone calls. And never before had we all been so ignored by Lyla—our common ground about that brought us all closer, too. Because we *all* missed her.

I round the bend, and there the swimming hole is. It looks drastically different than it did over the summer. Mainly because it's raining and dark out, but also because there's not a soul in sight. There aren't colorful chairs and towels laid out on the rocks and in the dirt. And the trees around it have leaves that are autumn colored. Leaves that are falling off of them. They are not green and lush and full of life. Everything looks cold and shriveled and hollow.

The snack shop is boarded up. There is a NO TRESPASSING sign staked into the ground. But that's the only thing to ward off trespassers like me. The parks and rec department probably figures that no one's going to even *want* to trespass since the water is too cold this time of year anyway.

There's a bridge that goes over the swimming hole. And past that is a high cliff. It's used for cliff-jumping. There are various levels of ledges to jump from in case you don't want to do it from the highest point. I've never been brave enough to jump from the highest point. Lyla used to do it all the time, though.

I stare up at that cliff's highest point and see the dark shadow of a man.

So, Eric *is* here.

I turn my flashlight off, cross the bridge, and climb the steps to the top of the cliff. Mom said that there didn't used to be stairs here. That they were added when this place became more popular. There didn't used to be a snack shop either. It wasn't a tourist attraction as much as it was just a place the locals all knew about.

"Hello?" Eric's voice calls when I near the top. I don't think he can see me yet. I think he just hears me.

"It's me," I say. I reach the landing and see Eric clearer now. He's in hiking boots, slightly muddy jeans, and a raincoat.

"Couldn't have picked somewhere indoors?" he asks. He's standing under a large branch of a big tree, which is shielding him from the rain. But he's still drenched like I am from the hike here.

"I didn't know it was going to be storming like this," I say. "Anyway, this shouldn't take long. I just wanted to ask you a couple of things."

"Yeah, I figured as much."

I keep a safe distance away. I stay by the staircase, in case I need to turn and run back down them. Why didn't I even bring pepper spray? Some sort of weapon to defend myself in case I needed it?

After all of these attacks, I should have learned my lesson by now. But maybe, *maybe* I don't see Eric as a threat. Am I stupid for that?

"Uh... I guess I'll just ask the main thing I want to," I say, swallowing audibly. "Why are you really here, Eric?"

"What do you mean?" he asks. "I've already told you that answer."

"I—I know." *Jeez, this is hard.* "Uh, the thing is, I've sorta heard otherwise."

"You're not making any sense here, Audrey."

"I'm not?"

He shakes his head.

"Do you want to kill Carson?" I ask the same time that thunder rumbles louder than it has in a couple of hours. Does that mean the storm is getting bad again?

As if on cue, the wind starts to pick up. The leaves and bushes around us rustle. Combined with the rain and the thunder, it's loud out here.

Eric doesn't look happy with my question.

I take a small step backward. Is he unhappy because I found out the truth? What's he going to do to me now that he knows I know?

He takes a step toward me.

"St-stay back!" I shout, holding out a shaking hand to stop him. When he listens, I'm surprised.

"Where did you hear that?" he asks.

"From your d-daughter," I stutter. My throat is tight and my voice is squeaky all of a sudden. My hand is still out, like I have some sort of magical power to keep him standing where he is.

"From... Harley?" he asks.

"Is it true? You didn't answer my question." I take another step back. I'm pretty close to the edge of the stairs. I need to be careful that I don't trip and fall down them.

Or that he doesn't *push* me down them.

"No, of course it's not true," he says, a little louder than I would have preferred. But maybe he's just talking loud because of the volume of the wind and rain. Lightning illuminates him. When I can see his expression clearer, I recognize confusion in his eyes. "My daughter told you that?"

I nod.

"What else did she say?"

I tell him what Mom told me.

Afterward, his hand reaches slowly toward his back pocket.

"W-what are you doing?" I yelp.

He pulls something out, and I'm ready for it to be a gun. Even though it wouldn't make much sense, I'm ready for him to admit he is the one behind all of this.

Instead, I see a phone in his hand.

"Is Harley seriously here in town?" he asks. "I'm calling her."

"Right *now*?"

He holds his phone to his ear. "I'll get this all figured out, Audrey. I don't know why she's lying to you. But I assure you, I mean no harm."

Slowly, I put my hand down. Maybe he's telling me the truth. Maybe he is going to get Harley to admit *she* is the one lying. Maybe he'll even get her to tell us why.

Or maybe they're conspiring together, and he's calling for his back up.

AMELIA

Harley doesn't seem too thrilled to be meeting up with Dean and me again. "You guys keep coming to me with so many questions. I'm beginning to think you're not fully trusting my answers," she says to us inside The Mix.

"It's nothing like that," I'm quick to tell her, wanting to reassure her that we're not suspecting her of anything. The minute she stops liking us is the minute she's going to stop giving us any answers. And I can't have that.

"Then what? Are you guys secretly cops or something?"

"Definitely not."

It's awfully loud in here. It's more crowded than usual.

"I'd still answer your questions if you were," Harley says with a shrug. "I don't have anything to hide."

"We appreciate that," Dean says. He's holding my hand under the table. Ever since I broke down earlier, he's been extra affectionate to me.

"So, what else do you want to know?" she asks. "I don't really know if I have anything new to say."

"You knew that Carson killed Megan Young, correct?" I ask.

"Yeah. Didn't we talk about this?"

"Right. But I was just curious... why doesn't he hardly remember killing her? What exactly did he tell you about it? I was wondering if you could go into specifics."

"Specifics? I hardly know them. I didn't exactly *want* all the details of it."

"But what exactly was it he said to you about it?" Dean asks.

"Uh... let's see..." She looks up at the ceiling for a moment. "I don't know. I think he regretted it. He *did* say how Megan was going to ruin everything. How he felt like he didn't have another choice. I don't know. Must've been one of those things where he was so traumatized by it that he blanked it from his memory. It's a real thing that happens. You can suppress stuff like that, if it's bad enough."

"Why was she going to ruin everything, do you know?" I ask.

"I don't know. Maybe she realized her job was more than she bargained for, and once she did, she wanted to come clean about it." She lets out a long, deep breath, and then her shoulders hunch a bit. "My brother is dead, okay? I know I didn't see him much over the years, but I tried to warn him. I tried to help him. Never once did it cross my mind that he would commit suicide. And if my dad is here in town? Then I think you guys can fill in the missing pieces."

It feels wrong to keep pestering her with questions when she's mourning the loss of her brother. But she's mourning the loss of a *terrible* human being. Of a man who kidnapped and tried to kill my daughters. Of a man who *did* kill another young girl. Of a man who is capable of killing again.

"You haven't heard anything that makes you wonder if maybe he's still alive?" Dean asks.

"Are you kidding me?" Harley jeers. "I'm sorry, what is this, some soap opera? It's kind of cruel for you to even try to get my hopes up. I think Carson is gone, and he's not coming back. I would have known otherwise."

"We're sorry," I say quickly, glancing at Dean. "We really hate to be bothering you, and we are so appreciative of everything you're doing. We don't want to take up too much of your time. I just wanted to ask one more thing."

"What?"

"My sister, Nora. She—"

I'm cut off when Harley holds her finger up and takes her phone out of her coat.

"Hold that thought."

She hops off the barstool and walks away.

"Who do you think that is?" Dean asks.

"Why, do you think it's Carson or something?"

"I don't know. Something seems off. Something's different."

"Yeah, I get the feeling this is the last time she's going to let us talk to her." I pull out my phone to check on my girls. "Is it really *this* late?" I gasp out when I see the time on the screen. The day has completely gotten away from me. I don't even think I remember the sun setting.

I start composing a text to Lyla and Audrey in our group chat. But before I can send anything, Harley comes hurrying back.

My head snaps up to her. Her shoulders are tucked under her ears. Her eyes are wide. "Amelia," she says in a completely different voice than the one she had just moments ago. She sounds out of breath. Concerned. "That was—that was my father. Your daughter is with him right now."

"*What*?!" Dean and I say together.

"We need to go," she barks. "*Right* now. We need to get her away from him. Before it's too late."

CHAPTER 70

LYLA

I have no idea where Warner and I are. We're somewhere in the middle of the woods. Following the tracked number is what brought us here, and we've completely deserted any hiking trails. We've just been trekking through the thunder and rain, trying to keep our sights on the little tiny dot on Warner's phone screen where the owner of the number that texted all of us is located.

"Whoa, whoa, watch out!" Warner whispers loudly, taking me by the hand and pulling me back behind him. Startled, I look down and see I had been close to the edge of a cliff. I didn't even know we had been walking at an incline.

"I... I think we're by the swimming hole," Warner says, still holding my hand. If we hadn't kissed earlier, I bet he would've let go by now. "I think we just got here the back way."

"It's closed for the season. Do you think Carson is using this as his latest hide-out? Maybe he's camping out inside of the snack shack."

"Probably."

We keep moving, but more cautiously. Thunder rumbles overhead.

"It's getting louder," I say. This probably isn't the safest place to be during a storm.

The wind picks up.

"Do you hear that?" Warner asks.

"What? The wind?"

He shakes his head and holds a finger to his lips. He leads the way, keeping me behind him. He's being protective, and it's completely adorable.

He stops short, and I bump into his back. But I don't even bother to apologize because I've quickly realize why he stopped—through the trees, up ahead, I can just barely make out two people at the cliff of the swimming hole.

Then lightning flashes through the sky. And I see who those two people are.

"Audrey?" I whisper, ready to break through the greenery to get to her. What the heck is she doing here? I'm assuming the man she's with is Eric. I don't know what other old man should be having a late night meeting with.

And I can't *believe* she didn't tell anyone.

Warner stops me from going anywhere. "Just wait," he says. We're talking in whispers, but the wind is so loud, and we're still so far away, that I don't think they would hear us if we talked at a normal volume.

"But Warner, doesn't this mean that Eric is the one who texted us?" I ask, shivering, and not just because I am freezing and drenched. "He could hurt her!"

"I... I don't get it," Warner says, looking back at the two of them. "It doesn't make any sense. I thought we'd be led right to Carson."

"Close enough. We were led to the man who probably killed him."

I move to make my way to her again. And again, Warner pulls me back. "Just *wait* a second, Ly" he says. "We can't just *burst* out there. We need to think of a plan. We need to... figure this out. I don't know."

"Warner?"

Our heads snap toward the voice. It came from the completely opposite direction of where Audrey and Eric are. It came from where Warner and I just were.

It's Maddy. She steps between two trees, pulling some branches back that are blocking her path. Then behind her, Craig steps into sight.

"What on earth are you—" Maddy starts, but Warner and I both interrupt her by shushing her.

She falls silent although she looks confused, and then she and Craig approach us.

"Audrey and Eric are here," Warner whispers to them. He points over his shoulder. "I don't know what's going on. What are you guys doing here?"

"And why are you with *him*?" I ask Maddy.

"I drove us here," she explains. Craig stumbles over some rocks to see Eric and Audrey for himself.

Warner mouths to Maddy, *Is he drunk?* behind Craig's back, and Maddy nods her head.

"Why are they here?" Maddy asks. "Why is Audrey with him?"

"Craig, stay," Warner commands, talking to Craig like a dog. And surprisingly, Craig obeys. But he's still eyeing Audrey and Eric down, and he's swaying a bit, too.

"Warner tracked the number of who sent all of us that text message," I explain to Maddy. "It led us here. So... I think it was Eric."

"How can that—?"

"Wait a second," Warner interjects. "How long have you guys been out here?" He stares down Craig intensely.

"I saw that you were wandering through the woods, so we came to find you," Maddy says. "We thought *you* were the trespasser at the swimming hole. I heard the call over the police scanner."

"So, Craig's been with you this whole time?" Warner asks. Is he beginning to think maybe *Craig* was the one who sent the text? Maybe Craig is the one we were led to?

The location of the tracked phone wasn't always clear at times. We lost service a bunch. The location wouldn't update as often as we wanted it to.

"Yes," Maddy says. "Why are we hiding in the trees instead of talking to this guy? If he did send that text to all of us, then you probably shouldn't leave Audrey out there alone with him." She steps past all of us, toward the clearing where Audrey and Eric are.

"Because!" Warner calls to her. Then he slaps his hand to his face when she doesn't stop to listen to him. "I was trying to think of a plan..."

Craig follows Maddy. So, I take Warner's hand, give him a reassuring nod, and then we go with them.

"What was that?" Audrey yelps when she hears the noise of us coming. Eric turns his head, and then we all come out of the darkness. Lightning and thunder go off at practically the same time. The sound is deafening.

"What are you guys doing here?" Audrey asks loudly. "Did you follow me? Did you follow Eric?"

Eric's squints at us. "They didn't follow *me*," he says. "I made sure I wasn't followed. Like you asked me to."

"Audrey, what the *heck*?" I ask, going to her side. I don't know how much protection I'll be able to give her, but I don't want her alone with this man.

"How did you find us?" she asks, looking more annoyed than anything. "I... I just wanted the truth. And honestly—"

"AUDREY!"

The voice yelling is coming from the bottom of the staircase. I hear the sounds of not only one pair of footsteps hurrying up, but multiple.

"*Mom?*" Audrey and I say together, recognizing her voice before we even see her. Everyone watches the landing, and then Mia, Dean, and a third person, a girl I've never seen or spoken to before, appears.

"How long have *you* guys been around here?" Warner asks them.

"Audrey! Lyla?" Mom is on high alert. And confused. "Stay away from that man!"

She pushes Audrey and me further away from the cliff's edge and Eric, and then she stands in front of us, and Dean stands in front of her. The third person looks at Eric.

"Hey, Dad."

That *is* Harley, then. But what is she doing with my mom and Dean? Where have they been all day?

"Maddy?" Mom asks when she sees her.

"Mia. Dean. What are you doing here?" Maddy asks.

"What are *you*?" Mom shoots back. She looks wildly around at everyone. Then her eyes fall on Harley. "You said it was just him alone with Audrey."

"It was...a few minutes ago," Audrey says.

"What did you do, Harley?" Eric asks.

I'm so confused by all of the people here. I no longer feel certain that it was Eric's phone that we tracked.

"Mom, maybe it's *you* who needs to stay away from *her*," Audrey says with a fierceness that makes my mouth drop. She's pointing at Harley.

"*Me?*" Harley asks. "You've got to be kidding me."

"Harley," Eric snaps. "What did you say to Carson?"

"What are you talking about?" Harley asks. I can tell they're related because they both get the same squinty eyes when they're angry.

Or maybe when they're lying.

"Why did you tell Carson that lie about the fire?" Eric presses. "Why would you tell him I wanted him dead? I don't know what's going on, and I don't know what you think happened, but... I was never mad at Carson for that night."

"Hang on a second," Craig says, and we all turn to look at him. I'm still so confused as to why he's even here. Why he and Maddy were together. Craig is addressing Eric. "Are you talking about the fire that killed Carson's mother?"

"Do you know about that?" Eric asks.

"Yeah. I remember him telling me about it when we were in high school. But... but he told me he never *actually* started that fire. He told me that his stepsister did. But that he took the blame because his stepsister was so young and scared and kept crying to him about how it was an accident."

"Oh my God," Mom says.

"Okay, but if you guys have learned anything by now, it should be that Carson has always been an excellent liar," Harley says. But there's too much of an edge to her voice. There's too much defensiveness in her tone.

Craig looks at her. "Are *you* his stepsister?"

She doesn't answer. But she doesn't have to.

"I take that as a yes," Craig says. "I don't know what need Carson would have to lie to me about that. It's not like he probably ever thought a day like this was going to come around. He told me that it wasn't until *after* he decided to take the blame—on your behalf—that he found out his mother even died."

I slap a hand over my mouth at the shock of it.

"Harley," Eric says, "that fire... it *wasn't* an accident, was it?"

"What?" Harley scoffs. "You—h-how should I know?"

"Don't lie to me," Eric demands. His voice is shaky but also very loud and severe. "You... you killed her, didn't you?"

"No!" Harley shrieks.

"Wait..." Maddy says, stepping forward. She points at Harley. "You *did*, didn't you?"

"Who even are you?" Harley asks her.

Maddy ignores her. "All this time, it's been you. You made Carson want to stay on the run. You... you killed his mom, and he took the blame without knowing she was dead. And you were so scared Carson was going to tell the truth, so, you came up with the lie about Eric wanting to kill him. You kept him running."

"You have no idea what you're talking about," Harley says, shaking her head repeatedly.

Maddy smirks at her. "I've seen you before. Years ago. When I was in high school. I was with you, actually." She looks at Dean. "We were at a CD store. Remember when I freaked out on you?"

"Sorta, maybe?" Dean says.

"It was because I saw *her* out the window. She was talking to Carson at his car." She looks back at Harley. "What were you telling him, Harley? That your dad was on his tail and that he was in danger? What lies did you feed him?"

"I don't believe it," Eric says, hanging his head.

But now I fully believe he's innocent in all of this. I don't think anyone can fake being heartbroken like that. It's as if his entire world just crumbled at his feet. He looks about ready to hurl himself off of the cliff.

And when Harley looks at her father, she must be able to tell that there is no way she is going to ever be able to convince him she didn't do it.

Her voice turns cold. "Well, it doesn't matter now anyway."

"Because... because you killed him, didn't you?" I ask. She didn't want to get found out. She didn't want her dad to know what she had done. And then she found out he was in town, getting closer to finding Carson. So, she hurried here to end him before Eric could learn the truth.

Harley rolls her eyes. "I bet you're all thinking that right now, huh," she says, her voice devoid of any emotion. "I bet you're all thinking that he never committed suicide. And that I had to kill him to keep my secret. But guess what. You're only half-right." She points a finger directly at Craig. "*He's* the one who killed him."

CHAPTER 71

WARNER

I don't understand it. I don't understand any of it.

Why is this Harley person saying Craig killed Carson? And why isn't Craig looking like he's going to try to deny it?

"Craig?" I think it's Amelia speaking, but the voice didn't come from her. It didn't come from my mom, either.

I hear Lyla and Audrey gasp, and my mouth falls open when Nora Flynn steps into the clearing out of seemingly nowhere.

How much had she heard? When did she even get here?

Who had she followed?

"Nora," Craig steps toward her. She holds her hand out to stop him. "I followed you here to see why you were sneaking off with *her*." She glares at Maddy.

"Hold on a second!" Amelia yells. "What is Harley saying, Craig? Why does she think you killed Carson?"

"Because he did!" Harley snaps.

"I..." Craig tries to take another step toward Nora, but when she doesn't show signs of wanting him anywhere near her, he decides to just stay where he is. He's still a little unsteady on his feet. I wonder how intoxicated he is right now. "In high school," he begins, clearing his throat. Maybe this whole experience is a bit sobering for him. "Let me tell you all something. Carson Price was never really my friend."

I look at Nora. She keeps her eyes trained on Craig. I move to look at Lyla and see that she's looking at me.

Craig continues. "I never trusted him. Right from the very beginning."

"You...had feelings for Nora, even back then," Amelia guesses.

Craig points at her and nods. "Just when I was beginning to wonder if you really are as smart as everyone says you are."

"What?" Maddy asks.

"He was in love with Nora," Mia clarifies. "So, he pretended to befriend Carson to keep an eye on him."

"Well, you did a horrible job," Maddy says to him.

Nora says nothing.

"Nor didn't know back then, of course," Craig says. "She was... well, she was in love with *you*, Dean, wasn't she?"

Dean doesn't reply.

Craig shakes his head at him. "Anyway. I never went for her because I just always assumed that she and Dean would end up together. I think everyone assumed that. But then Carson came into town. And all of a sudden, Nora set her sights on him.

"And then Carson died. And Nora was a mess over it, but yet, no one found Carson's body. I thought that Mia, Maddy, and Carson had all come together and conspired. I thought they were all angry because Nora loved Dean. I was always on Nora's side. Always."

"I don't understand..." Audrey trails off.

"When Nora came to town, we reconnected," Craig says. "We pretty much immediately started seeing each other. And she told me about Carson. About all the things he'd been doing. And I told her about how I've always wanted to find the truth about what happened to him. It took her some time to finally admit that Carson was still alive and blackmailing her. This is because she was scared. I only finally learned that it really was Carson doing this to everyone just before that night at the high school pool. I... I chased after him, after he attacked Warner. Lost sight of him, but I didn't stop searching. I found him at some point, may be a couple of hours later, deep in these woods. And I did what I thought I had to, to protect Nora."

"Craig," Nora says, her voice cracking. But I don't know why. I don't understand what she's thinking. I don't understand the look she's giving him. Is she in love? Is she sad? Did she know all of this? Or is she learning any of it for the first time?

"Nora," Craig says. "Why does this woman—how does she know... what I did?" He's referring to Harley knowing he killed Carson.

Craig killed Carson.

Why is Craig asking Nora that?

Everyone looks at Nora now.

Lyla steps forward, out from behind the protection of her mother. She looks paler than I've ever seen her. And as more lightning streaks across the sky and thunder slams in our ears, she looks at her aunt.

"Wait," she says. I can see her whole body trembling. "Y-you didn't follow Craig and Maddy here."

"Yes, I did, Lyla..." Nora says, looking at her like she is some sort of ugly alien creature.

"Warner and I tracked the person who texted all of us a threatening message." She looks at me, and I know exactly what I have to do.

I take my phone out. I go to the phone number, which I now have access to, since Parker's helpful friend unblocked it.

I call the number.

A phone rings. It pierces the night sky. The wind carries it into everyone's ears. But the wind doesn't distort where the ringing is coming from.

Slowly, Nora pulls the lit-up phone out of her old, faded hoodie.

I can't believe what I am seeing.

Nora declines the call.

"Wh-what's happening, Nora?" Amelia asks. "Wh-why do you have that phone?"

Nora's eyes become especially glossy. Is she about to cry right now? She only looks at Craig and ignores her sister completely when she speaks. "Craig, you have to know, I... I never lied about how I feel about you. Ever."

Everyone's asking questions now. Everyone's furious. Everyone's yelling things at Nora. Including me. I just don't understand it. I don't understand any of it.

What did Nora do?

"Are you pretending to be Carson or something?" Audrey asks.

This is the question everyone hears above all of the others.

It's also one that I think *I* can answer.

"She's not pretending to be anybody but herself," I say. "She just had Carson's help for a lot of it."

CHAPTER 72

AUDREY

Harley starts slowly backing away, toward the staircase. "You know, this is beginning to seem more like a...*family* situation," she says. "I think I should probably just see myself off now."

"You're not going anywhere!" Eric yells the same time Nora shouts, "No!"

Harley freezes.

"How could you do it, huh?" Eric asks his daughter, his body sagging like he can hardly carry his own weight. "How could you kill the love of my life?"

"Because!" Harley snarls. Suddenly, she's so angry that her face is red. When she speaks, she's so passionate that spit flies out of her mouth. "After Mom died, you moved on too fast! How *could* you, Dad? She had *cancer*!"

"So, you... you *kill* her? That's how you handle that situation? You couldn't just come to me? You couldn't just tell me how you were feeling? Or tell me to slow down? I had *no* idea you were that upset about it, Harley! You seemed completely fine with me moving on!"

"Well, I wasn't!"

"She's just one *heck* of a liar," Dean interjects.

"I *had* to get rid of that woman, okay?!" she yells. "Because you can't just replace my mom like that! You can't!" She pulls tightly on her own hair. "I have been *so* scared for so many years of you finding out! For *years*! Then, when the news came out that Carson was dead—for real this time—I had to come make sure for myself. To get proof. Because I thought if I could just guarantee that Carson really was dead, I wouldn't have to worry anymore. And my search for proof led me to Nora. And Nora said to me, 'I'm not so convinced he's really dead.' And foolishly, I teamed up with her. We both wanted the same thing. She completely played me. She had me convinced that Carson really was a bad guy. Heck, it made me even feel a little bit better about my big lie, because my I thought my 'brother' really was a killer. But then... then, when I was talking to Carson and he told me about that Megan Young girl. It was then that I realized the truth."

"Shut *up*, Harley," Nora shouts menacingly.

Mom has been shielding me so that I can't see Nora or Harley properly. But I need to see this interaction. So, I step out from behind her. I need to see Aunt Nora's face. I need to gauge if she's being genuine. Who can I trust? Who here is telling the truth?

"Sorry, Charlie," Harley says to Nora, still fuming as she tosses a look at her. "If my truth is out, then yours might as well be, too."

"You can't trust anything she says!" Nora cries. She *really* is sobbing. I see the real tears, even through the rain.

"What did you realize?" Mom asks Harley. "Tell us."

"Mia, come on!" Nora wails.

"I realized that Carson never killed anyone," Harley tells us. "I realized it was Nora who killed Megan. And once I figured that out, I figured *everything* out. It wasn't Carson who had a hold over Nora. It was Nora who was controlling *him*."

"LIAR!" Nora lunges at Harley.

Quickly, Eric and Dean stop them from attacking one another. As Harley stands there restrained by her father, she laughs darkly. Nora, held back by Dean, is still sobbing. She looks so childlike. So guilty. So much like she's just had her biggest secret finally exposed.

"*Fine*!" Nora screams, trying to get out of Dean's grasp. "Fine! I had to kill her! I had to kill her before she ruined everything!"

The news of my aunt being a murderer isn't the most terrifying thing that happens. It's what happens right after that. What's truly bone-chillingly, bloodcurdlingly terrifying, is watching how my aunt goes from a scared, sobbing, thrashing baby, to completely composed, no longer struggling against Dean. Her scrunched-up, twisted face completely smoothens out. The desperation and anger leave her eyes.

What replaces them is nothing but a piercing coldness.

"Nora," Mom whispers, a single tear trailing down her cheek. "What have you done?"

CHAPTER 73

Nora

Two Months Ago

That stupid little homeless, dishwater-blonde, brat!

Who does she think she is?

I stomp through the thick greenery of the Boldosa Redwood Forest. Carson and I have our little campsite set up about a mile away from where my nieces and Warner are, enjoying their school's camping trip. Megan was supposed to meet us hours ago, but she never snuck out. And I have a good sense about these kinds of things. I know why I haven't seen her yet. I know what she's up to. I've been able to sense it the past few days. I've seen that look in her eyes. The uncertainty. The fear, even.

It makes me laugh as I swat at yet another mosquito. How does Megan not realize it? She has nothing to fear as long as she does what we are paying her to do.

But now?

Now, she's going to have a reason to be afraid.

I'm so annoyed at this point that I don't care if I wake up Megan's tent mate when I go barging my way inside.

But I stop short of the pathway that'll take me the rest of the way up to camp, because in the middle of the trees, toward the back of the camp, I see her.

Megan's back is to me. She's speaking to someone.

It's Warner Carpenter.

Now, why would she be having a little rendezvous with him in the middle of the night when she is supposed to be having her meeting with Carson and me?

Warner looks deeply upset, and I fill with dread.

Is Megan about to spill our secret?

Trying not to panic, trying to remain as calm as humanly possible, I try to conjure up a Plan B. Someway to remedy the situation, ASAP. Before Warner figures it all out.

But then Megan calls out Warner's name as he's walking away from her.

What's this?

Megan sounds desperate.

She didn't get the chance to tell him.

I smile, feeling like I can finally breathe again, but then my smile is quickly replaced with a scowl.

I knew this would happen.

I approach Megan from behind. When she hears a twig snap under the weight of my foot, she spins around to me and gasps.

"What are you doing?" I ask. "You were supposed to meet us forever ago."

Keep it together. Keep it together.

"Oh." Sydney scratches the back of her neck. "I was just... I was trying to get away from Warner."

Liar.

She continues. "He ran into me when I was sneaking out, and I had to get him off my trail."

"Fine. Can we go now?"

"Yeah." But she sounds like coming with me is the last thing she wants to do.

Which is ironic.

I start leading the way. She knows she doesn't have any other choice but to follow. Right now, she has no idea that I know what she's doing. She has no idea that I know she wants out. And I intend to keep it that way.

We walk around the edge of Lake Oshwana until we reach another dock. Carson is already loaded up on the rowboat.

"Climb on," I tell Megan.

"Why?" she asks. "What are we doing now?"

"Stop asking so many questions. Just get on."

Carson is hunched over. He's on the floor of the rowboat, his back leaned up against what is supposed to be his seat. But this just holds him up better. He has his hood pulled deep down over his face. I have on the same exact outfit.

Megan takes the middle row. I take the back one.

"Help me row," I demand.

She does as instructed. "I don't want to get caught out here," she says. She'll hardly look at me. She used to look at me all the time. She used to not be afraid of me. She used to be completely on board with our plan. She used to not care who she hurt as long as she got her end of the deal fulfilled.

It's sad when things change.

"Why aren't you helping?" she mutters to Carson when I don't say anything to her. We row further and further to the center of the lake.

Carson doesn't answer her. What she doesn't realize, with Carson's hoodie pulled over his head like this, is that Carson isn't exactly awake at the moment.

"Are you seriously sleeping?" she asks him. Her poor attitude is nothing new. She's had it from the moment we, let's just say "adopted" her.

Still, Carson doesn't reply.

She rolls her eyes. "Seriously, Nora, what are we doing?"

"It's just another part of the plan."

"Okay... why don't I know anything about it?"

"You would know, if you had met us when you were supposed to," I say simply.

When we're far enough out, I stop rowing. So, Megan does, too.

"What is this?" she asks, looking around. She's probably noticing that she is surrounded by nothing but water on all four sides of her.

"Megan, you've been very helpful," I tell her. I might as well not beat around the bush about it. "And I want to thank you for that. However, I feel that our time has come to an end. Let's just say... Your services are no longer needed."

I pick up my wooden oar, and I hit her as hard as I can in the head with it.

She falls unconscious and tips over into the lake.

I wait a long time. Enough to make sure that she's not going to resurface.

I am a little shocked at how easy that was. I didn't know if I really had it in me. To kill someone? To really kill someone?

But all I feel right now is relieved that the plan worked, at least this far.

It's a shame because in other circumstances, I could've probably just paid Megan off and told her to never contact us again. But killing Megan wasn't just for her own punishment.

It's my safety net.

I smack Carson around a little bit. He doesn't stir. I splash cold water on his face. This does the trick.

I tuck my knees up under my chin and place myself as far away from him as I possibly can on this tiny little boat.

"W-what's going on?" Carson asks, his voice groggy. "Where are we? W-what are we doing?" The boat rocks violently as he moves around, not realizing we're in the water.

I drugged him as soon as we got onto the boat.

"Wh-what do you mean?" I ask in a shaky voice. My lower lip trembles. "Carson, why did you just do that?"

"What are you talking about?" Carson asks, holding his head, which is probably throbbing. "Where is Megan?"

"Stop messing around with me!" I squeak. "You –you just killed her!"

"What?"

"Carson, stop!"

"Nora, what is going on?!" He reaches a hand toward me, and I scream.

"Are you going to kill me next?!"

He stares at his hand. "I—why would I kill you, Nora?"

"Why should I believe you?!" Real tears stream down my cheeks.

It's a gift.

"I swear, I have no idea what happened."

"You're scaring me," I say.

He looks around the boat. "Where is Megan, Nora?"

"You hit her with your oar and pushed her into the water!"

He stares into the black lake. "But I... I don't remember it. I don't know what happened just now."

"Please, Carson. Just take me back. Take me back to the dock. I want to go back."

"Nora, I—"

"PLEASE!" I sob and curl away from him, hunching my shoulders to hide my face from him.

Slowly, wordlessly, Carson picks up the oar and takes us back to the dock.

CHAPTER 74

MADDY

I had to kill her before she ruined everything!

"You didn't," I say to Nora. But my voice is barely a whisper. I doubt she even heard me.

"Why?" Dean asks her, his voice much more audible. "Nora, did Carson make you?"

"No," Mia says, shaking her head. "No. P-please tell me that Carson is still alive, Nora. That everything they're saying isn't true. That Carson did all of this." Her eyes are crazed.

Her own sister...

Nora rolls her eyes. "Warner has it right, *Sis*. I had Carson's help. Not the other way around."

"*Why?*" Mia asks through clenched teeth.

"Do you really have to ask me that?" Nora asks. "Come on. I've only been trying to make yours and Maddy's life miserable since the 90s."

"It's because of Dean," I answer for her. Mia looks at me with tears in her eyes. I nod; I want her to know I'm just as upset. Just as shocked. Just as... shattered by all of this as she is.

A memory from when I was in high school, dating Dean, flashes to the front of my mind.

———

Nora and I hang in my bedroom. It's one of the rare occasions where we're at my house instead of hers and Mia's. Nora and I have both been getting really fed up with Mia and her bratty behavior lately. She never wants to have fun. Not like Nora does. I'm starting to feel that Nora may be a better friend than Mia. That maybe I should just stop being Mia's friend and start only hanging with Nora.

"I wish I lived here," Nora says as she jumps onto my bed, which is probably the size of her entire bedroom. "How come we don't always hang out here? I'm serious."

"I don't know. Mia always wants to do things at your house." It's not entirely true. Actually, I much prefer to be with their parents over my father, but I'm not about to admit that to Nora. I don't like people knowing about how sad I really am. These days, Nora and Dean are the only ones who make me happy. Them, and those extra-fudge sundaes from Delilah's.

"Where is Dean?" I ask Nora, since she always knows his whereabouts. "Do you think he'll call me soon?" I sprawl out on my rug. My phone is on the floor next to me. I want to be able to pounce on it the second I hear it ring. I don't want to take the chance that my dad will get to it first.

"I don't know," Nora says, her voice falling a couple octaves.

It makes me sit up and look at her. "What's wrong? You guys get in a fight?" I ask. I liked that Nora is younger than me, and that we both have a similar shade of long brown hair. I feel like we can pass for sisters. I decide that the next time we go to the mall together, we should pretend to be sisters.

"No," Nora says. "But...there is actually something I wanted to tell you about... him."

"Oh," I say, "what weird, gross habit does he have? He's a closet nose-picker, isn't he?"

She doesn't smile. It makes my stomach knot up.

"What is it, Nor?"

"I thought I would be fine with you and Dean being together. Especially since I have that thing with Carson. But... I guess I'm not so fine with it after all."

All I can do is stare at her. Dean and I have already been together for several weeks. "Why?" I finally manage to croak. "Are you serious?"

"Yeah. I'm really sorry, Maddy. It just really bothers me when I see you guys together."

I stand up. "Well, you should've said something before, then," I snap. "Before you gave me your approval and I allowed myself to like him."

"I know, I know. I just—"

I interrupt her. "Because now it's too late! I like him, Nora. A lot. And you already said I could date him. You can't just take that back."

"But, Mad—"

"You have Carson. You'll get over it. Come on. I'm hungry."

I leave my room in a hurry, stepping a little heavier than normal down the stairs.

It takes Nora a full three minutes before she finally joins me in the kitchen, where we pretend like the conversation never happened.

And we never discuss it ever again.

"I just don't understand, Nora," I say, speaking up a little louder this time. The memory makes me mad. Sure, I could've been a little bit more sensitive to her feelings. But still... "All of this because I dated Dean a million years ago?"

Her eyes light up with fire. "*You had his BABY!*" I've never seen her look like this before. She's feral. Enraged. Insane, even.

"Is that what it is?! Because we share a *kid*?!" I ask. "What, do you want my son dead because he's not *yours*?!"

Everything that's happened to us... to my son... Nora has been the one behind it. After all these years of me being her friend. Of giving her money. She secretly hated me?

"Oh my God," I say, putting a hand over my face and shaking my head. "It was you. You went in Warner's phone and sent that text to Jackson that night I had you over after Warner went to bed! I'm so stupid! I can't believe I didn't even consider that it could be you!"

"You had her in our *house*?" Warner cries to me in disbelief.

"You're not stupid, Maddy," Nora says. "Not *completely*, anyway. I only did that because I knew I wouldn't get caught, after all."

"I-I remember you going to use the bathroom... but then I also remember—*now*—thinking I could have sworn you just walked out of Warner's bedroom. I quickly dismissed it because...well..."

"...it was such a ridiculous thought to have," Nora finishes for me. "So, you thought."

"You went into my room while I was sleeping, put my thumbprint on my phone, and then texted Jackson to ruin our friendship?" Warner asks her. I hate the sight of the two of them even interacting at all. I want him as far away from her as possible. For the first time ever, I wish he was already in Florida, away from all of this.

"It was a two-for-one." Nora shrugs. "Your friendship with him, *and* Lyla's relationship with him. *Ugh*. Little had I known then that it would only bring you and Lyla closer together. I'm basically a matchmaker by mistake."

She seems so nonchalant about all of this. It's not normal.

Nora is a monster.

CHAPTER 75

NORA

1998

"Dean?" I ask as we sit inside his bedroom together. We're supposed to be working on homework. He's doing a much better job at it than I am. I'm sitting at his desk, re-organizing the stack of CDs that are all in their wrong cases next to his boom box.

"I know, I know. I need to put them away right," Dean says behind me, on his bed. "It's just easier when I go to switch the CDs out, to put the old one into the case that's already open. Come on—you know I'm right."

I spin in his chair to face him. "It's not about that," I say.

"Is it about homework?"

I make a fake gagging noise. "No."

He laughs. Then he puts his pencil down. He cares about homework way more than I do. He cares about school way more than I do. He and Mia have that in common.

It's no wonder he likes her more than me.

"Then what's it about?" he asks.

I chew on the inside of my cheek. "Is there anyone you like? At school?"

His beautiful, perfect, thick eyebrows bunch together, and the face he makes is so cute I could die. "I don't know. Why? Does Carson have some weird foster sister he wants to set me up with?"

I throw my pencil at him. He dodges it with the folder that he's using as a lap desk.

"Hey!"

"No. What do you mean when you say you don't know, though? Does that mean there is someone?"

He shrugs. "This is weird," he says.

"What is?"

"We don't talk about our crushes. That's not a thing you and I do."

"But you're my best friend," I tell him. "Who else am I going to talk about it with?"

"I had no clue about you and Carson," he argues, "You didn't talk to me about him."

"Just tell me who your crush is before I throw another pencil at you!"

He sighs. "I... I think I'm going to ask out Maddy Carpenter."

My eyes glaze over. All my thoughts about the possibility of a future with him, my hopes and dreams about a happy life with Dean Reeves go out the window. It's like I can see them all in a crystal ball. And then Maddy Carpenter appears out of nowhere, swinging a wooden bat and smashing my crystal ball into smithereens.

I already know Dean kissed my sister. I saw the whole thing. And that alone was enough to break me. That alone was the whole reason I was asking him about who we had a crush on now. I figured enough time had passed since their kiss, and that Dean had moved on from Mia. I figured that I could finally test the waters and try and see if Dean has any feelings for me.

Then I get blindsided by his feelings for Maddy? I get knocked down, completely crushed, all over again?

I wish I was a mouse that could burrow into a hole in the wall and hide forever. In the dark, where no one will find me.

Why do I keep losing you, Dean?

Why do I keep losing you to all these other girls?

Why am I not good enough?

"Nora?"

I have to snap out of it. I cannot show a reaction. The last thing I want is for Dean to know how hurt I am. The last thing I want is our friendship to end over this. I need Dean in my life. I don't care how. I can't let things change.

"Sorry," I say, giving a playful eye roll and totally putting on the act. "It's just weird to hear you say Maddy. Because I could've sworn you were going to say my sister."

He looks completely weirded out. "Why would I like your sister?"

You liked her when we were in junior high, Dean.

I shrug. "I thought maybe that was why it was weird for you to tell me about it. But I guess Maddy makes sense, too, since we're becoming closer friends and all these days anyway."

I just want to get out of here. I need to get out of here. I need to be alone.

"That would never happen," he says, closing the idea down quickly. I wonder why that is. I wonder what Mia said to him after their kiss. The second I saw it happen, I ran away. I have no idea what went down afterward. As far as I guessed, they had a make-out sesh and confessed their love for each other but then swore to never tell me. As far as I guessed, they were dating right now, still keeping it a secret all these years later, just because Mia is too afraid for me to find out.

But that can't be true. Or else Dean would never go for Maddy.

I am so heartbroken that my stomach physically hurts.

I nod at him.

"What's wrong?" he asks. "You look... weird."

"I don't feel so good all of a sudden," I say. "Um... I think I need to go home. I don't want to vomit all over your precious CDs." I force out a fake laugh. Then I collect all my stuff, and he gets up quickly to help me.

"Do you think you have food poisoning? I'm pretty sure we ate the same thing, like, all day."

"It could be from last night's dinner," I lie. He helps me put my backpack around my shoulders, and it's such a sweet gesture that it makes me feel even sicker. How can he be so sweet to me? How can he care about me so much and not feel anything else for me?

"Hey, what's on your jaw?" he asks, trying to get a closer look at me.

I swat his hand away. "It's nothing."

"Doesn't look like nothing," he says.

"I don't even know what you're talking about. There's nothing there."

He tries to look again. I turn so that he can only see the other side of my face.

"Stop!"

"Okay!" he cries, putting his hands up in surrender. "Do you want me to walk you back?"

"No," I say, a little too loudly.

His eyes widen.

I try to smile again. "I-I'll see you later. Oh, and that's cool about Maddy, by the way." I hate every second of getting these words out. I don't want to lie to him. But I have to. "You should totally ask her out."

The second I am downstairs and out his front door, the tears surge out of me.

I run home sobbing. I burst through our front door and storm up the staircase. I know my family can hear me. But there's nothing I can do about it. I held back as long as I could.

It doesn't take long for Mom and Dad to come up and check on me. They ask me some questions. They sit down on either side of me and rub my back and try to make me feel better. But I don't say anything. It's impossible to say anything. Because I can't stop crying.

Dean Reeves broke my freaking heart. Again!

All I want is to be loved by him. Why won't he ever choose me?!

Eventually, they give up and leave. Then a few moments later, Mia barges in. I know it's her just by the way the door flies open. I can't see her though, because I'm face-down on my bed, my face smashed into my pillow as I cry.

"Nora, what's going on?" she asks. "What happened?"

At this point, I am sick of having anyone in my room. I'm sick of Dean. I'm sick of her. I'm sick of everyone.

So. Sick. Of everyone.

"Can't you... all just... leave me alone?!" I say through my tears.

She does the opposite. She sits on my bed, by my feet. "Nora, just talk to me."

I finally lift my head, only to yell at her some more. "If I have to knock before coming in your room, then so do you!"

I don't expect it when she jumps up with huge eyes.

"Nora, what is that?!"

Oh. So, she's seen it. My jaw.

I turn away from her. "Nothing!"

She reaches a hand out to me. "Nora, you tell me how you got that right now!"

Just like I swatted Dean way, I swat her hand away next. "Don't touch me!"

I hate her. I hate her so much. I don't get what Dean sees in her. What Maddy sees in her. She's nothing special. She's not better than me.

"Did Carson do that to you?" Mia asks me. "Tell me the truth, Nora!"

I jump up off the bed and start backing her into a corner as I give her the dirtiest look I can. "Carson would never hit me!" I yell. "Nothing. Happened!"

"Then why are you crying?" she asks. She looks a little nervous. A little afraid of my behavior.

It's just what I want.

"It has nothing to do with him," I say. But as she stares at me, I know she doesn't believe a word of it.

"Nora, if he's hurting you, you can tell me," she says. Her voice is soft now. She actually sounds like a caring sister.

But it's probably all an act.

"I swear, Mia, if you tell Mom or Dad anything about this, and if you even so much as mention Carson's name to them, you're going to regret it. He didn't touch me."

"Nora," she whispers.

Is she seriously about to cry right now?

Way to make it about you, Mia.

"Besides," I say, done crying. I wipe my eyes and straighten up. "I'm having Carson over for dinner tomorrow night to meet Mom and Dad. You can't ruin it for me."

Then a rock hits my window. I recognize the sound because it happens often. I know that Carson is here. He's outside, waiting for me.

"What is that?" Mia asks, following behind me as I go to the window. I open the blinds, and there Carson is, on the side of our house between my home and Dean's.

I look at Mia. "Tell Mom and Dad I went to sleep." Then I start opening the window.

"Nora, no!" she snaps, grabbing me by the elbow. "You cannot go see him!"

But Carson is angrily waiting for me. We got into a bit of a spot earlier. "Nora, get down here!" he hisses from down below.

"I'll be right there," I bark at him, annoyed. He's such a drama queen.

"I mean it, Nora!" Mia cries as I yank my arm from her. "You need to stay away from him!"

I put my flip-flops on. "You don't know what you're talking about." Then I go fix my makeup-streaked face in the mirror. Mia grabs me from behind and turns me to face her.

"You're being crazy, Nor! That kid is a psycho!"

She wants to call me crazy?

I'll show her crazy.

Seeing red, wishing she could just disappear forever, I shove her as hard as I can.

Mia flies back into the wall and bumps into my dresser, making the contents on top of it shake. Then she sinks to the floor and looks up at me in horror.

Why couldn't it have been her head that hit the corner? That would've been so much more satisfying.

"You can't control me," I say to her. "I'm going."

CHAPTER 76

Amelia

I remember that day, when Nora stormed into the house crying her eyes out. She didn't want to talk to Mom or Dad. And when I tried to talk to her, she shoved me and snuck out to meet Carson.

I remember the bruise she had along her jaw line.

All this time, I thought she had been crying over what Carson did to her. But then I think about how the very next day, Maddy told us she and Dean were together. At the time, Nora had seemed totally okay with it, which I thought was weird because I knew very well how in love with Dean she was.

"That night when you shoved me, when we were in high school and you were crying in your room," I start, wanting my suspicions confirmed, "you were crying about Maddy and Dean, weren't you?"

"It was a long time ago," Nora says.

Nora was a mess that night. I had never seen that side of her. She had never put her hands on me like that before. How did I not see it then? How did Mom and Dad not see it? She was too in love with Dean. In a way that was dangerous. In a way that made her dangerous.

I could've stopped all of this from happening a long time ago.

"It was you who ran me off the road that one night," Warner chimes in. He's glowering at Nora. He looks like he wants to hit something.

"I don't think you guys understand," Nora says. Again, thunder booms loudly. "I've done everything."

"No. I don't get it," Audrey says, shaking her head repeatedly. "Carson... he—he was just as bad. Just as... violent. You're... covering up for him or something. He has something on you that you're afraid we'll find out about. Because it was Carson who tried to kill me and Warner in the pool room at school. Not you, Nora."

I notice how she no longer wants to put the "Aunt" in front of her name.

I don't blame her.

"That's because you were in contact with Eric!" Nora says. "And Carson blabbed about it to Warner. He panicked. Granted, at this point, he was pretty much a completely different person. Spending so many years hiding, realizing that his dad was this close to finding him, this close to killing him, after so long, it had him very much on edge. He was desperate to not get caught. He wanted to shut you both up. He didn't think he had any other choice."

"And who made him feel that way?" I ask, seething. Nora glances at me, but she doesn't answer me.

"But I was never going to kill him," Eric says.

Nora shrugs. "He never knew that."

Pain stabs at my chest at her words. Carson died thinking Eric hated him. And Eric will never get to tell him the truth.

"I think Nora is telling the truth about what happened in the pool," I say to Audrey.

She shakes her head at me.

"Carson threatened to shoot me when I found him in the woods. And his threat didn't feel empty. He had a gun even." I look at my sister. "Nora, you need some serious help."

How does Nora feel about Dean now? And if she has always known all of our secrets, does she know that we are together?

Dean has been trying to protect me, but what if I need to protect him from my sister?

"You've had me fooled," Maddy says. "All this time, I thought we were still friends. All this time, and I never had an inkling about you. Jeez, Nora. All of this because of Dean freaking Reeves?" Then she side-glances at Dean. "No offense."

Dean is as speechless as he's been since we got here.

"Oh, you've always been such a vapid idiot!" Nora yells at Maddy. "Dean is just the start of my hate for the both of you!"

"What else is there?" I yell. "What else have I done to you?! Nora, my entire life has been about you! My entire life has been dedicated to helping you!" My future was ruined because of her.

"Only because of your guilt over what you did to Carson!" she shouts back. "Of what you both did!" She slowly makes her way to the center of the circle we've all subconsciously made at the cliff of the swimming hole. "You've both just redirected your lives to try and make up for your mistake. I bet you feel pretty dumb now. Because I've always known!"

"Nora..." I trail off, the words getting lost in my throat as the crashing weight of realization consumes me.

She's always known.

"Then why pretend like you didn't?!" Dean interjects angrily. "Why do that to them, Nora?!"

"Shut up, Dean!" she snips. She casually paces around in the center of the circle. "First, you broke my heart by kissing my sister when we were in the eighth grade. Then Maddy showed up and you started dating her. And even after I told Maddy I didn't want her to be with you, she kept dating you anyway."

This is news to me.

Then Carson came into the picture," she continues, "and I thought maybe I could move on from Dean. Finally. I thought maybe I could get past my anger. I really liked Carson, ya know? He was the only one I ever liked besides Dean. And then you two tried to kill him!"

Maddy and I look at each other. Her eyes are as big as mine.

"Yes I know!" Maddy shouts. She stops pacing. "Of course, I know!"

"But... but he was beating you, Nora!" Maddy cries.

"No, he wasn't!"

"But... I saw your bruises, Nora," I say. I am drenched and freezing, and the wind feels like it's turning the water drops on my body straight into ice.

"He gave you a bloody nose!" Maddy adds.

"It's like I told you that night when we were in my room," Nora says to me. "Carson never laid a finger on me."

CHAPTER 77

NORA

1998

He can't do this. He can't do this to me. Not now.

"I'm sorry, Nora," Carson says. But he hardly even looks sorry. His jaw is tense. His hands are clenched into fists. He looks more angry than anything else. But it's not fair. He doesn't get to be angry.

"No," I say.

"No?"

"You're not breaking up with me, Carson."

It's the middle of prom. I'm lucky I even get to be here. I'm only a sophomore and got invited by Carson.

Invited by Carson.

He can't just bring me to his prom and then dump me during it!

"Yes, I am," he says. "That's exactly what I'm doing."

"What is your problem?!"

"You!" he yells back. We're standing in the parking lot at school. He finally brought me out here after acting weird the first half of the night. He's not normally one to dance, but not only did we not step foot on the dance floor, he's also hardly said a word to me. He's hardly even looked at me.

And that hurts. I worked really hard on getting pretty for him tonight. I'm looking my very best. I want to be irresistible to him. So why do I suddenly have the opposite effect? This isn't how tonight is supposed to go.

This can't be happening to me.

"What did I do to you?" I cry, stomping a foot. I'm too pretty to be crying and stomping my feet in such a beautiful dress. I'm too pretty to be hurt like this again.

I don't want to get hurt anymore.

"The fact that you even have to ask me, Nora, that says it all right there. You're... you're crazy. You're pathological. You're out to make it seem to everyone like I am some horrible, abusive boyfriend, and I'm not. I'm not that person, Nora. Do you have any idea what you're doing to me? Do you have any idea how hard my life already was before I came here?"

But I'm hardly listening to him. Instead, I'm planning. Plotting.

Carson Price can't break up with me. I finally found somebody to be mine. And I won't let him slip from my fingers like Dean did.

"I'm not crazy," I growl through my teeth.

"Of course, that's all you heard," he says, turning away from me. "We're done, Nora."

He starts walking away. I grab his hand.

"No!" he shouts, ripping it away from me. "Don't touch me. Just stay away from me. I mean it, Nora. We're over." Then he keeps walking.

"Carson!" I cry after him. Tears stream down my cheeks. My heart feels like it's combusted. I'm choking on the smoke filling my lungs. I fall to my knees, snagging my tights and not caring in the slightest.

Pick yourself up, Nora.

A few more sobs escape me before I finally listen to myself.

I'm stronger than this.

Besides, Carson and I are not done. He's wrong about that.

But to make sure that nobody else even thinks twice about wanting to be his next girlfriend, I'll have to take drastic measures.

I wipe my eyes. Now, they're fully dry. I don't have time for tears. Not yet. I need to save them. For now, I just need to remain focused on the task at hand.

I look around the parking lot.

What can I use? What can I use?

Then I spot it.

The tow hitch on the back of someone's pickup truck. That round metal ball. It's the perfect shape of someone's fist.

I make sure no one is around before I crouch down in front of it.

I shake my hands out, as if to rid the sweat from my palms.

Like that's going to work.

I slap my cheek a couple of times. If only a red, slapped cheek would be enough to do the job...

No. I have to take it further. I have to go to the extremes.

Carson cannot leave me.

I let out a slow, long breath. I tell myself I can't inhale again until I do it.

Yelling out, I get on my hands and knees and slam my face into the tow hitch. My nose cracks. The blood starts pouring from it instantly.

And it really, really hurts.

The plan has been put into action.

I run back into the school and make sure I am spotted by several people as I dash inside the bathroom and lock myself in a stall. Then I enact the tears again. The shocking sight of blood is what I needed. The bruises I had given myself before were weak, only seen by those who bothered to look close enough. I needed this to be seen by everybody.

It doesn't take long before somebody grabs my sister and Maddy, and they come barging in.

They ask me what happened.

I tell them Carson punched me. I tell my sister she was right about him. I make up some sob story about how he wanted me to spend the night with him when I wasn't ready. The plan always was to have a sleepover. At some cabin in the woods. He said he's been there several times. That he doesn't know who it belongs to, but it's always empty. He said we could have it all to ourselves. And I had been so excited.

And then he ruined it.

Then Maddy and Mia bring me into the hall. Dean, Parker, and Craig are all there. I tell them about how I have a record of every time Carson has ever hit me. In reality, I snapped pictures with my polaroid camera every time I hurt myself. When Carson and I first became a couple, I worried from the very start that it wouldn't last. But I need it to last. I need to be loved by him.

Dean brings me to his house. He comforts me. He's a complete gentleman. It seems like he's my best friend again. We have been distant lately. It's nice to be back here.

But I can't stop thinking about Carson. And it feels good that I can't stop thinking about him. I'm alone with Dean Reeves on prom night, but yet, I'd rather think about another boy.

Take that, Dean.

I just keep picturing Carson at a romantic cabin in the woods with somebody else. What if there is someone else? What if there has always been someone else, somebody who knows the truth already because Carson's been telling them this whole time?

I get sick to my stomach. I can't concentrate on anything else. Dean notices it. "Are you sure you're okay?" he asks with his arm around me on the couch in his living room. His parents aren't home. It's date night. Technically, I'm not even supposed to be in his house if they aren't here. But he's made a special exception for little ole me.

"Actually, can I have some water?" I croak.

"Of course." He disappears into his kitchen.

And that's my cue to leave.

I grab his keys off the coffee table. I dash out the front door. I steal his Bronco and drive to the address Carson wrote down for me back before, when he said he wasn't going to come to prom and that I should just meet him at the cabin after.

It's a long drive. I don't even know if Carson is really going to be there. The closer I get to the cabin—after having to pull over every few miles to double check the map—my panic and suspicion start to slowly dissipate.

It's ridiculous of me to be doing this, isn't it? I'm going to be in huge trouble with Dean and his parents for taking his car. And my parents, too.

But I've already come this far.

I drive the rest of the way until I can't take the car any closer to the address. I park on the road and follow the trail that the sign with the address nailed to a nearby tree is pointing to.

When I reach the cabin, I walk around the side of it because the inside looks dark. I see the pool first.

And then I see the sopping-wet lump beside it, in the grass and leaves.

It's Carson. And he's not moving.

I run to him. I see the gash on the back of his skull. I see the blood.

All I can think is that he's dead.

I sob and shake and lay over his body, and then his eyes open.

As it turns out, he's alive.

He pulls me to my feet and tells me that he needs to stay dead, and that I have to convince everyone that he's dead.

"I don't understand," I say, sniffling. "Carson, come on. Please just tell me what happened. I don't understand. You're hurt! Who did this?"

"Maddy Carpenter," he says, still gripping my shoulder. Only, his grip tightens. His face darkens. "And your sister."

All I can do is shake my head over and over again. Because they wouldn't do this. They wouldn't hurt him like this and then just leave. They know how I feel about him. And... they're not bad people. Especially not perfect, angelic Mia. Mia wouldn't do this.

"I don't know why you're shaking your head, Nora," Carson says venomously. "They pushed me off the balcony up there."

I turn and look where he's pointing. I see the broken-off piece of railing from the balcony of the A-frame cabin. Now it makes sense why he's drenched. He fell into the pool.

"How did you get out?"

"I don't know. I blacked out. I went over the edge, and that's the last thing I remember."

"It looks bad, Carson. I really think you need to go to the hospital."

"No. It's not gonna happen, Nora. You hear me? I can't. I can never show myself to anyone again. Anyone but you. Got it?"

"Why, Carson?" I ask, sobbing more. What does this mean? Am I never going to see him again? Why does he want to stay gone? I don't understand any of it. But I know that I'll do whatever I need to to help him. To make up for what my sister and Maddy did to him.

"I can't explain right now," he says. "There's not enough time. I'm dead, okay? I have your phone number memorized. I'm going to go now, and I will swing by somewhere on my way out of town and get some stuff for my head, okay? I'm going to be fine. And when I'm somewhere safe, and when I know that you've done what I've told you, I will contact you. But if anyone answers the phone besides you, I'm hanging up. And I won't call from anywhere that you could trace back the number and find me. And I'm not going to stay in one place long enough even if you try to. If I don't stay gone, Nora, then I might as well be dead. And if I don't stay dead, something horrible will happen to you, too."

I'm so overwhelmed. So confused. So angry at my sister and Maddy. I'm hardly even hearing anything he's saying. I'm just picturing what I'll say to people. I'm just picturing myself sitting on my bed, waiting to hear from him. Picking up the phone on the very first ring, desperate to hear Carson's voice again.

What if I never hear it again?

"But, Carson—"

"You owe me this, Nora."

I fall silent, still sniffling and shaking and trying not to sob anymore.

"After everything you've done, after the stuff you've pulled, you owe me this."

"I don't want you to go."

He shakes his head. He doesn't care what I want.

"You wanted me to stay with you, right? To stay in your life? Well guess what, Nora. You've gotten your wish. Because now, you're going to be the only person in my life."

CHAPTER 78

MADDY

Mia is delusional. Or she's choosing not to believe what is clearly right in front of her.

"But... no, Nora," she says to her sister. "I saw the bruises. I saw your bleeding nose at prom."

But I know exactly what happened.

"Mia," I say, "she's telling the truth. Carson never did lay a hand on her."

"What are you talking about?" she asks, her voice shrill. When the lightning illuminates her face, all of her features are pulled tightly back against her skull.

"Oh my God," Dean mutters. I think he's just caught on. "She did it to herself. She made it look like it was Carson."

"W-what?" Mia stutters. "N–no. Because that would mean... that would mean..."

"Did Carson ever hurt you at all?" Audrey asks Nora.

Nora shrugs. "I loved him. And things really are plain and simple when you love somebody enough. He needed to stay gone. And I was desperate to keep him in my life. So, I helped him."

"You hurt yourself to get him to stay with you," I tell her. "Nora, how *could* you?" I want a genuine answer from her. I want a valid explanation. I want something to make sense of all of this. Because that night, twenty years ago, Mia and I thought we killed Carson Price. And we did it for Nora.

What if all of this time, Carson had actually been a decent person?

No.

I can't think like that. It can't be possible.

It's too much.

"Carson didn't tell me for a long time why he needed to stay gone," Nora explains. "And I'm talking *years*. He didn't trust me. Go figure. But I was dedicated to proving to him that he could trust me. Even when all those rumors started spreading about me. That I was the girl who cried wolf. That Carson was alive. That he just *ran* away. And it was honestly surprising. I didn't expect so many people to turn on me. To think that I was some crazy person. And once people start thinking you're crazy, it sort of messes with your head. I started feeling like I *was* crazy. Why was I doing this? Why was I helping him? I hadn't heard from him. My life was flipped upside down. I couldn't go to school. I was miserable. And I missed him so much.

"And then it became too much for my parents to deal. And I got sent away. Locked up. In an *institution*. Because of the lie I was telling to help the boy I loved." Nora pauses in her explanation to look at Dean. "If you had given me a chance, you have no idea how fiercely I would have loved you. How I would have gone any lengths necessary to protect you."

"Nora, everything you're telling us, it's not healthy, okay?" Mia says. "It's not right."

"You think I don't know that?!" Her voice is loud, and she is furious again in an instant. She growls like an animal getting ready to fight, and then she resumes pacing around the circle. "What's messed up is that Maddy and my sister tried to *kill* someone, and *I* end up being the one who gets locked up! And what's even worse than that? My dear, *dear* sister never even visited me. Even though this was all her fault!"

"It's not," Mia tries.

"IT IS!" Nora yells at her. "If you would've never pushed Carson off the balcony, he wouldn't have ever had an excuse to fake his death! It *is* all your fault!"

"You made it seem like if we didn't do something about it, he would kill you, Nora!" I shout at her. How else can I make her understand? She's screaming, so maybe screaming back is the only way to communicate with her.

Only instead, Nora has the audacity to ignore me.

"Mia just got to move on with her life. And Dean, my best friend since diapers...I'm in an insane asylum when I know I don't need to be there, and my *best friend* can't even visit me. And when he finally sends me a letter, he's not even checking in on me! He's just telling me about his love for *my sister*!"

"You only chose one part of that letter to listen to!" Dean says. "I *did* check on you! I didn't know anything about those kind of places! All my parents told me was that you went somewhere to get help. It made me angry when kids at school said you went somewhere for crazy people. I never thought you were crazy, Nora. I just thought you were heartbroken. And I told you in that letter, that if you didn't write me back, I would take it as a sign that you didn't want to speak to me again. And you never wrote me back. So, I never visited. I thought you didn't want to see me, Nora. You were my best friend, and it sucked! I know it must've hurt you to hear that I was in love with your sister. I tried not to be, Nora. I swear to you, I did. Because I didn't want to hurt you. I never wanted that."

"So, that was it?" she asks him. "I get a little angry, don't feel like replying to your stupid letter, so you just give up on our friendship entirely? You don't keep trying to write to me? You don't come visit me anyway?"

"I didn't think you would see me," he says. "I'm not a mind reader, Nora. I thought our friendship was over."

"It's so nice to know how much effort I am worth to you, Dean."

He falls silent and shakes his head.

"The only person who ever visited me besides my parents was you, Maddy."

I don't even want to look at her.

She continues. "But I knew the whole time the real reason why you did it. I knew what you did. I looked you in the eyes while you pretended like nothing was wrong, when in the back of your mind, you thought Carson was dead. And you knew you and Mia were the ones who belonged where I was sitting. And you listened to everyone calling me crazy when you knew what you did."

She's right. I can't even say anything back to her because she's completely right. I thought we killed Carson. And I didn't know what happened to his body. I was always confused about that. Who had taken it? Was he buried in the woods somewhere? Did Nora bury him and not tell anyone where?

"I'm not stupid, Maddy," Nora tells me. "Your guilt, and your rebellious ways because of your filthy rich parents that you hated, your alcoholic father that you didn't want anyone to know about, they were all the reasons why you gave me your trust fund. After I left that place, you were the only reason I was able to fund Carson's disappearance."

"Mom, you didn't," Warner says.

But now they know. Now they all know where my money went. I didn't gamble it all away on a crazy Las Vegas trip when I was eighteen. I gave it all to Nora. I thought she deserved to have a good and happy life after she got out of there. That with all the other things she had to worry about, I thought money shouldn't have to be one of them.

I don't look at Warner. It's because of me that we live the way we live. Because of me, Warner doesn't have money for college and has to get a job to help me pay bills. I never tried hard enough to set up a good future for him. I never became more than just a stupid hairstylist.

"And then you gave yourself another reason to continue feeling guilty, didn't you, Maddy?" Nora asks me. "You never told me that you and Dean got back together. And you never told me that you were pregnant with his baby."

"That wasn't just you," I say. "I hid it from everyone."

"Because it was a scandal! Because so many people would've been outraged! Including me!"

Nora looks at Warner, and I wish she wouldn't. She thinks he's some sort of monster just because he was made by me and Dean. "You refused to tell anyone who the dad was, and you pretended like you didn't know. But I *knew* you, Maddy. If there were multiple prospects, I would've heard about them when you visited me. You would've told me about your guy troubles. But you weren't having any guy troubles. It wasn't hard to figure out. So, when I learned that you were pregnant, and when I got out of my little loony bin because I was a legal adult and voluntarily allowed to leave, I ran away. I disconnected from everyone. Including my own parents. I was mad at them. Because how could they not see what a horrible daughter they had, and how the wrong one was locked away?

"The only person I was in contact with was Carson. And occasionally, Maddy and I would connect. Guilty Maddy, always wanting to check in on me."

"You make it seem like that was the only reason," I say. "I *cared* about you, Nora. I saw you as a sister."

She chooses to ignore me. "When I proved to Carson that I had isolated myself, and that I wouldn't be followed by anyone, he finally let me see him again. And we stayed on the run together. I was smart with Maddy's money. I kept it safely put away and only used what I needed. I got remote jobs or did side-hustles any opportunity I had, and I made us live a very frugal lifestyle. I didn't want Carson to know that I had all that money. Because I wanted him to only be with me because he loved me. But I was stupid. I was forgetting the one huge reason why he faked loving me back—so that I would keep helping him. So that he wouldn't be completely alone. It took a few years, but eventually, I realized the truth. And it stunk. Eventually, I began to realize that what we had wasn't real. But still, what else could I do? Where else could I go? It was like Carson said—I owed him."

"You didn't owe him anything," Mia says. "You had a choice, Nora."

"Yeah, and I *chose* to stay with him. You don't get it. I loved him, Mia. I loved him so much that even when I knew he didn't actually love me back, I stayed."

"That's sad, Nora," I say. "Do you have no self-worth? Do you not understand that there are people out there who *would* love you back?"

"I know how to fight for what I want," she says. "I knew that Carson was worth the effort. I stayed on the run with Carson. He still wouldn't tell me why he was doing this. But I didn't need to know. And I liked being on the run. I liked not staying in one place for long. It was actually... fun. I went to so many places. I did so many things. I was still mad at people, of course. At first, I just did petty little things, like breaking up you and Parker, Mia. Oh, and you know that woman who got you fired from your first real interior design job? Yeah. I hired her to do that."

"Wait, what?" I ask. I don't remember hearing anything about this.

"You hired her to be an unhappy client?" Mia asks. Then she looks at me. "I got fired from my first interior design job outside of college because one of my clients was repeatedly complaining about what a horrible job I did."

"You were the only one I could still keep tabs on through Mom," Nora explains. "She never had updates to give on Maddy, so I had no idea what she was up to. I was too far away to be able to really wreak havoc in her life. But I was still so mad at you both. At the same time, I was having fun in my young adulthood with Carson. And then... as the years went on, I finally got what I wanted. Carson finally started truly falling in love with me. I knew it was only a matter of time. How could he not? I was his only connection to the world. Or so I thought. And after so much time of building up that trust and having a genuinely happy, loving relationship, he finally let me in. He told me what Harley did and how he took the blame. He told me that his dad wanted his revenge. And I didn't judge him. I understood him.

"You know, there did come a point where we tried to settle down. We actually got a little place. In North Carolina. We both got simple jobs. I still had plenty of money from Maddy. We liked our life. We were so in love. And we thought... why not try and start a family of our own?"

"But... you can't conceive," Mia mutters.

I never knew this.

Nora lets out a dark, sarcastic laugh. "Yep. The *one* thing I wanted, more than being with Dean. *More* than being with Carson, was to have a baby. To have a little child of my own that I could raise in a household full of love and protection. I tried. And *tried*. And when I went to the doctor and learned the truth..."

"You got mad all over again." Mia says. "You were mad because you couldn't have a kid, but Maddy and I could."

"When did you find out?" Audrey asks.

"Right before she and Carson began harassing us," Warner answers.

Nora smiles, and it makes the hairs on the back of my neck rise. "I guess you can say that's when I *really* lost it."

"You started blackmailing Carson," Craig says. "You made him help you torment all of them or else you'd out him to his father."

"It just wasn't fair," Nora says, silent tears blending in with the rain. "Maddy and Mia were happy in their lives. I wanted to ruin them. I was miserable, and I wanted *them* to be miserable. Especially when Dean came back to Toxey. Mom mentioned it to me so casually on the phone when it happened. She thought I'd be *excited* about it. But I knew why he was back. For *you*, Maddy. To be a perfect little family with you and your little brat."

"Nora," Dean says in a warning voice.

She ignores him. "Before I knew it, Dean was back in town, Mia was married and had a big house and a successful career. Neither of you deserve to be happy," Nora says to Mia and me. "*I* did. And yet, my chance of happiness was stripped from me *again*. So, I started plotting. Carson and I started going on the move again. We found Megan living in the streets of New York City and scooped her up. We came closer to home. Carson hated that, but I convinced him. I was the one in control now.

"And Carson *did* help me at first. With Megan in tow, Carson helped me spill your secrets, make you miserable, and scare you all. But eventually, he started pulling away. He thought I was getting too obsessed with my revenge. I was beginning to feel like he wanted out. I was beginning to feel like I didn't have enough to hold over him anymore to get him to stay. And that wouldn't do. Not when I had worked so hard to get him to let me in in the first place."

"No, Nora," Craig says. "*No.*" He looks like he's choking. He shakes his head and doubles over, his hands on his hips. Is he going to be sick?

When I look back at Nora, I see that she finally looks a little bit guilty. But only when she looks at Craig.

"I'm sorry, Craig," she says. "I'm sorry I lied to you."

"I..." He still can't speak.

"What?! I *had* to get Carson to stay with me!" Nora yells. "What don't you guys understand about that?! He was all I had. I couldn't lose him! I drugged Carson. I made Megan get in that boat. And I killed her. And when Carson came to, I told him he did it. And he believed me! And after that, I knew I'd get to keep them. I knew I didn't have to worry about him running off any longer. I knew that he'd keep helping me. He thought he was a murderer."

"You made me think he was!" Craig shouts. "You made me—" He cuts himself off and turns his back to all of us.

I don't think I've ever pitied Craig until now.

"I'm sorry, Craig," she says again.

Why is it he's the only one she wants to apologize to? Does she really not think anyone else is owed one?

I don't want to hear anymore, but Nora has more to tell. "I had Carson, but I still didn't have a kid of my own. And I was still so mad about it. I had already killed one person before, and it was surprisingly easier than I thought. I guess I just thought—I take yours away, and we're even."

Mia moves in front of her daughters. I reach out my hand and make Warner come to me.

"You had plenty of opportunities to kill us," Lyla says. "Why keep me locked up in that shed instead of killing me, then?"

"And why not finish me off after I fell and cracked my head open when you were chasing me through the house?" Audrey joins in. "Or why did you just turn and leave after chasing me through the woods? You were standing *right* over me. You could've done it right then and there!"

"When I was visiting you all, Craig kept coming around asking Mia questions about what happened during your camping trip, and he saw me. He asked to grab dinner and catch up."

"You actually *fell* for him?" Warner asks. "After all of that with Carson?"

"You wouldn't understand, Warner. Craig... he had always loved me. Since we were teenagers. All this time, he was always *right* there. If I hadn't been blinded by my feelings for Carson, I would have known. I could have been happy a long time ago. With Craig, there are never any conditions. Never any stipulations. He's always honest with me. He doesn't play any games with me. He wants to keep me safe. How could I not fall for that?"

"But you were lying to him," I say. "You made him think Carson *forced* you to do all of this."

All Craig had been trying to do was protect the woman he loved.

"*Anyway*," Nora says loudly, ignoring me again, "Carson could tell. He could tell that I was over him. That he was just... excess baggage.

And once he figured this out, he tried to pull what Megan tried to pull. When you came to see me at my rental, Lyla? He wasn't trying to hurt you. He was trying to get you to listen to him. So he could confess. So he could tell you about me."

"I—but... he was in the costume!" Lyla cries.

"Yeah. My theory is that he was planning on kidnapping you again, throwing you in the back of his truck and taking you somewhere where you couldn't escape. Where you had no choice but to actually listen to him. Where you couldn't just call him crazy and run off. Not until he had you completely on his side."

"He didn't want to chance you seeing his face again and getting away before he could tell you everything," Dean says.

"So, everything you told me in your car that night was complete bull," Lyla says to Nora. "Jeez, Aunt Nora, you had a gun. You showed it to me. You might as well have just shot me right then and there."

There is so much hate and betrayal in her eyes.

And I completely empathize.

"My God, Ly, I'm not a *complete* monster," Nora says. "There was that TikTok account. You guys were being followed by so many people. I had to be extra careful everywhere I went. Anyway. When I met Harley when she came to town to investigate, I told her that we could help each other get what we wanted. And what we wanted was..."

She looks at Craig again.

All Craig can do is shake his head in disbelief.

"Carson had contacted me multiple times during the years he was on the run," Harley says. "He always thought I was on his side. I meant it when I told you I knew more about him than anyone, Amelia. Because Carson told me everything. What he *didn't* know was that he told me *exactly* what I needed to know to devise a plan to get rid of him for good. Thanks for doing that by the way, Craig."

"I thought I had no other choice," Craig says, looking at me and Mia. He's in complete agony. He's white as a ghost. And he's never seemed soberer. "When I found Carson in the woods, I thought there was only one way I could make sure he never hurt Nora again. I thought he was a monster. I swear. I didn't know. I didn't know how wrong I had it."

Mia and I were played by Nora.

Craig was played by Nora.

And Carson was played by her, too.

"She fooled us all," Mia says.

"Until you went and opened your big mouth," Nora snarls to Harley.

"Hey, if I had to get found out, so did you."

They stare each other down. But then it's Harley who waivers, her expression turning uneasy. I watch as her eyes dart to the left.

She's looking for an escape route.

"She's going to bolt!" I yell right as Harley tries making a run for it.

With Eric having been warned by me in time, he's grabs hold of her again.

"LET ME GO!" she screams. But Eric has a good, strong grip on her. Harley isn't going anywhere.

"Everyone knows everything now," Mia says, taking a step into the circle toward Nora. "You're my *sister*, Nora. I know you don't want to kill anyone. I *know* you, Nor. Deep down, this isn't you. You're our family. You don't want to hurt us."

Everything feels so unpredictable. Is Nora going to try running next? Is she going to hide out for the next twenty years, until our kids have kids of their own that she can mess with?

When is this going to be over?

"You don't get it," Nora says, shaking her head at Mia. "I've tried to kill Audrey so many times already."

"No, you didn't."

"I did, Mia. She only lived because she got lucky. At your house, it was Carson who chased her, I told him to kill her. I told him to end it. He told me he thought that when she slipped and cracked her head open, she died then. But I know the truth. He knew she survived it—he was just too chicken to finish her off. I knew *I'd* have to be the one to do it. *I* chased you through those woods, Audrey. You're right. And trust me, I had every intention of doing it then. But then I got a text from Carson, telling me that Lyla had escaped from the shed. So, I had to hurry back to fix that problem, which was *extra* annoying, because it wasn't even supposed to be Lyla in that shed. I had tried to kidnap Audrey."

"Why do you hate me so much?!" Audrey yells. "Huh?! Why me?!"

"Because!" Nora yells back, stepping toward her. "Lyla is more like me! In fact, the more I got to know her when I was staying with you guys, the more I started to like her. And Joey—he's not even really your kid, Mia. I feel like having to be fostered by you is punishment enough for him. Poor kid. But you, Audrey?"

"What?!" Audrey yells. "What is so *wrong* with *me*?!"

"You're exactly like your mother!"

In the flash of a second, Nora reaches into her hoodie pocket, and I don't even see what she pulls out until I hear the earsplitting bang.

Then I hear screams.

My ears ringing, I look at Audrey, who Nora just shot a gun at. But she's still standing, and I don't see any blood.

However, in a heap on the ground in front of her is Craig.

CHAPTER 79

LYLA

"**A**UDREY!" Mom screams as Nora drops her gun to her feet.

Craig jumped in front of Audrey. Craig took a bullet for her.

And now, Craig is curled up on the ground, in the mud, and there's a lot of blood.

"Craig!" Nora cries out, both of her hands covering her mouth. She's frozen where she stands.

"Oh my God," Maddy gasps, running to Craig's side. "You shot him!"

"I-I didn't mean to!" Nora says. "Craig, I-I'm sorry!"

Craig is still conscious. His face is scrunched up tight as he holds his hand over his bleeding abdomen. It's doing nothing to stop all the blood pouring out of him.

"We... need to get help!" Warner says, dropping down next to Craig beside his mom.

Audrey looks like she's about to faint.

"I didn't mean to," Nora says again, shaking her head repeatedly and slowly stepping backward. "Craig, I really do love you. I'm so sorry."

She turns to run for it.

"No!" Dean shouts, lunging for her. "You don't get to run away again, Nora!"

"GET OFF OF ME!" She thrashes and kicks and yells, and Mom moves to help him hold her down. "LET ME GO!"

"Audrey, call 911," I instruct. She nods and sinks to her knees in front of Craig while taking her phone out.

"He's... he's dying!" Warner shouts, his shaking hands hovering above Craig's wound with no clue how to help him. Craig's twisted face starts relaxing, and his body grows stiller.

"No, no, *no*," Maddy says. "Craig, we're getting you help!"

Mia and Dean are pulling Nora further away from Craig. Or maybe from Audrey. At this point, I don't know anymore. They're closer to the edge of the cliff. We're over by the tree line.

Audrey tells the 911 operator what's happened. Craig rolls onto his back, his eyes open so he can look around at everyone. I get on my knees next to him, too. He saved Audrey's life. And I want to save his. But I just don't know how. We're in the middle of the woods. In the middle of *nowhere*. We're about a mile away from any cars.

"I'm so sorry, Craig," Maddy says to him, sobbing and clutching his arm.

"Try to stay awake, Craig," Warner says. "You have to stay awake, okay?"

"I..." Craig is struggling to talk or breathe. "I loved her. I..."

"I know," Maddy says through her tears. "It's okay."

"No!" Warner shouts. Craig's eyes start to close. "No, no, no!" Warner grabs his face and shakes it.

But Craig's eyes do not open again.

"This isn't happening," Warner says, shaking his head repeatedly. "No!"

Maddy and Audrey are both sobbing, Audrey still trying to talk to the 911 operator. Tears silently cascade down my cheeks, too, as I stare at Craig's lifeless body. My aunt killed him. My aunt killed Megan. My aunt tried to kill Audrey.

I turn my head to Aunt Nora. She is a crying, yelling mess. I look at Harley. She's given up struggling against her father, but he still has a tight hold on her. She fumes while Eric wears a morose expression. He won't look at anyone. I think he's just trying to give Craig his privacy.

I get to my feet.

"You need to tell the police what she did when they get here," I say to Eric. "You wanted to help Carson. But your daughter is the one who needs help now."

He nods. "We're not going anywhere," he reassures me.

Harley gives a halfhearted tug of her arm in a lame attempt to free herself. Eric tightens his grip.

"I don't know who you think you are," Harley says to me.

I approach Mom, Dean, and Aunt Nora.

"It's over, Nora," Mom says. "It's over, just accept it!"

Aunt Nora seems to calm down a bit when she sees me standing there.

"How do you do it, Lyla?" she asks me. "How can you stand existing with these monsters?!"

"I'm not like you," I tell her.

"What?" My words are enough to make her stop crying and struggling.

"You heard me," I say in a shaky voice. "I'm nothing like you, Aunt Nora. You've done horrible things. And you need to get help."

"Lyla, stay away from her," Dean demands. "Just stay back."

"Oh, I bet you think you're a *real* hero!" Nora hisses at him. "I bet you think you've redeemed yourself after all these years, don't you?!"

"Nora," Dean says, his grip on her strong. "I'm so sorry that I hurt you."

"How could you even want him back in your life, Maddy?" Nora yells to her. Maddy, still crying next to Craig's body, looks at her. "He abandoned you! For years! And what, you've *forgiven* him?!"

"I have," Maddy says, getting to her feet. "I have, Nora. Because I am capable of forgiveness. Unlike you, I can understand that people make mistakes and that people deserve second chances."

"So, that letter I sent him pretending to be you was all for nothing then!" Nora snaps as Maddy grows closer.

"What letter?" Maddy asks.

Nora looks at Dean. Realization crosses his expression, and for a split second, he loosens his grip on her. But it's all she needs. Out-strengthening my mother, she pulls herself free from both of them. But we have her surrounded. It's all of us and the edge of the cliff. She has no way out. Nowhere to run.

"Dean knows what I'm talking about," Nora says, flashing a quick, senseless grin.

We look at Dean.

"I got a letter from you, Maddy," Dean says in a low voice. "Just before you gave birth to Warner. You told me that you didn't ever want me to come anywhere near you or our son. You sounded so... hurt. So... *angry*."

"I... I never sent you a letter," Maddy whispers.

Dean looks at Nora. "You knew," he says. "You know exactly how to get me to stay away. *Exactly* how to prevent me from being the father I always should've been."

"You... *wanted* to be there?" Maddy asks him.

"Of course I did!" Dean cries. "I know I freaked out at first, but I was willing to pull it together and step up. When you had him, Maddy, I *wanted* to be there. I thought you sent that letter. So, I didn't come back."

"What is *wrong* with you?!" I yell at Aunt Nora. "You're pathetic, you know that?! How do I put up with *these* people? No, Aunt Nora. The real question is how anyone *ever* put up with you! You should've never been let out of that institution! You were right where you belonged!"

"Well, *you* killed your best friend!" she says. "So, you belong in there with me!"

"It was an *accident*!" Mom yells at her. "Don't even *think* you can compare yourself to my daughter! Both of my girls are just like *me*! Lyla will never be like you! You switched my pills, Nora. You tried to make me think *I* was the crazy one! But that gene had always been passed on to you!"

"Just add it to the list of reasons why my sister is so much more perfect than I am!" Nora bellows. "Add it to the reasons why Dean always preferred you over me!"

"I'm *sorry*!" Dean yells at her. "*God*, Nora, I am so, *so* sorry! I never meant to hurt you! You were so, *so* important to me. You were like my sister! And I know that's not what you want to hear, but I hope that you'll listen to me anyway! I didn't love you in the way you wanted me to, but I *did* love you."

"I don't care anymore!" Nora shrieks. She takes a step backward. "I don't love you anymore, Dean! And Carson is dead. *Craig* is dead. I don't have anyone else! I don't have anything more I can lose!"

"Nora, Stop," Mia says.

Nora takes another step backward.

"Nora," Dean jumps in. "Just *stay* there, okay?"

"Why? So I can go back in that place? Spend the rest of my life locked up?"

"Aunt Nora, don't," I say.

She takes another step back.

People jump off this cliff all the time. She'll be fine if she jumps, right? It won't kill her, right?

"I've fallen from this cliff before," she says. "I was so heartbroken over you, Dean. I remember, when my head was under the water, hoping that the jump would kill me. That I'd drown. That I'd never resurface. And it was peaceful. Quiet."

"Nora, get back from there!" Mia shouts.

"But then Carson jumped in and saved me," Nora continues. "Imagine all that he could've prevented if he hadn't."

"Nora!" Maddy yells.

But Nora is done listening to anyone.

She turns to the cliff.

"No!" Everyone's yelling at her.

But she doesn't care. She doesn't even look back at us.

She's really going to do this.

"Nora!"

Dean jumps out, wrapping himself around her. Nora clings to him tightly, a glimmer of a smile on her face. She tugs hard on his shirt as she falls backward, and then they both go over the edge.

CHAPTER 80

WARNER

I had a father once.

He was smart and tenacious and brave.

It took me nearly eighteen years to learn the truth about who he was.

For so long, I wondered about him. For so long, I dreamed about what it would be like to know him. To have him in my life. To have someone I could talk to about becoming the best man I could be. To finally know what it was like to have that type of a role model in my life.

Dean Reeves was my English teacher first. He was my football coach second. And then he was my Dad.

I didn't want to accept it. Not at first. I was angry. I felt abandoned. Betrayed. By not only him, but by my mother as well.

I wish I let him in sooner. I wish I had had more time with him.

I had a father once.

He was...

Well, I never got to learn what else.

Because now he's gone.

CHAPTER 81

AMELIA

Dean Reeves' life was taken from him last night. I loved him. My sister loved him.

And then my sister killed him.

People cliff jump all the time at the swimming hole. The fall shouldn't have killed anyone. But the way Nora pulled Dean off the cliff with her, the way their bodies entangled as they spiraled down, down, down...

Nora survived.

Dean didn't.

And there are no questions about it this time. There's no wondering if Dean is really dead. If maybe he is still out there somewhere, in the shadows, looking out at us all. There's no wondering if he swam far, far away and started a new life in another town. Another state. Another country.

Dean's body was pulled from the water. I saw it. Maddy saw it. My girls saw it.

Nora was also pulled from the water, by the police. She and Harley were taken into custody. I don't know what is going to happen to them.

While dealing with this tragedy, while feeling this giant, gaping hole in my chest, which is so painful I feel it could actually kill me, I've been on the phone with people left and right. Already, my mom has mentioned how Nora might be found "not guilty by reason of insanity". She might be deemed incompetent to stand trial. She might just get put away in her cozy psych ward, comfortable and numbed by various meds. Even after everything she did to me, my family, and Maddy's family, my mother is more worried about her than anyone else.

And that's always how it's been.

I don't know what to tell my girls. They've been asking about what will happen with their Aunt Nora. With Harley. But I don't know how to talk to anyone.

Dean is dead.

I distanced myself from him for years. for my entire life, practically. Even though I loved him.

I did it for Nora

I did everything for Nora.

And this is what I get for it.

Dean is dead. After I just *finally* let him in. I finally opened my heart to him. I was finally going to get the full experience of what it was truly like to be loved by him.

And then, like with everything else in my life, Nora ruined it.

I'll never understand it—Nora's hate for Maddy and me. *Me*. Her own sister. She hates me for the things I cannot control. She hates me for the life I have. The one she never got to experience. And there is absolutely nothing I can do to change her mind.

Dean isn't the only one who died last night.

Detective Craig Fritz is dead, too. He didn't survive the gunshot wound. Nora took two lives, thinking she'd get to take one more—her own.

Maybe that she did survive the fall is part of her punishment. Her karma. She didn't want to live, and now she has to face everything she's done. She has to think about it day in and day out. She killed the first man she ever loved. And she killed the last one she ever loved.

Poor Craig. He was blinded by her. He was manipulated and gaslighted by her. He couldn't see the truth. He killed someone who never deserved it. Because of Nora. Everything he ever did was because of Nora. Since we were kids.

And this is where it led him.

And then there's Carson.

All this time, he wasn't who we all thought he was. All this time, we saw him as a monster. He saw *himself* as a monster. He thought he killed Megan Young. He thought he had to kill Audrey to keep his dad from killing him. He never even got to learn the truth. His sister is the reason he spent so much of his life in hiding when he never needed to.

I can't help but think about how everything could have played out so differently if just a single different choice was made. Maddy and I could have confessed what we did. We could have called the police after we thought Carson was dead, and then we could have waited with his body until the police got there. We would have been with him when he woke up. It would have saved twenty years of so much guilt, fear, and pain.

I don't think everything happens for a reason. I think the choices we make in those quick, split-second moments are meant to force us to deal with the consequences we hadn't stopped to consider. I think each horrible thing that happens is life's way of teaching us a lesson. It's life's way of getting us to see just how important every decision is. Make the wrong one, the rash one, the quick and easy one, and life will kick you for it.

I don't know what is going to happen now. I don't know where to go from here. I don't know how to pick up the broken pieces of not only myself, but my daughters, too, and get us all to move on. To *finally* move on.

But we have to. We must be capable. Bad things happen every day. The world doesn't stop moving, no matter how much it feels like it should. No matter how much I want to just lay and think about Dean. About what I lost. I want to pause everything. I want to take as much time as I need to heal, and then hit PLAY and have nothing around me change until I do.

But it just doesn't work that way.

In the end, Nora didn't get what she wanted. In the end, everyone she wanted to suffer is still here.

We're all still here.

There is a long road ahead, for all of us. I suppose what matters most is that we can get through it. We *will* get through it.

Together.

CHAPTER 82

WARNER

Twenty-One Months Later

I step onto a plane when the weather is blistering hot, ridiculously humid, and annoyingly sunny. When I step off of it six hours later, it's pouring rain, cold enough to need a jacket, and just as I remember it.

I am finally back home. The Toxey airport is small, and it's usually not this crowded. At least, it wasn't the handful of times I've been here during my nineteen years of life.

"Warner!"

I grin immediately even though I can't see her yet. I can only hear her. She's here, somewhere, in the crowd.

A body slams into me, and I'm nearly knocked flat on my butt. I drop my bags, grab onto her tightly, and scoop her off the ground.

"You're finally here!" Lyla squeals before kissing me deeply. I've waited an agonizingly long nine months—since winter break—to be able to do this again.

"God, I missed you," I say to her when we stop kissing. I press my forehead to hers, still holding her in my arms. I don't care about the PDA we're flaunting. I don't care how cheesy we look. The girl I love is finally in my arms again. And I'll never have to go this long without seeing her again.

"Ditto," she says, giggling. I love seeing her this happy. I love how luminous she is. She is the sunshine in Toxey.

We walk out into the rain and run to her car, our hoodies pulled up over our heads. During the drive to my house, we have so much to talk about, which is almost weird because we talk on the phone every day, several times a day.

But I could never run out of things to talk about with her.

Especially since she's so excited about Florida and keeps asking me millions of things about it.

"Is there a good place for dessert?" she asks while pulling up to a red light. I am a bit distracted—I'll admit—because I keep looking out the window to see if Toxey has gone through any changes while I've been gone. And it's only been a few minutes, but already, I've seen that a commercial building that has sat vacant forever is going through a remodel. And was that a drive-thru coffee stand under construction we just passed by?

"Huh?" I ask, turning away from the window, back to her.

"You *know*, like Delilah's. Please tell me there is. Or else I don't know if I can go."

I playfully tickle her side over the console. She yells at me and swats my hand away.

"Shut up," I joke.

She pretends to be offended, gasping at me with her jaw dropping. "*You* shut up!"

We laugh, and I tell her, *again*, about all the great things to do around University of Miami. I completed my first year there, back in May. Now, my second year is about to start, and I am all moved-in to my new apartment with Logan and Mateo. I befriended them last year when I lived in the dorms and Logan was randomly assigned as my roommate. Mateo lived on our floor. Lyla knows all about them. And she's going to be meeting them very soon, because in just a few days, she's going to be in Florida with me.

"You won't even want our regular hangout spot to be anywhere indoors, I promise you that," I tell her. "Although the humidity... it takes some getting used to."

She smiles so big it makes my stomach flip. I can't describe how happy it makes me to see her like this. She's so excited. So full of hope. And she deserves this. She's worked so hard over the last year to get back on track in school and accepted into the same college as me. I can't wait to take the long road trip back in my Jeep—Mom's been borrowing it since last year because living in the dorms, I didn't really need it—with her and show her a whole new world.

"Maybe I'll finally get a real tan!" she cries.

"Or you'll just get super bad sunburns."

"Ha ha."

I tickle her again as the light turns green, and when she yells some more and moves my hand away, I grab onto hers tightly, and our fingers remain linked together the rest of the drive.

She drops me off—I have to have dinner with Mom tonight, and Lyla doesn't exactly want to be in attendance for it, plus she has some last-minute packing to do anyway—and Mom runs out of the house, screaming.

The rain has slowed, but it's still coming down, and even though Mom doesn't have an umbrella, or even shoes on, she doesn't care as she throws her arms around my wet hoodie and squeezes me tightly.

"Hi, Ma," I say, hugging her back. As I do, I can see Steven standing in the doorway over her shoulder. He smiles and waves at me.

"Welcome home!" Mom cries. We pull apart and I smile at her.

"Welcome to *your* home, you mean," I say. We no longer live in the small, rundown two-bedroom shoebox. When I came to visit over winter break, she broke the news to me that it was finally happening. She and Steven are moving in together.

Mom rolls her eyes, helps me with my bags, and drags me inside Steven Hall's mansion. I can't believe this is where I'll be staying. I can't believe I have my own room here—even though I don't plan on ever coming back long enough to really get settled into it.

"How was the flight?" Steven asks, shaking my hand when we get back inside.

"Good, thanks," I say. I have to admit it. I like Steven. I like my mom and him together. I've never seen her happy like this with anyone else.

They show me to my new room, give me a tour of the rest of the house as if I hadn't been here many times already because of the house parties Wrigley used to throw, and then the part I have been dreading most has finally come.

"Wrigley!" Steven yells up the staircase while I sit at the kitchen counter next to Mom.

"Coming," I hear Wrigley grumbling, probably from in his room. I watch him slowly come down the staircase, dragging his feet and looking like he just rolled out of bed. From what Mom has told me, Wrigley is doing online community college and working part-time at The Viper. I asked her why he had to work, and why he wasn't going to some fancy, expensive school since Steven has all that money, and she said it's because Steven has decided to make Wrigley work for what he wants instead of just spoiling him and coddling him as he had always done before.

He looks just as I remember him. T-shirt and dark jeans. Coily red-brown hair. An I'm-too-cool-and-mysterious-for-anything-and-anyone expression on his face. But I'm sure in the last nearly two years, I haven't changed too much either. I'm just taller and a little tanner.

Wrigley reaches us. "Sup," he says to me in a dull voice

"Hey," I say back, sounding just as thrilled.

Yeah. Wrigley and I still don't like each other.

After some forced small talk is made, Wrigley is allowed to go back to his room, and Steven has a work call to take in his office, so it's just me and Mom.

Mom. My best friend. Who would have thought I'd ever call her that? But it's true. Sometimes, when I get all into my feelings about what happened with Nora, I think pettily about how I at least have *her* to thank for bringing my mom and me closer than ever.

"You look so different," she says to me as she whips me up a snack in the kitchen. She's still dressed in her business-casual attire because she just got home from work a little before I arrived. She manages The Viper. She loves her job, and she does it even though she doesn't need to. I guess Steven told her she didn't need to work another day in her life because he'd always take care of her. But she's always had a job, since she graduated high school, so she said with me gone, she'd go crazy without one.

"What are you talking about?" I ask, smiling at how ridiculous she is.

"I'm serious. I don't know what it is. Florida... it looks good on you."

"Thanks, Ma. Living the wealthy lifestyle, you were always supposed to looks good on you, too."

"*Hey* now," she scolds jokingly.

I play innocent. "What?" If she never gave her trust fund away to Nora and cut herself off from her parents, she would have probably lived in a house like this a long time ago. The last time I visited, she drove me past her old house, the one she lived in when she was in high school, with her father. Even so many years later, it was still a really awesome house.

"I'm not with Steven for his money," she reminds me.

"No duh," I say. Anyone with eyes can see how gaga she is over her boyfriend. I just wish her boyfriend didn't happen to be the father of my girlfriend's ex.

Mom and I chat for a long time, and then since there's still a couple of hours until dinner, I hop in my old Jeep, which I've missed a *ton*, and drive down to the cemetery.

By the time I get there, it's no longer raining. The sky is still dark and dreary, but at least when I go visit Dean, I won't get completely soaked.

The gate creaks when I gently push it open. I stuff my hands in my pockets and follow the path to his grave.

Dean Reeves.

A wonderful teacher, a brave fighter, and a beloved father.

It's the last word that I stare at the longest.

Father.

"Hey, Dean."

I still don't call him Dad. I didn't get to know him well enough to reach that point. But Dean is a good middle-ground between "Dad" and "Mr. Reeves."

"Uh, I finished my first year at University of Miami."

It had never been my idea to visit and talk to Dean's grave like this. Lyla convinced me. She told me it would feel weird and ridiculous at first. but that I would get used to it the more I did it. And she was right. It feels much easier now.

But it's still hard, too.

"I might play football next year," I tell him. "I miss it."

My respect for him grew so much when I learned the truth about him. He tried to be there when I was a baby. He stepped up way before any of us knew he did. But all because of the letter he thought my mom sent, he stayed away, wanting to do as he thought she asked.

"I wish you were here," I tell him. "I wish I got to spend more time with you. I wish the guest room at your house had turned into a bedroom for me. Or maybe you would have moved in with Amelia, and I would have gotten to live with my girlfriend."

I smirk at the joke.

"Kidding."

Dean cared about all of us. And even after everything she did, he never stopped caring about Nora, either. He risked his life to prevent her from ending hers. And I know he would have done the same for any one of us.

After all this time, Dean really was a good father.

CHAPTER 83

AMELIA

I slide into the small, quiet booth of the little Italian restaurant. I'm nervous as I stare at the empty seat across from me, and I don't even really know why. It's not like this is the first time we've had dinner together. And I'm *far* from worried that it's going to be the last.

I unroll my silverware and put my napkin on my lap. I take my compact mirror out of my purse and check my reflection. My lipstick still looks good. My hair is freshly colored and sleek in its updo. I *don't* look almost forty. Maybe I'll even get carded by the waiter when I order my glass of wine.

"Hey, sweetie."

He kisses the top of my head before sitting down across from me. His hair is pretty much fully gray now, but he still has a lot of it. And he still has that gentle, kind face. The one I looked at nearly every day for almost eighteen years.

"How did your meeting go?" I ask, smiling at him.

"First, let me just say—you look beautiful."

My stomach dips. And it's silly because its Gentry. His compliments should have lost their effect years ago. And for a while, they did.

"Thank you," I reply.

He smiles and reaches across the table to take my hand. After we tell the waiter our drink orders—I did get carded, yay! Who cares if he just did it to be nice?—Gentry goes to answer my question.

"I actually wasn't fully honest with you when I told you I had a work meeting," he says.

I lean back and tilt my head at him. "Oh?"

Why does he look mischievous like that?

"I just didn't want to tell you about it until I saw you again in person."

I let go of his hand and cross my arms. "What did you do, G?"

He licks his lips and leans in closer to me, his chest hovering over the white-clothed table. "I was meeting with my realtor. I just put my house on the market."

"*What*?!"

Heads turn at the volume of my voice in the quaint, quiet establishment.

Gentry laughs.

"Are you kidding?" I ask, talking quieter now.

"Not even a little bit. I can show you the listing, if you'd like."

"I—but—Gentry..."

I can't form words.

The drinks are delivered, and I gulp from my stemware without even doing a toast with him first.

"Mia," he tells me, and I know exactly what's coming next. I'm downing the wine because I want to prepare myself for it.

It's not that I *don't* want him to say it. I do. I'm excited. But I am also terrified. A million thoughts are swarming through my mind. What will the kids think? What will it be like? How different will life become?

"It's time for me to come home."

I stand up so I can go around the table and kiss him. I bend over, cup his scratchy, stubbly face I my hands, and he holds my waist as our lips lock. While it's so familiar to kiss my husband, it feels new all over again.

"Thank you," I breathe when we break apart.

He smiles. "Sit down, sit down. You've been on your feet all day."

It's true. I have. It was a long day at work preparing for my new intern's first day coming up.

I kiss Gentry one more time before going back to my rightful side of the booth. I sort of wish we had a bigger table so that I could sit on the same side as him like those cheesy couples everyone makes fun of. That's how happy I am right now.

Gentry and I started dating again nine months after the night Dean passed and Nora was taken away. I originally had no hope of us ever reconnecting, of me ever getting to live with Joey again. I had no hope of ever feeling happy again. I thought—and still sometimes feel—that Dean's death was a punishment. I made a mess of everyone's lives, and I had to pay for it. I thought I deserved to be heartbroken and miserable. Gentry bought a house and moved in with Heather, and I thought they were going to have a happy ever after together. But then things just...changed. Gentry brought Joey over to visit me, because Joey had made the decision that he wanted me in his life. That he had forgiven me, and that he missed me. And while visiting with him, Gentry and I got to talking.

And then we never stopped talking.

And before I knew it, he told me Heather was moving out. That it wasn't working. That he just didn't love her.

And shortly after that, he asked me to dinner. He took me somewhere fancy. He spared no expense on it. And he admitted that the reason it wasn't working with Heather was because he was still deeply in love with me.

We started going to counseling together. And we need it. There is so much we still have to work on. It hasn't been all rainbows and butterflies, getting back together with him. He's still upset and hurt by my past and the things that transpired. He's hurt that he was my second choice. That Dean was my first.

But seeing a therapist alone, too, has helped me understand something. I loved Gentry. But with Dean always in the back of my mind as that "what-if" scenario, since I always loved him, too, I'd never be able to fully open my heart to Gentry. Now, Dean is gone. Now, there is no "what-if." Dean no longer has this claim over me. And although it's hard, it's sad, and I miss Dean so much, I can finally see Gentry in a much clearer light.

And Gentry is the one for me. He always was.

CHAPTER 84

MADDY

On our way to dinner, Steven is acting weird.

"Is something on your mind?" I ask him in the passenger seat of his Mercedes. Wrigley and Warner are driving separately and are going to meet us there.

"Think they'll ever be friends?" Steven asks.

"Who?"

"Who do you think?"

"Oh. I'm guessing you're referring to our sons."

He nods. "It was like pulling teeth to get them to talk earlier."

"I know. It always is." Resting my chin on my hand and my elbow on the door frame, I stare out the window. I am trying to think of a solution to it. When Warner isn't at school, and until Wrigley moves out and gets a place of his own, they are going to be living together. At first, I thought it was just the thing with Lyla that made them dislike each other so much. But Lyla's been with Warner for nearly two years now. You'd think Wrigley would be over it by now. Maybe Warner and Wrigley just never liked each other. Maybe they're just... too different.

"I guess we will try again in a few months, or whenever the next time we see Warner is," Steven says.

"Maybe we should drag Wrigley with us to go visit Warner, and then ditch him and force them to spend some quality time together."

He snickers. It's like we're plotting some evil plan. It makes me laugh. But then he's quiet again, and his grip on the steering wheel is tight.

When we get to the restaurant, outside of Toxey near The Viper, my jaw drops at the sight of it. It has complimentary valet, for one.

"*This* is where we're eating?" I ask. "Steven, you didn't have to do this, it's just *Warner.*" What lengths is Steven willing to go to make sure Warner likes him?

"What?" Steven says casually as a valet worker opens my car door and helps me out. "It's got good food."

"I'm sure it does," I say, still in disbelief. Luckily, I don't feel underdressed to be eating at a five-star restaurant like this because I just bought a new, expensive dress when Steven took me shopping last weekend. I tried to tell him no when I saw the price tag, but he insisted on me getting it. And I bought it with my own hard-earned money from The Viper. So what if I have a lot of money now that I no longer pay any other bills because Steven won't let me? So what that he's the one supplying me with my bi-weekly paychecks? He could honestly just save himself the payroll because I'd work there for free, but he likes to joke that it's my spending allowance. He not only wants me to buy myself things all the time, but I've also been helping him spruce up his mansion—with Mia's help, of course.

We're seated at a surprisingly large table, and I think a mistake must have been made.

"Oh, there's only four of us," I tell the hostess.

Steven smiles at her. "No, this is great, thank you."

He sits down, and even though the chair is pulled out for me, I don't join him. "Steven, this table is huge. This can't be our reservation."

"Whoa," someone says behind me. I turn and find Warner strolling in, Lyla with him.

"I didn't know you were coming," I say, smiling at Lyla and hugging her. We hug now. So do Audrey and I. I love Mia's girls. And Mia loves Warner. We are all one big family.

That's when it hits me.

"*Wait* a minute," I say as I notice more people walking in. Before I know it, Amelia, Gentry, Audrey, Joey, and Wrigley are all sitting with us at the table. They are full of smiles and cheerful chatter as they make themselves comfortable after greeting us. All of them except for Wrigley, but I hardly even notice because of all the other surprise guests.

"Steven, what is this?" I ask, my heart beating faster.

He grins at me. "We're just having dinner, babe."

"No. Nuh uh. What's going on?" I'm not going to let it go. I want an explanation or I'm not sitting down.

"Yeah, take a seat!" Mia calls, grinning at me from the other end of the table, everyone else joins in trying to convince me.

I cross my arms like a defiant toddler. "No! Not until you tell me why you did all of this," I say to Steven. "You said it was just going to be me and you and our boys." I'm certainly not mad that all of my favorite people are here, but I am definitely suspicious.

Steven simultaneously groans and rolls his eyes while keeping the smile on his face. He gets up from his chair begrudgingly and stands before me. "I was going to wait until *after* dinner, but I should have known this is exactly how you'd react."

"What do you mean?" I ask.

He shakes his head. Then he reaches into his coat pocket and gets on one knee.

I gasp.

From his pocket, he pulls out a black velvet box and opens it in front of me.

There's a ring inside.

"Mads, I love you so much," he says. "I want nothing more, than to—"

"Yes!" I scream, jumping up and down with my hands over my mouth.

"I—I didn't even ask you yet!" he says, everyone laughing.

"You don't need to! Yes, yes, *yes*!" I don't even know what the ring looks like because I am too happy to pay any attention. *Steven wants to marry me!*

He gets to his feet as I practically lunge at him and smother his face with kisses. There's lipstick all over him. I don't care. He doesn't either.

"I love you," I tell him.

"I believe you," he says, his face flushed.

Everyone cheers. Not just everyone at our table, but the entire restaurant.

I am on cloud nine. All I have ever wanted was to find someone to settle down with. Someone good. Someone Warner would be proud to call his stepdad. Someone I could see growing close with him. I don't want Steven to take Dean's place in Warner's life as his father, but I hope Steven can be something like one to him. I hope he finally gets to know what it's like to have a whole, complete family.

All I've ever wanted was for that person to be someone I'm madly in love with, too. It only took me thirty-eight years to get here.

But we're finally here.

CHAPTER 85

Audrey

"There," I say, putting my hands on my hips and stepping back to admire my work. Now, with the added touch of the framed photo of me, Joey, and Lyla, my desk is perfect.

"Love it," Mom says, coming to stand beside me and wrapping her arm around my shoulder in a side-hug.

I shrug out of it. "*Mom*," I complain. "Here, I'm not your daughter, remember?"

She smiles and nods her head exaggeratedly. "Oh, *right*, you're Audrey, the *intern*."

I scowl. "Take me seriously."

"I do, I do!" she says. "Sorry. I really do, I am so excited for you, hon—Audrey."

I'm excited, too. Today is my first day as an intern at my mom's boutique interior design firm. I'm ready to be put to work after a long, relaxing, quiet summer of really doing nothing but spending time outside—when the weather permitted—and hanging out with my family and Danielle. No torments. No drama. No boys, even. It was peaceful, which was exactly what I needed. Plus, interning at Mom's firm puts me ahead of the game when it comes to finding a job after college—even if I don't go the interior design route. Mom says my internship can be about all sorts of areas of business. Leadership, marketing, social media, I can even shadow her accountant, if I'm interested.

I'm *so* not.

I'm starting the internship before I even start school, but it's on purpose. I wanted to find a way to keep my mind occupied so I wouldn't think about the horrible, awful thing that is happening to me tomorrow morning

Lyla is leaving.

I'm staying here, in Toxey, to be with Mom. No one asked me to. I am doing it because I want to. And that's the best part about it.

Ever since everything that happened with Aunt Nora, I've completely done a 180 with my life. I have stopped living to please other people. I have stopped doing what I think is expected of me. What I think people want me to do. I have decided to be me and only me. I have decided to choose things for myself and only myself.

And it's been the best thing I have ever done.

I didn't put the pressure on myself to get immaculate grades so I could get into an amazing college so my parents would be proud of me. That had always been the plan, but eventually, I changed my mind. I don't even know what I want to do when I'm done with school. What I want to even go to school for. So why waste the money? I'm completely fine with going to community college in Toxey.

It's really not such a bad place after all.

The town has been increasing in population recently. Mom is busier than ever with remodels and even new builds, which she's super excited about. More tourists are coming around, too—because of the TikTok account and the media frenzy over everything that happened to us. Mom told me the other day that there are talks of a documentary on one of those streaming services being made. Everyone wants to know our story. Everyone wants to know how and why so many awful things happened to our two families, and how it went back to events that occurred all those years ago. But I try and stay away from all of that. I don't even have any of my social media accounts anymore. I only posted on them because I felt like I had to. Now that I do things for me and me only, I don't need them anymore. I don't care about what everyone at my old high school is doing next. The ones I do care about, I reach out to personally.

Because I want to.

The possibilities for my future are endless. And I am so grateful for it. I'm thankful that I even have a future to live at all. I am thankful that all of this is over, and that I finally feel like I am in a spot where I feel significantly healed from all the trauma. Where the nightmares occur much less frequently. I feel good.

Mom claps her hands together loudly to snap me out of my thoughts. "Alright! Work meeting in five minutes in the conference room. Chop, chop!"

She leaves me to myself.

I look at the photo of Lyla, Joey, and me again.

It's going to be okay. You're going to be fine.

I grab a cup of coffee from the lounge to drink during the meeting, as well as a notebook and a pen from my desk. I set my phone down so I won't be distracted by it in the conference room, but when I do, it lights up, and I see I have a new text message.

"Oh my," I whisper as I immediately put everything else down to pick my phone back up again.

Did I really read that name right?

I did.

Ryan Copeland.

We completely lost touch after I ended things with him my junior year. I think I remember him trying to reach out a few times, but since I was busy working on myself, I didn't engage. And eventually, he stopped trying. Then, after he graduated, I still had a year left at Blackfell, and he moved out of state to somewhere on the east coast.

It's so strange to hear from him now, after so long.

I open the message, my breath quickening.

Ryan: *Hey Audrey! I wanted you to hear this from me before you find out from all the gossip that will surely start going around soon. I'm back in Toxey. Permanently. Long story, but my dad is sick. I was talking to Austin Booth about who is still around, and your name came up. I'd love to meet up if you're ever interested. I get it if not. I just figured it can't hurt to try...again.*

"Where's Audrey?" I hear my mom's voice saying in the conference room. Shoot. I've read the message over so many times I didn't realize the meeting is already about o start.

I click my phone off, grab my stuff, and dash down the hall to join everyone in the conference room. I'm a grinning, excited mess as I sit down in my chair with my mo—*boss*—the receptionist, and the other designers. I'm at my very first work meeting. I start college next week. Mom and Dad are back together, and I have the feeling it won't be long before Dad and Joey officially come back home. And Ryan Copeland, who is probably the only boy besides Warner I have ever had a crush on, has moved back to town and wants to reconnect, and I am finally at a place where I am open to the possibility of it. I might actually be ready to finally let someone else in.

I have no doubt in my mind about it—it's going to be a good year.

CHAPTER 86

LYLA

This is it. I am all packed up. My room at Mom's looks cleaner than it's ever been. It hardly looks like my room anymore. It doesn't really feel like it is, either. Because I'm moving out. I'm moving hundreds of miles away. I've waited so long for the chance to start somewhere new, to be someone new, and the time has finally come.

"I hate this." Audrey sits on my neatly made bed, her shoulders sagging. Her hair is in two long braids, and she's fiddling mindlessly with one of them. When I catch a glimpse of myself in the mirror above my dresser, I look so much different than her. My hair is chopped to a short bob. I've added some darker colors to it, and I curl it most days. Audrey is still the same blonde she's always been, and she's been growing hers out ever since she had to cut it. I hardly wear any makeup, just a dash of mascara and some tinted foundation. Audrey, like Mom, likes to get fully ready every day, even if she doesn't have any plans to do anything or go anywhere. I like comfort over style when it comes to clothes, so I'm wearing black biker shorts and a loose band tee that's tied in a knot at the bottom. I'm also wearing my black Doc Martens. I am obsessed with them. Audrey is preppy and cute every day with her outfit choices. She has a pastel floral wrap dress and summery, strappy sandals on right now, for example. She's also adapted a bit of a professional style since she works three days a week at Mom's job.

We rarely go into each other's closets anymore.

"Are you going to help me carry any of this downstairs, or...?" I ask her, duffel bags and suitcases all around my feet.

She defiantly shakes her head and crosses her arms. "No. If you want to travel hundreds of miles across the country to leave me, you can carry your own bags."

I go to reply, rolling my eyes, but then I hear the front door opening downstairs.

"Lyla!" Joey's voice calls.

"I'm still here!" I yell down. He must be with Dad, coming to see me off. Warner will be pulling up in his old, freshly tuned-up Jeep any minute.

"Take me with you!" Joey complains. He's about to be an eighth grader, and he's in this phase where school sucks and he just wants to sit around and play video games with his friends. Or go to Florida with me, apparently.

In my room with a pouting Audrey still, I chuckle.

"You can still change your mind," Audrey says.

I walk over to my bed, grab her hands, and pull her to her feet. "I love you, Ree. I'm going to miss you every day."

I see the tears forming in her eyes. Crap. I didn't think we were going to do this. But seeing her crying makes me start to as well.

"But we've only been apart one other time our whole lives," she whines. She's right. The only other time I have been separated from Audrey was when I was kidnapped by Carson and our aunt.

"This will be nothing like the last time, though," I reassure her, even though it should go without saying. "I'll have my phone. We can FaceTime every day. You guys and Mads will be coming to visit for Thanksgiving, and that will be here before you know it."

We make sniffling noises at the same time, and then we both pathetically laugh about it.

We're still holding hands. Neither of us are ready to let go. But I need this. And she knows I need this. Before Warner, I had no intentions of going so far from home. I had no idea what I wanted to do with my life after high school. I think I figured I would follow in Mom's footsteps, like Audrey might. I always thought *she'd* be the one to leave. She was always talking about how she wanted to live in California.

What happened those twenty-one months ago changed all of us in such big ways.

It was Warner who convinced me that getting out of Toxey might be best for me. And seeing how much he's grown and changed over the last year, it's only convinced me further that it's a good idea.

There's a knock on the front door downstairs. I look out the window and see the Jeep parked on the street. Warner has the top off. It's another amazingly clear and sunny day. Toxey has been full of them lately. It's the least rainy summer we've had in over two decades, according to the news.

"Warner's here!" Dad calls up. Then we hear the door open, and he, Mom, and Joey start excitedly talking Warner's ear off.

Butterflies flutter around in my stomach. A week-long road trip with the boy I'm in love with, then college together—near a *beach*. I'm not going to live with him; we both decided we're much too young and it's much too soon. But Warner insisted I do the dorm-thing for my freshman year. He says it's the easiest way to make friends and get used to being on my own. I'm nervous to meet the roommate I was randomly assigned, but I stalked her online as soon as I learned her name. Liza Marino. She's from New York. She likes to paint super realistic portraits of people. She is best friends with her older brother. She smiles in all of her photos and rarely posts selfies, so I think it's safe to say she's not conceited, and that's a good sign. Granted, I don't know if I will immediately be able to jump into a friendship with her. I have learned my lesson about that. I am overly cautious when it comes to people I don't know. I haven't made any new friends in forever. Part of me doesn't want to. But part of me knows that it's time to try. The chances of my next new friend being someone who was paid to learn all of my secrets and expose them to the world have to be pretty slim.

Audrey squeezes my hands tighter at Dad's words. "I can't believe this is really happening," she says.

"Me neither."

For so long, it was just talked about. It never felt quite real. Even when I got my acceptance letter. Even when I went shopping for all of my dorm room furniture. I've learned that every day is not promised, so I don't see anything planned in the future as a real possibility until it actually happens.

"You better not like your roomie more than me," she says. "And you better not tell her any juicy stories that happen to you before telling me first."

I laugh.

"It's not funny! I'm serious!"

"Okay, I promise."

She groans loudly and dramatically and then pulls me into a tight hug. "I love you, butthead," she says before letting me go and finally grabbing some of my bags.

I wipe my tears and grab the rest, and we go downstairs together. Dad and Warner immediately grab my stuff for us and bring it out to load it up in Warner's car.

Joey nods at me—he's too cool for hugs now—but instead of nodding back, I force him into my arms, even if over this past summer, he's shot up in height and is actually freaking taller than me now. I only recently learned that his biological father is over six and a half feet tall.

Joey resists the hug, but I know deep down he is probably happy about it.

"You just call me the second you need me, and I'll be on the next flight there," Mom says, beaming at me.

"I'm sure I'll be fine, Mom."

"It feels wrong that your father and I aren't the ones taking you. It's like a parents' rite of passage to drop their kid off at college."

I start walking outside, and they all follow. "Warner and I have been looking forward to this trip all summer, though." It might be our only chance to have this much time together. Sure, we will be attending the same school, but who knows how much time we will actually spend together once classes start and we're both slammed with homework and tests to study for?

"I'd really rather you at least take *your* car, Ly," she says as we reach Dad and Warner on the curb. She addresses Warner next. "Are you sure this old thing is going to make it all the way to Florida?"

Warner smiles at her. "Positive. I've spent the last few days getting her all ready." He slaps the side of it like he's patting an old buddy on the back.

"They'll be fine," Dad says, slinging an arm around Mom's waist and kissing her temple. "I have full trust in Warner. He'll take good care of our little girl."

"Dad. Ew," I say. I'm a legal adult. I'm definitely not a little girl. "Okay, we're going to go now..."

The long hugs begin. But while Dad smothers me with his iron grip, Audrey cries out, "Wait one sec!" before she dashes up the lawn and back inside the house.

"What's she doing?" I ask while physically pushing Dad off of me so I can breathe.

"Dunno," Dad says.

I almost wonder if she's going to reappear with all her bags packed, smiling at me and yelling, "Surprise! I'm coming, too!"

If I had my twin by my side during the next adventure, I'd be more excited than ever.

When Audrey returns, she has no bags. She's not coming with. This is really happening. I'm leaving my sister. My best friend.

She's holding something small. "I found this when I was digging around looking for a picture of us for my desk at work," she says, handing it to me.

It's a photo strip from the photo booth at the Halloween Carnival at Blackfell High back when we were freshman. I don't remember where Danielle, Sophia, and Olive were when we took these—probably finding boys to flirt with—but in these photos, Audrey, Trinity, and I are crammed into the tiny seat, cracking up in our ridiculous costumes and making funny faces.

I start crying all over again. "I didn't even know you still had this," I say. There had only been two copies. Trinity kept the second one. I lost the fight over getting to keep this one.

Audrey is crying again, too. "I was going to keep it pinned up in my room...but I think you should have it. Take Trin to college with you."

I hug her again. All my hard copies of photos with Trinity are buried in the Boldosa Redwood Forest, because I wanted Trinity to experience the upperclassman trip she had always been so excited about. I can go back and look at the old photos of us on my phone anytime I want, but something about holding this strip in my hands, photos of us I had completely forgotten even existed, makes it feel much more meaningful.

I still haven't talked to Trinity's parents since that day I went to their house and apologized. They hadn't forgiven me then, and I have no idea if they've forgiven me now. It used to be so important to me for them to not hate me or be mad at me over their daughter's death. But, with time, I was able to realize it wasn't their forgiveness I needed.

It was my own.

And I have forgiven myself. I'm no longer consumed with my guilt over texting and driving that night. I can't change the past. All I can do is move forward.

It's all any of us can do.

CHAPTER 87

NORA

I can't believe I have finally agreed to this. She's been trying forever. And I've turned her away every time.

So why did I say yes *now*? Is it my meds? They were adjusted recently. I'm on new stuff. Maybe its altering my ability to think rationally. Because talking to my sister, especially face-to-face, is not a rational decision. Maybe I need to tell my doc they're not working.

When Amelia Bailey sits across from me at the round table in the community room, where visitors are allowed on Sundays, I'm annoyed at how she looks exactly the same as she did the last night I saw her, nearly two years ago.

Has it really been that long already?

"Hi, Nora," she says to me, looking perfect and healthy and happy. I worked so hard for so many years to ruin her. She's much stronger than I thought.

"Hey," I say, slouched in my chair, hoping my long hair is covering most of the visible evidence that I'm dressed in the same thing I wear every single day. The plain white shirt and white pants and slippers that I will be wearing for the rest of my life.

Or so they say.

"I'm really glad you finally let me see you." She isn't smiling at me. But I do see the hopeful sparkle in her eye.

Barf.

I shrug. "What do you want?"

"Um..." she starts, picking invisible lint off of her pretty, expensive-looking blouse. "I just wanted to see you, really. I just want you to know that I'm here."

"I do know," I say. "Every single week they tell me you're here to see me."

She nods. "I was kinda starting to think they were just turning me away without even bothering to check with you first."

"No. They ask me every single time."

It's silent for a second. She takes a slow breath before continuing.

"It doesn't matter. I don't care if we just sit here for an hour and not say a word to each other. I don't care if you let me see you this one time and never agree to it again. I'll still be here, Nora. Every visiting day. And if for some reason I can't, I will send you a letter or leave you a message explaining why."

How insufferable.

I don't say anything. I just stare at her. Why is she doing this? Why would she even *want* to come anywhere near me? I killed Dean. I tried to kill her daughter. I kidnapped her other one.

"I... I did it wrong before, Nora," she says. "I wasn't there the last time you were in a place like this. But I should have been. I thought only of myself back then. But I am here now. You're my sister. You're my family. I let you down in the past. I am not going to do that again."

"Whatever."

She leans in closer and looks me dead in the eye. "I'm sorry. For everything."

"Kay."

I won't give in to it. I won't show emotion. I won't give her what she wants. I won't let her leave today thinking we're ever going to be okay.

But at the same time, I can't bring myself to tell her to bug-off. I don't tell her that a visit with me is never going to happen again.

Can our relationship really be repaired? Even if it's years from now? Am I actually sitting here thinking it's a real possibility? Maybe I'm just *that* lonely in here. Or maybe I just want a connection to the outside world, because one day, I'm going to be back in it.

I've been told I'll likely be in here for life. I've been told that even if I am found someday competent to stand trial, I will still have to be on trial. But I've met some of the other patients in here. I've made some friends. I've heard some stories.

I'm getting out of here someday. And when I do, I am going to stop at nothing to have the life I've always wanted.

I'll do whatever it takes.

Up Next

BUT WAIT! THERE'S MORE...

Well, not more of the *"Moms Who Lie"* series, but if you liked that one, you'll love our new series *"The Turquoise Mist Thrillers"* beginning with *"Summer Bodies: Turquoise Mist Thrillers Book 1"*.

Can a troubled teen uncover the mysteries buried in the desert without joining them there?

After getting unjustly expelled from her elite private high school, Summer is forced to leave her trendy Boston home and live with her estranged half-brother in a sleepy Arizona ghost town. She's more lonely and isolated than ever, which usually gets her into trouble.

While partying at a creepy abandoned hotel outside town, a teen she barely knows gets murdered. And the evidence points to *her* as the likely culprit.

To find the real killer, she teams up with a couple of other misfit teens. But she's not sure if she can trust them, or anybody else, because nobody in this small town is who they seem to be.

Can Summer solve the murders and clear her name? Or will she end up in prison, or a grave?

"Summer Bodies" is the first book in the 4-Book *"Turquoise Mist Thrillers"* series by Brett Monk and McKenna Langford.

If you like unputdownable psychological thrillers with relatable teen and adult characters and a drop-the-mic cliffhanger at the end of each book, then you'll love the *"Turquoise Mist Thrillers"* series!

Can We Keep In Touch?

Seriously. Especially if you've now read three or more of my books.

I'm an independent author and my loyal readers are really important to me. I'd like to know what you like and what you'd like to see more of.

I've gone to a lot of work to create an email newsletter, a private Facebook community, and other ways that I can interact with my fans, and that my fans can interact with each other.

You might want to become an ARC READER. (Someone who gets free e-book copies of my books before they're published in return for feedback to me and reviews on Amazon and other places.

You might even want to become part of my "STREET TEAM." That's for folks who would like to help me share news about my books and movies on their blogs and social media platforms. I provide memes and fun graphics for people to use, and I've been known to send gifts of appreciation to my highly active Street Team Members.

I correspond personally to my emails and to comments in my social media, especially with my ARC readers and Street Team Members.

Also, If you want to learn **all the details about what happened back when Maddy and Mia were in high school, the night Carson disappeared**, you can download the free bonus novella, *"The Lying Begins"* at the link below.

More details are available at this link: **https://www.brettmonk .com**

www.BrettMonk.com

About the Authors

Brett Monk

Brett Monk is an author, movie director, and voiceover artist.

He holds degrees in Communications and Psychology and spent over 30 years writing and directing films for businesses and government agencies in the Washington, DC area before turning his focus to creating books and audiobooks.

He also directed and co-wrote two feature-length murder mystery movies which are in worldwide distribution.

Originally from the Shenandoah Valley area, he now lives in Northern Virginia with his family and a rambunctious Bernedoodle named Merlin.

McKenna Langford

McKenna lives in Arizona with her husband and two goofy Box-ador brothers.

Before she dove into the world of ghostwriting and co-writing, she got her bachelor's degree in interior design and published her first five novels. She worked in a boutique interior design firm in the valley for two years, moved to Seattle with her husband to explore for another two years, then moved back to Arizona and made writing her full-time career in 2021.